DUTY AND DESIRE

"It would help if you didn't see us now as Warrior Chief and Liege. This isn't a contest of wills, Nazleen. I'm a man and you're a woman, and we want each other. But I can't take more from you than you're willing to give."

She searched his face, too, seeking some clue as to the truth or lie behind his words. It was true that he couldn't take from her what she was unwilling to give, but was this too a part of his scheme to gain the power he craved?

He reached out to stroke her cheek softly. "I can give you pleasure or merely give you an heir. That choice is up to you."

Greenfire

SARANNE HOOVER

LEISURE BOOKS   NEW YORK CITY

A LEISURE BOOK ®

September 1990

Published by

Dorchester Publishing Co., Inc.
276 Fifth Avenue
New York, NY 10001

Printed in the United States of America.

PROLOGUE

His face was incredibly clear, leaping out of the blackness of sleep as though he brought his own radiance. Then he was gone just as quickly, leaving only an imperfect memory imprinted on her brain.

But she did remember some things—thick hair of burnished gold and a curling golden beard outlining a strong, handsome face that was totally, unrelentingly masculine. There was a small scar just above his left brow, a thin white line on bronzed skin.

And those deep-set green eyes, eyes that couldn't be.

And in the background was the sacred fire, the awesome green fire.

She awoke in an icy, sweating fear to hear the echoes of her inner self saying, "Yes, this was meant to be."

CHAPTER ONE

"How certain are you of the accuracy of these reports, Miklav?"

"The Warrior Chief shrugged his broad shoulders. "As certain as one can ever be of anything the Trens tell us, Milady."

Nazleen regarded him with a frown. The Mountain Trens were generally reliable, but this report had come from their desert kinfolk—and therein lay the problem. The wandering desert clans were only nominally under the rule of Hamloor. There was no way to force them to swear allegiance. They roamed a vast sea of sand where no sensible Hamloorian would go, not even the ever-restless Warriors.

"It seems unlikely that they would fabricate such a story, Nazleen," Haslik put in. "What purpose could it serve?"

Nazleen gratefully turned her attention upon her brother. The Warrior Chief's dark eyes disturbed her. She saw the bloodlust of a Warrior catching the scent of battles to come.

"So you believe it then, Haslik?" If he did, then she had no choice but to accept the accuracy of the report about the aliens. Haslik was a Warrior, too, but he was still her flesh and blood. Furthermore, she continued to think of him as a reluctant Warrior at best, forced by birth to join that caste.

Haslik nodded gravely, his dark eyes meeting the brilliant green of his sister's. "I do—or at least I give it enough credence to believe that we must act upon it."

Nazleen stared at him, realizing belatedly that his presence here was no accident. Miklav had brought him along to help make his case.

"And what would you have me do?" she asked, still focussing on her brother and ignoring the larger man beside him.

Haslik's gaze slid off to the Warrior Chief. He might be her brother, but Miklav was his superior officer. As always, Nazleen had to stifle her resentment of Warrior discipline that placed military rank above blood ties. It reminded her all too clearly of the uneasy relationship between the warriors and their Liege. Haslik remained silent, so it was Miklav who finally answered her in his gruff, precise manner.

"We should send out a surveillance squad as soon as possible."

Nazleen knew that on the face of it his suggestion made sense, but she also knew that such a seemingly innocent action held many dangers. First of all, even a surveillance squad could give rise to that bloodlust that simmered just beneath the surface of any Warrior, and spying could so easily turn into an attack. Furthermore, the Desert Trens might be very angry about an intrusion into their territory which could lead to still more trouble.

She moved away from the two men, lost in thought. They both silently watched her, a diminutive figure with hair the color of the setting sun, and a face where delicacy and strength vied constantly for supremacy. She was dressed in a formal white robe decorated with emeralds and embroidered gold threads. From her neck hung a gold chain with the unique circle and flame insignia of the Cerecians, indicative of her two loyalties.

Miklav watched her, outwardly impassive but inwardly seething with volatile emotions. She was too young for this responsibility. He wished her mother were still alive. He'd clashed with her often enough, but at least he hadn't been forced to contend with the raging desire that was even now making him uncomfortable in his tight-fitting dress uniform.

Haslik worried about her, too. Even though he knew she had a mind that was easily a match for their late mother's, she was still his little sister, and he feared that her determination to maintain peace at any cost in order to further her own goals could one day cost them all dearly. He only hoped that this wasn't that day—or that she would agree to finding out more about these aliens on their borders.

Then, abruptly she turned to face them again,

framed by the large archway that led into the palace gardens. The lowering afternoon sun flared around her golden-red hair that was piled into elaborate braids and sprinkled with tiny emeralds.

"I will leave tomorrow for Cerece to attend an Augury. You will have my answer when I return."

Even as he chafed inwardly at her imperious tone, Miklav managed a brief bow. "With your permission, Milady, I myself will accompany you to Cerece. That way, I will have your answer sooner. The desert storm season will arrive within the month, so we cannot afford to delay."

Nazleen frowned again. She'd forgotten that the storms that made desert travel impossible would come soon. Even the Desert Trens left their home then, coming to pay their annual visit to their mountain cousins.

She didn't want Miklav to accompany her, but she couldn't deny the wisdom of his suggestion. Furthermore, he knew perfectly well that he didn't need her permission. As Warrior Chief, he already had the right to decide which Warriors accompanied her on any journeys. She nodded her assent anyway, then asked her brother if he would be coming, too. That would make the trip much more bearable.

Once more, Haslik deferred to his commander. Nazleen considered insisting that Haslik join them, but just as quickly rejected the thought. Under the terms of the Compact, she had no authority over any Warrior save Miklav, their Chief.

"Haslik will be returning immediately to Denra. He has important work there."

Nazleen's eyes met Miklav's in unspoken challenge. She knew he was sending Haslik back because she wanted him to stay. For a few seconds, only the Compact stood between this silent clash of wills—but it was enough. She gave a barely perceptible nod, then left the reception room.

Two hours later, she was dressing for dinner, rejecting the low-necked, clinging gown her maid had chosen in favor of a simple pair of embroidered pajamas, loosely billowing with a high neck. In the past, she'd occasionally deliberately taunted Miklav by wearing gowns such as the one her maid had selected, but this night she found that she had no appetite for such a game.

In order to prolong as much as possible the moment when she would be forced to go down to the dining hall, Nazleen went out onto the terrace of her personal suite. Twilight touched the land, but there was still enough light in the sky for her to see the great mountains to the west—the land of the Trens. Beyond that lay the desert, and beyond that . . .

The land beyond that was said to be rugged and almost barren, unlike the lush, fertile hills and valleys of Hamloor. There were even tales of great mountains that belched fire and smoke and places where the very earth itself trembled in fear.

For years the Warriors had wanted to explore that land, but the Desert Trens had made it known that they would not welcome incursions into their territory, so to avoid almost certain conflict, successive lieges had forbidden it. Nazleen could recall several stormy arguments between her mother and her father—the Warrior Chief before Miklav—on that very subject. She'd been hiding in the next room, fascinated as always by those brief glimpses of her father.

The Desert Trens would be very unhappy if she gave permission for this expedition, although perhaps after so many years of peace they might be somewhat more sanguine about it. Besides, according to Miklav, they, too, were concerned about the aliens they'd seen.

She'd been too busy thinking about the implications of Miklav's request to give much thought to the aliens themselves, but now she began to wonder about them. At any rate, it would make for safe, interesting dinner conversation.

Miklav made her nervous, chiefly because his presence always reminded her that she should be choosing a mate. She was young and healthy, to be sure, but there still needed to be a daughter and heir. Otherwise, if something happened to her, the succession would fall to her cousin, who was clearly unfit to rule.

She didn't *have* to choose Miklav, of course. The Compact stated only that the Liege's mate must be chosen from among the Warriors. But for three generations now, the Liege had taken the Warrior Chief as her mate.

From Nazleen's perspective, one Warrior was just about as bad as another, although there *were* times when she looked with relative kindness upon Miklav. But those feelings certainly didn't whet her appetite to lie with him in the royal bed. In fact, the thought of it was quite enough to ruin her appetite.

She turned slightly to face the dark hills to the southwest, thinking of Cerece. Did they know how truly fortunate they were to spend their lives in the beauty and serenity of that sacred place? Her years there had been the happiest of her life.

The daughters of the royal line who bore the distinctive traits of the Cerecians were always sent to the Sisterhood at the age of 12, just as the Cerecian daughters of all Hamloorians and Trens were. There they were educated and grew to womanhood under the gently watchful eyes of the Sisterhood. But unlike the others who went there, the future Liege had to return before taking the final oath.

A sound behind her pulled Nazleen's attention reluctantly away from the past. Her maid had come into the room to remind her that it was time to go down to dinner. She knew she had kept Miklav and the others waiting for as long as she dared, so she left her quarters and descended the wide staircase, then passed through the formal reception rooms to the great dining hall.

Silence descended quickly over the large, high-ceilinged hall as she entered. The room was lit by flickering oil lamps whose glow suffused the magnificent murals with bejeweled colors. Some 50 people were present, already seated at three tables that formed a large "U".

Scattered among the members of her court were the Warriors who had accompanied Miklav, and he himself was seated at the head table with her Council of Advisors. His place was next to hers—a chair left empty when he was absent, which was less often in recent months.

Nazleen noted with pleasure that old Andras was seated on the other side of Miklav this night. Perhaps that garrulous old gentleman would keep

Miklav occupied during dinner, thereby preventing any opportunity for intimate conversation.

She moved slowly down the length of the room as all rose to bow to her. As always, the Warriors bowed minimally. They had long ago perfected the art of according the Liege as little respect as possible. Even the independent Trens, one or two of whom were often present at court, showed more courtesy.

Miklav had risen from his chair, his dark eyes fixed intently upon her as she approached the head table. He, too, accorded her that half-bow, then stepped down from the dais to offer his arm. He was a big man, both tall and broad, but his size and his dark, rugged appearance had long since ceased to frighten her. At times, she could almost think of him as attractive in a crude sort of way—but never attractive enough to make her want to take him as her mate.

They ascended the few steps to the table where a servant immediately filled their golden goblets with wine. She raised hers and intoned the formal toast required when the Warrior Chief was present.

"To the Compact, by which we live in peace and vigilance."

Then she turned to Miklav as required, touched her goblet to his briefly and met his eyes just as briefly. The modest pajamas clearly hadn't worked; barely leashed desire glittered in those dark eyes like hot ice.

That simple toast formed the very basis of the society. In the years before the Compact, various Warlords had ruled and their entire world was in a constant state of warfare. The Cerecian Sisterhood had remained apart from it all in their mountain compound, contenting themselves with their intellectual and mystical pursuits. But when it appeared that the total destruction of their society was at hand, they had finally unleashed their unique powers, and the Compact was the result.

Under its terms, those men who so chose could become Warriors, but they were relegated to a series of ancient forts in the hills that had previously been the strongholds of the various Warlords. But they were expressly forbidden to make war upon each other, a rule that had nevertheless been broken from time to time up until the days of Nazleen's father, the Warrior Chief before Miklav.

At that time, an outbreak of war with a renegade band of Trens had united the Hamloorian Warriors, and after the Trens' defeat the unity had held, first largely thanks to the iron rule of Hektar, Nazleen's father, and now thanks to Miklav's own personal authority.

For more than 20 years now, there had been no wars at all. Only the oldest of the Warriors had ever been "blooded"—their term for service in battle. Miklav, now 41, had been a young aide to Nazleen's father in that final battle.

But the peace was a very fragile one, and Nazleen was more than ever aware of that fact when she was presented with the news of an alien presence just beyond the desert.

Servants began to bring in the spicy, aromatic dishes that comprised the dinner. Because of the presence of Warriors in their midst, red meat was served. Cerecians, including Nazleen, eschewed red meat, and the court followed that custom. But it

15

was considered a gesture of respect to their guests to serve it, and in any event, they brought it with them.

A platter of vegetables and spiced fish was set before her just as Miklav seized a momentary silence in the ramblings of old Andras to address her.

"I am grateful for your decision to ride to Cerece, Milady. We cannot afford to lose even a few days."

Nazleen merely nodded. Her decision had less to do with Miklav's desire for haste than it did with her own fear of staying away from court too long. Leaving the government completely under the control of her frequently scheming Advisors was dangerous, but she certainly couldn't tell Miklav that.

"I enjoy riding," she said finally, "and I have so little opportunity." That was true enough, and it also served to let him know that she didn't consider the situation to be as threatening as he did.

How carefully we communicate, she thought. More is implied than is ever spoken.

"What will you do if the Augury isn't clear?" he asked.

It was a question she didn't want to answer because, unfortunately, Auguries were often unclear. They could be open to many interpretations, but she hoped fervently that would not be the case this time.

"I don't know," she replied. "That's why I want to be there to see it myself."

Then she quickly shifted the conversation before he could start lecturing her on the foolishness of Auguries. She already knew his thoughts on the subject.

"Tell me more about these aliens," she requested, trying to avoid looking at the slab of nearly raw meat in front of him.

"The Trens' description was vague and filled with their usual circumlocutions, but there were seven of them, near those old ruins Hektar discovered."

Nazleen's interest was piqued. She'd heard about the ruins as a child from her father. In order to establish once and for all that the Desert Trens were under the control of Hamloor, Hektar had taken his men on a long march across the desert. It was a typical case of Warrior overkill, since the Desert Trens hadn't joined their mountain cousins in making war on Hamloor.

The ruins to which Miklav referred lay a short distance beyond the desert and were the furthest west any Hamloorian had ever ventured. Beyond them lay the land of the Fire Mountains and earth tremors.

She recalled her father's description of the ruins, how they didn't resemble any building style known to have existed in Hamloor and how much of them lay buried beneath the fine gray dirt that covered the area. But she had no opportunity to dwell on them now as Miklav continued.

"Apparently, the Trens frequent the place to gather medicinal herbs, and they came upon the aliens not far from the ruins. Depending upon whom you choose to believe, either three or four of them were clearly Warriors, wearing uniforms and carrying weapons."

"What about the others?"

"They were carrying things, too, although the Trens didn't know if they were weapons. And one of them might have been female."

"*Might* have been?" Nazleen asked curiously.

Miklav chewed on some meat before responding, then turned to her with a slight smile. "Opinion was about evenly divided on that. She—if it was a she—was wearing pants and carrying something that might or might not have been a weapon."

Nazleen rather unsuccessfully fought down a smile of her own. The Trens, like the Warriors themselves, considered pants on a woman to be an abomination. In fact, that was the reason she'd chosen to wear them this night, and Miklav's sense of humour about such things was, in her opinion, one of his greatest assets.

"What did they look like?" she asked, intrigued more than ever by these aliens.

Miklav shrugged. "Not much different from us apparently. In fact, the Trens thought at first they might be Hamloorians, despite their strange clothing and the weapons they were carrying."

"Did the aliens threaten them in any way?"

"No. Apparently they were as surprised to see the Trens as the Trens were to have come upon them. The aliens started to speak in some strange language, and that's when the Trens knew they weren't Hamloorian and fled back into the desert."

"Seven aliens hardly constitute a threat to Hamloor or even to the Trens," Nazleen observed drily. "And if there was a woman with them . . ."

"The Trens *saw* only seven, but there must have been more. They were on foot, with no sign of horses or supplies. My guess is that they were just a small group out exploring the territory. The rest probably weren't very far away. As I recall, there

18

are some well-protected ravines in that area that would make an excellent campsite for an army.

"And as for the presence of a woman among them, if there was one, she might well have been a camp follower." He gave Nazleen another smile.

"Although, from the Trens' description, they'd have to be pretty desperate to have camp followers like that."

There was general laughter among the males at the table over that, their conversation having been closely followed by all within hearing.

Despite the traditional mistrust between the court and the Warriors, Miklav was quite popular with many in the palace, the men in particular. He was an excellent raconteur and rather less arrogant than his predecessor had been, though not by much. Warrior Chiefs were never known for their humility.

"Milady, I think it would be wise for you to send word to the Chieftain of the Desert Trens, requesting his permission for a possible march through their lands."

"I've already done so," Nazleen replied, "although it could take quite a while to locate him."

Miklav nodded his approval as he continued to devour his meat. "He shouldn't be too hard to find. It's near enough to the storm season that he won't be too far into the desert."

Nazleen glanced at him, suspecting that he knew exactly where the Trens' Chieftain was. Both Nazleen and her mother before her had always harbored suspicions that the Warriors ignored the ban against venturing into the desert.

Old Andras took over the conversation once

more, asking about the current state of Warrior relations with the Mountain Trens. All seemed peaceful to the court, but they could never really be sure. Warriors and Trens lived too far from the city and in too close proximity to each other in many cases.

"They're behaving," Miklav stated, his tone suggesting that they'd do well to continue to do so. "There have been some minor skirmishes over hunting rights here and there, but that's about all."

"Do you mean that they've been invading your territory?" Nazleen inquired, even though she didn't believe any such thing. In all likelihood, it was the Warriors who had encroached upon Trens territory.

"Occasionally—and we've strayed onto their lands a few times, too." Her disapproving look moved him to further explanation.

"There aren't any clear boundaries out there, Milady, and sometimes the game flees from their territory to ours or vice versa. There was also a problem a few months ago when some Trens stole horses that had been let out to pasture at Treba, but that's been settled."

"Settled in what way?" Nazleen asked archly. Such disputes should have been brought to court.

"We went out and brought them back," Miklav replied with an innocence that scarcely suited him.

Nazleen exchanged a meaningful glance with her Minister for the Trens. This matter would have to be looked into. No protest had been registered with the court by the Trens, but they were a strange people who might well have decided to settle things their own way. And that way could easily lead to violence with the Trens getting the worst of it.

The dinner concluded with the traditional herbal tea preferred by the court and the strong brew enjoyed by the Warriors. Nazleen was looking forward to retiring to her quarters. Miklav's presence was far more disturbing to her this night than usual, perhaps because she knew that deep down inside she'd already reached a decision regarding him but wasn't yet ready to face the consequences. She rose to signal her intention to retire, but Miklav forestalled her.

"Would Milady care to walk in the gardens? The mizias are blooming now, aren't they?"

His voice was just loud enough to attract the attention of those around them and held a carefully calculated note of challenge as well. She couldn't refuse, and she knew he was aware of that. To refuse might give rise to rumours that she feared the Warrior Chief, and no Liege could afford that. There were still many men in Hamloor who doubted a woman's ability to rule and would prefer to see the Warrior Chief in control.

So she acquiesced with formal politeness and left the dining hall on his arm.

The lush, heavy fragrance of the mizias surrounded them the moment they emerged from the palace. The night-blooming flowers held their scent during the day in tightly closed cups, then released it as they opened at night. Their faintly iridescent blossoms were everywhere, shimmering against the blackness.

Miklav breathed deeply. "It's unfortunate that they won't grow in the mountains."

Nazleen didn't reply, recognizing an ingratiating

comment when she heard one. Warriors were about as interested in flowers as they were in art—which is to say, not at all—and it was very well-known that Nazleen, like her mother, loved the rare and delicate flowers.

They strolled along the pebbled paths, moving deeper into the deserted gardens. Her hand continued to rest lightly on the Warrior Chief's heavily muscled arm. To remove it now might signal fear on her part.

She was thinking that perhaps she should just take him as a mate now and get it over with. With any luck at all, she would conceive quickly and the first child would be female. Thereafter, she could remain celibate or, if she chose, take a consort from among the men at court as her mother had done.

Nazleen was 27, a very young age to be Liege. She'd been barely 21 when her mother had succumbed to a sudden illness. For that reason, she'd made the advancement of medicine one of her highest priorities, and the results thus far had been very encouraging. Just the other day, her medical advisor had informed her that a cure for the disease that had killed her mother might have been found.

But if war came, all progress would halt. War would deplete even Hamloor's considerable resources. And yet, she thought, war is just what Miklav wants. With that thought, she unconsciously moved away from him.

"Milady?" he inquired.

She turned to face him in the darkness. "I do not want a war, Miklav. In only twenty years of peace, we have advanced further than in the previous one hundred, and the future promises so very much."

He looked down at her, his expression unreadable in the dim light. "We may have no choice, Milady."

"And that is just what you want, isn't it?"

Miklav said nothing. A lie would be unconscionable, and the truth would displease her. If he didn't desire her so much, he might be willing to risk her wrath. What could she do, after all? He might have sworn allegiance to her, but he'd never promised to agree with her at all times.

The only thing the Warrior Chief wanted more than his beautiful Liege was power, and under the terms of the Compact, true power came to him only in time of war. Despite what he knew she believed, it wasn't really war he wanted—it was power. Both as a man and as the Warrior Chief, power should be his right.

He admitted to himself, though, that she wasn't likely to see much difference between his wanting war and wanting power.

As she walked on ahead of him, he let her go for a moment, watching as she moved with a slow grace along the path. He knew that she'd chosen her outfit this evening to put him off, just as she often found ways to torment him. What she didn't know was that he was just old enough to find it almost as amusing as it was frustrating.

But you will be mine, he told her silently. You don't want any of us, but you will choose me. And he hoped that she wouldn't conceive too quickly and that the first child would be male.

She had stopped at the end of the path, where an ornately carved gazebo stood against the edge of the royal forest. As he walked toward her, she turned suddenly to face him, her expression one of rigid determination. He sighed inwardly, certain that he was about to receive yet another lecture on the bloodlust of Warriors in general and of him in particular. But this time, he was wrong.

"It is time I chose a mate, Miklav. If anything should happen to me, my cousin would become Liege and she is clearly unsuitable—by her own admission. When we have settled this matter of the aliens, I will announce that I have chosen you. But I want you to know that I would rather not choose *any* of you."

Miklav stared at her, keeping his expression carefully neutral. For a moment, he was tempted to remind her that he had the right to refuse her. Under other circumstances, she might have found that amusing, given the fact that his desire was certainly well-known to her. Since her sense of humor was nowhere in evidence at the moment, he resisted the temptation.

He also suspected that her timing indicated an ulterior motive, but he refrained from suggesting that, too. Instead, he bowed slightly, thinking that like her mother, she could be a first-rate schemer.

"I am honored, Milady."

Then, impulsively, he reached out and took her hand and brought it to his lips briefly, a court gesture he frankly found foppish. But he knew it would catch her off-guard, and her surprised expression proved him correct.

"Has Milady taken a lover yet?" he inquired, knowing perfectly well that she hadn't. He had his spies, even in the royal palace.

"No." The question wasn't really presumptuous

under the circumstances, but it wasn't necessary, either. She knew exactly who his spies were.

"And you will not be my lover, either, Miklav. We will mate because we must. Understand that."

He merely smiled, always amused at that imperious tone she used so well. Perhaps she would never speak of him as her lover, but she would enjoy their nights together, nevertheless. Miklav knew he was as skilled in the arts of lovemaking as he was in the arts of war. He'd learned many years ago that pleasing a woman only increased his own pleasure.

"I would like to be left alone now," she stated in that same tone, "and I'm sure you would prefer the company of Shara."

"I intend to remain in the palace tonight, Milady, since we will be leaving at dawn." He made another bow and strode away quickly. Nazleen watched his black-clad form blend quickly into the darkness. Her remark about Shara was ringing unpleasantly in her ears. He might very well believe that she had spoken in jealousy.

Shara was a craftswoman in the city who had borne Miklav a son and a daughter. Her sources told her that he actually appeared to be faithful to her and, even more surprisingly, that he was known to spend time with his children.

It wasn't unusual for a Warrior to spend time with his sons, particularly as they approached the age of decision. Every Warrior wanted his sons to follow his path. But Miklav's son was only three and his daughter eight, and Warriors generally had little interest in such young children.

But then, Miklav's present behavior wasn't so unusual for him. He had another son, now 13, who had gone to the great fortress of Denra to live with his father when he was only seven. The boy's mother had died, and Miklav had petitioned Nazleen's mother to permit the boy to go with his father, rather than being put into the care of relatives. Granting his request had been one of her mother's last acts as Liege.

The truth was that Nazleen had never really settled her mind about Miklav. At times, she actually liked him—particularly when she remembered his kindnesses and attentions to her when she was a child and he visited the palace often as an aide to her father.

He was quite popular, not only at court but even among the general populace. He spent far more time in the city than had past Warrior Chiefs, and she was often uneasy about that. When she'd once questioned him about it, he'd replied with apparent sincerity that a modern Warrior Chief had to be a soldier-diplomat and gain the trust and affection of the people.

Even his faithfulness to Shara had endeared him to a small but growing minority in Hamloor who were life-mated. Such relationships, while not actually illegal, were nonetheless frowned on by the court, because through such means had men controlled women for centuries, so they could make war upon each other.

Most Warriors fathered children to women in the city or in the farm communes, but they also spent most of their off-duty time in the pleasure houses on the fringes of the city. If her sources were correct, Miklav hadn't been seen there since his youth.

Well, she thought, still staring into the darkness after him, now I've done it—and the sooner it's over with, the better. She would consult the Healers at Cerece about the optimum time for conception, and if fortune were with her, she would have to lie with Miklav only once.

By the time the morning mists had burned off, the royal caravan had left the city behind and was moving along the wide road that wound through Hamloor's fertile farmlands. Workers in the fields, seeing the fluttering green banners carried by two court pages, left their tasks and hurried to the roadside, where they bowed deeply as the royal retinue passed. No one appreciated the reign of peace more than these farmers, whose lands and animals had been constantly ravaged by war in the past.

Dressed in a short green cloak embossed with gold and a wide, split skirt of the same shade, Nazleen moved with the easy grace of an accomplished horsewoman. When she rode in the privacy of the royal forest, she wore pants, but such attire would be offensive to the farmfolk and the Trens whose lands she would be passing through. Her mount was one of the Royal Whites—small, elegant horses whose delicacy of appearance belied great stamina and speed.

At her side, Miklav rode a huge black stallion, one of the steeds of war bred in the Warriors' mountain fortresses. He was dressed as always in the traditional Warrior's black uniform, decorated in his case with the green insignia of the royal court. His rank was further evidenced by twining ropes of gold that crossed his broad shoulders and banded his sleeves.

The other Warriors—more of them than Nazleen would have preferred—also wore black, but their uniforms were less heavily decorated and the insignia showed only their fortress. Only the Warrior Chief wore the royal insignia because only he swore allegiance to the Liege. The others pledged their fealty to their commanders.

As Nazleen acknowledged the homage of her people, she noted the slight uneasiness with which some of their gazes rested on the Warriors, especially Miklav. Still, it was a great improvement; they no longer fled in terror whenever the men in black approached.

For that, she knew she had Miklav to thank. Her father had done little to prevent Warriors from galloping through planted fields and terrorizing rural males and raping the females. Miklav had put an end to that in typically brutal Warrior fashion by having any offenders executed.

Nazleen cast a sidelong glance at Miklav, understanding completely why the rural folk still feared them in spite of their much improved behavior. Even with no possible enemy in sight, they all bristled with weaponry. A pistol was sheathed in a holster at his side, a long rifle rested in a scabbard beside the saddle and a small dagger was visible along the top of his high boots. Even his helmet, with its pointed crest, looked deadly.

"Milady?" he queried, breaking the long silence.

Nazleen fought down her irritation. He noticed too much. "I dislike all this show of weaponry. It isn't necessary, and it frightens the people."

"Milady, there are aliens just across the desert. It is not unreasonable to believe that they might have sent spies or even assassins into Hamloor."

Nazleen turned to him sharply. "Do you truly believe that?"

He shrugged, and the morning sun glinted off the gold ropes on his shoulders. "It is what I would do in their place . . . what, in fact, we will be doing."

"*If* the Augury shows danger," she reminded him acerbically. But the thought of aliens actually within her borders troubled her greatly. The Warrior fortresses were widely scattered, and although the city was well-protected, the surrounding countryside was highly vulnerable in many places. She recalled unhappily how she'd refused Miklav's request to build more fortresses.

Then she grimaced as she realized that she was thinking like a Warrior. Even if aliens *had* entered Hamloor, might not their intentions be entirely peaceful?

They had reached a small stretch of forest where the road narrowed beneath huge old trees that nearly formed a canopy overhead. Six Warriors had spurred their horses and moved ahead of them, and one now rode on either side of Miklav and her. Miklav had unfastened the holster that held his pistol, and the other Warriors now carried their rifles. Heads swiveled constantly, searching the dense forest on both sides.

Nazleen looked around her at the dark, bearded men and felt almost more frightened than protected. Even her little mare shied from the closeness of the huge horses. Miklav reached for her reins just as she tightened her own grip on them.

29

Then, apparently satisfied that she had the mare under control, he merely touched her hand briefly and withdrew.

"We'll be back in the open soon," he said quietly.

Nazleen chafed inwardly at his behavior. She'd never been able to separate the Warriors' overprotectiveness toward her as Liege from their similar attitude toward women in general. As her mother had once remarked, "They would protect us to keep us in our places."

But the Compact required the Warriors to protect the Liege at all times, whether or not the Liege felt it necessary. It was another of the compromises worked out to guarantee the future of their society.

As soon as they emerged once more into open farmland, the other Warriors withdrew to a discreet distance, leaving her alone with Miklav. The closeness of so many bearded men brought to her mind yet another curious thing about Miklav. Warriors by tradition had always worn beards, harking back to the days when their lives were spent in battle with no time to shave. Other males, particularly those at court and in the city, were clean-shaven. She'd always assumed that here was yet another means by which he sought to portray himself as a so-called warrior-diplomat.

"Why do you not wear a beard, Miklav?"

He smiled at her, as though pleased by her personal interest in him. "It's a matter of personal vanity, Milady. My beard is reddish in color and therefore looks strange."

She glanced at him, her expression conveying her skepticism at that explanation. Warriors weren't known for their vanity in such matters, and Miklav certainly had never seemed vain in any other way.

"Also, Shara has very sensitive skin." His gaze lingered for a moment on her own very fair skin.

"You talk as though you're life-mated," she said scornfully, choosing to ignore his double meaning.

"In a manner of speaking, I suppose we are," he replied equably. "Since the days of my hot-blooded youth, I've never considered variety to be a desirable quality when it comes to women. Besides, as you surely know, Shara is the mother of my two children."

He paused briefly, then went on in a surprisingly subdued tone. "My parents were life-mated. They lived on one of the eastern communes."

Nazleen wondered why he was telling her all this. Was it possible that he was discreetly suggesting she look elsewhere for a mate? It didn't seem likely, given his behavior toward her, but she now decided to face the issue squarely.

"Are you trying to tell me that you would prefer my choosing another mate? Because if you are, I will certainly honor that request."

His gaze locked boldly onto hers as he shook his head. "No, Milady. If that were the case, I would have told you. What I have said I've said to make you understand that I take fatherhood very seriously, unlike your own father and most Warriors."

She stared at him for a moment longer, then let her gaze slide away. "Sometimes you truly surprise me, Miklav."

"And I may surprise you still more in the future, Milady."

Nazleen lapsed into silence, thinking about the implications of his statement. It was certainly true that her father had spent virtually no time with either of his children. He hadn't even bothered much with Haslik, since he had no need to persuade him to become a Warrior. The Liege's sons were required to become Warriors.

A part of her had always resented her father's lack of interest, despite the attention showered upon her by everyone else. But now she began to think of the problems presented by an overattentive father, and she found she didn't like that idea, either. What influences might he gain over a future Liege? Furthermore, what would it mean for her own authority if he were always around? She wouldn't be able to deny him access to his own children.

He is issuing yet another challenge, she thought. Boldness was a quality one expected in a Warrior Chief, but Miklav might well be the first of his kind to combine boldness with intelligence—and that could make him very dangerous indeed.

They took their noontime meal at an inn along the Western Road. The innkeeper had prepared a marvelous repast, providing the Warriors with their disgusting meat, while Nazleen and the courtiers who accompanied her enjoyed delicate mountain nuts and fresh fruits and cheeses.

Afterwards, Miklav politely inquired whether she might like to rest for a while—a suite had been prepared for her use—but Nazleen demurred. She was a little tired from the unaccustomed long ride, but she was more determined not to show any sign of weakness.

So they set out once more, coming by midafternoon to the intersection where the Western Road split, with one branch veering off toward Denra and the other going more southerly toward Cerece. Miklav called a temporary halt, and the party dismounted to stretch their legs by walking through a pretty glade.

Nazleen quickly set off alone. Her aides were accustomed to her solitary strolls and understood that someone who was almost constantly surrounded by people needed to be alone from time to time. But Miklav apparently had no such understanding, because she had gone only a short distance when she heard someone behind her and turned to see him following at a discreet distance.

"This is not the royal forest, Milady. It isn't wise for you to be walking alone now."

She started to protest, then remembered his warning about possible alien spies and instead nodded her acquiescence. He took that as a signal to close the distance between them.

His earlier comments about his parents and his relationship with Shara had set her thoughts to the subject of life-mating. Although the majority of her people did not live that way, the numbers who did were apparently growing, and some of her female Advisors were pressing her to outlaw the practice. As one of them had said, "Life-mating is by definition a form of bondage."

"You said earlier that you were more or less life-mated to Shara, Miklav. Are you in love with her?"

"I am content with her."

"That isn't the same thing."

He cocked a dark brow in amusement. "How can you be sure of that, Milady?"

Well, he had her there. She remained silent.

"My parents certainly loved each other and were very happy together," he went on in what was for him a gentle tone, "but such a thing really isn't possible for me. A Warrior Chief has too many responsibilities. Like a Liege," he added after a pause.

She nodded. "You are right. Perhaps we understand each other better than I'd expected."

But she was stunned to feel a strange sadness. His mention of his parents reminded her of another discussion long ago with someone whose parents had been life-mated—her old friend and Cerecian mentor, Loreth.

Nazleen was glad that she would soon be among the Cerecians again. Obviously if she was thinking such foolish thoughts, she needed to draw strength from the Sisterhood. Loreth had certainly given up such absurd romanticism long ago.

As though he had tuned in on her thoughts, Miklav suddenly broke the silence. "How many Cerecians are there now, Milady?"

She frowned at him. He should know better than to ask such a question. No Warrior had any right to information regarding the Sisterhood.

"I ask only because it's possible that we may have need of them, and my sources tell me that there are far fewer of them these days."

His candor astounded her. Now he was even admitting to spying on them. "How many do your sources tell you there are?"

"Fewer than two hundred."

"That's about right." In fact, there were just barely 170 including the elderly and the Novices.

He grunted unhappily. "That's not good news."

"Not good news? I would have thought you'd be very pleased."

He shook his head. "No, Milady. The days when Cerecians fought Warriors is long past. If another war is to be fought, we will be allies."

His tone troubled her. He seemed to be taking it for granted that war lay ahead. A tremor went through her, leaving icy shards of fear in its wake. To cover it, she sighed.

"I will be happy to reach Cerece. I've not been there for over a year."

Miklav nodded, knowing that because he always knew of her movements. But the tone of her voice emboldened him to ask a personal question of his own.

"If you hadn't become Liege, would you have been content to remain at Cerece?"

"Yes," she said without hesitation and with a regret she couldn't quite conceal.

"Then the prospect of lying with me—or with any man—does not please you."

"No, it does not. But the Compact must come before my pleasure."

She turned then and started back to the others. Miklav followed, determined he would prove her wrong. As far as he was concerned, the terms of the Compact would assure her a pleasure that the life of a celibate mystic could never provide.

Miklav was a happy man. Two challenges lay ahead—the aliens and the woman in front of him. He faced two challenges and two paths to power.

CHAPTER TWO

THE ROYAL PARTY STAYED THAT NIGHT AT AN INN THAT catered primarily to families who were traveling to visit the Cerecians. Some were relatives of members of the Sisterhood, who were permitted annual visits, and some were families bringing a sick relative to be treated by the famed Cerecian Healers, who could often cure by the laying on of hands.

Nazleen went directly to her suite, where she took her evening meal and remained for the night, foregoing even a stroll through the gardens behind the inn. As she drew closer to her spiritual home, she had less and less desire to spend any time in the company of Miklav.

The Warrior Chief passed most of his evening playing cards with his men and drinking the potent mountain brew favored by the locals, who were a mixture of Trens and Hamloorian miners. But late in the evening he received two Warriors who had ridden hard from Denra to inform him that the Chieftain of the Desert Trens had been found and "persuaded" to agree to the passage of Warriors through his land.

The Chieftain had also been told to make haste to the campsite where the royal representative would be most likely to find him quickly. Naturally, he would say nothing about his visit from the Warriors.

The method of persuasion, used occasionally in the past by Miklav, had been the taking of a hostage, one of the Chieftain's sons. The boy would be held at Denra until the Warriors had passed without interference through the desert. It worked quite well—and without bloodshed—although Miklav doubted that his Liege would have approved.

There was another benefit to this method, too. All three of the Chieftain's sons would now have spent time at Denra, the most powerful of all the Warrior fortresses. They were always given free run of the place, although under discreet supervision. Miklav knew that the boys would report back to their father their impressions of Warrior strength and power, and they would remember that visit when one of them became Chieftain some day. To further the impression of limitless power, Miklav imported both Warriors and weaponry from other fortresses for the occasion.

So Miklav went off to bed satisfied—except for the potential problem of the Augury. Since he didn't understand it, he therefore had no faith whatsoever in it and even suspected that it might be falsified in some manner to show whatever the Cerecians decided it should portend.

He was determined to do battle with these aliens regardless of the outcome of the Augury, however. He knew that once a war had been started, how it actually began became a matter for historians.

In the meantime, however, he would bide his time, prepare his troops and play his Liege's game.

Once again the party was off with the rising of the sun. Up here in the foothills of the great mountains, there was no morning mist; the air was clear and fresh and cool. Nazleen rode enshrouded in a heavy green cloak, and even Miklav had donned a black woolen cape.

The horses were rested and eager to run, but their riders held them in check, knowing that ahead of them, the road rose ever more steeply. As the birds flew, the distance from the inn to Cerece wasn't far, no more than 20 kilometers, but the road twisted and turned upon itself as it avoided the steepest grades.

After less than an hour's ride, they spotted the first of the distinctive stone mounds the Trens used to mark their lands, and shortly thereafter they approached a Tren village. Since royal heralds had been there the day before, the villagers weren't taken by surprise, but even so, many of them looked with suspicion upon the Warriors. Their memories of the havoc once wreaked upon them by the Warriors were still clear, and because they lived in close proximity to the Cerecians and were in many cases indebted to the Sisterhood, they were unwilling to let go of old enmities.

The party stopped in the village square to water the horses and to receive the traditional gifts of potent berry wine and creamy, delicate cheeses for which the Trens were justly renowned. Nazleen accepted these gifts graciously and in turn presented the headman with the first shipment of a new herbal medicine for kwati, a dread disease that often claimed the lives of young children.

Nazleen was always slightly saddened by these visits, because although the Trens were respectful toward her, they clearly did not regard her as one of their own. Despite the fact that Tren blood flowed in her veins, she was seen as being Hamloorian and therefore more closely aligned to the Warriors who guarded her. Not even the fact that she was also Cerecian could overcome that handicap.

The life of a Liege was not easy. She was rejected by her kin, the Trens, for her alliance with the Warriors, she was resented by the Warriors for her power over them, and perhaps worst of all, at least from Nazleen's standpoint, she didn't even truly belong to the Sisterhood.

"We are the embodiment of the Compact and nothing more," her mother had stated many times. But Lieges could take heart from the certainty that the Compact was the adhesive force that held together their fractious society.

Throughout the ceremony in the Tren village, the Warriors, to Miklav's credit, tried to remain as unobtrusive as possible. But since Miklav himself stayed very visibly at her side, this made little difference and certainly did nothing for the already nervous state of the village headman.

Nazleen did her best to put the man at ease, but her command of the difficult Tren language had slipped from disuse, and several times she was forced to turn to Miklav for assistance. She suspected that her kind words spoken in his gruff military manner lost most of their intended meaning.

Finally, they were on their way again, moving up the steep road in double file—two rows of Warriors in the lead, followed by Nazleen and Miklav, with alternating rows of courtiers and Warriors behind them and more Warriors bringing up the rear. The forest grew ever more dense, making it difficult to see into it for more than a dozen or so meters. All the Warriors save for Miklav himself were once again carrying their rifles. Miklav allowed his weapons to remain partly hidden. Knowing it was a concession to her, Nazleen found herself rather touched by that.

Miklav could so often do that to her, she thought ruefully. He frequently irritated her and sometimes even angered her, then he would do something that touched her in some strange, unexpected way. Like that awkward attempt to kiss her hand the other night, they were often things that she knew were against his true nature.

After her mother's death, when she was still in a daze from the suddenness of it all, it was Miklav who had bolstered her confidence by reminding her that her mother had had every confidence in her ability to rule. Others had extended sympathy, but it was the Warrior Chief who had given her the will to assume her new position.

And of all the tears she'd seen in the eyes of everyone around her at that dark time, it was the wetness in Miklav's dark eyes that stayed in her memory. She hadn't known that Warriors could cry, and later she realized that it was even more surprising that he had allowed her to *see* him cry.

She glanced at him just as he turned his head in her direction, and without thought, she smiled at him. He returned the smile and started to draw closer to her, but then his eyes shifted suddenly to a spot behind her and he shouted a warning.

In a flurry of motion that she never quite sorted out, he grabbed her reins and forced her mount into a tight circle of Warriors who appeared from nowhere. Then he disappeared from her view, although she could hear him shouting orders. Because both the Warriors and their horses were so much bigger than Nazleen and her mare, she could see nothing but black uniforms and black horses.

The Warriors surrounding her had their weapons trained on something ahead of them, but as yet no shots had been fired. Then she heard shouting in the Tren language. Miklav's voice was recognizable to her as he commanded someone to stop and throw down their weapons. The excited response was too garbled for her to understand, and Miklav's next words were muffled by the movements of the Warriors around her. As soon as they began to relax their vigilance, she urged her mare through the space between them.

Miklav and four other Warriors sat astride their chargers, blocking the narrow road, while a short distance away two Trens sat nervously on their sturdy little mountain ponies. Their rifles lay in the road between the two groups. The discussion was continuing, but between the Trens' obvious agitation and their heavy local accents, Nazleen could understand nothing.

As soon as the Trens spotted her, they were visibly relieved and stumbled off their ponies to bow to her. Then the older of the two gestured to her as he spoke excitedly to Miklav. Nazleen understood only two of his rapid string of words: "danger" and "Liege". For the first time, she began to feel real fear and unconsciously moved closer to Miklav.

"What has happened here?" she demanded of the Warrior Chief. But he ignored her and began issuing orders to his men, then acceded to the Trens' request to take back their weapons.

A few moments later, two Warriors left the group with the two Trens, riding hard up the road in the direction from which the mountain men had come.

The party was quickly reassembled, with two Warriors now flanking each pair of courtiers, all of them packed so closely on the narrow road that bodies and animals touched. One very large Warrior rode up beside her, and after surveying the lineup, Miklav closed in on her other side. Nazleen repeated her question in an exasperated tone as she tried to calm her nervous mare.

"Aliens, milady. The Trens spotted four of them in the woods about five kilometers from here, headed toward the Cerecian lands."

"Aliens?" Nazleen gasped. "At Cerece?"

"No, they hadn't reached Cerece, but they were definitely headed in that direction. Two of my men and the Trens have gone after them, but it's rugged country and they'll have to go most of the way on foot. The Trens were fleeing from them when I spotted them. Naturally, I thought they were planning to attack *us*. That's why I reacted the way I did."

He paused long enough to look her over carefully. "Are you all right, Milady?"

Nazleen nodded mutely. Aliens near Cerece! It seemed unthinkable! Then, for one brief moment, she remembered that strange dream she'd had several months ago. No, there couldn't be any relationship. Miklav had described the aliens seen at the ruins, and she quickly dismissed the thought.

It seemed that Miklav had been correct to worry about her safety, and she told him so. In response, he reached over to cover her hands briefly with one of his.

"I'm sworn to protect you, Milady," he said formally as he withdrew his hand. Then he added in a lower voice, "And inclined to do so in any event."

"What were the aliens doing?" she asked, trying to ignore his intent gaze.

"Walking through the woods up the mountain toward Cerece. The Trens were out hunting and just stumbled upon them. They fled because they had no way of knowing if there might be more of them."

He paused, then added, "And now we know that they've crossed the desert."

They had reached a short stretch of open land where a fire had cleared away most of the trees and all of the underbrush. After surveying the land on both sides, Miklav ordered the Warrior who was flanking Nazleen to move ahead with the others, leaving the two of them alone.

"Could they invade the Cerecian lands, Milady?"

Nazleen hesitated; the same question was on her mind. Under normal circumstances, it would be impossible for anyone to reach Cerece without the Sister's foreknowledge. Watchers were stationed along the perimeters at all times. It was an ancient tradition no longer necessary for protection (or at least so they'd believed), but it had long ago been made a part of Novice training and thus still continued. She herself had stood many watches. Being the daughter of the Liege hadn't conferred any special privileges in Cerece.

But at this particular time, the Sisters would be preparing for the Augury, and it was possible, given their diminished numbers and the lack of danger for so long, that at least some of the perimeters would be left unguarded.

She hesitated a moment longer, then told Miklav this, having decided that the safety of Cerece outweighed any concerns about divulging such information to Warriors.

"Then we must escort you up to the compound," he stated flatly, "and we will remain there until watchers can be posted and guards obtained from Denra."

"You know that's forbidden," Nazleen protested. "No Warrior can enter Cerecian lands."

"Milady, your safety—and the safety of the Sisters—comes first. Unless we have guards around the compound itself, you're all in danger."

"No one could get over the compound's walls," Nazleen scoffed.

"There are breaches in that wall that should have

been repaired long ago."

She stared at him, aghast. "You have trespassed on Cerecian lands?"

"The Sisterhood is under Warrior protection just as everyone else is, and I can't guarantee protection if I don't know what defenses exist."

"But how could you possibly have gotten all the way up to the compound without the watchers knowing of your presence?" At the moment, her curiosity exceeded even her outrage.

"We didn't trespass on Cerecian lands," he explained. "We found a high spot on Tren land and used our scopes."

She might have pointed out that trespassing on Tren land was forbidden as well, but instead she asked what scopes were.

Surprisingly, Miklav gave her an apologetic smile. "If I answer that, Milady, I will be ruining your birthday present from Haslik. He invented them and I have given him permission to present you with one."

"I insist upon knowing what they are, Miklav. If Warriors have trespassed on Cerecian lands . . ."

"I gave you my word that we haven't," he cut in testily. "Scopes are tubes with glass that is bent in several ways. When you look into them, they bring distant objects very close."

For a moment, Nazleen was so fascinated by her brother's ingenuity that she forgot about the nefarious purpose to which it had been put. Haslik had always liked to build things.

"In any event, from the description I received, that wall isn't impregnable. Why has it been allowed to deteriorate?"

Now it was Nazleen's turn to be testy. "There were more important things than rebuilding walls that weren't really needed."

"Well, since we'll already be breaking the rules by escorting you up there, I'll put together a work detail of Trens and Warriors to rebuild it right away."

"No."

"Then you and the Pavla can give me your word that you'll stop your chanting or whatever you do and rebuild it yourselves—immediately."

"Loreth won't see you, and you aren't the one giving orders there, Miklav."

"So Loreth is Pavla, eh?" He chuckled. "That doesn't really surprise me, and I do think she'll see me."

"You . . . you know her?" Nazleen stared at him in astonishment.

"We grew up together on a commune. Our families were close friends. She's a few years older than me, so she left for Cerece before I left to become a Warrior."

"She still won't see you, Miklav. Pavlas never grant audiences to anyone from the outside world. The only Sisters who see outsiders other than their own families are the Healers."

"We will see—and that wall will be rebuilt one way or the other."

"Miklav, I don't like your attitude." Nazleen glared at him, her eyes like green ice. It was the kind of look that froze her courtiers in place.

"And I don't like the thought of your being at the mercy of the aliens," he retorted, meeting her glare with a dark one of his own. "Your protection is my business."

She could not believe that she would be at their mercy, certainly not at Cerece, but the truth was that she couldn't be sure—although she certainly couldn't tell him that. It was commonly accepted among the Warriors that the Sisterhood could no longer wield the fire as they had once done, and successive Lieges had said nothing to either confirm or deny that. It was generally agreed that the Warriors were better left in the dark.

No one—not even the Pavla—knew if they truly *could* wield the fire in battle now. A few of the Sisters still occasionally practiced the exercises, but no one now alive had ever attempted it. There had seemed little point.

They'd all felt so safe at Cerece, and until today that had seemed a reasonable belief. But perhaps they'd been living all this time in an illusion.

The road had again become narrow and winding, and the thick forest closed in around them. The other Warriors surrounded her once more. A short time later, they reached the small cluster of stone houses that marked the outer boundaries of Cerece. A low, crumbling stone wall snaked off into the woods on both sides. This wall existed only to mark the outer boundaries of Cerece, and the rugged little houses had been built long ago to accommodate visitors to the Sisterhood.

When the party came to a halt, Miklav gave orders for most of his Warriors to remain there with the courtiers, then summoned three of them to accompany him up to the compound. There was great consternation all around.

Nazleen remained silent as he explained the situation to them. She knew he could legitimately claim that there was a threat to her life, which meant, according to the Compact, that it was he who was in charge now. That didn't give him the right to enter Cerecian lands, but to prevent that she herself would have to remain here—and that she couldn't do. It had become absolutely essential now that she see the Augury for herself.

The small group crossed the boundary into Cerece. Nazleen saw with considerable satisfaction that the Warriors seemed nervous. It could be that they were simply concerned about encountering aliens, but she suspected that they were more worried about offending the Sisterhood. Warriors tended to dismiss the Sisters as a group of harmless mystics at best, but she was certain that was nothing more than typical Warrior bluster.

Miklav, by contrast, seemed unaffected. Unlike the others, he rode casually, though he still regularly surveyed the lands through which they passed. Perhaps his discovery that the Pavla was an old childhood friend made him less wary. Nazleen was still astonished at that coincidence. Loreth knew that Miklav was the Warrior Chief, and yet she'd never mentioned that she'd grown up with him.

But instead of pondering the strangeness of that, Nazleen emptied out her mind and reached out in the unique Cerecian manner. She had been right; there were no watchers, at least along this side of the compound. She glanced at Miklav to find him watching her intently, but neither of them spoke.

Several miles further along, Nazleen suddenly

felt something brush against her mind. For a fraction of a second, she was frightened; it had been a long time. Then she opened herself quickly and felt the question. She sent back a calming message, a "don't worry" signal. Her skills were rusty, and she could only hope it would be understood.

"They know we're here," Miklav said into the silence. It was a statement, not a question.

She nodded. That Cerecians could communicate telepathically with each other was well-known to the outside world. It was another talent that had proved invaluable to them in their long ago battle with the Warriors.

"Well, even if they do still know how to wield the fire, we're safe enough with you in our midst," he stated.

Nazleen knew his words were intended for the visibly nervous men around them. "Yes, she replied. "But they will be very disturbed."

They rode on toward the compound, with Nazleen feeling more and more a traitor to the Sisterhood. She could only hope that her close friendship with Loreth, her old mentor, would survive this breach of the rules. As Liege, she couldn't actually be banned from Cerece, but she *could* be forbidden to take part in ceremonies, including the Augury.

Then she began to feel the unique pull of the sacred fire-pool, and her fears dissolved into longing. A part of her that remained dormant in the palace began to awaken, rather like a sudden flexing of mental muscles. It felt like coming home.

The road rose and dipped, rose steeply again, and then the ancient home of the Cerecians lay before

49

them. The outer wall and the buildings beyond were all composed of a native stone that had a mellow amber cast to it, and in the late afternoon sun it glowed with a warmth and serenity.

Beside her, Miklav made a sound of appreciation, but Nazleen barely heard him as she stared at the repository of her youthful dreams and her awakening to a world far removed from ordinary life.

They were less than 100 meters from the open entrance to the compound when three riders appeared on the shaggy ponies supplied to the Sisters by their Tren neighbors. Two were older women well-known to Nazleen, and the third was a young Novice, the only one of the trio who betrayed any nervousness.

One rider was the Chief Healer, chosen, Nazleen assumed, because of her regular contact with the outside world, but there was no doubt about why the eldest of the trio was there. Ecara had obviously been chosen for her extraordinary ability to read minds—all minds, not just those of her Sisters. Miklav would never know it, but his thoughts would be carefully and delicately probed to determine his true purpose for being here.

Nazleen was not unaware of the great significance of this moment. This was the first meeting between Sisters and Warriors since the signing of the Compact nearly 100 years ago.

It was the Healer who addressed Nazleen in the Cerecian tongue. There was no gesture of respect to her as Liege; the Cerecians, like the Warriors, swore their allegiance only to the Sisterhood. Only Loreth, as Pavla, would greet her as Liege. Instead,

Nazleen was greeted as a Sister, even though her position had prohibited her from taking the final oath.

As the formal greetings were exchanged, old Ecara gazed steadily at Miklav from beneath her half-concealing hood. Even as she intoned her part of the ritual greeting, Nazleen was wondering what would happen if Ecara discerned any hidden purpose to Miklav's presence.

Then the Healer's gaze swept over the Warriors. "What is the meaning of this, Sister? Why have you brought Warriors into our midst?"

Still using the Cerecian tongue, Nazleen explained as briefly as possible. Beside her, Miklav was stirring restlessly in his saddle. The other two Warriors were a few paces behind, but the creaking of their saddle leather indicated that they too were uneasy.

Some Hamloorians and Trens spoke the Cerecian tongue, particularly those among whom the Cerecian blood flowed strongly. But Nazleen knew that Miklav didn't speak it, and she doubted that the other Warriors did, either.

She quickly finished her account by mentioning the breach in the compound's wall, which was not visible from where they were now.

"You have told them of this?"

Nazleen hesitated. For a moment, she wondered if it might be better for the Sisters to think she had told the Warriors, rather than having them learn that they were being spied upon. But she finally told the truth, knowing that she must.

All three women stared very hard at Miklav, who met them stare for stare. *Either he is very brave*

51

indeed, Nazleen thought, or he truly believes that fire-wielding is a long-lost skill.

Finally, the Healer exchanged a brief glance with Ecara. Even Nazleen could feel the old woman's approval. Miklav had passed the test: he harbored no secret intentions.

"Follow us," the Healer said as the trio turned their ponies and started back to the compound.

"What did you tell them?" Miklav demanded softly as they urged their mounts forward.

"The truth," Nazleen replied. "Including about your spying on them."

"We want no trouble with the Sisterhood, Milady, but they must be made to understand the danger they're in now."

"I'm sure they do," Nazleen replied, knowing that Ecara understood that *he* at least believed they were in danger.

The Novice had hurried on ahead, and by the time they reached the gate she was nowhere to be seen. The other two came to a halt, blocking the entrance to the compound.

"We will wait here," the Healer announced.

They didn't have long to wait. In a few minutes, Loreth's aide appeared in the entrance. Nazleen stiffened, certain there would be trouble when the aide told Miklav that he could not see the Pavla. But the woman greeted Nazleen in Cerecian, then turned to Miklav and spoke with cool formality in Hamloorian.

"You may enter, Warrior Chief. The others must remain here."

"With your permission, Sister, I would like to send my men to examine the compound's walls."

Nazleen turned in shock to Miklav, who seemed to be taking this incredible announcement in stride and making further demands at that!

"You will instruct them to remain here," came the soft but firm reply.

Miklav gave the order, then followed Nazleen into the compound. They turned over their horses to two nervous Novices, then followed the aide into the main building. The place was normally bustling with activity at this time of day, but today it was totally empty. No doubt everyone had been sent elsewhere.

Miklav made no attempt to conceal his interest in this forbidden territory. He walked along easily beside her, but his head was in constant motion as they passed through the spacious building. Nazleen quickly realized that they were being led to the Pavla's personal quarters, but she was still too stunned at the invitation extended to Miklav to be further shocked by that.

She was also beginning to worry anew about Loreth's reaction to her breach of the rules. The lure of the fire grew ever stronger, and therefore so did the fear of being banned from the pool.

The aide left them in Loreth's small reception room. Miklav immediately walked over to a painting that hung prominently on one wall. Nazleen had always disliked it, even though she admired Loreth's talent as an artist. It was a somewhat abstract rendering of a small child clinging to a limb just beyond the reach of a wild tor-beast, a vicious creature now believed to be extinct. Though the child seemed about to be devoured by the great jaws, she wore a calm, faraway look.

53

Nazleen had just begun to explain to Miklav that Loreth had painted the picture herself when the Pavla appeared in the doorway. Her brilliant green gaze swept briefly over Nazleen, then came to rest on the broad back of the Warrior Chief as he continued to examine the painting.

"It is a reminder, old friend," the Pavla said softly.

Miklav turned around quickly, his face wreathed in the warmest smile Nazleen had ever seen on him.

"There were far better things to remember, old friend."

"When one's life is given back at death's door, it is wise not to forget," Loreth responded as she closed the distance between them and stretched out both hands to Miklav. "I promised myself whole-heartedly to the Sisterhood at that moment, just before you saved me."

"Yes, I guessed that. You'd had your doubts before that day," he said, taking both her hands in his. "The years have been kind to you, Loreth, and I was not surprised to learn that you had become Pavla."

"Nor was I surprised to see you become Warrior Chief. You were always very good at commanding those around you." She gave him a wry smile.

They stood there, holding hands and smiling at each other, while Nazleen remained off to one side, totally ignored and too shocked even to notice that fact.

Finally, Loreth must have remembered her presence, since she stepped away from Miklav and turned to her former pupil, greeting her formally both as Liege and as a Sister of Cerece. Nazleen managed to make the appropriate responses, but as soon as the ritual was completed, she could no longer contain herself.

"I don't understand this. Miklav told me that you had known each other as children—but are you saying that the child in that picture is you, Loreth?"

"I'm afraid so," the Pavla replied with a rueful smile. "I was always wandering off alone. As Miklav said, I had doubts about joining the Sisterhood, so I had a lot of thinking to do. One time when my mother couldn't find me, it was Miklav who guessed where I might be and came looking for me. He was unarmed when he found me in that tree with the branch about to break under my weight, so he diverted the tor-beast's attention to himself and then barely made it to the pond in time. They never went into the water, you see." She turned back to Miklav with a fond smile.

"Even as a boy, the mark of the Warrior was upon him."

Nazleen stared from one to the other in amazement. The Pavla speaking fondly of the Warrior Chief! Her mother would never have believed this. Nazleen wasn't sure that she herself did.

A Novice came in then with tea and pastries, laid a small table for them and departed quickly with one last frightened look at the Warrior Chief. They all sat down.

Nazleen repeated her reason for bringing Warriors into Cerece, and Miklav explained further about the aliens. Loreth sat quietly, listening to them and nodding from time to time. Then Miklav went on to talk about the condition of the wall and

55

how they'd seen it.

"You should not have been spying on us, Miklav," Loreth said in a mild rebuke when he had finished.

"It wasn't spying, Loreth. We're responsible for your protection, too."

The Pavla sighed. "So you undoubtedly believe. Very well, I forgive you, even though I'm sure that curiosity about us was at least equal to your interest in our protection. But there is a condition to my forgiveness." Her green eyes glinted with humor. "You must promise to give me one of those scopes. Then we can spy on you as you spy on us."

Miklav chuckled and quickly agreed.

Then Loreth got up and began to pace about the room, her face turned away from them. After a few moments of silence, she turned back, her expression now grave.

"I will agree to the repairs, and there is also a second place you couldn't have seen from your vantage point. Until the work has been completed, I will be grateful for the protection of Warriors."

"I will see to it immediately," Miklav promised.

Loreth hesitated, this time looking at Nazleen before she spoke. Nazleen saw something in those eyes that sent a chill through her.

"The Augury will be held tomorrow, but there have already been certain portents."

"What do you mean?" Nazleen asked, forgetting for the moment that she would have to spend the entire night preparing herself if it was being held tomorrow.

"Vague portents, but definitely threatening. It is perhaps unwise to speculate at this point, but the threat appears to be directed at us more than Hamloor."

"Those aliens the Trens saw were headed up here," Miklav reminded them, "so you may well be right. But unless we capture them, we'll have no way of knowing if they knew where they were going."

Then he stood up and made a brief bow to both women. "With your permission, Milady and Pavla, I will return to my men. I intend to have a force on its way from Denra by tomorrow to guard the compound and another preparing to leave for the desert."

"No!" Nazleen stated, rising herself. "Miklav, I will not permit you to assemble war parties until we are sure they mean to attack us. We agreed that you would send a scouting party only and not even that unless the Augury shows danger."

"Milady, the danger already exists. The Sisterhood senses a threat, and aliens were seen on their way up here. What more proof do we need? The Compact states that when a threat exists, it is the Warrior Chief who makes the decisions." He paused briefly, then looked sternly at her.

"And I want you back to the safety of the palace as quickly as possible."

"I am safe here, Miklav, and you are stretching the Compact too far."

The two of them glared challengingly at each other until Loreth's quiet voice intervened.

"Miklav speaks only of preparations, Nazleen. Surely that is wise under the circumstances. Will you remain here until after the Augury, Miklav?"

"Yes. Outside the compound, of course."

"We will see that you are made comfortable, then."

Nazleen walked through the dank, stone-walled tunnel, carrying a torch that illuminated the darkness for only a few meters around her. Every Cerecian who walked this path thought of the labors that had gone into its construction—the lives lost, the injuries suffered. There were indeed ghosts here, but they were benevolent spirits, gentling urging on those who traveled this way.

The tunnel had been built nearly 200 years ago, together with the compound itself, by the founders of the Sisterhood. In those days, they had all been Trens, descendants of Stakezti, the revered mother of the order.

Many within and outside the order believed that the compound and the tunnel had not been built entirely by human labors. No proof existed, but many within the Sisterhood were of the opinion that ancient magic had been employed, magic lost through the generations.

The founders of the order had been illiterate, so the early history, like their unique language, had been passed down by word of mouth and only written down much later in the Hamloorian language, when intermarriage between Trens and Hamloorians had become common. Cerecian to this day remained a spoken language only.

Little was known for certain about Stakezti, the first Cerecian. The old stories had it that she'd appeared one day in a Tren village, half-starved and babbling in a strange language. She had referred to herself and her language as Cerecian, a name unheard of among the Trens. It was said that she had been about eight or nine years old at the time.

She was taken in by a kindly Tren family, where her striking golden hair and green eyes contrasted sharply with their darkness. Stories about her differentness in other respects grew as she herself grew. She was said to have strange powers, powers that frightened even her new family.

According to the tales, Stakezti never spoke of her origins, but as she grew older, she was known to have wandered great distances through the hills, seeking something she couldn't or wouldn't name. By all accounts, she was a solitary child, tolerated by her adoptive family but often shunned by others.

Finally, in her mid-twenties, she married a Tren artisan. Eight children were eventually born of this union, six of them girls. All of the girls bore a striking resemblance to their mother, and all were said to have inherited her mysterious talents.

Over the generations since, golden-haired, green-eyed girls continued to show up regularly among the many descendants of Stakezti. Finally, a group of them founded the order. The compound was built at the site of that which Stakezti had sought and failed to find, the place to which Nazleen now came.

A surge of energy rushed through Nazleen as she neared the end of the tunnel. She set aside the torch because it was no longer needed. A flickering green glow danced before her.

The cave was not large, perhaps 30 meters in diameter and very nearly circular. Luminescent walls surrounded her as she stepped onto the ledge around the pool. She quickly stripped off her robe and walked eagerly into the glowing green fire.

The sensation was incomparable, ecstatic. A unique warmth permeated every fiber of her being, soothing and energizing at the same time. That faint, indescribable scent filled her nostrils as she waded deeper into the very center of the pool, where the liquid fire reached almost to her neck. Then she closed her eyes and began to recite the ancient words.

The incantation lasted nearly an hour. Nazleen lost all awareness of her own body, of her very self, and became one with the fire. She was no longer Liege, no longer Cerecian. She was part of an ancient force, a power that was old even when their world was young.

Finally, the incantation completed, she slowly groped her way back to an awareness of herself and walked out of the fire-pool. Her naked skin was luminous, glowing with a pale green light. She put on her robe once more and paused at the entrance to the tunnel to pick up a fresh torch and light it. Then she made her way back through the tunnel and the maze of hallways to her quarters.

There she sank onto the thickly cushioned sleeping mat, but there would be no sleep for her this night. The hours would instead be spent in exercises and incantations learned years ago. This would draw forth the powers conferred upon her by her immersion in the sacred fire, focusing her mind into a razor-sharp awareness and then opening it to the ancient rhythms woven into the very atmosphere of Cerece.

From time to time during the night, her hands would move in sudden slashes or graceful arcs, and pale green fire traced the paths they took.

Finally, when a pink dawn crept into the room, she rose from the bed feeling both refreshed and strengthened. The tiredness would come later, but for now there was a light eagerness to her step as she left the room to go once more to the fire-pool.

This time, she was not alone in the tunnel. A steady procession of silent, green-robed women moved in single file through the stone channel, every fifth one carrying a torch to light the way. Beneath the hoods, green eyes shone from shadowy faces.

Nazleen entered the cave once more, then took her place along the ledge. Her eyes sought out Loreth, and the Pavla beckoned her to her side. With heartfelt gratitude, Nazleen moved toward her. All of them would by now know of her breach of the rules, and this was Loreth's way of telling them that she was to be forgiven. Loreth took her hand briefly, then let it go as they both turned their attention to the fire-pool.

Twelve heads were visible in the shimmering greenness, arranged in a circle in the center of the pool. Their eyes were closed as they chanted silently.

Nazleen felt a moment's sympathy for them. She herself had once stood an Augury. These women had been here for five hours, holding hands and speaking the ancient words over and over again, the phrases that united them with the flames and made their request known to the ancient powers.

When it was over, they would have to be carried back through the tunnel and would then sleep for an entire day and night. And perhaps worst of all, they would miss the Augury because they were part of it, part of the energy that would flow from the fire-pool.

When the procession from the tunnel had ended, Loreth held out her hands to the green fire and began the Pavla's recitation. A long tendril of shimmering green reached out to her, curling itself about her outstretched arms. Nazleen and the others then joined in, until they too were touched by the swelling green flames.

Voices speaking in the Cerecian tongue echoed off the cavern walls and roof, while in the pool itself, the 12 heads were no longer visible in the roiling flames.

Then at last the moment came. The chants died away as the fire surged ever more restlessly. Total silence fell upon the scene as the images began to appear, shifting and changing, becoming crystal clear and then fading, reappearing and then disappearing forever.

A Novice brought fruits and cheeses and herbal tea as Nazleen and Loreth reclined on cushions in the Pavla's quarters. Then the girl returned with paper, quill pens and ink and took her place on the floor before the two women. Novices were not permitted to attend Auguries because the energy released at such times was too powerful for the inexperienced. So instead, they served as scribes, recording the images recalled by the participants.

Elsewhere in the compound, other Sisters were also gathered in small groups, recording their memories of the Augury. When all had been written down, the results would be scrutinized by the Pavla and her aides and the results announced. Different women saw different images or sometimes variations of the same images. Using their knowledge of their Sisters and noting the frequency with which the same images occurred, the senior members of the order would pronounce the interpretation.

Neither woman had spoken since returning from the pool, and they devoured their meal in silence, too. Then, when the food was gone and more tea had been poured, Loreth began. Her voice was taut with suppressed emotion.

"The image that kept reappearing to me in various forms was the destruction of the order. I saw the compound silent and empty—except for the cave, where all hid in fear—but then I saw it filled again, except that some of the figures were male. I couldn't see them clearly because they wore hoods, but their robes were green like ours and they were clearly male. Finally, I saw ancient stone tablets with strange writing on them displayed in the great room. A form of picture-writing, it seemed to me." She paused, frowning, then went on in a low, puzzled tone.

"But the truly strange thing was that all the time I was seeing what I knew was the destruction of the order, I was thinking that this was a good thing."

Nazleen listened to the Pavla with an increasingly heavy heart, because she too had sensed the end of the Sisterhood, but she had also seen more.

Nazleen was not a strong believer in Auguries. She'd insisted upon this one more as a way in which to buy some time to consider the matter of the aliens than as a mystical guide to the future. But this time, she was uneasy—perhaps more than uneasy.

"I too saw an end—and a beginning," she admitted. "But I also saw war and death."

"Miklav's death," Loreth said quietly.

Nazleen nodded, and their eyes met. In the Pavla's eyes, she saw pain, but Loreth made a dismissive gesture.

"We will talk of Miklav later. Did you see anything else?"

Nazleen hesitated, not wanting to give credence to her other vision by speaking of it. Then she nodded slowly.

"I saw a man with golden hair and green eyes, and I saw him wield the fire." She hesitated again, her voice dropping even lower.

"I've seen him before."

Loreth stared hard at her. "When?"

"I dreamed of him two months ago—not really a dream, I suppose, but a vision."

Loreth continued to stare steadily at her, then she reached out to grasp Nazleen's hand. "I saw him, too, but not his face. I saw him in the fire-pool with someone. I couldn't see the other person, but I think it was you."

"No!" Nazleen's protest was automatic, then she lowered her head and shook it slowly. "No," she repeated more softly.

"There will be war, Nazleen, and Miklav will die. And this man, the man who wields the fire, will be the one who brings down the order. This I believe!"

The two old friends stared at each other while the scribe wrote furiously upon her tablet. Shadows moved in the depths of vivid green eyes where the sacred fire still lingered.

"You must rest now," Loreth said after the long silence. "It will take several hours to compile the Augury. I will send for you then."

Nazleen got up slowly and went to her own room. Despite her very troubled spirit, she fell asleep quickly, exhausted by the energy required for the Augury after a sleepless night.

When she was awakened several hours later, she felt as though she hadn't slept at all. Barely remembered nightmares taunted her. She was certain of only one thing in those terrible dreams—the golden-haired Fire Warrior.

Zaktar awoke suddenly, with that brief disorientation that comes when one is torn unwillingly from sleep, but his hand had already closed around the butt of his revolver by the time he became fully conscious. With the reassurance of that cold, deadly metal in his hand, he sat up and looked around.

They were camped in a narrow ravine, closed in on three sides by steep walls of rock. He peered first at the open end of the ravine and saw with relief that the guard was still there, sitting on the hood of one of the trucks with his rifle across his lap.

More relaxed now, Zaktar turned in a slow arc, seeking the other sentries. All were in place and none appeared to be trying to call to him. The rest of their party were a series of dark, humped shapes on the uneven ground as they slept in their sleeping bags. The only sounds he could hear were soft snores coming from some of them.

Only then did it occur to Zaktar what might have

awakened him. He hadn't expected contact at such a distance, unless the scouting party was already on its way back across the desert. He sucked in a big lungful of the cool night air and began the exercises to open his mind.

It came quickly—that soft, insistent brushing against his mind that had obviously awakened him. He reached out to the boy.

They'd found a fire-pool! But they'd also encountered people. All were safe, however, and they were now in the desert on their way back.

The details would have to await their return. The distance was too great for the boy's inexperienced mind. Zaktar closed off the contact, not wanting to strain the boy.

Taka had apparently obeyed orders and avoided conflict. Zaktar had been forced to send him because he was the only other Cerecian in the expedition, a political decision he'd noisily disagreed with. Taka wasn't in charge of the scouting expedition, but Zaktar had worried that he might try to exert his authority as a Cerecian to countermand the officer in charge. Young ones like Taka were often altogether too impressed with themselves. Zaktar knew that from personal experience.

He pulled himself out of his sleeping bag, shivering in the night air until he had put on his pants and jacket. Even though he'd been very quiet, he saw that the sentries were aware of his movements. After waving to the ones at the top of the ravine to let them know that all was well, he walked carefully past the sleeping bodies to the open end of the ravine where the other sentry had scrambled down from the truck hood and now stood at some semblance of attention.

"Anything wrong, sir?" the youth asked nervously as Zaktar came up to him.

Zaktar shook his head. If he'd had any reason to believe they faced trouble here, he wouldn't have allowed this kid to stand guard, but since he'd volunteered to take his turn, Zaktar hadn't wanted to hurt his feelings. Besides, they were shorthanded with several of the best men away on the scouting party.

"I was awakened by a message from Taka. They found a fire-pool, but they also found some people. They're on their way back across the desert now. Everyone's all right."

The youth nodded, but his gaze slid away quickly. Zaktar understood this; it was a common enough reaction. Every Cerecian got used to such reactions very early in life. People always feared what they couldn't understand.

"So they should be back sometime in the morning, then?"

Zaktar nodded as he stared off into the darkness to the east.

"Do you think those people could know about the fire?" the boy asked tentatively. "I mean, could any of them have learned how to use it?"

"I don't know," Zaktar admitted. "I hope Taka will be able to answer that, although he might not have had time to find out." Then he smiled ruefully at the guard.

"It's very tempting to believe that Cerecians are the only ones with that knowledge, but it's also very arrogant."

The youth could not quite contain his surprise at

Zaktar's words, and Zaktar understood that, too. Arrogance was a term frequently used to describe Cerecians—and with good reason. He certainly wasn't entirely free of that particular trait himself.

He stood there, staring off to the east a few minutes longer as he thought about Taka's discovery. Then he bade good night to the sentry and returned to his sleeping bag.

The youth watched him walk away. After nearly a month in Zaktar's company, he should be getting used to him. He'd been around other Cerecians from time to time, but Zaktar was different; there was no doubt about that.

First of all, he was the greatest war hero of their time. It was said that no one could wield the fire as he could. In battle, he'd been invincible. The boy was a pacifist, but the blood of warriors flowed in his veins, and he could not avoid at least a degree of hero worship—and maybe a little fear, too. A man who could kill instantly without weapons was inclined to inspire fear, no matter what the circumstances. He'd seen others in their group actually quaking with terror when Zaktar had delivered a mild reprimand. They all knew that no Cerecian ever killed without just cause, but still . . .

He continued to watch as the Fire Warrior undressed and slid back into his sleeping bag. There were so many stories about him. No other Cerecian was talked about as much as Zaktar, not even their Pavla. Not only was he the greatest Fire Warrior, he was also a brilliant inventor. Before this expedition, it had been rumored that he'd designed a flying machine. The boy had asked Taka about it, and he'd said it was true. The machine was even now being built.

He'd observed in Zaktar that restlessness that all great minds seemed to have. He often seemed lost in his thoughts, faraway in some place only he could go, but he could also show an unexpected kindness and consideration for others, too. He was always polite and kind to Shaba, for example, even though in the boy's opinion she'd been pursuing him shamelessly from the beginning.

Then the boy turned and stared off to the east himself, wondering what other news the scouts would bring. He was eager to cross the desert, to see what wondrous things the land beyond might hold. He was a botanist and had already discovered several dozen new plant species; surely there would be even more over there.

But there was now an element of fear in him. The green fire was over there, and if someone else had learned to use it, he didn't want to be in the middle of that battle.

Most Cerecians began their day with the complex mental exercises that kept their unique powers honed to a fine edge. But Zaktar preferred physical exercise, a deviation that never failed to draw disapproving looks from the Pavla and other elders when they saw him. He ignored them in this, just as he ignored them in many other things as well. He tolerated them because they were, nominally at least, his superiors. They tolerated him because they had no choice.

He crawled out of his sleeping bag and dressed quickly in the cool morning air, then jogged out of camp just as the others were beginning to stir. No one joined him; it was understood that he preferred to be alone. He jogged along the uneven bottom of the ravine until he had reached the open plain beyond, then picked up his pace considerably. A little more than a kilometer away, the ruins beckoned him.

When he reached the outskirts of the ancient village, he stopped to strip off his outer clothing, then began the rigorous set of calisthenics that kept his body younger than its 39 years.

To an observer of this scene, Zaktar might easily have resembled an ancient god come to life. The morning sun gleamed on his sweat-slicked body, outlining its hard, muscular contours. His tousled hair was thick and lustrous, a shade of gold that could vary from very pale to deep-burnished as the light played over it.

Zaktar was very tall, even by Cerecian standards, with broad shoulders, a narrow waist and hips and long, muscular legs. Beneath the beard he'd grown for convenience on this expedition was a face of chiseled masculine perfection—square jaw, wide mouth, cleft chin. The only flaw amidst all this perfection was a small scar above his left brow, the result of a childhood accident.

But as with all Cerecians, it was Zaktar's eyes that immediately drew one's attention. They were deep-set eyes of a very dark but vivid green, eyes that no non-Cerecian could meet for more than a few seconds. Even into their modern society, the myth persisted that looking too long into the eyes of a Cerecian could spell madness or even death. Within those eyes lay all the awesome powers of the Cerecian race—the ability to control the green fire.

Furthermore, the Kaptis, the people with whom the Cerecians lived, had excellent reason to fear them. Scarcely more than a century had passed since the Kaptis had felt the full fury of those powers.

Nearly three centuries ago, the first Cerecian, a boy named Metak, had been found wandering the forests on the edge of the Kaptis' lands. Since he was a tall, strapping youth, he was taken as a slave by the leader of the group who had found him. He spoke a strange language, but even after he'd learned the Kapti tongue, he refused to say anything at all about his origins.

Eventually, Metak fathered a total of 12 children to various female slaves. Every one of the boys— but none of the girls—inherited their father's strange golden hair and green eyes. Generation followed generation and still those traits continued to show up, always in males.

Owning the strange-looking slaves became a mark of distinction among the Kaptis, and as they continued to make war on each other, the slaves exchanged hands. They came to be known as Cerecians because that was how the boy Metak had described himself.

Forced breeding of the Cerecian slaves became a common practice as their owners sought to increase their numbers and therefore their own wealth.

It was a slave named Jedar who finally led his people to freedom. Sent into the hills to find game for his master's table, he stumbled upon a fire-pool and upon his hitherto unknown powers.

Word of Jedar's discovery was passed along secretly through the marketplaces and the slave quarters, and within the next few years virtually every Cerecian had found his way in secret to the fire-pool. Words that had previously had no meaning but had been passed on from one generation to the next now became clear.

By the time the Kaptis discovered what was happening, it was too late. The slaves revolted and easily defeated their former masters by unleashing the ancient fire.

But the Cerecians were magnanimous in victory. Recognizing that they were too few in numbers to control the Kaptis for long, they made a treaty with them that allowed the Kapti to control their own society, as long as they remained peaceful. In truth, the Kapti themselves had begun to grow tired of their incessant wars, and some of the more enlightened ones had even begun to speak out against slavery.

So Cerecians and Kapti alike then turned their attention to the advancement of their society. Both races proved to be resourceful, and a Golden Age was soon upon them.

The Cerecians had built for themselves a beautiful city surrounding their fire-pool. They lived there apart from the Kaptis and developed their own social order. Partly because an intense racial pride had been awakened in them and partly because of old resentments over forced breeding, they chose a life of celibacy. Reproducing themselves seemed unnecessary; each new generation of Kaptis produced more Cerecians, the male offspring of females in whom the Cerecian blood flowed.

Then an expedition into the unknown lands to the west brought war once more, this time with

Kaptis and Cerecians allied against a common enemy. It was this war that made the young Zaktar into a hero.

He was 29 at the time of his great victories. The praise heaped upon him by everyone, plus a strongly rebellious streak in his nature, led him to break his oath of celibacy. Choosing to remain for a while in his parental home instead of returning to the austere regimen of his spiritual home, he met a young Kapti woman he'd known as a child. Their attraction was instantaneous and mutual, and nature followed its course.

But the fire-pool beckoned; Zaktar knew he belonged there. So he returned to his spiritual home with considerable guilt, both at having broken his oath and at having left the girl. The Pavla had lectured him sternly and set him a long penance, but he could scarcely turn away their greatest hero.

For the next ten years, Zaktar had turned his excellent mind to the development of new technologies, but his was a restless spirit, not given to long periods of contemplation or scientific research. As soon as his period of penance was finished, he began to agitate for an expedition to the unexplored lands to the east.

Two circumstances finally combined to make Kapti and Cerecian leaders decide that such an expedition was worthwhile. First of all, fewer and fewer Cerecians were appearing in each new generation, and the new science of genetics suggested that the race might well die out. And secondly, their society had become heavily dependent upon gewa, a unique type of crystal that could be bathed in a chemical solution and used to power engines of all

73

types. Since the conquered lands to the west had neither more Cerecians nor gewa, a decision was made to journey to the east, where volcanic and earthquake activity seemed to have quieted down in recent years.

After nearly a month's leisurely journey, the expedition headed by Zaktar came upon the ruins where he now performed his calisthenics. From the moment Zaktar first saw the ruins, he knew he'd discovered an ancient Cerecian town. Both he and Taka could sense a fire-pool buried deep beneath the layers of volcanic ash and hardened lava.

Zaktar theorized that Metak, the founder of their race, might well have been an escapee from that devastation—and if he had escaped, so too might others, perhaps into the desert to the east. He thought it possible that some of their people might even have migrated across the desert before that final cataclysm, if fire-pools existed there. Hence, the scouting party was sent across the desert to seek more Cerecians and evidence of gewa deposits.

Zaktar was intrigued by the possibility that other Cerecians might live beyond the desert, and Taka's discovery of another fire-pool only heightened that curiosity. But he also knew that a race so long separated might not easily be brought together again. Who knew what kind of people they might have become?

They'd already had one brief encounter with a small group of very primitive aliens at the edge of the desert. Zaktar hadn't seen them himself, but from the reports they couldn't pose much of a threat unless their numbers were very great.

In any event, after that encounter, he'd decided

to proceed very cautiously, not wanting to repeat the mistakes that had gotten them into war on their last expedition. So the orders to the scouting party had been very clear—fight only to save their own lives and return to camp immediately at the first sign of trouble.

What would happen next would depend on the report he received when they returned this morning.

CHAPTER THREE

THE WARRIOR CHIEF WAS OBVIOUSLY VERY ANGRY. Nazleen felt rather sorry for whomever had borne the brunt of his wrath. Unfailingly polite and gentle toward her, Miklav was nonetheless known to possess a fiery temper and to suffer insubordination or incompetence badly indeed.

He strode furiously into the Pavla's quarters, and both women received a minimal bow and slight nod.

"They got away," he rumbled ominously. "Somehow they managed to vanish into the desert."

He refused Loreth's invitation to be seated and instead paced heavily around the room, a brooding black figure amidst soft blues and greens. Finally, he turned to Nazleen, his expression very grim.

"Milady, there is something I must tell you now,

something I had hoped to confirm through my own men before bringing it to your attention. I did not translate for you all that those Trens said about the aliens."

He paused for a moment, as though daring her to reprimand him. When she wisely remained silent, he continued.

"The Trens claim that one of them was a youth with golden hair and green eyes."

Nazleen and Loreth both drew in their breaths sharply, then exchanged quick glances. The Warrior Chief had been given an expurgated version of the Augury. He'd been told that the Augury appeared to forecast war and that the threat seemed to be directed against the Sisterhood, although there was some dispute about that. Nothing had been mentioned of the vision of his death shared by Nazleen and Loreth or of the Cerecian Fire Warrior seen by all of them in various forms.

"Perhaps they were mistaken, at least about his eyes," Miklav went on, oblivious to their shock. "After all, there is light hair among Hamloorians, although it is rare enough that these Trens might never have seen it on anyone other than Cerecians. This group could have been nothing more than a renegade band of Hamloorians. They've come here from time to time, usually to escape the law."

"But green eyes?" Nazleen said in a taut voice. "Green eyes exist only among Cerecians."

"They might well have seen the pale hair and imagined the green eyes. They admitted that they didn't get all that good a look at him. He was some distance away from the rest of the group, but he was the reason they fled."

"You said he was young," Loreth inquired. "How young?"

"They described him as being in his early twenties."

"Miklav," Nazleen said quietly, "you don't really believe they were Hamloorians, do you?"

"No, I don't, Milady. We've seen two groups now, and both times the Trens have described similar weapons and clothing. I'm less certain about one of them being Cerecian, however. None were seen the other time. They might well have light-haired people, even ones with green eyes, but that doesn't mean they're Cerecian."

He paused a moment, then went on musingly. "They did say that he was dressed differently, though. He wore a green uniform, a shade darker than your robes. And they appeared to be headed in this direction."

"But how could they have just vanished into the desert?" Nazleen asked quickly, wanting to end this speculation about male Cerecians.

"They used some sort of strange vehicle, apparently. My men found unusual wheel tracks but no animal tracks of any kind."

"A carriage that moves by itself?" Loreth asked in astonishment.

"So it would appear." Miklav stopped pacing and threw a brooding glance at Nazleen. "Haslik has spoken of such things; they're a dream of his. He believes that some sort of engine could be built that would replace a horse and do many other things as well."

"But the Desert Trens saw no such vehicles,"

Nazleen reminded him.

"No, but they were probably close to their camp at the time and may have had no need for them. The two groups must be together. To believe otherwise would be to stretch credulity, and that is always dangerous."

"They've not given any indication that they seek war," Nazleen said in desperation.

The look Miklav gave her was the kind one would give a cherished but hopelessly naive child. "Milady, do you forget the Augury? War will come, and we must know what we are fighting. We have secured the approval of the Desert Chieftain to cross his lands, and a scouting party must leave quickly. The storm season is nearly upon us."

"But surely the storm season would also prevent them from attacking us," Nazleen persisted.

"Not necessarily. Who knows what those vehicles of theirs are capable of? The scouting party has been assembled and leaves tomorrow."

Nazleen opened her mouth to protest his arrogance, but he cut her off.

"And as for you, Milady, you will return to the palace the day after tomorrow. A squadron from Fetezza is on its way to escort you. I do not wish to draw down Denra's defenses at this time." Fetezza was the Warrior fortress closest to the city and second in size only to Denra.

"Do not attempt to order me about, Miklav," Nazleen stated with imperial haughtiness. "You have no right to do so. And I am safe here, with the Trens rebuilding the wall and your men guarding us in the meantime."

She had no intention of returning to the palace,

where she would be too far away to know just what the Warrior Chief was doing.

"Milady, the Compact . . ."

"The Compact states that you are in charge only if there is war, but there is no war, Miklav—and if I can help it, there won't be, either."

"The Augury . . ."

She waved an angry hand. "Blast the Augury! Many of us believe that it shows only one version of the future, and that the future can be changed. Stop throwing the Augury at me, Miklav. You yourself consider it to be nonsense, and if it had shown peace, you'd be saying just that."

A smile flickered in his dark eyes, although he managed to keep it from reaching his mouth. Then he turned to Loreth.

"Is that true? Do you believe that the predictions can be changed, Loreth?"

Loreth hesitated, glancing briefly at the angry face of her former student, "No, I do not believe it. I believe there is only one future—and that in this case, the Augury was very clear. But it is true that some believe differently."

"Well, Augury or no Augury, I sense danger," Miklav stated, "and I cannot guarantee your safety here, Milady."

Nazleen glared at him. "What you cannot guarantee with me here is that you can have your war, Miklav. "That is why you want me to return to the palace."

In response, the Warrior Chief's scowl disappeared and was replaced by a much softer look. Even his voice lowered to a mere growl. "How could you have chosen a mate you distrust so much that you would put your life in jeopardy just to keep an eye on him?"

The sudden intake of breath on Loreth's part was barely heard by them as they stared at each other. Nazleen had not yet told the Pavla of her decision.

"I trust no Warrior, Miklav. I told you that I would rather have none of you for my mate. And until I announce my choice, I can still change my mind."

A brief smile now touched his mouth. "But you won't. Very well, Milady. Remain here for now if you wish. You should be safe enough for the time being. When the squad from Fetezza arrives, I can set them up along the perimeters of the desert until the scouting party returns."

Then he bowed. "With your permission, Milady, I am returning to Denra. There is much that demands my attention there."

"Preparing for war, you mean," Nazleen said disgustedly, unwilling to betray her pleasure at having faced him down.

"Preparedness is the watchword for all good Warriors," he replied, then strode from the room.

The two women stared at each other as the room seemed to settle back into its normal tranquillity. But both pairs of green eyes were troubled. Between them hung an unspoken question that had been there since the Augury. Could there be male Cerecians?

"The face in my dream was not that of a boy of twenty," Nazleen stated. "He seemed close to Miklav's age."

"The one I saw in the Augury was no youth, either," Loreth confirmed. "Even if I didn't see his face, I'm sure he was older."

Nazleen shivered, remembering the rest of the Pavla's vision.

"I keep thinking about the stories of Stakezti's origins and how they found her wandering near the desert, her skin burned as though she might have come from there," Loreth mused quietly. "The most common story was that she had come from the land beyond the desert."

"And there were stories of a great explosion just before she appeared, an explosion in the fire-mountains," Nazleen added. "When my father discovered those old ruins on the far side of the desert, my mother wondered if that might have been Stakezti's home. He said they were nearly buried by a black powder that the Desert Trens believe results from such an explosion."

Loreth nodded. "I have often wondered about that, too. And if Stakezti *did* come from there, isn't it possible that others might have fled in the opposite direction or even that there were other Cerecian villages beyond the fire-mountains?"

Nazleen nodded slowly. It had been years since she'd spent time speculating on Stakezti's origins. Novices invariably spent hours in such discussions.

The Sisterhood itself espoused no particular doctrine where the origins of Stakezti were concerned. Most of them were inclined to believe that she had been the offspring of Trens who had abandoned her because of her differentness. Crippled and otherwise freakish children had often been thus abandoned in those days. "Left to the gods" was how the Trens had put it. It also had happened among Hamloorians centuries ago.

There had been a certain romance to the notion that their founder had been abandoned and then been somehow touched by the old gods and sent back, accompanied by thunderous explosions.

"But the problem with believing that she merely came from some land across the desert is that it doesn't account for the fact that no male Cerecians have ever been born here. Surely only the gods could cause that to happen."

Loreth nodded. "But what the gods decreed for Stakezti and her descendants might have been very different from what happened to the others. Neither explanation excludes the other."

She looked at Nazleen levelly. "At the very least, we must consider the possibility that there could be male Cerecians."

Both women stared at each other, realizing just how fragile their position was. If there were male Cerecians, and if they were Fire Warriors, how could they fight them? No Sister had wielded the fire since the battle that preceded the Compact.

And what in the name of the gods would happen if fire fought fire?

"They were both short and dark, like the ones we saw before, and they were carrying these old muskets. Even their clothes were old-fashioned— homemade, by the looks of them. They looked like they'd stepped out of the pages of a history book."

Zaktar listened to the descriptions of the scouting party with interest. They were all fascinated by these people who seemed to have come from a different time period. It was also becoming increasingly clear to him that they had little to fear from

83

these backward people.

"It was Taka who really scared them," the party's leader stated with a wry grin. "They didn't see him at first because he was still climbing out of the gully behind us. But they were more afraid of him than they were of us, even though we were closer and had rifles."

"That's true," the young Cerecian confirmed. "They looked at me as though they were seeing a ghost or a devil. And that's when they took off."

"I'm sure there must be gewa there," the party's geologist put in. "The rock formations were right for it."

Zaktar finally dismissed them so they could go regale the rest of their expedition with their tale. But Taka lingered behind.

"I've been trying to figure out why they were so frightened of me," he said with a shake of his golden head. "Do you think it's possible that there *are* Cerecians there and that they misuse their powers?"

"It's possible," Zaktar conceded, "but it's also possible that they just found you strange-looking. If you forget about the clothing differences, the Kapti and these people probably look pretty much alike."

But he frowned thoughtfully. "On the other hand, it does seem strange that you'd find a fire-pool and then run into people who are afraid of you."

"But if there were Cerecians there, why didn't I sense them? I don't think the pool was all that far away."

"Maybe they operate on a different frequency," Zaktar suggested with a grin.

Both men laughed. The old Pavla hated their use of such terms in regard to their unique powers. But the Kapti and many younger Cerecians were prone to referring to the Cerecian frequency, as opposed to normal radio frequencies. The radio had been invented by a Cerecian, and no gift they gave the Kaptis had ever been more gratefully received, since it allowed them to communicate as easily as the Cerecians did.

Still, Zaktar knew that there just might be some truth to his facetious remark. A race separated for so long might well have developed differently.

He wanted to believe there were Cerecians at that fire-pool and wished that the scouts had been able to establish that fact. It now appeared that they'd found gewa, but the other part of their quest was still very much in doubt.

The reaction of those primitive men to Taka disturbed him very much. He was inclined to agree with the younger man that it seemed to indicate the presence among them of Cerecians who'd abused their powers, something his own ancestors could so easily have done.

The Kapti Council of Ministers had traveled to the Cerecian city named Jedara for the slave who had discovered the fire-pool and then led the Cerecians to freedom. They came for a meeting with the Pavla, who was an elderly and rather frail man.

All had been apprised of Zaktar's radio message. The Pavla graciously permitted his Kapti counterpart to conduct the meeting.

"Both Science Ministers recommend immediate

funding for excavations at the ruins under the supervision of Felka. Is there any dissent?"

There was none. Archaeology had recently become quite popular among the Kapti upper classes, and of course the Cerecians were eager to learn more about this ruin that might have been their ancient home.

"Very well. Now we move on to the other discovery. Do we cross the desert and seek out the gewa the geologist believes is there? If we do, we know that we risk war with these people. We would, of course, attempt to trade with them, but they are apparently very primitive and may be difficult to deal with."

The discussion went on for some time. Everyone present knew that their situation was becoming ever more desperate. They had to find more gewa or their entire society could be plunged into chaos. Already, unpopular plans for rationing were being made as scientists struggled to find a substitute for the scarce fuel.

All claimed that they didn't want war, and most of them meant it. On the other hand, the area seemed sparsely populated and the people so very primitive that it would surely be a very quick war—unless, of course, Zaktar's warning about the possible presence of Cerecians was accurate.

The Pavla stated their position that war was to be avoided at all costs, but they also must make some attempt to determine if indeed there were other Cerecians there.

One of the Kapti ministers expressed a common concern. "What if it's a whole tribe of Fire Warriors, Pavla?"

The Pavla nodded. He too worried about that possibility. From time to time, he observed Zaktar's small force at their practice, and the thought of such a battle troubled him greatly.

"What would happen if fire met fire?" one of the two women present inquired of the Pavla.

"No one knows. No Cerecian has ever turned the fire upon another. It would be unthinkable."

"But perhaps it wouldn't be unthinkable to them," another stated.

In the end, they reached agreement. Kapti troops would be sent immediately to the site of the ruins. By moving more quickly than Zaktar's leisurely expedition had done and by traveling at night as well, they could be there within ten days.

The Pavla would also send the Fire Warriors, the group Zaktar had led since the war, and the only Cerecians who still trained to wield the fire. The Kapti troops would remain at the ruins, but the Fire Warriors would proceed across the desert to seek out their kin, hoping to arrange trade agreements.

With little further debate, the two Councils agreed that the entire expedition should continue under Zaktar's command. As several of the Kaptis pointed out (with the Pavla's silent agreement), Zaktar would do as he damned well pleased in any event, and none of the Kapti commanders would be willing to stand up to him.

Their decision was quickly relayed by radio back to the camp near the ruins, and Zaktar fell asleep that night with a satisfied smile on his face. If the Pavla had refused his request for the Fire Warriors, he would have gone back and gotten them himself.

There wasn't one of them who wouldn't have been willing to disobey the old man and follow Zaktar. Now that inconvenience had been avoided. And while he awaited their arrival, he could do some scouting himself.

"Captain, we will leave for Denra tomorrow."

The Warrior gaped at her in astonishment. "But . . . but, Milady . . ."

"The Warrior Chief commanded you to protect me, Captain, and with or without you, I leave for Denra in the morning. I intend to be there when the scouting party returns. If you choose not to accompany me, then I will ask the Trens for protection. I'm sure they'll be happy to comply."

"But, Milady, no Liege has ever visited Denra. The Compact . . ."

"I'm well aware of what the Compact states, Captain, and you are wrong. A Liege did visit Denra many years ago and was murdered by Warriors. I can only hope that Warriors have become more civilized. I would also remind you that no Warrior is permitted to visit Cerece, either, but your Chief was not harmed."

The Captain knew when to give up. He nodded curtly, bowed and then stood there staring after the Liege as she walked back into the compound. He was annoyed, but he had to admire her courage, not that she had to worry about suffering the fate of that long ago Liege, who may or may not have been murdered by Warriors. The Captain knew, as they all did, that the Warrior Chief would never allow her to be harmed; he was too determined to have her.

Still, he wasn't at all certain that she would be welcome at Denra just now, with the scouting party soon to return, war preparations underway and the son of the Desert Trens' Chieftain being held hostage there. He hurried off to send word to his Chief.

Loreth was awaiting her when Nazleen entered the Pavla's quarters. "Will he take you to Denra?"

"I gave him no choice. If he doesn't, the Trens will. And he knows full well that if I show up at Denra with them, he'll be fortunate if he's only stripped of his rank." Using Miklav's well-known temper to her own ends pleased her.

"Nazleen, are you going only because you fear that Miklav may distort the scouts' report, or is there another reason?"

The question didn't really surprise Nazleen— Loreth knew her well—but she wasn't at all sure that the Pavla would approve of her other reason.

"Yes, there's another reason. Perhaps Miklav will be less determined to make war if I am carrying his child. The Healers tell me that the timing would be right for conception."

Loreth merely nodded, but in one of those moments that can happen between Cerecians who are close, Nazleen saw into her old friend's thoughts. She shrank away automatically, courtesy demanding that one avoid such intrusions upon another's privacy, but as they exchanged looks, Nazleen knew that Loreth had felt her brief presence.

"Yes, I love Miklav," Loreth said quietly. "He was always so kind to me, and he saved my life at great risk to his own."

Badly shaken by this revelation, Nazleen immediately protested. "Then I will not take . . ."

"Yes, you will. I want you to take Miklav as your mate. The two of you are the most dear to me in all the world, and it pleases me to think of you together. I only wish that you too loved him."

Nazleen found this conversation almost surreal. A Pavla speaking of romantic love? She struggled to find acceptable words. "I don't dislike him. He has many good qualities, even if he is a Warrior. Besides," she shrugged, "Miklav doesn't love me. He merely lusts after me, in much the same way he lusts after war."

"Perhaps you are right," Loreth acknowledged, "but Miklav is a very complex man, not as easily understood as you may think. Nevertheless, if your plan will prevent war, then it will also prevent his death. And even if Miklav can't be saved, your union might one day give me a child to raise here."

But Nazleen barely heard her, for at that moment her mind had spun back to Loreth's vision of her in the sacred fire-pool with the Fire Warrior. A shiver went through her, which Loreth incorrectly interpreted as being distaste for mating with Miklav.

At dawn the next morning the party prepared to leave for Denra, two days' ride to the southwest. Loreth came to see them off and embraced her former student. It was an emotional moment for them both, because their instincts told them they might not see each other for a long while, and the prospect of war hung over them both, darkening the beautiful day.

Nazleen had decided to return to the palace after her visit to Denra. She'd sent her Advisors back already, keeping only her personal maid. If war could be prevented, she would return to the city of her own accord, and if not, then Miklav would order her back to the protection of the palace.

As they rode out into the early morning, Nazleen turned in her saddle for one final look at the glowing golden stones of Cerece. A great wave of sadness washed over her as she wondered if she would ever see it again as it was now. If the Augury came true . . . She turned away and urged her spirited mare forward.

Zaktar first saw the compound from a hilltop about a kilometer away. The sun had risen less than an hour earlier, and its rays infused the stones with a warm, bronzed glow. The lure of the sacred fire had drawn him here, just as it had Taka. He knew it was there, deep within the walls of the compound.

Inside the walls, he could see no sign of life, although from his vantage point, he was peering down through a heavy forest and able to see only a small portion of the place. Nevertheless, he was struck by the air of serenity to the place and began to wonder if he might not have misinterpreted Taka's encounter with those people. It was difficult to imagine the compound being the headquarters of a violent people.

Instead, he began to wonder if it might not be deserted, perhaps a relic of times past. Every fiber of his being protested at the thought that he might have found yet another place where his people had once lived, but the fear Taka had described could be explained that way, too. Those primitive people might have thought they were seeing a ghost of a race long vanished.

Bending low to avoid being seen in case anyone *was* down there, Zaktar moved along the top of the hill, seeking a better vantage point. The other men with him were doing likewise but apparently without success. Then he stopped and quickly flattened himself against a rocky ledge.

He could now see the entrance to the compound, and in front of it was a group of black-clad Warriors, bristling with the weapons of their trade. They wore big old-fashioned helmets, so it was impossible to see their heads. He admired the big, handsome steeds they rode even as he smiled derisively at their ancient weapons. They did indeed look like figures from a history book.

Could they be the residents of the compound? More importantly, could they be Cerecians? If they were, they might not know how to wield the fire; otherwise, why would they be so weighted down with weapons?

Zaktar watched them through his high-powered glasses, trying in vain to see their faces. Then one of them lifted his head to scan the hilltop near Zaktar, and before he flattened himself to avoid detection, he got a brief look at the man's face. He wasn't Cerecian. Zaktar lay there, wondering if he should be happy or sad about that.

Then his attention was distracted for a few moments by the other two men, who had crept up beside him, crawling like snakes on the rocky ground.

"Warriors," he whispered. "Keep down!"

They obeyed, slithering up beside him. "Are they Cerecian?"

Zaktar shook his head and noted the relief on the faces of the Kapti soldiers.

By the time they risked looking again, the group was disappearing from view into the thick forest along a road whose outlines the men on the hilltop could barely see. Zaktar had just a moment to glimpse something white in their midst before they were gone.

"So they have an army," the one Kapti said. "Do you think that's their headquarters down there?"

Zaktar looked again at the compound. "I doubt it. If it were, surely they'd have it better fortified."

"But there's fire down there?"

"Yes." He turned away, resisting that unique pull.

The men moved across the hilltop, seeking a vantage point that might permit them another look at the black-clad Warriors. A short stretch of road lay below them on the far side of the hill. The group concealed themselves behind some low shrubs and waited. They couldn't be sure that the Warriors were taking this road, but it was the only one in sight. They settled down to wait.

Zaktar thought some more about the compound and its hidden fire-pool. There was another peak some distance away on the far side of the compound that should offer an unobstructed view, but that would have to wait for another time.

Those Warriors made him uneasy. They might not be equipped with modern weapons, but if there were enough of them, they could still pose a threat to the expedition, at least until the reinforcements arrived. Much as he wanted to stay here and discover the secrets of that compound, he knew he had to return to camp.

He was just about to give up waiting for the reappearance of those black Warriors and return to their truck, when the first pair of them came into view on the road. They were riding two abreast, rifles at the ready.

Two more pairs passed by below, and then Zaktar discovered what that glimpse of white had been. Another Warrior, an officer to judge by his insignia, rode beside a much smaller green-robed figure on a pretty little white mare.

A woman? Certainly the size and the little horse argued for that, but he couldn't be sure. The cloak was long and hooded and hid the body beneath completely. Clearly he or she was a person of rank. Golden threads woven into an elaborate design were worked into the cloak.

Then another small figure appeared, riding just behind the first. This one was clearly female, since her hood had been thrown back. From her attire, Zaktar guessed that she was a servant, and she also was not Cerecian.

The line of Warriors disappeared from view once more, and although Zaktar knew it was time for them to get back to their truck, he couldn't resist seeking one last look at that green-robed figure. So he led his men across the hill to yet another place where the road came briefly into view, even closer to them this time. They hid and waited, a short wait this time.

"Look at those muskets," the man beside him whispered. "I have one of them. It's over two hundred years old."

But Zaktar was paying no attention at all to the

Warriors at this point. His gaze was riveted on that small figure on the white horse. Her cloak was just a shade lighter than his own uniform, and the significance of that struck him for the first time.

Then he caught his breath with a barely strangled cry as she suddenly reached up and pushed the hood from her head. Beside him, the other two made sounds of surprise, too.

A mass of golden-red hair gleamed brightly in the morning light, hair the shade of the setting sun. Zaktar knew that he was seeing for the first time a woman of his own race!

Without conscious intent, he let go of powerful emotions. Below him, he saw the woman suddenly jerk her body and reach up to put a hand to her head. Then she began slowly to turn in his direction. He quickly reined in his thoughts and flattened himself behind the shrubs.

He'd made contact! She'd felt his presence! He lay there trembling with suppressed emotion.

"Milady, what is it?" The Captain leaned toward her with a frown.

Nazleen waved him away rather shakily. "There was a sudden pain in my head, but it's gone now. I'm fine."

"Is Milady ill? Do you wish to return to Cerece?"

Nazleen shook her head firmly. She knew she should tell him of her suspicions, but if she did, he would insist that she go back to Cerece while they searched that hilltop. She turned once more, carefully reached out with her mind—and felt nothing.

They rode on, with the Captain watching her closely and Nazleen struggling not to let her inner turmoil become evident to him.

For one brief moment, she'd felt a pain in her head unlike anything she'd ever experienced before, raw and very powerful. Almost, she thought, like a huge wave of pure emotion. She was very sure that the source of the pain wasn't physical; it had the feel of telepathic contact but magnified many times. She was also certain that it had emanated from that hilltop.

In that moment, she'd been certain it was that Fire Warrior. Now, as rationality returned, she began to question whether anything at all had happened. Hallucinations weren't uncommon in the days following an Augury. Many of the Sisters experienced them, but she never had before.

What if it *was* the Fire Warrior and he meant to attack the compound? She hesitated, uncertain what to do.

And then it came again, not with a pain this time but with a deep, strong feeling.

"Safe. No harm."

"Who are you?" she asked, sending the question hesitantly.

"Zaktar," came the response in that same low, powerful tone.

She turned again, but the hilltop was now blocked from her view by the forest. There was nothing more. She rode on, repeating that name over and over as she recalled that strong, handsome face from her vision. Zaktar!

They stopped that night at a small inn in a Tren village about halfway between Cerece and Denra. Nazleen was tired from the long ride, but even so she couldn't sleep. Round and round in her brain went the question that had no answer—had it been real or simply an hallucination?

She'd heard others describe such hallucinations. They were always connected in some way to the Augury, and from what she'd been told, they seemed very real. Some were visions, some were voices, and occasionally they affected all the senses.

In the end, she decided that it had been an aftereffect of the Augury and nothing more, perhaps fed by her fears for the future. That would explain that message. She wanted to believe there would be no war, and that's what she'd heard.

But in her dreams, the Fire Warrior awaited her, his green eyes glowing. And had there been anyone there in her bedchamber, they would have heard her whisper the name "Zaktar".

The next morning, she discovered a second contingent of Warriors from Denra awaiting her. As soon as she saw them, she feared they might have come to force her to return to the city.

The officer in charge strode up to her, bowing rather more deeply than most Warriors, and when he had removed his helmet, Nazleen immediately recognized him. Captain Mevak was a close friend of her brother's and had often come to the palace with him. Nazleen rather liked him and at one time had toyed with the idea of choosing him over Miklav, but her fears for the man's future had forced her to give up the thought. She was convinced that Miklav would have found some way to take out his anger on the handsome captain.

"Milady, the Warrior Chief has sent us to accompany you, so that the others may return to Cerece."

"Accompany me to Denra, Captain?" She inquired imperiously, not about to be tricked into returning to the palace.

"Yes, Milady," he replied with a barely concealed smile. "And I was instructed to tell you that the Warrior Chief is eager to show you his hospitality."

Nazleen wondered just what Miklav's idea of hospitality was. Rather belatedly, she realized that for the first time she would be confronting the Warrior Chief in *his* territory. Although she wasn't actually afraid of Miklav, the thought still wasn't comforting.

It was nearly sunset when they finally began the tortuous ascent to the hilltop fortress. For miles before they had entered the thick forest at its base, Nazleen could see the great walled fortress perched on its rocky pinnacle. It was a very forbidding sight and did little to calm her nervous thoughts about her meeting with Miklav.

When they came at last to the broad clearing below the fortress, Nazleen gasped in amazement. The walls were the highest she'd ever seen. No wonder the Warriors had chosen to make this their headquarters. It was impregnable. If they had stayed within its walls all those years ago, not even Cerecian fire could have touched them.

"Milady is impressed?" the Captain inquired in an amused tone.

"Rather too impressed, I think," Nazleen responded drily.

As they rode slowly toward the huge wooden door set into the stone walls, the stillness was suddenly pierced by a loud screeching sound. Nazleen's little mare reared up in terror. When the

Captain tried to grab the reins, he succeeded only in frightening the animal still further. Caught off-guard both by the sound itself and by her mare's reaction to it, Nazleen fought to keep her seat, then tumbled off as the animal reared once more.

She landed in a heap on the ground, then scrambled quickly out of the way of the mare's flailing hooves. The ground was muddy and uneven, and before she could stop herself, she slid down an embankment.

Shakily, she pulled herself into a sitting position. There were anxious cries and a thunder of hooves at the top of the hill, and then Miklav was scrambling down the bank toward her.

"Are you hurt, Milady?"

Nazleen, who had been gingerly testing all her extremities, shook her head as he came to a sliding stop before her. She looked down at her mud-splattered cloak, then put a hand to her face and felt streaks of mud there, too. Miklav was bending over her, his rugged features taut with concern, and at the top of the embankment other anxious faces peered down at her.

She had a sudden image of how she must look to them and did the only thing she could do under the circumstances—she laughed.

"I'm not hurt, but I'm afraid that my dignity has been fatally wounded," she managed between giggles.

The Warrior Chief sank to his haunches beside her as his own laughter rang out across the hills. Above them, the others contented themselves with smiles and low chuckles. It was a scene never to be forgotten—the Liege and their Chief sitting in the mud and laughing together.

Finally, Miklav helped her to her feet, then assisted her up the steep bank. He lifted her up into the big saddle of his charger and swung himself up behind her. The Captain told her that several men had been dispatched to catch her mare, who had galloped off back down the road.

She asked what the noise had been and learned that it was the sound of the huge gate being opened. Just as they reached it, she heard hoofbeats behind them and turned to see that her little mare was being led back to her, still nervous but unharmed.

"Welcome to Denra, Milady," Miklav said in a low, amused tone near her ear as they rode past the honor guard assembled just inside the gate.

"What you may have lost in dignity you have gained in the admiration of the Warriors."

A short time later, she was comfortably ensconced in a big tub in Miklav's personal quarters. He'd explained that the fortress had no guest quarters to offer, "except for the dungeons," so he had turned his suite over to her. After escorting her there, he had left with one final amused look at her bedraggled appearance.

The tub had been filled almost to the top, and Nazleen sank into it gratefully, then dismissed her maid, who'd been fluttering about nervously ever since their arrival. The girl's presence was doing little to soothe Nazleen's jangled nerves.

She picked up the scented soap the maid had packed for her and began to lather away the lingering traces of mud. Then she leaned back in the warm water and thought about Miklav's reaction to her accident.

It could so easily have been an opportunity for him to have embarrassed her before his Warriors, and she knew he must have realized that. Yet his own humor had helped her. Furthermore, his concern for her had been very genuine, despite the fact that her death or even serious injury at this time could have presented him with the perfect opportunity to seize power.

There is good in him, she thought once again, but he was still a Warrior. Kindness and gentleness did not get a man elected Warrior Chief.

Her mother had once made some shrewd observations about Miklav, whom she'd gotten to know well over the years when he'd been an aide to Nazleen's father and then Warrior Chief himself.

"Hektar was the last of the old breed of Warrior Chiefs—not a truly evil man but essentially a killing machine. Miklav, on the other hand, has the intelligence for diplomacy as well as making war, and that makes him even more dangerous. Hektar took what he wanted—or tried to—but Miklav will work in much more subtle ways to attain his goals."

She'd also advised her then 18-year-old daughter to take Miklav as a mate one day and bind him to her through their children.

And that, thought Nazleen now, is just what she planned to do.

War had to be avoided somehow, because once the Warriors had tasted blood, they would never be content to return to their war games. And once Miklav had tasted true power, he would never willingly hand the reins back to her. Even if he died in battle, some other Warrior would take his place with the same result. If there were no more enemies without, they would turn upon each other as they had done long ago.

She and Loreth had debated whether telling Miklav of the prediction of his death would keep him from plunging into war, and they'd reached the sad conclusion that it wouldn't matter. A Warrior's greatest glory was to die in battle. She recalled Miklav's sadness that her father had died peacefully in his bed.

Then, as the soothing warmth reached into her, her thoughts began to drift away from this place and its bloody history, back to that hallucination she'd had at the beginning of this journey. Normally able to set aside troubling memories, Nazleen found that this one could not so easily be avoided.

His face was still so incredibly clear in her mind's eye, and the name "Zaktar" had attached itself to that face, despite her certainty that the whole thing had been only an illusion brought on by the Augury. She didn't believe in Auguries, so why did she persist in believing in the Fire Warrior's existence?

When the water began to cool, she climbed out of the tub and called to her maid, who dried her with a big, rough towel that left her fair skin flushed. After that, she dressed in a simple robe and let her still-damp hair tumble in soft curls about her shoulders. A supper had been laid for her in the small sitting room of the Warrior Chief's quarters, and she realized that she was quite hungry.

But she stopped in the doorway when she saw Miklav there. His back was to her as he stared out the unshuttered window into the gathering twilight.

Then he turned to pick up a wine goblet and saw her there.

If Nazleen had ever doubted that he wanted her, those doubts vanished the moment his dark eyes met hers. In the past, he'd kept his desire under tight control most of the time, but what she saw now was raw, undisguised lust. She thought unhappily that it wasn't much different from the bloodlust she'd seen there when he'd come to tell her about the aliens on their borders.

He waved a big hand toward the food. "Our kitchen can't compare to the palace or to Cerece, but the cooks have done their best for you, Milady."

She murmured her thanks and sat down very carefully on the chair that had been drawn up to a small table. The warmth of the bath had begun to wear off, and her body was starting to protest its recent rough treatment.

Miklav noted her careful movements. "We have ointments that will ease the pain, Milady, but the scent isn't quite so pleasant as the one you carry with you from the bath."

How carefully he skirts along the very edges of impropriety, she thought with a certain admiration. "I may use them anyway, since it will undoubtedly be much worse tomorrow if I don't."

When she began to eat, he drew up another chair to sit across from her. "So you didn't trust me to report the findings of the scouts accurately."

"I decided that I would like to question them myself. I have that right, Miklav," she stated, not really knowing whether or not she did but determined to brazen it out anyway.

"But you would surely trust your brother?"

"So he is with the scouting party," she said, having suspected that when Haslik had failed to appear after her arrival.

Miklav nodded. "His expertise in weaponry made him a natural choice, and his relationship to you meant a report you would trust."

Nazleen chewed some fruit as she admired his strategy, but then, as Warrior Chief, he would naturally be good at second-guessing the enemy.

"Do you regard me as being an enemy, Miklav?" she asked, following her thoughts without considering that he might find the question strange.

If he did, he certainly hid it well. He shook his head. "No, I regard you as my Liege. That means that you can't possibly be an enemy, although you could be a problem from time to time."

He finished his declaration with a smile that she found impossible not to return. "Such as now, for example?"

"No, not at the moment. Now you're in *my* territory."

Both his expression and his tone were light, but Nazleen couldn't quite suppress a small quiver of uneasiness. All the bloody history of their people seemed to be weighing down on her here. Warrior Chiefs and Lieges had fought throughout their history, and a Liege had once died here under mysterious circumstances.

Miklav had been watching her closely, and when he spoke, his voice was surprisingly soft. "Do you regard me as an enemy, Milady?"

She met his gaze steadily, despite her unpleasant

thoughts. "No, I don't. In fact, I think that you and I have gotten along better than all our predecessors. Don't you agree?"

"Until now, yes."

"Until the return of the scouting party, you mean?"

He nodded.

"Then you will want war, and I won't."

"No, you will continue to want peace at any cost, and I will want war if the cost of peace appears to be too high."

"Miklav, if the scouts report no warlike intentions on the part of these aliens, there will be no war."

"I agree. In that event, we will send out a peaceful party to meet with them and find out what they want. But remember this—if they have superior weapons, we run a great risk by believing their intentions to be peaceful. True peace can only exist between equals."

"And you think they have such weapons?"

"On the basis of what I've heard thus far—yes. They carry weapons that are almost certainly superior to ours, and they must have some new type of vehicle. And we can assume that at least some of them are Warriors. Peaceful civilians do not wear uniforms. Besides," he shrugged, "the Augury points to war."

"The Augury you don't believe in in any event may very well be pointing to a war that you started, Miklav. That vehicle may be nothing more than a new means of conveyance, and only a few of them wore uniforms. They could well be there simply to protect a peaceful group of explorers. I think you

105

are misconstruing the situation deliberately."

"We shall see," he replied, crossing his muscular arms over his broad chest and leaning back in his chair.

A servant came in at that moment and cleared away the remnants of Nazleen's meal, then refilled Miklav's goblet and poured her some tea. They were both silent until he left.

Miklav continued to lounge in the chair, totally at ease as he regarded her through half-closed eyes. His posture was a none-too-subtle reminder of the difference in their situation. At the palace, his bearing and manner had always been formally correct. Now, as he had said, she was in *his* territory.

She'd never before seen him in anything other than his formal dress uniform, but now, although he still wore black, he was dressed in a loose-fitting shirt and casual trousers. Even the high, gleaming boots had been replaced by soft shoes. And there was no weapon in sight. It was impossible for a man like Miklav to appear soft, but he did indeed seem far less harsh.

"Did you perhaps have a second purpose in mind when you decided to come here?" he inquired casually as he lifted his goblet to his mouth.

Nazleen had been thoroughly schooled for her profession, which frequently required a careful control over her emotions, and she put that skill to a severe test now. It simply hadn't occurred to her that he might guess her other purpose. She thought uncomfortably that she was making a habit of underestimating this man, or perhaps she had come to overestimate herself.

"Why would you think that?" she responded, her voice adopting a tone of polite formality that showed just a trace of annoyance at such presumption.

"It occurred to me that you might also have come here to offer me a bribe—a bribe to stay out of war."

"I'm afraid that I don't understand, Miklav. What bribe could I possibly offer you?" She was determined that he should be the one to state it, so that she could dismiss the notion with an imperious gesture of annoyance.

But instead, he cocked his head to one side and grinned at her—a very insolent grin. "Is it possible that Nazleen, Liege of Hamloor, Protector of the Trens and Sister of the Cerecian Order, is behaving like an ordinary female and dissembling?"

A self-righteous anger swept away her nervousness. She glared at him. "No, it is not possible."

"My mistake, then," he replied with a careless wave of his hand. "Somewhere, I got the notion that you might offer yourself to me as a way of distracting me from thoughts of war."

She narrowed her eyes challengingly. "Would it have worked?"

He looked at her with a thoughtful expression and stroked his jaw slowly. "Well, as the Warrior Chief, I would have to say no, but as a man, I'll admit that it could possibly work."

"*That* sounds rather like a bribe to me," she replied. The truth was that she found herself rather relieved that her subterfuge hadn't worked. Now she could postpone the inevitable a while longer.

"No, it was only a statement of truth. There are

two parts to me, but I'm the Warrior Chief first and a man second. Unfortunately," he added with what sounded like genuine regret.

"Then we needn't discuss this any further," she stated as she stood up. "I'm tired, Miklav, so you will have to excuse me."

He, too, had gotten to his feet. "There will be war, Milady. The Augury foretold it, and I myself feel it. If you wish to bear my child, it might be wise to consider the possibility that I may not survive that war."

Nazleen gasped at his seemingly casual words. For one irrational moment, she thought he might have found some way to spy on the Augury. She could not bring herself to meet his eyes and instead started to turn away, but he put out a hand to grasp her arm lightly. The gesture was certainly presumptuous on his part, but she said nothing. She simply stopped and forced herself to meet his gaze.

"I think you also understand what it is to be two people in one body," he said softly. "As Liege, you must be self-confident at all times, but as a woman you're very nervous right now."

She opened her mouth to protest, then closed it again. To protest the obvious would be to embarrass herself.

"Yes, you're right, Miklav. I have many things to be nervous about just now."

He slid his hand slowly down her arm until he was holding her hand instead. Then he raised it to his lips, brushing them against her skin lightly.

"Then you'll agree that it's better that one of us has some experience."

She searched his face, trying to decide if he were

referring to war or to their union—or both. Perhaps it didn't matter. She withdrew her hand and turned again toward the bedchamber.

"Good night, Milady. Rest well. We have three nights at least before the scouts return."

Nazleen did not fail to note that he had said "nights."

CHAPTER FOUR

NAZLEEN AWOKE THE NEXT MORNING TO NOISES IN THE courtyard beneath her window and a lingering sense of unpleasant dreams. Her maid must have come in earlier to open the shutters to the morning air, forgetting that up here in the mountains that air was very cool.

She pulled herself from bed, shivering until she had wrapped herself in the bedcovers. Her nose wrinkled at the unpleasant odor of the ointment provided to her by the Warriors' physician, but as she stretched and tested her abused muscles, she was pleased to find that the aftereffects of her accident weren't as bad as she'd feared.

Dragging the bedcovers with her, she went over to the window, taking care to stay well back as she peered out into the bright morning sun. Scores of black-clad Warriors were engaged in their morning exercise routines, led by a very loud drillmaster whose colorful encouragements and admonitions reached even to her ears.

Then she noticed a group of very young Warriors, the newest recruits, no doubt. Most of them appeared to be no more than 12 or 13. She watched them, wondering if one of them might be Miklav's son.

Miklav. What was she to do about him? As she watched the boys, his statement about the responsibilities of fatherhood came back to her. A brief union with him to satisfy the terms of the Compact was one thing—she'd always known she would have to face that one day—but an involved father who intended to take an active role in the upbringing of his children was quite another.

But he won't be an involved father if he's dead, she reminded herself. From a purely practical standpoint, that was a solution to the problem, but the simple truth was that she didn't want Miklav to die. If he died, then war would have become a reality. And if he died, what was the likelihood that the new Warrior Chief would be as enlightened as Miklav was? At least she could trust Miklav—up to a point, that is.

If the Augury was wrong and he lived, then he promised to be an constant source of trouble to her.

She sighed, hating her own ambivalence and hating the uncertainty that plagued them all right now.

Loreth might believe that this Augury had been clear, but Nazleen thought no such thing. It was true that all had agreed there would be war—and that was highly unusual—but the rest of it was open to different interpretations. An end to the Sisterhood—yes, they'd all seen that, too. But a new beginning? Only some of them had foreseen that—the younger ones, Loreth had said.

And the Fire Warrior? Most of them had seen him, and some had even seen a whole group of them. Were they out there across the desert, waiting for some sign? Would they know Haslik and the others were spying on them? If they were indeed Cerecian, they would know. She shivered, thinking of her brother confronting a Fire Warrior.

She continued to stand at the window watching the boys as they attempted the rigorous exercises of the Warriors. How much they wanted to be like those bloodthirsty killers, but at least now they also received a decent education.

She'd learned a few years ago from Haslik that since Miklav had become Warrior Chief the boys spent far more time in classrooms. That revelation had surprised her, even though she'd always been aware of the fact that Miklav himself was an educated man. She wondered how he had come by that learning. He'd grown up on a commune, and at that time such children were generally not educated. Loreth herself had said that she was barely literate when she came to Cerece.

She was about to turn away from the window when the boys finished their routines and were given permission by their drillmaster to rest for a while. One boy in particular caught her attention. She'd never seen anyone but a Desert Tren sit in that manner, an uncomfortable-looking sort of squat.

She edged closer to the window, peering at the boy and noticing now that he seemed to be darker than the others, even though all of them were tanned at this time of year. He was also shorter and had very straight black hair.

Nazleen frowned. She knew that Miklav, ever the diplomat, had begun to permit a few boys of mixed Tren and Hamloorian blood to enter Warrior training, but they were the offspring of Mountain Trens and as far as she knew never sat that way. Neither were they inclined to be as dark as their desert kinfolk.

As soon as they'd broken ranks, the boys had gathered into small groups. The dark boy she was watching had been left to himself at first, but now a tall, athletic youth came over to sit with him. The tall boy sat facing in her direction, and all of a sudden he lifted his face and stared directly up at the window where she stood.

Nazleen retreated quickly, but not before she got a brief look at the second boy. Even at this distance, his resemblance to his father was striking. So she'd found Miklav's son after all. But who was that dark boy?

Her maid came in then, followed by servants who brought water for her bath. After washing away the pungent odor of the ointment, Nazleen breakfasted in the sitting room of the Warrior Chief's suite, wondering if her host intended to put in an appearance during the day.

The prospect of several days with nothing of

consequence to do did not sit well with her. It was difficult to relax in such surroundings, and she doubted that Denra boasted much of a library. She also didn't know just how much freedom she had here and was disinclined to test the limits. No doubt there were many Warriors who privately disapproved of her presence here as it was.

After she had finished her breakfast, she asked her maid to summon one of Miklav's staff. She had decided that one thing she should do is exercise her mare, even if she had to do it inside the walls of the fortress. After the animal's behavior yesterday she would need to be ridden.

The maid returned quickly with the Captain who had accompanied her to Denra. She told him of her need to exercise the mare and inquired if she might ride outside the fortress.

"Milady, I'm sure that the Warrior Chief would not want you to ride unaccompanied outside the walls. However, with his permission, I will be happy to accompany you."

But the Warrior Chief did not give his permission; instead, he himself appeared just after she'd changed into riding clothes. Nazleen was both amused and irritated. She wondered if Miklav might not be jealous of the handsome Captain. Surely he had far more pressing matters on his agenda, and she was irritated because she would have preferred the Captain's company. The less she saw of Miklav during her stay here the better. Having failed in her scheme to turn his thoughts away from war, she was quite prepared to let matters between them remain unchanged for now.

"It was not my intention to take you away from

your duties," she stated after he had greeted her and announced that he would take her riding.

"On a fine day like this the prospect of riding in the company of a beautiful woman is far more appealing than reviewing war plans," he replied with that lazy smile that could soften his rugged features.

Nazleen gave him a look that signaled quite clearly her lack of susceptibility to flattery, but he merely continued to smile as he led her through the corridors to the courtyard. There she found two youths with her mare and Miklav's stallion. She saw immediately that the one youth was the one she'd seen looking up at her window—Miklav's son. Up close, the resemblance to his father was even more apparent.

"Milady, this is my son, Kyetki. You may recall that your mother gave permission for him to come here with me when his mother died."

"Yes, I do remember, and there is certainly no doubt that he is your son, Miklav." She smiled at the boy and acknowledged his nervous bow.

Miklav assisted her into the saddle, then laid a hand briefly on his son's shoulder before mounting his charger. The boy's look was one of such pure adoration that Nazleen felt a sudden catch in her throat. Certainly neither she nor Haslik had ever felt that way about their father. They'd barely known him.

As they walked the horses toward the open gate, Nazleen glanced at Miklav. It was surely no coincidence that his son had been the one to bring her horse to her. Had that little scene been another reminder to her that he took fatherhood seriously?

If so, she had to admit that it had worked. He might have staged their meeting, but the boy couldn't be faking that love for his father.

Then, as they rode out through the gate, she recalled the other boy she'd seen with Kyetki earlier. She turned to the Warrior Chief.

"Earlier this morning, I saw Kyetki and the other boys out in the courtyard. There was a boy with him who seemed different. He was very dark, and he sat in that peculiar manner I've seen only among the Desert Trens."

"I've permitted a few boys of mixed blood to enter training," was the Warrior Chief's casual reply.

"Yes, I know that, but such children aren't generally that dark."

Miklav was silent for so long that she thought he had nothing more to say on the subject, but finally he turned to her.

"He's the son of the Desert Chieftain."

"But . . ." Nazleen stopped, frowning as the significance of his words began to dawn on her. "Miklav, is that boy a hostage?"

"In a manner of speaking," he replied. "As you saw, he has the run of the place and the company of the other boys. Kyetki tells me he's quite content; in fact, he's even expressed an interest in staying here."

"But you brought him here against the Chieftain's will."

"Yes. He's a guarantee that there won't be any trouble about our crossing the desert."

"By the gods, Miklav, you have gone too far! You . . ."

"I do what I believe to be best for the protection of my men which, I might remind you, includes your brother."

"Don't bring Haslik into this!"

"Why not? Ask him when he returns what he thinks of the idea."

"Haslik won't say anything that is contrary to your beliefs and your orders, and you know that."

"I know nothing of the sort. When you see him out of my presence, I have no way of knowing what he tells you."

"I don't want to talk about Haslik. I want that boy returned to his father with an apology."

"Milady, with all due respect, if you feel the need to apologize, by all means, do so. Your envoy can claim ignorance of the entire matter in good conscience."

"The boy cannot stay here, no matter what his own wishes."

"That's true, although I may speak to his father about his returning here to enter training, if the boy truly wants that. There have been no problems having the boys of mixed blood, and several Mountain Trens have approached me about Warrior training for their own sons. One is close kin to the Desert Chieftain, so it might work out."

Nazleen was silent as her anger subsided. There was nothing in the Compact to prevent Trens from becoming Warriors. That had scarcely been necessary at the time of its negotiation, since the two groups were still warring periodically with each other.

In a sense, the fact that Trens were actually asking to send their sons into Warrior training was the best indication possible that the Compact had worked. The old hatreds and distrust were ending.

"I can see the value to that," she admitted reluctantly. "And I am reminded of my mother's comment about your being both a Warrior and a diplomat."

He smiled at her. "I will take that as a compliment, Milady, and pay you one in return. As much as I admired and respected your mother, I also found that she was nearly always unwilling to change her mind. You have not inherited that troublesome trait, and you are the better for it."

"And I will take that as a compliment, but do not think you can bend me to your will, Miklav. If I change my mind, it is because facts I had never considered have been brought to my attention."

"That's exactly what I meant, Milady."

After that exchange, they rode in silence, crossing the wide, open area in front of the fortress and entering the thick, sloping forest, where a narrow path snaked its way through the aromatic evergreens. The mare seemed very much herself despite her ordeal, but Nazleen felt her own muscles still protesting their abuse.

"She seems to have recovered well," Miklav said at length as he glanced at the little white mare. "Kyetki exercised her last evening in the courtyard. He's very good with animals."

"I must thank him for his thoughtfulness. You must be very proud of him, Miklav. He's a fine boy."

"Yes, he is. And he shows a great aptitude for building things. He spends most of his free time

118

with Haslik and the others."

Nazleen began to think about how her perceptions of Warrior training were being challenged by her visit here. It had always troubled her to think of Haslik being forced to become a Warrior and how the same thing would happen to any son she bore. But she realized now that Haslik himself had never expressed any unhappiness with his lot, even though he'd missed life at the palace for a while.

Contrary to Miklav's stated opinion, Nazleen was sometimes very reluctant to change her mind, to give up her cherished beliefs. Like most people born to great power, she had a subconscious belief in her own infallibility. However, unlike many others, she did chastise herself for that trait from time to time.

At the moment, she felt herself in danger of revising her opinion of Warriors too quickly. So she turned to the comforting certainty that Warriors were still nothing more than killers, no matter how they might present themselves from time to time. Haslik was, of course, an exception.

She could not, she told herself, afford to think otherwise with the prospect of war looming over them.

Miklav was wondering what had possessed him to tell her the truth about that boy. He knew he could have deceived her. People are easily deceived if they want to be, and he knew she didn't want to believe it. Was she gaining some sort of hold over him?

He felt himself treading on dangerous ground. The truth was that in addition to his desire for her, he actually liked her. He respected intelligence and personal integrity, and Nazleen had both those qualities.

But however much he liked this woman who rode beside him, Miklav could never let himself lose sight of the fact that she was the chief roadblock in his quest for power. He had no intention of trying to subvert the Compact because he too was a man of integrity, but that Compact could give him power. He had only to be sure that war would come.

They came out of the forest onto a wide rocky ledge, where he signaled a halt and dismounted, then hurried to her only to have her dismount without his assistance. He could see the slight awkwardness in her movements and knew that she must still be in some pain. He admired both her behavior yesterday after the accident and her insistence upon riding again today. Most women would not have shown such courage.

The view beyond the ledge was spectacular, the most breathtaking panorama of mountains and narrow ravines that Nazleen had ever seen, and she told him so.

He nodded. "I come here as often as possible. It's a pleasant place to pass a few hours reading."

Once again, Nazleen found herself caught between her former beliefs about Miklav and the image he now presented. "It's difficult for me to imagine a Warrior Chief spending his spare time reading."

He chuckled. "Possibly that's because you base your notions of what a Warrior Chief should be on your father."

"That's true enough. Mother told me that he was

barely literate."

"Oh, Hektar could read well enough. He simply had no interest in it."

"But you do."

"I have a curious mind, and when I came here, I found someone to feed that curiosity."

"Who?" she asked, unable to imagine such a person at Denra.

"His name was Sektav. He was an old man by the time I came to Denra. He'd lost a leg in battle when he was only twenty-four, and he came from a wealthy merchant family who provided him with books. By the time I arrived, his eyesight was failing and he chose me to read to him. I'm not sure why. In any event, I would read to him, and then he'd question me about what I'd read. In that way, he improved my reading skills and taught me to think."

"Didn't the others tease you about it?"

He laughed. "A few of them did, but only once. Like every other boy here, I had to fight to maintain my place, and as it happens, I fight very well."

Nazleen didn't doubt that, but his words made her wonder about the difficulties Haslik must have faced—and the problems a son of hers might face one day. No boy who grew up in the palace learned to defend himself the way she assumed a commune boy like Miklav would have.

"Did Haslik have problems when he came here?"

"No, not really. He's not a fighter, but he has a very likable nature. And most importantly, he instinctively found the middle ground between flaunting his position and denying it. Also, it became evident very early on that he had important

121

gifts—his ability to build things. When war comes, I will not send him into battle; his value lies elsewhere."

A great wave of relief washed over her, though she tried to hide it. She couldn't bear to think of losing her brother. "Does he know this?"

"Yes. We discussed it before he left with the scouting party. I made it clear to him that if they should run into trouble, I wanted him to beat a hasty retreat, not stay and fight. I think he was greatly relieved. As I said, he isn't much of a fighter."

Then he looked directly at her. "If you are concerned that any son of ours would have a difficult time here, you can rest easy. Warrior training places much more emphasis on intelligence these days, and if there's one thing we can say for certain about any children of ours, it's that they would be bright."

Nazleen met his smile with one of her own, but this talk made her uneasy. She wanted children, although perhaps not as much as most women seemed to, but the begetting of them was another matter altogether.

As Liege, she was essentially untouchable. Normal affectionate contact with people just didn't happen to her, and in her case it had always been that way. Her mother hadn't been a very demonstrative woman, and the servants who had cared for her as a child had, for the most part, taken their cue from her.

Added to that, of course, was her Cerecian upbringing, which taught that the sexual act interfered with spiritual training.

They turned and started back toward the horses. Nazleen lifted her foot to the stirrup and couldn't quite suppress a gasp of pain. Miklav caught her about the waist, but instead of lifting her into the saddle, he drew her around to face him. They stared at each other in a suddenly charged silence. Then he slowly brought one hand up to cup her chin.

"Fear is best gotten over one step at a time."

His tone was gentle, but she could hear a raw edge to his voice, as though he were controlling himself with great difficulty. He searched her face carefully and perhaps saw what he wanted to see, because he began to lower his own face to hers.

His grip on her was light, and Nazleen knew she could end this now. But to her surprise, she felt a curiosity growing in her, a need to take that first step now. Instead of moving out of his arms, she closed her eyes and then felt his mouth on hers.

The intimate contact both repelled and intrigued her. Unaware of having done so, she made a low sound in her throat. Immediately, his lips moved over hers with increasing pressure, teasing hers apart to allow his tongue entrance. At the same time, he drew her more fully into his arms, surrounding her with his strength.

Nazleen was so fascinated by this new experience that moments passed before she began to panic, but as soon as she felt that fear well up within her, he released her. She stared at him, knowing now that she truly had to guard her inner self against this man. This, surely, was what the Sisters had meant.

He ran one long finger slowly along the line of her jaw, then across the achingly sensitive flesh of her lips.

"There is a place within you that I may never reach, Nazleen, but I *will* give you pleasure."

After dining alone that evening in Miklav's suite, Nazleen tried to interest herself in one of the books she'd selected from the library. The obliging Captain Mevak had taken her on a tour of the fortress; apparently, Miklav had decided that he didn't represent a threat, after all. She'd been surprised to find such a good library and had selected an old favorite she'd read as a child.

But as the night came on, Miklav's presence loomed over his quarters. She half-expected to turn around and find him lounging there somewhere, perhaps on the thick cushions that were tossed haphazardly before the fireplace. Or did he plan to appear after she had gone to bed?

One part of her was still very curious and actually wanted to know the pleasure he had promised her, but another part urged caution, lest she allow him into that inner self she must protect.

She remained dressed and awake until a very late hour, keeping the shutters partly open despite the evening chill just in case he was out there waiting for her to go to bed before coming to her. She was no longer certain that he would wait for a specific invitation which she might well have issued this afternoon.

Finally, when she heard the fortress gong announce the midnight hour, she prepared for bed, her ears pricked for any unusual sound. When her maid had departed for her cot in an anteroom, Nazleen climbed into bed, certain that she'd never sleep. But she did indeed fall asleep, even as she continued to listen for any sound that could mark the Warrior Chief's arrival.

From the top of the fortress wall directly across from his quarters, Miklav saw the lamps go out in his sitting room. He chuckled to himself. She'd certainly waited long enough, but he had no intention of going to her this night.

Forcing himself upon her now might relieve the ache in his loins, but a temporary pleasure couldn't compare to mutual desire. And he knew that he'd set her on that road this afternoon. He could wait, although probably not for much longer.

When Nazleen awoke the next morning, it was to the startled realization that she'd slept the night through without interruption. She sat up in bed and contemplated the implications of that. So he had meant what he'd said about small steps. Somehow that failed to reassure her, perhaps because it seemed to mean that they were playing this game by his rules, and it was a game at which he was an expert while she was a complete novice.

She could change those rules by inviting him into her bed—or was that just what he wanted her to do? It wasn't in her nature to await action on the part of others, but in this case she was disinclined to take any action herself.

The Captain showed up shortly after she had breakfasted and inquired if she would like to ride again.

"With you as escort, or has the Warrior Chief sent you?"

"Both, Milady. I would be happy to escort you,

and the Chief suggested it."

So they rode out of the fortress, taking a different route from the one she had taken the day before with Miklav. She was pleased to discover that her soreness was just about gone, allowing her to truly enjoy the ride this day. Captain Mevak was good company as well, amusing her with stories about the young Warriors with whom he apparently spent much of his time. She inquired about Kyetki, wondering aloud if it was difficult for him because of his father.

"He demands too much of himself sometimes," the Captain replied, "although I think that's probably just his nature. But he shows much promise, and he's popular with the other boys. In a sense, he's far ahead of the others, since he's been here for six years now."

"Does he spend much time with his father?"

"Not as much as he once did, since he's busy with his studies most of the time. It's a demanding routine designed to keep them from having much free time, but they spent a great deal of time together when he was younger, since he shared the Chief's quarters until he joined his class of recruits."

"Miklav appears to be a devoted father."

"Yes, he is. In my opinion, that sets a good example for the rest of us. Many, as you surely know, Milady, tend to ignore their children, except when the time comes to recruit their sons as Warriors."

He went on to talk about his own six-year-old son and about other Warriors who spent much of their free time with their children. Nazleen was surprised to discover that Miklav's behavior wasn't all that unusual. She wondered why no one had told her about this change. It seemed important for her to know, since it meant that the Warriors were involving themselves far more intimately in the lives of their society.

At the time the Compact was being negotiated, the Warriors had rarely set foot in the city or in any of the farming communes, except to frequent taverns and pleasure houses. An attempt had been made to restrict them to those places, but the powerful Warrior Chief of that time had refused to accept such restrictions, declaring them to be more appropriate to prisoners than to citizens of Hamloor, and the Cerecian Pavla had acceded to this argument.

Now she wondered about the wisdom of that decision. If the Warriors came to be seen as no more than ordinary citizens, didn't that spell danger for her and for future Lieges?

They had circled through the forest and came now to a road she recognized as being the one she'd traveled to get to Denra. Just as they turned onto it, a small party of Trens came into view on their sturdy little ponies. The Captain greeted them by name, seeming unsurprised at their presence here on Warrior property. The Trens, for their part, showed no fear of the Captain, but they were obviously shocked to discover their Liege here.

Seeing their surprise, Captain Mevak explained that she was a guest of the Warrior Chief for a few days, an explanation that produced still more astonishment.

Then the group rode together across the open

space in front of the fortress and passed through the gate without challenge. A group of young Warriors appeared quickly to take their horses and the Trens' ponies, and one of Miklav's aides led the Trens off across the courtyard.

"Why are they here?" Nazleen inquired.

"They come once a month, Milady. The Warrior Chief holds regular meetings with the headmen of the closest villages. So do the commanders of the other fortresses—on the Chief's orders. That way, no problem is permitted to grow too large before being resolved."

Nazleen thanked the Captain and returned to her suite, lost in thought. It appeared that her visit to Denra was proving to be far more instructive than she would have guessed.

She bathed and then waited for the two boys she had requested to see—Kyetki and the Desert Chieftain's son. The Captain hadn't appeared to be surprised at her request, although she wondered if Miklav would allow her to talk with the Tren youth, given the circumstances under which he was here. But both boys arrived in short order.

She thanked Kyetki for his kindness toward her mare, and he expressed his admiration for the animal. He'd never seen a Royal White before. When she asked if he were fluent in the peculiar dialect of the Desert Trens, he assured her proudly that he was. Warriors were being taught all the languages spoken in Hamloor, he said, including even Cerecian.

Nazleen tried not to look shocked at that. "Then please tell him that I deeply regret that he has been brought here against his will and that I had no foreknowledge of this."

Kyetki looked somewhat uncomfortable, but he quickly translated to the other boy who stood there silently, his dark eyes upon her.

Nazleen could follow him well enough to be reasonably certain that he was translating accurately, but she had more difficulty with the boy's response, which was accompanied by shy smiles at her and several awkward bows.

"Tarabdi says that he likes being here. His brothers had visited Denra and told him about it."

Nazleen stared hard at both boys and was forced to conclude that they were being honest with her. "But his father must be unhappy about this."

Through Kyetki, the boy stated that he believed his father understood the necessity and respected the Warrior Chief. Then the boy spoke up again in an excited voice, directing his words at Kyetki but sending what seemed to be pleading looks at her.

"He says that he would like to become a Warrior. He is the third son, so there is no chance of his becoming Chieftain. He wonders if you could assist him, Milady."

"I will not object, but such a decision must be made between his father and the Warrior Chief. I will be happy to send a representative to be present if they discuss it."

When Kyetki had translated this, the boy smiled delightedly and bowed very low. She dismissed them and sat lost in thought for a long time. Then she got out her journal and sat down to begin to write.

Like her mother before her, and like most other Lieges throughout their history, Nazleen found a journal a good way to organize her thoughts and help her shape her decisions. During her lifetime, it would be for her eyes only, but when she was gone, her daughter would have it. She had read and reread her mother's journal and had often found help there with her own problems. She dipped the pen into the inkwell and began to write:

I have been at Denra for less than two days, and yet I feel that I may have learned more about the Warriors than in all my earlier studies and discussions with my Advisors. What I have learned seems to have important implications for the future, perhaps even for the present.

The Warrior Chief has assumed such authority to himself as I would never have guessed from the reports received at the palace. He has taken hostage the son of the Desert Chieftain to guarantee safe passage through the desert for his men—and moreover admits to having done this before. This makes a sham of our own emissary's discussions with the Desert Chieftain, and that Miklav would admit to having done such a thing is even more troubling than the act itself.

Furthermore, it would appear that he has cast himself into the role of diplomat far more than either my mother or I had believed. Miklav has taken it upon himself to hold regular meetings with the headmen of the Tren villages near Denra and the other commanders are said to be doing likewise at their fortresses. This action clearly undermines the authority of the Court, since it has always been the Court's responsibility to mediate disputes between the Warriors and Trens. Why else am I called Protector of the Trens?

Also, I have learned that Miklav is not the only Warrior who is taking an active role in the upbringing of his children. This means that the Warriors are assuming an ever larger role in the daily lives of Hamloorians. I cannot but see danger in this to the Court.

Too much power is being concentrated in the hands of the Warriors, particularly the Warrior Chief. To a large extent, the Compact is based upon the assumption that the Warriors need to be controlled, that they are feared by Hamloorians and Trens alike, but that fear may be rapidly vanishing.

I fear for the future of our society. The Sisterhood believed that women are clearly more fit to rule, since they are far less inclined toward war, and they further believed that women must lead independent lives, free from the slavery imposed upon them by that ancient tyranny called marriage.

But now we have Warriors beginning to assume power in the lives of Hamloorian citizens, and we also have an increasing tendency toward life-mating despite the Court's clear disapproval of such arrangements.

Is there some grand scheme at work here, some plot on the part of Miklav? It is certainly possible. No Warrior Chief has ever hungered for power more than he, and I will never again underestimate his intelligence or his cunning.

If war comes, I fear that more than lives will be

lost. The Compact itself may be the greatest victim. Miklav will never relinquish power once it is in his grasp, and his alliances with the Trens and with ordinary citizens, plus his popularity with many of my Court, may mean that he can discard the Compact without fear of reprisal.

Only the Cerecians would stand between him and total power, and their numbers are sadly diminished. There may be no one left who can wield the fire, and no will to learn it again, either. I studied it while I was at Cerece and continue to practice the required exercises, but to what purpose? Even if I am Liege, I'm only one person.

Loreth has admitted that she loves Miklav. I know that she would never choose him over the Sisterhood, but who knows what gradual shifts of power she may accept because of that love? She trusts him, and if he tells her that he has not usurped the Court's authority, she may well believe him.

And what about the aliens across the desert? Are there really male Cerecians—Fire Warriors—there? If so, and if war comes and Miklav dies, I may have an even worse enemy to contend with. Would even the Sisterhood stand with me against members of our own race?

Deep inside, I believe that this man Zaktar exists, and I believe that it is he, not Miklav, whom I should fear most.

"It's just a small scouting party," Zaktar whispered to Taka. "The same as we sent out."

"So what will we do?" Taka whispered back. "Shall we let them be?"

Zaktar nodded. The two of them were hiding behind some large boulders on a hillside between the ruins and the campsite. Below them, the five men in black moved quietly through the forest. Thanks to the guards posted along the edges of the desert, they'd had plenty of advance warning. Before he and Taka had climbed up here, they'd gathered the expedition together and told them to go about their business as usual. Sharpshooters had been posted at various intervals, concealed but ready to fire if the invaders gave them any cause.

Zaktar and Taka had positioned themselves so that they had the Warriors in sight over a considerable length of their journey. They'd been watching them from the moment they'd broken camp at dawn to circle the ruins, where they'd watched the activity for several hours. Now they were on the move again.

It was obvious to Zaktar that they knew the lay of the land, since they appeared to be headed toward the narrow ravine where the expedition had made camp. After observing that they had no radios, Zaktar had permitted the use of their own radios. As soon as the Warriors were far enough away, he switched it on and spoke into it.

"They're headed for the camp. Keep them in your rifle sights, but hold your fire unless they threaten the camp."

Then, when the order had been acknowledged, he and Taka left their hillside and hurried off toward the forest behind them. There was one thing he didn't want the Warriors to see, and it had been hidden deep in the forest. With any luck, it would permit them to find out where these men had come from.

Nazleen had grown increasingly curious about Miklav's absence as the day wore on and evening approached. After recording her thoughts, she found herself with an even keener interest in the Warrior Chief and his plans. Where, she wondered, did she herself fit into his schemes? She was still convinced that he would never harm her or allow her to be harmed, but he must surely have some plan for her. Perhaps he believed he could bend her to his will once she'd borne his children.

And yet, what else could she do? She'd chosen him, and if she now tried to renege on that, she would be showing her fear of him. Besides, she had no other choice. He would never allow another Warrior to have her. He might even have permitted her to spend time with the handsome Captain Mevak just to torment her with the certainty that she could not have him. She didn't want Mevak, but Miklav might well believe that she did. She knew she'd spoken well of him to Miklav on several occasions, and he was her brother's closest friend.

In short, Miklav had been brilliant, and she had been very blind not to have seen all this before. But it wasn't all her fault. Isolated as she was within the palace, she had to rely on reports gotten through her Advisors, and they had certainly not been supplying her with the information she needed.

What remained for her now was to decide how to respond to this threat. Should she embark upon some subtle campaign of her own, or should she confront him here and now?

Her tendency was to believe that his subtle strategies could best be countered by equally quiet moves on her part, but the imminence of war cast that in doubt.

She pondered all this as the object of her thoughts became ever more conspicuous by his absence.

CHAPTER FIVE

"THE WARRIOR CHIEF ASKS TO JOIN YOU FOR DINNER, Milady."

Nazleen wanted to refuse, but even as she thought it, she was nodding. "It will be my pleasure."

Miklav's aide departed. It would certainly *not* be her pleasure. Her pleasure would be to return to the palace without having laid eyes on him again. Her pleasure would be to learn that the aliens had departed for their own lands. But her pleasure was no longer important.

She still had no idea how to proceed and decided to let his behavior and his words guide her. Extensively schooled in all the nuances of human behavior, she had been taught to trust her instincts.

When he arrived a short time later, she extended

both hands in an affectionate greeting, and he took them quickly, his eyes sweeping over the simple but alluring gown she had chosen. The gown revealed nothing but promised much, and the message was received.

As dinner was being served, she inquired about the scouts.

"They should arrive tomorrow, but much depends upon how easily they found the aliens and how easily they were able to get away again."

Her thoughts turned once more to Haslik's safety, and then something else struck her. She waited until they were alone again and voiced her new fear.

"Miklav, if there are Cerecians among them, the scouts may not be able to observe them without being caught. Trained watchers will have detected them."

He nodded. "Yes, but that was a chance I had to take. We must know what we face."

"But if they are caught . . . Haslik is with them," she finished with fear in her voice.

"Haslik is a Warrior, and he, more than anyone else, should be able to determine what sort of threat their weapons pose to us."

"You've risked his life!"

"A Warrior Chief is often in the position of risking lives, even, occasionally, of sending men to certain death."

He saw the look on her face and reached across the table to take her hand. "Nazleen, I don't believe he is in danger. Certainly it's possible that they could be captured, whether or not there are Cerecians among them, but I don't think they would be killed. It isn't likely that there are very many of them, and they can't have any idea how many of us they'd face. So they're not likely to risk a battle with us at this point over a scouting party."

She withdrew her hand, having in that moment made up her mind about how to proceed. "But if they *are* killed, it would further your plans, especially because my judgment could be clouded by the death of my brother."

He didn't respond at once, turning his attention instead to his dinner. After some wine, he nodded.

"Yes, such an occurrence would further my plans, but I am neither so desperate nor so depraved that I would seek such a means to war—and you know that. You would never have chosen such a man to be your mate."

"You seem to place great store in that fact, Miklav. You've said such a thing before, but it's possible that you believe you can do exactly that *because* I'd never believe it."

He chuckled. "The intricacies of this conversation are soon going to be beyond me and into the realm of some of your courtiers."

"I have reached the conclusion that nothing is beyond you when it comes to hatching plots and devising grand schemes to gain power."

"Oh?" he inquired, arching a dark brow as he continued to smile at her.

So she carefully enumerated what she had learned and how she interpreted it. He said nothing, continuing to enjoy his meal as she spoke in carefully measured tones. When she had finished, he drained his goblet and partially refilled it. Nothing betrayed anger or fear or any other emotion.

"I commend you. I never doubted your intelligence, but I'm surprised to find such an analytical mind in one so young."

"So you admit it."

"I admit to everything you've accused me of, yes. The facts are indisputable. And I have to say that your Advisors have not been serving you well if they didn't bring all this to your attention before."

"Don't stray from the subject, Miklav. I want an answer! Are you plotting to subvert the Compact and rule Hamloor yourself?"

"If I were obsessed with ruling Hamloor myself, we would not be having this conversation— because you'd already be dead! There have been ample opportunities to have you killed and let it seem that the aliens had done it. In that case, I could have both war and the rule of Hamloor."

Nazleen stared at him. She could find no fault in his reasoning. Aliens *had* been seen in the area. She might well have "disappeared" en route to Denra, her body to be "discovered" later, and her death attributed to them. Miklav would declare war as a result of this evil deed, and with no one to succeed her, the power would remain in his hands. No one would challenge him—not even Loreth.

"No, I do not believe you capable of such an act," she said finally.

"Now tell me why you don't believe it. Is it because you think that my desire for you exceeds my desire for power, or is it because you believe that I am a man of honor?"

"Why do you want to know?"

"It's important to me."

She stared into his eyes and knew that it *was*

important to him. "I believe that you are a man of honor, Miklav. You were right; I would never have chosen you otherwise."

"But you might well have chosen me because you saw no alternative. My desire has been plain enough, and you might have believed that choosing any other man—Captain Mevak, for example— could result in his death."

"What would you have done if I had chosen him or someone else?"

He shrugged. "I would have made his life so miserable that he'd have been forced to leave. For a Warrior, that could be worse than death. But in all likelihood, if you'd chosen anyone else, he would have refused for that reason."

"I did consider Mevak, as a matter of fact. He's Haslik's closest friend, and I like him very much."

"So do I. It may also be that, in his case, being forced to leave the Warrior life would not be so difficult. He likes to teach and could pursue that profession outside as well."

"Are you suggesting that I should change my mind and choose him?"

"I am giving you that option. That's why I asked him to accompany you here and then to take you riding today. You may discuss it with him if you wish, and you have my word that I will do no harm to him if he accepts and then leaves."

Nazleen remained silent as she finished her dinner. Why was he suddenly giving her this option? Certainly he still wanted her. What possible advantage could there be to his plans in such a choice? None that she could see.

That left only the possibility that Miklav wanted

her to choose him freely—or as freely as the Compact would permit. It was somehow important to him. She thought about Loreth's cautionary words that Miklav was far more complex than she'd assumed.

She met his steady gaze, and for one fleeting moment she thought she saw fear there, the fear that she might accept the option he offered.

"I do not wish to choose Mevak—or anyone else."

She saw all the subtle signs of a man relaxing while attempting to hide that fact. And for one brief moment, she allowed herself to think of Miklav not as the Warrior Chief but as a man.

When the servants returned to clear the table, Miklav rose. "Unfortunately, there are no gardens here for us to walk in, but it's a pleasant night and the moon is full. Would you like to see the view from the fortress roof?"

Nazleen nodded. It would, she thought, be far more clear than the view in her mind, which at present was very clouded indeed.

He led her out of the suite, through dimly lit hallways and up several flights of stone steps, where they emerged onto a wide, flat roof.

She gasped, pleasantly surprised. The full moon was floating just above the tree line, illuminating the dark, silent forest surrounding the fortress and casting silvery shadows on distant valleys. A gong sounded in the distance, announcing the hour, followed by the ritual calls from the guardposts on the outer walls. She turned to him with a delighted smile.

"This is as beautiful in its way as the palace

141

gardens." She thought that she might well have misjudged Miklav's capacity to appreciate beauty that night in the royal gardens.

They were both unconsciously staring off to the west, where the desert was hidden beyond the far hills. Nazleen's thoughts turned once more to Haslik, and she shivered. Miklav, who stood just behind her, slid his arms about her waist, drawing her back against him.

"He will be safe."

"You can't be sure of that," she protested, as an image of that Fire Warrior returned to torment her. "Safe," he'd said. "No harm." Hadn't that been just an hallucination or a projection of her own hopes?

"No," Miklav admitted, "I can't be sure, but I trust my ability to think as the aliens would think."

"Or you trust them to think as you do," she pointed out.

"Yes," he replied, his voice muffled as he lowered his face to her hair.

Nazleen willed herself to relax as he drew her still more closely to him, and her softness molded itself to his hard, muscular body. It wasn't as difficult as she'd expected.

Then he lowered his face still more, burying it in the curve of her neck and shoulder where his mouth and tongue moved lightly against her sensitive skin. Even through the layers of clothing, she could feel the hard evidence of his desire, and she also felt something stirring inside her.

I will not let him have *me*, she thought. I will give him my body, but not *me*. Then, just as he began to turn her to face him, she saw again that man with golden hair and green eyes. The sacred fire shimmered briefly, and then he was gone as Miklav drew her against him again.

His kiss was different this time, beginning as a subtle teasing of her senses and moving slowly into a promise of pleasure to come. He had said he would give her pleasure, and she no longer doubted that.

Perhaps he sensed her acquiescence, because he released her, then extended his hand. "Let us go back inside."

They were back in his suite far too quickly. Fear was writhing inside her despite every effort to keep it down. Every movement and every gesture was magnified. Desperately, she tried to remind herself of her duty to the Compact, of the need to provide a future Liege. Her mind accepted that knowledge, but her body wouldn't.

As soon as the door closed behind them, Miklav lifted her into his arms and carried her into the bedroom. She felt helpless and resented that feeling, then wondered if that were his intention. For the first time in her life, she felt a situation moving beyond her control.

Instead of laying her down on the big bed, he set her on her feet, his dark eyes searching her face carefully.

"It would help if you didn't see us now as Warrior Chief and Liege. This isn't a contest of wills, Nazleen. I'm a man and you're a woman, and we want each other. But I can't take more from you than you're willing to give."

She searched his face, too, seeking some clue as to the truth or lie behind his words. It was true that he couldn't take from her what she was unwilling to give, but was this too a part of his scheme to gain the power he craved?

He reached out to stroke her cheek softly. "I can give you pleasure or merely give you an heir. That choice is up to you."

"I distrust that kind of pleasure," she replied, but did not move beyond his reach.

He dropped his hand, took a few steps away from her and began to undress in a methodical manner. She stood there watching him and wondering if her pleasure truly mattered to him.

Nazleen had never seen a naked adult male, and when he had finished undressing, she stared at him in undisguised shock. It wasn't that hairy, muscular body that shocked her, and it wasn't even the two long scars that marred his chest and one thigh. It was that jutting instrument of male potency.

She'd been educated by the Cerecians to understand and monitor her own body, but since the Sisterhood disdained the sexual act, they wasted no time discussing male anatomy. Her mother had explained the act to her only in the simplest terms, and Nazleen, who had seen Haslik naked only when he was a young boy, had simply never considered the possibility that that part of a male grew to such proportions.

Miklav shook his head with an amused look. "I can see there are some disadvantages to a Cerecian education."

No matter that she herself had been thinking the same thing, Nazleen drew herself up haughtily. "I've changed my mind, Miklav. Please leave."

"Like this?" he asked, gesturing to himself.

"You can dress first."

"That isn't what I meant. I'm sure the Sisters never explained the facts of life to you, but surely your mother did."

She turned away. His proud display of his body made her angry, and the heat she could feel stealing through her own body made her even angrier. So this was how women became enslaved to men. She longed for the all-female security of Cerece.

Then she heard him move and whirled around, for one brief moment fearing that he would force himself upon her. She'd once heard her mother argue with her father over his failure to prevent his Warriors from raping women, and she recalled now her father's dismissal: "They want it, even if they protest before and after." But Miklav was the one who had put an end to such violence.

He had walked over to a large wardrobe and pulled out a black robe, embroidered with an intricate gold and scarlet design. Shara's work, she guessed. He wrapped the sash tie around his waist and went over to pour a goblet of wine.

"All right, maybe I rushed things. I should have taken into account your innocence and your Cerecian training."

"You said that you intended only to please yourself," she reminded him, relaxing a bit now that he was covered again.

"That doesn't include rape. Any man who would force a woman isn't a man to my way of thinking."

She sat down on a big chair before the fireplace, where a small fire fought the evening chill. Her legs were still shaking, but she couldn't let him see her weakness. "May I have some wine, please?"

"No. Wine can muddle the brain, especially this wine. You're not used to it, and I don't want you to wake up tomorrow and blame me for getting you drunk so I could take you to bed."

Then he walked over and sat down on the rug before the hearth. "Are you afraid that I'll hurt you?"

"No. You said you wouldn't rape me, and I believe you."

"That's not what I meant. You've never seen a naked man before, have you?"

"No, how could I? I told you . . ."

He nodded as he drank some wine. "I know—my fault. It's not comfortable for a woman the first time, Nazleen, but I'll be careful. And if you could just forget for a while that you're the Liege and let yourself be a woman, you could make it much easier for yourself."

"That's absurd," she said dismissively. "Are you going to forget that you're the Warrior Chief?"

He nodded without hesitation. "Right now, I'm a man with the need all men have when they find a woman they desire."

"I don't understand that kind of desire."

"You just saw the evidence of it. And you desire, too, Nazleen. You just don't want to recognize it. That's the trouble with being born into your position. It means being born to the assumption that if something displeases you, it just doesn't exist. I remember telling you once when you were perhaps ten and surrounded by costly toys that where I grew up, children didn't have any toys at all. You didn't believe me, because you didn't want to believe me. Now, instead of toys, you disbelieve the needs of your own body."

She opened her mouth to protest that, then closed it quickly. She remembered the incident, because she'd been troubled for days by it before she'd managed to dismiss it. She pushed herself out of her chair, then went over to the window where the shutters were still partially open to the night air. Through her mind ran all the times when she'd silently accused her mother of just such arrogance. Miklav, damn him, was right.

As she stood there, staring out into the night where pinpoints of flickering light marked the guard stations along the walls, she thought that perhaps she did indeed need Miklav, but in a very different way from that he'd been talking about.

None of her Advisors ever talked to her the way he did. Her Cerecian teachers had challenged her intellectually, but even they had never forced her to examine herself.

She wrapped her arms about herself, partly because of the cold air and partly because of the chill of uncertainty. He came up beside her to close the shutters.

"The nights are always cold up here. Come back and sit by the fire."

Still clutching herself, Nazleen returned to the chair before the fire, and Miklav resumed his seat on the rug near her feet. When he bent one knee to rest his wine goblet on it, she saw one long, hairy, muscular leg.

There was something, she thought, that is essentially repulsive about men. All that hair and those bumpy muscles—not to mention that emblem of his manhood that was thankfully hidden by the folds of the robe.

And yet he was right—she *did* want him. Or maybe she just wanted to know how it felt. "Uncomfortable," he'd said. Her mother had never told her that, but perhaps she'd long since forgotten by the time she'd talked with her young daughter. Perhaps it was like the pain of childbirth that her mother had said was quickly forgotten.

Nazleen felt terribly alone, more alone than she'd ever felt in her life, save perhaps for those first weeks after her mother's death. There was no one to whom she could confide her fears and no one to whom she could turn for advice. She could never discuss such intimate matters with her Advisors, and there was no point in discussing it with Loreth or the other Sisters.

She glanced at Miklav and remembered again how he'd been there in the terrible aftermath of her mother's death, silently attuned to her thoughts and fears. Haslik had been faraway, and days had passed before he had gotten back.

It was, she thought, a singularly strange relationship—enemy and confidant.

Then he saw her staring at him in the flickering firelight. "Did the Healers at Cerece tell you that conception was likely at this time?"

She nodded before she could stop herself. How unfair it was that he knew about a woman's body, but she knew next to nothing about a man's. She vowed that no daughter of hers would ever grow up so ignorant.

"Well," he said matter-of-factly, "then we should get on with it, shouldn't we? If you conceive quickly, that'll be the end of it."

"If it's a girl and a Cerecian," she reminded him, not at all surprised now to hear him echoing her own earlier thoughts.

"The firstborn in my family have been males for generations," he said. "And in yours, also."

She hadn't given that fact any consideration. Was it important? She just didn't know. Perhaps he didn't either.

Silence fell over them once more as they both stared into the fire. Half-hypnotized by the leaping flames, Nazleen unconsciously sent her mind into the future. Some Sisters could do this quite easily, although without the power of the Augury, the visions were generally limited to themselves alone. Nazleen had tried it but had never been successful. As Loreth had said, not all gifts are equal.

She saw nothing, but she felt an emptiness inside her, as though something once there had been torn away. And then, although no vision accompanied it, that name rumbled through her: "Zaktar." She started nervously.

"What is it?" Miklav asked, his own rougher voice replacing that deep, ghostly one.

She shook her head, then suddenly turned to him. "Miklav, do you seriously believe that there could be more Cerecians out there among those aliens?"

His eyes narrowed speculatively. "There was more to that Augury than either you or Loreth told me. I knew that. Neither of you is very good at lying."

"You haven't answered my question."

"It's possible. If they exist and they can wield the fire, they would be formidable enemies. If you

149

know more than you've told me, you owe it to your people to tell me, Nazleen."

She met his level gaze, then let hers drop away. It was she who had insisted that they not tell Miklav about the Fire Warriors, and it was she who had kept silent when she thought someone was on that hilltop. But as Miklav could not afford to underestimate the danger to Hamloor, she could not afford to overestimate the chances that the aliens' intentions, no matter who they might be, were peaceful.

"In any event," he continued, "we should know when the scouting party returns."

Yes, she thought, we can both wait for that. If they've discovered no Fire Warriors, then the Augury was wrong and my vision was only an aftereffect of it.

Suddenly, she was conscious of her growing tiredness. The warmth of the fire, the distant sound of the gong striking the hour before midnight and the small amount of wine she'd drunk with dinner —all combined with her heavy thoughts to make her long for the oblivion of sleep.

She got to her feet. "I am very tired, Miklav. Good night."

He rose from the hearth, seemingly distracted himself, and left the room. Lost in thought, she took off her gown, then climbed gratefully into the bed her maid had prepared for her.

She nearly had descended into that welcome sleep when a sound drew her back sharply. She rolled over to see Miklav standing beside the bed, his face shadowed by the faint firelight as he stared down at her.

"My clothes," he said, gesturing to the pile on the

floor. But instead of retrieving them, he sat down on the edge of the bed.

She didn't move, and encouraged by that, he bent over her, his face descending slowly as she stared at him.

His mouth was warm and gentle against hers, betraying none of the urgency he felt. Leaving his clothes behind had been a calculated gambit. Now he was determined not to make the same mistake again by rushing her.

He slowly drew back the covers she'd pulled up to her neck and moved from the soft ripeness of her lips to the satiny skin of her throat, tasting it with his lips and tongue and feeling the vibrations as a low sound came from her. He smiled even as he continued to kiss her throat and one exposed shoulder. He knew that sound far better than she herself did. He'd won.

Nazleen trembled slightly as he drew back the covers still further, then reached for the lacy straps that held up her chemise. His callused fingers rasped against her softness. It felt strange but not unpleasant.

Then he drew down the silken fabric until her breasts were exposed and, with a deep groan, bent to kiss each rosy crest. When she cried out at the wave of charged heat that swept through her, he raised his head and gave her a quizzical look.

"Have I hurt you?"

She shook her head mutely, wanting and not wanting that feeling again. But he made her wait, instead covering her face and throat with more kisses before returning his attention to the taut nipples that awaited him.

Hesitantly, she lifted a hand to touch his hair. It was thick and coarse beneath her fingers, not at all like her own soft curls.

Miklav felt that tentative touch and felt her slender body arch to meet him as he slid its flimsy covering still further down. He smiled once more. There was passion there, just as he'd guessed.

He moved away from her, enjoying her silent protest as he stood up to shrug hurriedly out of his robe. And this time, when she stared at him he saw not shock but hunger.

He stripped away the chemise and lowered himself down beside her to draw them together. His hands moved carefully over her even as his own need roared through his body.

Nazleen felt herself entering a new world as Miklav's big, heavy body touched hers. Here was the place where thought ended and sensation began. His kisses grew ever more demanding as his hands roamed over her. When he began to nudge her thighs apart, she protested, but he swallowed that sound with a hard, insistent kiss. His fingers invaded her, creating a heavy ripeness that made her cry out again.

After that, some part of her moved away, disconnecting itself from a body that had grown damp and aching with need. By the time he moved on top of her, she was writhing beneath him, arching to meet him and wanting just what he wanted.

There was a sudden fullness as he entered her, followed by a brief, tearing pain that vanished quickly as he thrust into her again and again. He tensed, then cried out in triumph and finally sagged against her, nearly crushing her until he realized her discomfort and moved away to stretch out beside her.

But her need remained, a throbbing yearning need. She was confused, but not for long. He propped himself up beside her and bent to kiss her as his fingers once more invaded her. She stiffened.

"Relax," he murmured hoarsely against her mouth. "Let it happen."

Let what happen? She didn't understand. But then her silent question was answered as her body was suddenly suffused with a ripening heat that built until she could no longer tolerate it, then exploded into great waves of shock. She clung to him as an anchor against this storm.

He held her silently for a long time after that, his big hands absently stroking the long curve of her back as the tremors gradually subsided. Finally, he leaned over and stared down at her, his dark eyes gently mocking.

"Have I pleased you, Milady?"

She knew the question didn't require an answer. She reached up to touch those smiling lips with hers.

"Yes, Miklav, you have pleased me."

Miklav stood ramrod straight in the bright morning sun, watching his troops in their hand-to-hand combat exercises, but his gaze kept straying upward to the windows of his quarters. She had been asleep when he'd reluctantly left her and might be sleeping still.

He envisioned her as he'd seen her when he left their bed—a small, huddled shape beneath the covers, nothing visible but those golden curls that spilled across the pillow. He wanted her again.

He'd even awakened in the night hard with desire, but he'd denied himself the pleasure of having her again. He could wait until she'd soaked away the soreness in her morning bath and remembered only the pleasure.

He forced his gaze back to his men, then to the trainees, but not even the son he loved could hold his attention this morning.

He hadn't expected to want her so badly, just hours after having her. He wasn't young anymore, and it had been years since he'd wanted Shara twice in one night, even though she knew all the ways to please him.

He couldn't afford to let that wanting get completely out of control. Too much was at stake here. If she didn't already know, she would soon discover the hold she had over him, and he knew sadly that he didn't have the same control over her. He'd awakened passion in her and would always be able to do that, but some part of her remained beyond his reach.

Then the drillmaster signaled the end of the exercises, and Miklav returned to the world that *was* within his grasp. He didn't look up at the high windows again.

Nazleen leaned gratefully back against the small pillow her maid had provided and luxuriated in the scented bath water. Her thoughts were not on the night just past. She was once more the Liege, a role she understood.

Her jaw set determinedly as she thought about the Warrior Chief's remark that her Advisors were not serving her well. As in so many things, he was right. Were they deliberately deceiving her, or were they merely incompetent? The distinction was important, because if they were incompetent, she could always replace them. But if they were deceiving her . . . ?

The women she could trust; she was sure of that. Her mother's Advisors had been almost all female, many of them holdovers from Nazleen's grandmother's time. But as they'd retired, Nazleen had replaced some of them with men, thinking to stifle the discontent of the male courtiers, and most of them were the ones in positions to know what the Warrior Chief was up to.

Her mouth set even more grimly as she remembered that it was Miklav himself who had recommended several of them. Since they were already members of court in good standing, she'd chosen them, foolishly believing that if the Warrior Chief approved of them, they would be able to spy on him more effectively. Now she saw that they must have been under his influence from the beginning.

Miklav. It always came back to him. She picked up the sponge and began to soap herself, finally allowing herself to think about last night.

She'd awakened a short time ago to a sense of differentness about her body, the aftermath of an invasion—a gentle invasion, but an invasion, nevertheless.

Long ago, when she and Haslik were inquisitive children, they'd managed to elude their caretakers and sneak off to the dusty storerooms of the palace. There, in an ancient trunk covered with centuries of dust, she'd found some very old books, the oldest she'd ever seen. They were books of poetry, love poems penned by some long-dead writer.

Haslik had been more interested in some old wooden soldiers he'd found in the trunk, but she had taken the books back to her room. She'd managed to read only a little of them before her mother had discovered them and had them destroyed, berating her for wasting her time with such foolishness.

The exact words hadn't stayed with her, but the meanings had. Love was supposed to be a union of two people, a merging of bodies and souls. For some years thereafter, the idea had intrigued her, until her mother and the Sisters had driven it out. Nazleen found it ironic that one of those Sisters had been Loreth, who herself now admitted to loving the man who had prompted these memories.

What had happened between them last night had been pleasurable, but it hadn't been that union the poet had written of. She and Miklav were as far apart as they'd ever been.

When she stepped from the bath, her maid brought a big towel. Perhaps she could still avoid taking Miklav as her mate. Was there more to be gained by refusing him or by keeping him? They weren't at the palace, and there had as yet been no formal announcement. As long as she wasn't yet pregnant . . .

The door burst open and the Warrior Chief strode into the room, his eyes raking her as the maid rushed to cover her. But he seized the towel from the nervous girl, then wrapped Nazleen in it and picked her up. The poor girl stood there trembling until Nazleen was forced to dismiss her.

Miklav carried her over to the bed, then set her down and began to rub her with the towel.

She struggled to get away from him, but since she was still partially wrapped in the towel, it was impossible.

"Miklav, what's the meaning of this?" she asked in a voice that shook with outrage but also held a trace of memory.

"Perhaps I've decided to take up a new career—lady's maid to the Liege. Being Warrior Chief seems to be difficult this morning."

"How dare you do something like this? You must know that servants are the biggest gossips in the palace."

He paused to look at her quizzically. "Why should that concern you? When you return to the palace, everyone will know that you've chosen me."

And then she understood. Somehow, he'd already guessed what had been in her mind just before he burst through the door. It terrified her to think that he could know her so well, when all she had were questions about him.

"Or were you planning to change your mind after the fact?" he taunted in a low voice. Then, when he saw her expression, he laughed.

"Don't credit me with mind reading, Nazleen. I leave that to the Sisterhood. I operate on pure logic, an understanding of human nature in general and of your nature in particular. Don't forget that I watched you grow up and that I knew your teachers well, both your mother and Loreth."

And so he did. He'd spent much time at the palace as her father's aide and then later as Warrior Chief himself. Always he had singled her out, taking her riding on his big charger, bringing her small gifts, and probing her developing mind. She remembered that now—how he'd questioned her and challenged her. Had he actually laid his plans that long ago?

While she thought about all this, he had finished toweling her dry, then tossed it aside. He propped himself against the bed pillows and drew her naked onto his lap.

"Is that what you were planning to do?" he asked softly.

"I am considering it," she answered with a defiant tilt to her chin.

"If you do, you'll be signing someone's death warrant," he growled.

"You assured me that I could choose Mevak or anyone else, for that matter."

"But that was before you took me into your bed. I won't let anyone else have you, Nazleen—not now, not ever."

"Don't be ridiculous! We're not life-mates. We're only fulfilling the terms of the Compact." Then she narrowed her green eyes.

"And what about Shara? You said that you were life-mated to her."

"Shara bore me two children and made me content, but I never swore any oaths with her. I'll continue to see that she lacks for nothing."

"Miklav, understand this! You cannot prevent me from taking a consort once you and I have produced a daughter."

"How many men do you think would be willing to share your bed if they knew death was the price they'd pay?" he challenged.

158

She pulled away from him. "You're behaving like a crazy man, not the Warrior Chief! We will both forget that this absurd conversation ever happened."

"On the contrary, I'd advise you not to forget it," he said as he reached for her.

She put out her hands, pushing against his vastly superior strength. He had just loosened his hold on her and leaned forward to kiss her when they were both startled by a loud knock at the door of the bedchamber.

"What is it?" Miklav roared.

"The scouts are returning, Chief," came the muffled voice. "They will be here within the half-hour."

The two of them stared at each other, and he saw the question in her eyes.

"Are they all returning?"

"Yes, Chief."

"I'll be along in a few minutes," Miklav said, then reached out to twine one damp curl about his finger.

"I never got around to asking how you feel this morning. Would you like to ride out to meet Haslik?"

Caught off-guard by the sudden softening of his manner, Nazleen nodded. "Yes, I'd like that very much. I'm sure he'll be surprised to see me."

Miklav wrapped a hand around the back of her head and drew her to him for a brief, gentle kiss. "Perhaps he'll be surprised to see you at Denra, but he won't be surprised to see you with me."

No, she thought, he won't. Her brother both liked and respected the Warrior Chief. He always spoke highly of him, even when they were alone together.

She got up from the bed, and this time he made no attempt to stop her. But he too got up, then circled her from behind and drew her back against him. She suddenly felt terribly vulnerable in her nakedness as her skin rasped against his uniform.

He bent to bury his face in the curve of her neck as he cupped her breasts. "I meant what I said, Nazleen, even though I shouldn't have said it. I wouldn't be able to let another man have you, and I want no other woman. You belong to me. You always have."

"I belong to Hamloor," she replied as forcefully as possible.

Then she moved away from him and hurried off to the dressing room. He stood there breathing raggedly as he watched her, admiring both her womanly curves and her regal carriage. He'd lost control again, but he'd meant every word he'd spoken. No other man would have her as long as he drew breath.

"Haslik," she cried as soon as she spotted her brother among the group of Warriors approaching them. She had to suppress an urge to spur her mare and fly to him. The moment he saw her, she knew that he too was fighting that urge, but instead he contented himself with that lopsided grin she so loved.

The Warrior Chief sat beside her on his black stallion, and the group saluted him smartly as they stopped a few yards away. Miklav surveyed them all silently, assuring himself that there had been no injuries. His eyes met Haslik's, and the younger man gave him a slight smile and a barely perceptible nod. Miklav counted himself lucky that Haslik approved of him. He knew how close brother and sister were and envied that closeness.

To Nazleen's irritation, they rode back to the fortress with only minimal conversation about the journey. She was eager to hear what they'd learned and wondered if Miklav would try to prevent that.

But when they dismounted in the courtyard, Miklav took her arm and led her with the group through a door into the main building. The room into which they all crowded was austere. Huge maps covered the stone walls, except for one portion where a collection of swords hung, their blades gleaming in the sunlight that poured in through the open windows. Several tables were lined up against the walls, their surfaces covered with more maps and papers. The chairs in the room were large, wooden and uncomfortable-looking. Miklav glanced at them, then ordered that a comfortable chair be provided for her.

As soon as she was seated, Miklav waved the scouts to a bench and took a large, ornately carved chair for himself. The group's commander, a Warrior Nazleen had never seen before, began his report.

"We found them, Chief. There are thirty-four of them, only ten in uniform. Most of them were busy at those old ruins Hektar discovered years ago, and the rest were at their camp in a nearby ravine."

"Did they spot you?"

The man shook his head. "We watched them for the better part of the day, and they never saw us. They were all too busy digging and measuring those ruins."

"You mean they didn't even have a guard posted?" Miklav asked with a frown.

"No. The Warriors were working, too. They had their weapons with them, but most of them set them down somewhere."

Miklav nodded thoughtfully, and Nazleen spoke up, unable to wait for the Warrior Chief to ask the question uppermost in her mind.

"Were there any Cerecians among them?"

The man turned to her, then glanced at Miklav for permission before responding. "No, Milady. We did see one youth who could have been the one the Trens saw. He had lightish hair, but we studied him through the scopes and his eyes were dark."

Nazleen's response to that was outward relief but a deep, inner regret. Some part of her had actually wanted to discover Cerecians among them, even though the rational side of her was glad the Augury had been wrong—and her hallucination had been just that.

"What about a vehicle? Did you see what they used to escape back across the desert?" Miklav inquired.

The commander nodded, his face becoming grimmer. "We saw it, all right, and many more like it. Haslik said the wheels matched the marks described to him by the ones who chased them."

"What are they, Haslik?" The Warrior Chief turned his attention to him.

"They're just as I guessed, Chief—vehicles that can move by themselves. While we were watching them, two of them got into one and drove it back to the camp. It made a humming sort of sound, and it moved fast, at least as fast as a horse at full gallop.

Probably it could move faster on a road."

"What about weaponry?"

"I got a good look through the scope at one of their rifles. It looks to me as though they can fire many shots. I'll draw you a sketch of them. And they have what looked like a scope mounted on them, too. Several of the Warriors had small guns in holsters, too—much smaller than our pistols, maybe half that size—but I couldn't get a good look at them."

"And there were those things they talked into," the commander reminded him.

Haslik nodded excitedly. "They were small boxes with a long wire that they pulled out when they talked into them. It's a way of communicating, I think. The ones back at the camp had some, too. They'd talk and then listen and then talk again." Haslik could no longer restrain himself.

"Just imagine what it'd be like to have something like that, Chief." He shot a quick grin at his sister.

"It would be almost like the Sisterhood's way of communicating."

Nazleen listened as they continued their report, describing in detail the tools the group at the ruins used, the tents they had set up, the other gear they couldn't identify. The commander also reported that three of the group were females, wearing pants and working right alongside the men.

When he had finished, Nazleen addressed Miklav. "This doesn't sound like a war party to me."

Miklav let a smile cross his face briefly. "I agree, Milady, but I don't like the reports of those strange vehicles and weapons. There have to be more where those came from. And why are they there in the first place? Why should they be interested in those old ruins?"

No one answered, and he dismissed the scouts. Nazleen rose from her seat. "Haslik, will I see you soon?"

He smiled at her and rubbed his shaggy beard. "As soon as I bathe and make myself presentable— if the Chief agrees, that is." He shot a look at Miklav, who stood just behind her, his hand curved familiarly about her waist.

"She'll be in my quarters."

CHAPTER SIX

Nazleen paced back and forth in the Warrior Chief's suite, thinking about the information brought back by the scouting party. Their failure to discover any Cerecians continued to trouble her. The Trens claimed to have seen one, the Augury indicated that they existed, and then there were her own visions.

But the news brought back by the scouts had been good, even better than she could have hoped. The aliens were surely nothing more than a group of explorers. Apart from a curiosity about where they'd come from, she felt no concern about them.

How did it happen, though, that they had found those old ruins, the very same ruins that had always intrigued her, the ruins she'd often thought might provide a clue to the origins of Stakezti? Was it nothing more than pure chance that they'd come to that mysterious spot?

But that was nothing more than a matter for idle speculation. The important thing was that it was clear—and must be clear even to Miklav—that no danger to Hamloor existed. Not even his considerable persuasive powers could bring about a declaration of war now, and she knew he had recognized that because she'd seen the troubled look on his face before she'd come back up here.

She heard the outer door to the suite open, and a moment later a clean and smiling Haslik appeared in the doorway. She ran to him, meeting him in the center of the room with a hug. Dear Haslik, how she wished he could be at court with her.

"So you can still surprise me, Nazzie." He grinned, using his old pet name for her that he claimed was the way she'd first referred to herself.

"I would never have guessed that you'd show up at Denra. Whose idea was it?"

"Mine. I wanted to be here when you returned with your report. I didn't want to have to hear it secondhand."

"You didn't trust Miklav," he stated flatly.

"I still don't." She knew this was a delicate subject because Miklav was Haslik's superior, and her brother had sworn an oath of loyalty to him.

"Are you using his suite—or sharing it?"

She sighed. "Sharing it. I had to choose someone, Haslik, and you know Miklav expected it to be him."

Haslik nodded. "If you'd chosen anyone else, his life wouldn't have been worth much."

"Do you really believe that?" she asked curiously

as Miklav's words echoed through her mind.

"Yes. As far as he's concerned, the choice was made long ago, and I don't know anyone who'd want to stand between the Chief and what he wants."

"But you like him. You've said so many times."

"I do like him. He has his faults, but he's undoubtedly the best Warrior Chief we've ever had."

"Why? What makes him the best?"

"He understands human nature, he values learning, he's a born leader, and he's a very fair man."

She just nodded. There was obviously no point in discussing the Warrior Chief with Haslik. Just like her, Haslik had worshipped Miklav when they were children, but unlike her, he'd never really looked at him through adult eyes.

"Well," she said, "thanks to the information you brought back, at least he won't be able to start a war."

Haslik was silent for a moment, then asked about the Augury. "Rumor here has it that it showed war."

"Some interpretations put it that way," she admitted. "What it really seemed to show was a threat to the Sisterhood."

He stared at her in disbelief. "Do you believe that?"

She shrugged. "You know that I've always been ambivalent about Auguries. They're open to too many interpretations." She neglected to add Loreth's assessment that this had been the clearest one she'd ever witnessed.

Haslik walked over to the window and stared out,

his back to her. "I think there will be war," he said quietly.

"But you said that they were nothing more than a group of explorers."

"I think that's true, but they do have Warriors, and Warriors like to make war. Who knows how much they've seen of us? That group the Trens saw might be just one of many scouting parties they've sent over here, and if they've seen us, they know that they have superior weaponry. Whether it's now or a year from now, I think there'll be war with them."

Nazleen shuddered. Haslik wasn't pessimistic by nature, and despite being a Warrior, he wasn't bloodthirsty, either. So his words had a far greater impact upon her than Miklav's had.

He turned suddenly to face her, his expression grave. "Nazzie, brother-to-sister, can the Sisterhood still wield the fire?"

Nazleen knew he meant that her response would go no further. It was an expression they both used since he became a Warrior and she ascended to the throne.

"I don't know," she admitted. "It's not possible to test such a weapon. A few Sisters have more or less kept up the exercises—but only a few. And even if they could, I'm not sure they would."

"You mean that they'd just sit there and watch Hamloor be destroyed and do nothing?"

"I don't know," she repeated. She was back to thinking about the possibility of other Cerecians among the aliens. She just couldn't dismiss it.

Then suddenly something occurred to her, something she should have considered earlier. She made a small sound of surprise, and Haslik looked at her questioningly.

"Haslik, just because you didn't see any Cerecians doesn't mean that they weren't there. They would have known you were coming and might have hidden themselves. They could have spent the day watching you watching the others."

He nodded slowly. "I never thought of that because I just hadn't given much credence to the idea from the beginning. And when we saw that light-haired one who seemed to fit the Trens' description, I think we all forgot about it. But it could explain why they didn't have any visible guards."

Since they were standing near the windows with their backs to the doorway, both of them started nervously as a deep voice spoke behind them.

"I agree," the Warrior Chief said as he strode into the room. "That lack of guards kept bothering me. They knew there were strangers nearby. No Warrior would allow a party of civilians to be out there without a guard. But if they knew in advance that you were coming, they could have hidden themselves, couldn't they?"

Nazleen drew herself up imperiously. "This was a private conversation, Miklav."

"Not when it involves a possible war, Milady."

Haslik stood there thinking. "I can recall several places where they might have hidden to observe us."

"That's what I wanted to talk to you about," Miklav said. "Of the group, you're the one with the best memory for details. Is there anything else you recall?"

Haslik nodded slowly. "We told you that Cheka

went to have a look at their campsite. While he was observing them, he saw one of them talking into that device. He told us about it when he came back, and I wondered at the time if I might be wrong about them being communications devices, because during the time he was gone, I didn't see any of the ones at the ruins talking into it."

"I don't understand." Nazleen frowned.

Miklav gripped Haslik's shoulder briefly. "That's exactly what I meant by your attention to details." He turned to Nazleen.

"What he means is that the one at the camp was talking to someone, but it wasn't anyone at the ruins."

"But that still doesn't mean there were Cerecians there," Nazleen protested. "All it means is that there must have been others the scouts didn't see."

The Warrior Chief stared hard at her. "What I would like to know is why you continue to believe there might have been Cerecians among them."

Nazleen affected a casual reply. "Because the Trens thought they saw one."

"And possibly because the Augury foretold their existence?"

She said nothing, turning away from him.

"Milady, may I remind you of your duty to Hamloor? If the Augury foretold the existence of more Cerecians, especially Fire Warriors, you have an obligation to tell me."

She kept her back to both men. Loreth had made the same argument, but she had refused to accept it. But they were both right.

She turned to face both men and found two pairs of eyes watching her intently.

"We saw a male Cerecian—a Fire Warrior." And she saw him again, as clear as the first time. Zaktar.

Haslik let out a low sound of surprise, and Miklav swore loudly. "How are you certain he was a Fire Warrior? Did you see him wield the fire?"

She started to shake her head, then stopped. She hadn't seen that in the Augury, but she *had* seen it in her earlier vision. She told Miklav that, explaining about her vision months ago.

Then, after pausing to draw a shaky breath, she told them about the incident on the way here to Denra.

Miklav's face darkened in anger. "Captain Treba told me that just after you left Cerece you seemed ill for a moment. You knew there was someone spying on you and you said nothing to him?"

"I told you, I thought it was merely an aftereffect of the Augury. Hallucinations are fairly common then. It still may have been nothing more than that," she added defensively.

"That judgment was not yours to make," Miklav replied severely. "Treba was charged with your protection, and you withheld information he should have had."

Then his expression gradually softened. "Nazleen, for the love of Hamloor, do not let yourself be infected with misplaced loyalty to them just because they may be Cerecians."

Haslik, who had been silent through all this, now spoke up. "The Chief is right, Nazzie. Cerecians or not, they're aliens. You can't have any idea what they're like, even if he did send you that message."

She looked from one to the other of them—her beloved brother and the man she'd chosen, the man

171

whose child she might even now be carrying. They were right; misplaced loyalties could be dangerous to them all.

Miklav took her arm and led her to a chair, then took a seat across from her and beckoned Haslik to join them. "Is there anything else about the Augury that you didn't tell me?"

She shook her head even as she thought about Loreth's vision of her in the sacred fire-pool with the man who might be Zaktar. That had no bearing on any of this.

"What made you say there was a threat to the Sisterhood?" he asked.

"We all felt an end to things as they are now. Each of us felt it in her own way."

"And that corroborates what we've just said. You can't trust them even if they are Cerecians."

She nodded, but she didn't tell him that many Sisters had seen that as a good thing. She could never explain that.

"If there are Cerecians, in addition to more modern weaponry, they also have the fire . . ." Haslik let the sentence dangle as he looked at Miklav.

Nazleen saw the dark gleam in Miklav's eyes. It wasn't the fear any sensible man would have. He wanted war, regardless of the odds.

"I should go to their camp," she said suddenly. "If there are Cerecians there, I will know it, and perhaps I can talk to them."

"No!" Miklav stated firmly. "I will not allow you to put yourself at such risk. If necessary, I'll tie you up and carry you back to the palace myself."

"Is it my protection that concerns you or the possibility that I might prevent the war you want?"

"Your safety comes first," he replied, meeting her anger with equanimity, "before anything else—and not just because you're Liege."

Haslik cleared his throat and stood up. "I think I'd better go check on some projects." He bent to kiss his sister on her cheek, then left after exchanging a glance with Miklav, who dismissed him with a nod.

Alone now with the Warrior Chief, Nazleen felt the tension in the room beginning to rise uncomfortably. She got up, wanting to put as much space between them as possible, but he too rose and followed her to draw her into his arms.

"Much as I want to keep you here with me, I'm sending you back to the palace tomorrow. Then I'll know you'll be safe."

And you can continue to make plans for war, she thought. Aloud, she said, "But you'll be coming to the city for the Anniversary?"

He looked surprised. "I'd forgotten. Of course. Will you wait until then to make the announcement?"

She nodded. The Anniversary of the Compact seemed an appropriate time to announce her choice. It was less than two weeks hence.

"Will you promise me one thing, Miklav?"

"If I can."

"Promise me that you will do nothing to start a war between now and then—nothing! That means no more scouting parties, either."

"I promise," he said easily. "The storm season is

173

almost upon us in any event. The men could feel it as they crossed the desert."

The sun was rising to meet them as they drifted eastward. The great balloon reflected its rays and changed from blue to a strange purplish pink. Zaktar stared at the fiery disc and was immediately reminded of the golden-red hair of the woman he'd so briefly glimpsed. He thought wryly that it took very little to remind him of her; she hadn't been far from his thoughts in any event.

She wasn't the reason he'd decided to launch the balloon, but that didn't prevent him from hoping he might discover her again. In fact, finding her again was uncomfortably close to becoming an obsession.

But he'd set out on this particular journey because the balloon was the easiest and fastest way to learn the lay of the land and, if they were fortunate, to discover the location of the Warrior force.

It was also the safest way to gain that knowledge. He wasn't concerned about any attacks. Even if they too had balloons, the great bags of super-heated air weren't fighting weapons; they were surveillance machines. But he doubted very much that they had such devices; they seemed far too primitive for that. After all, balloons had been in use among his people for only a few decades.

Still, he knew that different people developed at different and strangely uneven paces, depending upon necessity and the minds and natural resources available to them.

He wished that his flying machine could have been built in time for this. He smiled to himself as he imagined their reaction to that. The prototype was being built during his absence by engineers and workers he trusted, but he had a clear understanding with them that he would be the first to test it. The idea was his, the design was his, and if he'd erred, the death would be his.

Off along the eastern horizon, a dark smudge was gaining definition. They were nearly across the desert already. They'd hauled the balloon by truck out into that vast sandy wasteland, then gone aloft in the first evening breeze.

The pilot checked his compass and made some adjustments to their course. Zaktar had decided to make a wide arc over the area to the southeast of the compound with the fire-pool. The woman and the black-clad warriors had been headed in that direction. He doubted that a noble lady would be riding horseback for any great distance, so something must be there.

The winds were kind, and before Zaktar had finished his meager breakfast, they were drifting over thickly wooded, rugged terrain. He took out his high-powered glasses and began to scan the land far below.

"Ahh," he said with a smile of satisfaction a short time later. A narrow road lay beneath them, winding its way through the lush forest. It was probably the same road, but if not, all roads led somewhere.

Then, in the distance, he saw an open area where a hillside had been mostly deforested, but even from this distance he could tell that it was no city, only a small village. By the time they passed over it, dipping lower for a good look, he knew this could not have been the woman's destination.

But they still scanned the village with keen interest. The small houses were stone with thatched roofs, reminiscent of the few remaining primitive villages of the Kapti that had been preserved for their connection to the past. The glasses were powerful enough to let him see blurred, upturned faces in front of the houses and in the village square. They'd been spotted. He wondered what they were thinking. They might well believe that some ancient god was coming to pay a visit.

Then they were following the road again, up into the high mountains. The pilot turned up the fuel jets so the balloon could ascend. Navigation became much trickier here, with the currents being disrupted by the jagged peaks.

It was beautiful country, Zaktar thought admiringly, much wilder and more rugged than his homeland. He was so busy taking in the scenery below him that it was one of his companions who spotted it first.

"Look! What's that?"

Zaktar trained his glasses on the far peak the man had indicated and identified it just as one of the others named it.

"It's an old fortress!"

Nazleen awoke to find sunlight streaming through the slits in the shutters—and Miklav still sharing her bed. She sat up and watched him for a moment. Even in sleep, his face never quite lost its harshness, although a faint smile curved his slightly parted lips.

Her body once again felt ravaged and invaded,

even though Miklav had again been careful and gentle with her. In any event, the fault was hers, not his. He'd asked to join her, and she'd assented. She'd wanted that mindless pleasure last night, however much she might wish to berate herself this morning.

And yes, it *had* been pleasurable. Miklav gave as much as he took—perhaps more. Twice during the night the passion had flared between them. Probably that was why he was still asleep. Even as he'd reached for her the second time, he'd joked that he was "too old" for this.

But Nazleen trusted that pleasure no more than she trusted the man who had given it. It wasn't a complete absence of trust, just a limit.

Moving carefully so as not to disturb him, she climbed out of bed, dragging one of the covers with her. He shifted his position slightly and made a sleepy, guttural sound. She held her breath, then let it out with a soft sigh when he settled down again. She wanted him to sleep as long as possible so there'd be no repetition of last night now.

Wrapped in the blanket and nothing more, she walked over to the window and pushed open a shutter. Her body felt ugly and bruised, worse than after her accident. She also felt as though the woman who had moaned with pleasure the night before was someone else who had temporarily taken over her body, then vanished in the morning light to leave her with the uncomfortable reminders.

She looked down into the courtyard. The Warriors were at their calisthenics, dressed in the loose-fitting black pajama-type uniforms they wore here in the fortress. She spotted Haslik almost immediately, his lean, agile body easily recognizable among mostly bigger and heavier men.

Off to one side as before, the young recruits were mimicking their elders. Miklav's son, Kyetki, was leading them this morning, but the son of the desert Chieftain was nowhere to be seen. He must already be on his way home.

Captain Mevak was supervising the boys' exercises this morning, and suddenly she saw him lift his head and stare into the sky. Then she heard him shout something, and other heads also began to swivel upwards. Nazleen shifted her own gaze to follow them.

She gasped, the sound lost amidst the sudden clamor of voices below. As men broke ranks and began to rush off, Mevak was hurrying the boys toward a door. She glanced briefly back at them, then looked back at the sky and turned to awaken Miklav just as the Warrior Chief leapt from bed.

"Look!" She pointed. "Miklav, in the name of the gods, what is it?"

He leaned out the window and squinted at the huge blue balloon with its dangling basket-type attachment, then turned to her just as the door to the bedchamber burst open and his aide rushed in.

"I've seen it," he stated before the aide could speak. He was grabbing his clothes that were scattered about the room.

"Take her to the dungeon—now!"

Nazleen, who stood there clutching the blanket about her, was slow to realize who he was talking about. A huge man, even bigger than Miklav, appeared behind the aide, and both men stared at

178

her uncertainly.

"Dammit, I said *now*! This is no time to stand on ceremony. Pick her up and get her down there!"

"No," she said, but the protest was lost upon the men, who heard only their Chief's roar. The giant swept her off her feet and ran out the door. Behind her, she heard Miklav's aide tell her maid to follow.

The huge Warrior ran through hallways and down the stairs, carrying her as though she weighed no more than a sack of flour. They ran past other Warriors, who flattened themselves against the walls to let the giant pass, then ran on again, rifles in hand. None of them showed any surprise at seeing their Liege wrapped in a blanket and being carried through the fortress. Their faces were intent upon their missions.

"Why?" she gasped, even though she wasn't the one running.

"Safety, Milady," he replied, not breaking stride or even sounding winded.

Safety? In a dungeon? And from what? A giant balloon, not unlike the ones she saw children play with at parties?

The Warrior paused at the bottom of a narrow stairwell to kick open a heavy door. It was then that Nazleen caught sight of her poor, red-faced maid who had been running along behind them. Then they were through the door, and it clanged shut behind them with a frighteningly final sound. The Warrior paused before the door to the first cell and finally set her on her feet on the cold stone floor.

"You'll be safe here, Milady," he said with a surprisingly gentle tone. He urged Nazleen and the maid into the cell, paused for a moment, then slammed the door behind them. Before she could say anything, he was gone, his footsteps receding into the distance.

She wrapped the thin blanket more tightly about her as she shivered in the damp cold and, forgetting entirely about her dignity, began to hop about on one bare foot, trying to keep the other warm. The cell was small and crudely furnished, to say the least. A rickety wooden chair sat in a corner, with its one leg tilted at a crazy angle. A wood slab was suspended by chains in another corner as a crude cot and an old chamberpot rested in the semidarkness in the back, undoubtedly responsible for the malodorous air to the place.

The silence was suddenly broken by a thin wail from the maid who was cowering in the corner nearest the cell door. When Nazleen saw her pale, terrified face, she went to her and put a soothing hand on her shoulder. The poor girl had been in a constant state of nervousness ever since they'd come here.

"We were brought here for safety reasons, Miska, not for punishment." She knew that the girl must be thinking about the tales of that long ago Liege who'd supposedly died here, the victim of poisoning if the stories were correct.

Then she realized that the maid probably didn't know about the balloon and told her about it. The girl's eyes grew round with a mixture of terror and wonder.

"Why should they be so afraid of a balloon?" Nazleen asked irritably, more of herself than of the maid. "It must be the aliens, out on another scouting expedition. Miklav is making too much of this."

As she spoke, she went to the cell door and tugged at it. Just as she'd suspected, they were locked in. No doubt that giant Warrior had feared she'd run back upstairs, which is exactly what she'd intended to do.

She sighed and went over to the wooden cot. After testing the rusty chains, she sat down and pulled her feet up under her, then wrapped the blanket more tightly about her. At least, the maid was dressed better for the occasion. She was wearing a thick woolen sweater over her pale green servant's dress, and she had on sturdy shoes. She invited the girl to join her and the two of them huddled together in the dim light that came from the hallway outside the cell.

Nazleen began to lose track of time. The chill and dampness of the dungeon quickly found its way through the thin blanket, raising gooseflesh all over her naked body. She tried to use her Cerecian training to withdraw into herself and think warm thoughts. It seemed not to help. The Sisters evidently never anticipated one of their own being imprisoned in a cold dungeon.

She may have slept a bit, because her head jerked up painfully when she heard the sound of running footsteps outside. A moment later, the Warrior Chief's face appeared at the barred window in the cell door. He tugged ineffectually at the door as he peered through the bars at her. Then he disappeared and returned a few moments later with an old ring of keys.

The maid had gotten up as soon as Miklav appeared, but Nazleen remained huddled beneath the blanket, her feet still drawn up under her. When he finally opened the door, she tried to unfold herself and climb down, but her frozen limbs refused to respond and she tumbled to the floor.

The maid knelt beside her with a sob, but Miklav pushed her out of the way and bent down to tuck the covers more securely about her. Then he picked her up and peered closely at her, his expression clearly worried.

"J . . . just get me out of here," she ordered through uncontrollably chattering teeth.

He left the cell, with the maid scurrying along after them. Several others were coming down the steps, and he ordered them to get back to his suite and get a fire going, then bring some heated wine.

Nazleen shivered in his arms, but the warmth of his body began to thaw her a bit. Miklav walked swiftly through the corridors of the fortress and up the stone staircases. Others moved quickly out of his way, this time casting curious glances at his well-wrapped burden.

Finally, they were back in his suite, where he deposited her before the fireplace in his sitting room as he told the maid to bring more blankets. Someone else was ordered to find the physician. The maid handed her a cup of heated wine, and when Nazleen's trembling hands couldn't hold it, Miklav dismissed the girl and held the cup to her lips himself.

After a few sips, she felt warmth spreading through her, but she also began to feel light-headed. He set the cup aside and began to rub her bare feet with his fire-warmed hands.

"I'm sorry," he said contritely, "but I was think-ing only of your safety, not your comfort."

Nazleen stared at him through the hazy filter of wine. Her teeth had stopped chattering, but her jaw ached and it seemed too much effort to respond. Then the physician arrived, and Miklav explained the situation.

The thin-faced, gray-haired man bent to peer at her closely, then asked for her hand and pressed his fingers against her pulse point. Miklav continued to massage her feet.

"Is Milady ordinarily subject to chills?" the physician asked.

Miklav answered for her. "No, she's always been healthy. She never even had the usual childhood illnesses."

"In that case, I foresee no problems. I'll prepare something for her, but no more wine. Too much and it can have the opposite of the desired effect."

The physician left, and Miklav ceased his minis-trations to her feet, which by now were almost warm. He sat back on his heels, and a smile creased his rugged features.

"You must be feeling bad to be so quiet. I'd have expected you to be shrieking at me by now."

"Why did you send me down there?" she asked, unable to summon her usual imperious tone.

"Because I didn't know what might be in that balloon. They could have been planning to drop explosives or fire of some sort on us. The old dungeon was the safest place I could think of."

"Where is the balloon now?"

"Gone—headed back toward the desert."

"There were men in it?"

He nodded. "We could see several of them through the scopes. We didn't see any weapons, but it looked as though they had some sort of scopes of their own."

"Could you see them clearly enough to . . . ?" A vague image of the Fire Warrior named Zaktar swam in her wine-befuddled brain.

"No, we couldn't tell if any of them were Cerecian, but it did look as though one of them had light hair. And he was wearing what looked like a green uniform."

"Zaktar," she muttered, then shook her head when Miklav asked her to repeat it. "I might have been able to contact him."

"Your safety was more important than contacting them."

She couldn't really fault him, just as she couldn't blame him for vetoing her suggestion that she cross the desert to find them. But she also wondered if he were using the powerful weapon of his responsibility for her safety to keep her from the Fire Warrior.

He *is* real, she thought. Zaktar is real. And she thought again about Loreth's vision. The warmth drained away from her body, and she shivered again.

Nazleen gazed out the window of her palace suite, trying to recapture the excitement she'd once felt when Anniversary Week arrived each summer. How she wished that she could be a child again, caught up in all the revelry!

The palace was abuzz with activity, filled to capacity with guests and extra staff. Her personal privacy wasn't impinged upon, of course, but beyond the wall of her garden she could see the tops of the tents set up for the arts and crafts exhibition.

The lucky artists and craftsmen who were chosen to exhibit their creations on the palace grounds would be out there now, setting up their displays and then sleeping there to guard them overnight. All over the rest of the teeming city, those of lesser talent would be plying their wares or selling foodstuffs and livestock.

People were streaming in from the outer edges of the realm. The Mountain Trens came and even some of their desert cousins who, in any event, had to leave their home because the storm season had begun.

Fortunately, Hamloorians and Trens managed to mingle peaceably these days for the most part, and the large Warrior presence for the celebration augmented the small city police force to discourage any outbreak of violence.

The Warrior Chief had not yet arrived, but he'd sent word that he'd be here the next day, the actual beginning of the week-long festivities. Nazleen had already informed her Advisors of her decision to take him as a mate, and the formal announcement would be made later during the week.

Returning to the palace had had a salutory effect upon her. Here in these placid surroundings, resplendent with the trappings of her power, she felt in control again. She was still concerned about the presence of the aliens across the desert, but war now seemed a distant thing, perhaps nothing more than echoes from the ancient walls of Denra.

Even Zaktar, the Fire Warrior, had begun to

assume mythical proportions. As one of her more astute Advisors had observed, the evidence of his existence was slim indeed.

What troubled her now far more than the possibility of war was the memory of her conversation with Haslik last night.

He'd shocked her by going on at considerable length about changes that needed to be made in the governing of Hamloor. He claimed that there was a growing restlessness among the people, a desire to have some say in the rules and policies that affected their lives. There was, he said, a belief that she and her Council of Advisors were too far removed from the people and out of touch with their needs.

Nazleen had reasons of her own not to trust her Advisors, but she certainly wasn't ready to turn over the realm to the common people.

"Why not?" Haslik had countered. "Thanks to free education, they're all literate now. And thanks to better health care, their lives are improved in other ways as well."

She'd pointed out that it was her policies that had given them all these benefits, though she didn't mention that many of her Advisors had opposed her.

"That's true," Haslik had agreed. "But they need to have more control over their improved lives, and they need to aspire to something more than the menial work of their parents. That's why so many of them are entering Warrior service. We don't discriminate. With us, they can aspire to the highest ranks."

Nazleen had stared at him, shocked. "But I understood that fewer and fewer boys were choosing to become Warriors these days."

Haslik had shaken his head. "I've no doubt that that's what your Advisors have told you, since fewer of their sons are making that choice, but that's not true among the common people. Each year, the recruit classes get bigger and bigger. If Miklav decides to let Trens enter, we'll be bursting at the seams."

Nazleen had gone to bed sorely troubled. Miklav again. Either he was plotting to make war, or he was plotting to subvert her rule in other ways.

After a largely sleepless night, she'd summoned her Finance Advisor to her breakfast table and demanded to know if the Warrior Chief had been getting a larger budget these days. In truth, she paid scant attention to financial matters. The treasury was well-filled, so she concentrated on programs that interested her.

The man assured her that the Warrior Chief had received regular, small increases in his allocation but no more than any other segment of the government, so she was left wondering just where Miklav was getting the funds to take care of these increased numbers of recruits. It was a question she certainly intended to put to him when he arrived.

In times past, Warrior Chiefs had often exacted tributes from the farming communes and mines and from the Trens, but she doubted very much that Miklav would flout the law in that manner. And with fewer sons of wealthy families entering the Warrior ranks, it wasn't likely that private fortunes were involved—unless, of course, Miklav had secret support among the nobility, many of whom were among her Advisors.

Later this day, she planned to meet with a small group of her most trusted Advisors—all of them female, of course—and she intended to raise her concerns about Miklav with them.

But regardless of those concerns, she would still announce that she had taken him as her mate. Her mother had once expressed the opinion that it was better to have an intimate enemy than an unknown one, and Nazleen could now see the wisdom to that. It would surely be far easier to keep an eye on him if he were her mate.

That night, Nazleen tossed and turned once more, drifting through sleep without ever really settling into it. Her closest Advisors were indeed concerned about Miklav. Once she herself had raised the issue, their fears had poured forth. They'd known of her nearly lifelong relationship with him and had guessed that she would take him as her mate, so they'd been reluctant to voice those fears.

Unfortunately, for the most part they'd just echoed her own fears and had been unable to provide her with any new information. However, the oldest of them had ventured a guess as to where Miklav had been getting the additional funds required to expand the ranks of the Warriors. She'd heard tales many years ago of caches of gold and precious jewels hidden in the fortresses, tributes that had once been extorted from mine owners and wealthy Tren families.

Additionally, they'd all agreed that it was not just possible, but perhaps even likely, that Miklav was being secretly funded by a few members of the nobility who either had centuries-old grievances against Nazleen's family or who objected to being ruled by a woman.

Several of the Advisors had even agreed with Haslik's assessment of the people's growing unrest, though they didn't agree with his proposed solution to the problem. That, Nazleen knew, was to be expected, since Haslik's solution would require them to give up at least some of their power.

As she turned these matters over and over in her mind, Nazleen felt less and less secure. Outside, beyond the walls of the palace, things were happening that she could neither control nor understand.

Finally, she began to wonder if the Augury might have been true, after all, but badly interpreted. Perhaps the Sisterhood was indeed in danger, but only because the entire realm was in danger—and from within, not from without.

When she finally did fall asleep, the Fire Warrior was there waiting for her, this time with his green eyes flashing a warning.

It took all the considerable skills of Nazleen's maid to cover the ravages of a second sleepless night, but by midmorning she was ready to begin a long, tiring day of official duties. She might not be burdened with the preparations, but as the embodiment of the Compact, she was its star and her presence was required at numerous official functions.

The first of these was something she usually enjoyed—a tour of the arts and crafts that had been singled out for palace honors. Nazleen, who sometimes painted in secret, was always fascinated by the talents displayed in this exhibition. She had far more interest in the arts than her mother had, and because of her interest and royal patronage, art had flourished in recent years.

She left the palace in the company of her ever-present Warrior guards and more than a dozen of her Advisors, plus other court notables. The honored artists stood at their booths and tents, eager to sell something to their Liege. There was never any haggling over prices. If the Liege saw something she wanted, the Keeper of the Purse simply bought it at the price asked. But even more desirable than the money was the opportunity to display the royal seal since what Nazleen bought, others had to have as well.

She moved slowly among the displays, selecting a few paintings and a lovely handwoven shawl with a very intricate design done in gold thread. Then, a short time later, she came to another booth that displayed handweavings. The breathtaking beauty of the designs and the obvious quality of the workmanship so enchanted her that it was only after she glanced at the children of the craftswoman that Nazleen thought to look at the small sign with the woman's name.

The sign confirmed what she'd known the moment she'd seen the boy. This was Shara, the mother of two of Miklav's children. The boy was the very image of his father, just as Kyetki was, and Nazleen wondered wryly if Miklav were incapable of fathering sons who were not perfect replicas of himself.

The little girl, however, more closely resembled her mother. She would never be a true beauty, but her very large, dark eyes were so striking that one failed to notice the deficiencies.

Nazleen's eyes met those of Shara as the woman rose from her curtsy. Strange, but she'd expected that the woman would be a great beauty. After all, the Warrior Chief could have his pick of the women of the realm, but Shara could more appropriately be termed "handsome". She was quite tall, and her features were strong rather than beautiful.

Nazleen was so struck by this incongruity that it took several seconds before she realized that Shara looked as tired as she herself felt. Unfortunately, the craftswoman had no expert maid to hide the results. There was no resentment in the gaze that met hers, but Nazleen couldn't help wondering if Miklav might have already arrived and told her the news. In that brief moment when their gazes locked, Nazleen was certain that she saw a great sadness there.

But why should Shara be unhappy? She must have known this could happen; everyone knew the Liege was likely to choose the Warrior Chief as her mate. And Shara could still have him. In fact, a certain degree of respect was accorded to those the Liege's mate slept with, at least among the common people like Shara herself.

Then she recalled Miklav's declaration that he intended to be faithful to her. At the time, she'd dismissed the notion. Her father might well have said the same thing to her mother, and he'd certainly had women all over the realm. But Hektar and Miklav were two very different men.

Deeply troubled by the implications of this and feeling guilty that she might be causing this woman such pain, Nazleen was lavish with her praise of Shara's work and bought several jackets and shawls. She admired her work in any event, but she also felt that she was taking the only means open to her to make amends.

She returned to thoughts of Miklav with distressing frequency during the long day, even as she met with various important personages and rode in a huge parade through the streets of the city to officially open the festival. On the final day, the actual anniversary of the signing of the Compact, she and Miklav would ride to the great square, where a wondrous tower had been constructed to honor that signing.

But as her entourage circled it this day, Nazleen stared up at it and wondered if it might not outlast its purpose.

By late afternoon she was able to steal away to her quarters for a nap, but as soon as exhaustion pushed her down into sleep, the Fire Warrior awaited her. Miklav tormented her conscious mind, and Zaktar haunted her unconsciousness.

Zaktar was seething with frustration and had been doing so for over a week now. In all his life and through all his wanderings, he'd never seen the like of the storms that had been lashing the desert. He stood on a hillside near the ruins and scowled at the murky gray heavens. Even here, kilometers from the desert itself, a fine rain of sand poured down upon them several times a day. Out in the desert itself, it was far worse. He knew, because he'd ventured just a few kilometers out in one of the trucks. In what should have been daylight, and even with the headlights on, he hadn't been able to see more than a meter or so.

How long could it last? The reinforcements would be here soon, including his Fire Warriors, and then he'd have even more restless men like himself, confined to their tents much of every day by the sand-rain.

Only the diggers were undeterred, although they grumbled that their progress was being slowed. They'd set up several tents near the ruins and retreated to them when it got too bad.

Zaktar knew he should be far more interested in the ruins. Taka, the Cerecian youth he'd brought along, was fighting his own frustration by helping the diggers, but Zaktar, although he was sure that the ruins had once been a Cerecian village, could not summon up more than a fleeting interest in them.

He stared out into the midday twilight of the desert and thought about the people on the other side. They knew now, to their considerable relief, that none of the Warriors were Cerecians. When the balloon had drifted over their mountain fortress, he'd gotten a look at them without their ridiculous helmets.

But even in the midst of his relief there'd been disappointment. There was no sign of the woman among the group that had brandished their rifles helplessly. Perhaps they'd taken her somewhere else, after all, or maybe they'd hidden her to protect her against what they might have perceived to be a weapon.

Or maybe, despite her regal bearing and attire, she was a prisoner of the men in black, locked away in some dark dungeon.

Zaktar smiled for the first time in days over that thought. The next thing he knew, he'd be picturing himself as the rescuing hero, fighting the men in black to save the beautiful woman in distress.

She was never far from his mind. During the day, his thoughts were at least rational, but at night he descended into fantasies that became increasingly improbable.

Could there be perhaps only a few Cerecians, all living in that compound where the woman had come from? His rational thoughts about her had centered on that possibility. They might well be regarded by the Warriors and those other primitives they'd seen as mystics or religious folk of some sort. Given the unique Cerecian talents and the times in which those people were living, it was entirely possible that was the situation.

Zaktar still hadn't decided what to do when the reinforcements arrived, but a plan was slowly forming. If, together with his Fire Warriors, he could return to that compound and make contact with its occupants, then perhaps some sense could be made of all this.

Obviously the woman with whom he'd made brief contact wasn't totally loyal to those Warriors. She must have known of his presence yet hadn't told them. Even after centuries, the ties embodied in the sacred fire remained.

He stared unseeing at the distant sandstorms and thought again about her. A long-suppressed hunger began to awaken once more.

CHAPTER SEVEN

IT WAS TIME FOR THE FIRST OF THE FORMAL BANQUETS that were held in the palace each year during the Anniversary Festival. Nazleen's Advisors struggled annually with the guest lists, since the occasion was used to honor various residents of the realm for their accomplishments or services to the government.

For ordinary citizens, this was the invitation of a lifetime. There were wealthy merchants, farm commune leaders, mine owners, Tren leaders, artists, writers and those who had performed acts of heroism.

And, of course, there were the Warriors, whose presence was never more noticeable in the city than during Anniversary. Even many from distant fortresses journeyed to the city for the various athletic contests they held as their contribution to the festivities. One of Nazleen's Advisors had once remarked that if an enemy were seeking a time to attack the realm, Anniversary would be the perfect time, since most fortresses maintained only a small defense force during that week.

This year, however, could be different. Except for the Court and the Warriors no one knew about the aliens, but since they'd been spotted by the Trens who would now be coming into the city, that secret could not be contained for long. Many Warriors were disappointed this year to learn that they must remain on duty to guard the boundary that faced the desert. Long years of peace could make even some Warriors forget their true purpose.

As Nazleen was being prepared for the banquet, she kept expecting the Warrior Chief to show up at the door to her suite. Although no one else even requested permission to intrude upon her privacy here, there was a long tradition of Warrior Chiefs assuming that the rules of court behavior didn't apply to them, and in the past Miklav had shown himself to be no exception.

A suite was kept ready for the Warrior Chief at all times, since he rarely sent any advance warning of his arrival. This time, he had, and yet he'd failed to appear. Nazleen had inquired several hours ago and learned that he had not yet been seen in the palace, but the look on Shara's face had told her that he was indeed in the city.

Where was he—or more importantly, what was he doing? Where she had paid scant attention in the past to Miklav's comings and goings, Nazleen now found herself obsessed with his every move. Still, she could ill afford to let that concern be seen by anyone. As her mother had said, "Even if you're at your wit's end, never betray that fact. There are always those who would take advantage."

This week, when so many of the most important people in the realm were gathered together in the city, would be a perfect time for the Warrior Chief to plot and scheme against her. But what could she do?

When at last she went down to the great dining hall, Miklav was there in his accustomed place, rising to pay his respects to her along with the other hundred or so guests. On this formal occasion, he not only wore his best dress uniform with all its heavy gold braid, but also the heavy gold medallion with the symbol of Hamloor and the gold-hilted, jewel-studded ceremonial sword of the Warrior Chiefs.

She too was bedecked with the symbols of her rank. She wore a high-necked gown made entirely of gold threads, partially covered by a lavishly embroidered, floor-length cape that was studded with tiny jewels. Suspended from her neck was a smaller version of the medallion worn by Miklav and hanging just beneath it the symbol of Cerece.

Her gleaming hair had been piled high on her head in loose curls into which had been woven strands of gold and tiny, glittering green gems. On her right hand was a ring of Cerecian design and on her left yet another golden symbol of Hamloor. Both wrists were encased in hammered gold cuffs of Tren origin. Hamloorian, Cerecian and Tren were all represented on one slender, graceful body.

On such occasions, Nazleen frequently felt herself lost beneath all this—and never was she more aware of her responsibilities to all three factions.

Miklav stepped forward to escort her the last few steps to the dais, an act that caught her by surprise and produced a low ripple of interest among those assembled. When their eyes met, she saw a glimmer of amusement in his.

"Don't worry," he said in a low voice. "The woman is still there beneath all that."

In spite of herself, Nazleen smiled. She'd complained to him at the time of her first Anniversary as Liege that she felt lost. Trust the Warrior Chief not to forget that slip of the tongue. In fact, it seemed that he rarely forgot anything she said, no matter how casually stated or however long ago.

Wine was poured into the golden goblets, and the two of them intoned the ritual words, her soft but clear tones providing a perfect counterpoint to the Warrior Chief's deep, gruff voice. She thought about all the times she and Haslik had sat here, listening to their parents speaking these same words, and she tried to envision her own children doing the same. But the images refused to come; the future remained dark.

She barely heard the Pavla's message, which was read by one of her senior Advisors. Since the Pavla never left the compound, the message was delivered to court each year and read at the official opening. Nazleen had already seen it and knew that it contained nothing about the Augury.

Why can I not see the future? she asked herself. She hadn't expected a true vision—those happened only rarely for her—but why did the future suddenly seem so dark and forbidding? Had she lost faith entirely in her ability to bring about the future she desired?

She was so lost in her thoughts that she was slow to realize that Loreth's message had been completed. They had all remained standing during the reading of the Pavla's message, and, of course, it was she who would take a seat first to signal the end of the formalities and the beginning of the feasting.

The light pressure of Miklav's hand at the back of her waist drew her sharply from her bleak thoughts, and she took her seat. The Warrior Chief leaned close.

"Are you all right?"

No, she wanted to shout, I'm certainly not all right, and you know why I'm not. But she merely nodded instead, then remained silent as servants scurried about with the food.

"I expected you to make an announcement," the Warrior Chief said quietly as soon as they'd been served.

"I thought this night should belong to the Pavla's message," Nazleen replied. "I intend to make the announcement on the final night."

Their eyes met, and once more Nazleen saw amusement there. Did he think she was still trying to get out of her decision? Well, maybe he was right. There was no reason why she could not have made the announcement this night, but it felt like a further capitulation to the Warrior Chief, even if the choice had been hers.

Fortunately, general conversation began at the table then, and Nazleen was spared the necessity of any further remarks by the Warrior Chief, although there was not a moment when she didn't feel the force of his presence. Miklav was impressive under any circumstances, but dressed as he was this night, he was truly formidable.

She began to feel terribly isolated as the conversation flowed around her, even though court protocol demanded that she be the one to interject herself into any discussion. No such protocol existed regarding the Warrior Chief though, and he was the center of attention. Nazleen's mother had often despaired of Hektar's inability to carry on social conversation at such times, but Miklav was far more skilled.

The banquet proceeded, course after course. Strolling musicians provided a pleasant backdrop to the buzzing conversations. Nazleen was forced to eat far more than she would have chosen, because for the Liege to refuse anything would be an insult to the hard-working cooks who had prepared this feast.

At one point, when Miklav saw her glance at the large slab of nearly raw meat placed before him, he quietly offered to forgo that course if the sight of it bothered her. She shook her head and assured him that she didn't mind, then found herself begrudgingly touched by his thoughtfulness.

It was that unexpected side of his nature that seemed to keep her constantly off-balance. She thought wryly that life had certainly been much easier for her mother, since Hektar had been singularly lacking in thoughtfulness and kindness.

Overfilled with rich food that only exacerbated her tiredness, Nazleen rose from her seat as soon as possible, wanting nothing more than the welcome oblivion of sleep. Everyone else rose, too, but most of them would remain much longer before breaking up into smaller groups to drink and talk the night away.

When she turned to Miklav to say good night, he instead offered his arm. Nazleen knew that all eyes were upon them and once more felt obliged to accept. But as soon as they had left the hall, she told him that she wished to return to her suite. He obligingly led her up the stairs, and she assumed that he intended merely to escort her back there before returning to spend the remainder of the evening with his Warriors, as was his usual custom.

However, when they reached the doorway to her suite, which was guarded, as always, by two Warriors, Miklav followed her through. Nazleen became irritated. No one entered her personal quarters without an invitation.

"I did not invite you here, Miklav. You are taking liberties."

He merely stood there smiling at her. "That tone didn't work on me when you occasionally used it in the past, and it certainly isn't going to work now. Would you like to go for a stroll in your garden?"

"No, I am too tired tonight. I wish only to go to bed."

"Why are you so tired?" he asked, peering at her closely.

For a moment, she didn't understand that scrutiny, then she realized the reason. "I'm not pregnant," she stated firmly, even though she couldn't be certain that was the case.

"Perhaps you just don't know it yet. Too little time has passed."

"I'm not," she said peevishly, knowing only that

she certainly hoped that was the case. Whatever that meant in terms of her future with Miklav, this was not the time to undertake motherhood. Too much was uncertain just now.

"Then how do you explain this sudden tiredness in someone who has always had unlimited energy?"

"I didn't sleep well last night or the previous night," she stated in a tone designed to end the discussion.

Rather to her surprise, it seemed to work. He bent to kiss her lightly. "I too had a long day after a difficult night."

An image of Shara flashed through her mind. "Oh?"

"I arrived late, and then I had to see Shara and the children. I wanted her to hear the news from me, not from gossips or the palace."

"I saw her this morning," Nazleen admitted. "She's one of the artists selected for palace honors."

He nodded. "An honor long overdue—and one she might have received before if it weren't for her association with me."

"The committee is very fair," Nazleen stated defensively, having appointed them herself.

"In most cases, that's probably true, but I think they passed her over because they thought her presence might offend you."

"Then why would they have honored her this year?"

"It could be that they thought you might want to gloat over your triumph."

"That's absurd, Miklav. Why should I want to gloat, as you put it? It must be plain to everyone

202

that I chose you because I had no real choice in the matter."

"You know that, and you've certainly let *me* know that, but others might see it differently. Sometimes your understanding of human nature is rather limited, Nazleen."

She waved tiredly. "Miklav, I am too tired to debate this with you tonight. If I've hurt Shara, I'm truly sorry. She's lovely and talented, and your children seem quite nice. In any event, I purchased more from her than from any of the others, so her work will now be honored."

"So I understand," he said. "She was very pleased. Now shall we go to bed?"

"Miklav, I'm sure I made it plain that I'm tired."

"And so did I."

"Then why should you want to stay here?"

"I want to be with you."

Nazleen had turned to go into her bedchamber, but his simple statement brought her to a halt. There it was again, that side of him that could touch something in her. For just a moment, she wondered how great a hold she had over him, but she sensed that it would be folly to believe she could ever control him that way. He too had a hold over her, didn't he?

She walked into her bedchamber, neither denying his request to stay nor inviting him to join her. Her maid awaited her there.

"Leave us alone," Miklav ordered as he followed her through the doorway.

Nazleen opened her mouth to countermand those orders, then closed it again, ever mindful of providing grist for the palace gossip mills. The poor girl had started to flee in any event. Then she caught sight of herself in a mirror and remembered the intricate hairdo that had to be undone, but by the time she turned to recall the maid, the girl was gone.

"I need her," she said irritably. "I can't undo this hair myself."

In response, Miklav undid the fastener and removed her long cape, then he guided her to a chair. "Then I'll do it for you."

She stared at his reflection in the mirror as he bent over her, peering intently at the elaborate hairdo as though it were some thorny military problem. His expression was so serious that she had to laugh.

"Go ahead, then. I'd much rather see the Warrior Chief doing hair than making war."

He chuckled and began to unwind the gold threads that were strung with tiny gems. His touch was surprisingly delicate and sure. In no more time than the maid would have taken, her curls tumbled free to her shoulders.

Then he lifted the two chains from around her neck and stared for a moment at the Hamloorian and Cerecian symbols before laying them aside. He unbuckled the gem-studded belt that held his sword and added that and his own medallion to the glittering pile.

When he picked her up and carried her to the bed, Nazleen made no protest. He undressed her and bent to kiss each exposed breast, eliciting from her a soft moan that brought a smile to his face.

But after he had stripped off his own clothing and joined her in bed, he did no more than kiss her and fit her gentle curves against his angular hardness. She fell asleep almost as soon as her head touched the pillows.

The Warrior Chief continued to smile as he too fell asleep.

Miklav strode into the courtyard at Denra, accompanied by the commander of the Warriors assembled there. As soon as he saw the heavily armed group, he felt a sharp pang of regret that he wouldn't be joining them. As Hektar had once remarked, the only disadvantage of being Warrior Chief was that one had to be content to watch other men do what one wanted to do oneself. Miklav remembered those words well, because Hektar hadn't been a man given to philosophizing.

The Warriors came to attention, then at the order of their commander mounted the eager chargers amidst much clanking of armaments and creaking of leather. Miklav watched them impassively, only the hard glitter in his eyes betraying his emotions. Not since he was a young man serving under Hektar had he known the powerful, unique emotions of a battle to come.

The group's commander saluted before mounting his own steed, and Miklav returned the salute, then briefly clasped the man's shoulders and wished him victory. A few moments later, nothing remained but the waning echoes of hoofbeats as they rode out of the fortress.

Miklav climbed to the top of the wall to watch until the party disappeared into the dense forest. He smiled to himself. The first steps had been taken; war was now inevitable. Not even his peace-loving Liege could reverse the process now. Hamloor would be saved from its enemies whether she liked it or not.

Miklav had laid his plans well. Even the ancient gods had cooperated by ending the storm season early this year. When the Desert Trens had begun returning to their home a few days ago, disguised Warriors had gone with them under an agreement worked out with their Chieftain. It hadn't been difficult to persuade the old man this time; he was truly worried about the aliens who were camped upon the borders of his desert.

Miklav was certain that the aliens would soon be crossing the desert again. The Trens Chieftain would order his people's camps spread out in such a way that contact between them and the aliens would be inevitable. When that contact came, Miklav's men would make sure that an incident occurred. After that, war was inevitable.

The group that had just now left Denra would be close at hand to attack the aliens and destroy them before their numbers could grow. For all their superior weaponry and gadgets, they didn't seem very warlike; Nazleen was right about that. So Miklav reasoned that when the current group was annihilated, they'd be reluctant to send more. They'd simply move their explorations elsewhere.

One day, he might even tell Nazleen the truth— how he had carefully planned the war that had saved Hamloor from destruction. When it was over and their borders were once again secure, she might understand how a limited war could prevent the larger horrors neither of them wanted.

His thoughts turned to her as he left the wall and

started back across the courtyard. She was now at Cerece, and even though she'd given no reason for the journey, he knew it must be to consult the Healers about a possible pregnancy. Once again, the timing was perfect. Not only did he very much want her to have his child, but a pregnancy at this time would turn her thoughts elsewhere. Instead of causing him problems, she'd be concentrating on impending motherhood.

Miklav was feeling a great pleasure in life at the moment. Finally, it seemed, all his plans were coming to fruition. Over the years, he'd worked tirelessly to cultivate the various factions of the realm—the Trens, the communes, the ordinary people who were growing tired of a court increasingly remote from them, and the dissatisfied elements within the palace itself.

While taking care never to dispute his Liege's right to rule, he'd managed to let all these elements know that he too was dissatisfied with the current state of affairs. It had often been a very delicate balancing act, but he knew he'd succeeded. Furthermore, he could assuage his conscience with the certainty that he had not initiated any of this; he had simply taken advantage of a growing restlessness within the realm.

He'd also let it be known that the Sisterhood was much diminished in numbers now, so that no one would fear their intervention on the Liege's behalf. They had, he'd said many times, long since retreated far into their mysticism. He believed this to be the case and was convinced that not even his old friend Loreth, for all her abilities and strength, could resurrect the Sisterhood to its former power.

The imminent transfer of power to Miklav would be the end to his long quest. He couldn't have known that aliens would show up on their borders, but their arrival meant that he didn't have to find some other way to start a war—the only thing that had troubled his conscience in all this.

Nazleen was bright and had many good ideas and programs to help the people, and he admired her wisdom and generosity. But what she hadn't understood was that the healthier and richer and better-educated the people became, the more they resented the autocratic rule of the court.

What he envisioned was a future where Nazleen would remain the titular head of the government, tending to ceremonial duties and to those programs that interested her, while true power would remain with him. He'd get rid of that group of bumbling Advisors of hers and replace them with representatives from the restive population. The Warriors, not the Sisterhood, would be the glue that held their society together.

Nazleen would ultimately accept this change, though not without a struggle, but he would convince her that they'd make a good team, rather than the adversaries Warrior Chiefs and Leiges had always been.

"You are not happy."

Nazleen turned from the window to look at her old friend and mentor. "I've accepted it."

"Surely there should be more to it than that." Loreth frowned.

"Perhaps there should be, although I suspect that Mother felt much the same way when she was carrying Haslik and me. There is so much to do, and right now there is so much uncertainty. I should have waited."

Loreth disliked seeing Nazleen so apathetic. It didn't suit her nature. "Miklav, at least, will be happy."

Nazleen grimaced. "No doubt he will, but for the wrong reason. I don't doubt that he'll find some way to use my pregnancy to his advantage."

There was a small hesitation, then Loreth said with a sigh, "You may be right, much as it pains me to admit it."

Nazleen gave her a sharp look. Something in the Pavla's tone suggested private knowledge. She raised her brows questioningly.

"I received a report from a Tren headman in a village not far from Denra. He came here to tell us that yesterday morning a large force of Warriors left Denra in full battle regalia, headed toward the desert."

Nazleen struck her fist against a table. "How dare he? The aliens have done nothing to provoke an attack. For all we know, they might have returned to their home when the storms struck."

"It's possible that they were just going on maneuvers," Loreth said half-heartedly.

Nazleen shook her head, and the Pavla sighed. "Perhaps we could suggest to Miklav that I go to them and try to make contact with the Fire Warriors."

"You mean leave Cerece? But Loreth, no Pavla has ever left here." Nazleen was shocked.

"Sometimes traditions must be laid aside," Loreth replied calmly. "And I've already done that by permitting Miklav to come here."

"You would be in no less danger than me, and Miklav cares too much for you to permit that. Besides, he *wants* war, Loreth. He would only use his concern for your safety as a means of preventing it, just as he did with me."

Then she frowned. "But how could the Warriors be going into the desert? Has the storm season ended?"

"Yes. The Desert Trens began to return to their homes a few days ago."

"Then Miklav has either reached some sort of agreement with their Chieftain, or he has kidnapped one of his sons again."

"I think the Desert Trens would support him in this. My sources tell me they are concerned about the aliens, too. And Miklav has been quietly courting the Desert Chieftain for years. Those kidnappings haven't really been necessary."

"But why didn't you let me know this before, Loreth?" Nazleen asked in exasperation.

Loreth met the angry green eyes with a softer green of her own. "You forget, Nazleen, that the role of Pavla is one of mediator. It seemed to me that Miklav's attempts to win over the Trens and others was a good thing, that by becoming closer to the people he was making the Warriors less of a threat."

"And as a result, they've become more of a threat than ever," Nazleen replied disgustedly. "You were wrong, Loreth."

"Perhaps," the Pavla conceded. "But then war may have been inevitable."

"If you accept the Augury."

"But I do accept it, and you even accept it in part, since you believe in the existence of your Zaktar."

"Don't call him mine! He may well be an enemy of Hamloor, and my responsibilities to Hamloor come before any kinship with Fire Warriors."

"You protected him," Loreth pointed out gently.

"I half-believed it to have been an hallucination, and I feared the Captain would use it as an excuse to force me to return here. Besides," she sighed, "I still don't know that it wasn't an hallucination."

"I do not believe it was an hallucination, Nazleen. That same morning several of the watchers reported sensing something strange, but they were unable to identify it further."

Nazleen shivered and wrapped her arms about herself. "I don't want another Warrior to deal with at this point. Miklav is quite enough."

"If the Augury was correct, you will have only one," Loreth replied sadly.

Nazleen returned to her room. Amidst the timeless serenity of Cerece, she was a small figure of turmoil. She pressed a hand against her still-flat belly, wishing that the Healers could be wrong—but they never were. She was indeed carrying the child of the man who plotted to seize power from her.

No, she thought angrily, he is no longer just plotting. Now he has made his move.

And Loreth, the one person she should have been able to turn to for advice, now was lost to her. The Pavla clearly believed that war was inevitable, since that accursed Augury had foretold it.

What was she to do? Her mind refused to settle down long enough to consider her options.

She paced the small room restlessly, at first thinking she should go into the fire-pool, then rejecting that thought. She'd gone there when she'd arrived several days ago, but the sacred flames hadn't soothed her. And that night the Fire Warrior had haunted her dreams even more than before.

Finally, she sank to the floor cushions and began the demanding series of exercises that enabled one to wield the fire. Regaining that lost art seemed so important now.

Zaktar stood on the running board of the lead truck for a moment and looked back at the five similar vehicles behind him. Then, with the first smile he'd worn for weeks, he slid back into the truck and signaled the driver to move out.

The 60 Fire Warriors had arrived two days earlier, together with 400 Kapti troops. That very day, they'd all noted a decrease in the ferocity of the sandstorms. A very good omen, he thought, even though he wasn't inclined toward superstition.

He'd spent these past two days discussing the situation with his men. Although he was their acknowledged leader, the Fire Warriors operated on a far more democratic system than the regular military ever did. Discipline was tight when they ventured into battle, but that hadn't happened in a very long time. In any event, Cerecians were never very accepting of autocratic rule. Pavlas were usually chosen for their ability to mediate more than their leadership qualities.

All had agreed that their mission should be to contact their kin across the desert. There was a palpable hunger among them for that contact, and

212

not just because some of them were women.

He'd warned them carefully and repeatedly of the dangers of attempting contact by telepathy. They might have to resort to that if those in the compound had somehow lost their common tongue, but clearly it should be a last resort. He had no wish to cause the pain to them that he'd obviously caused that woman.

Several of the Fire Warriors had ventured a thought that had also occurred to Zaktar. What if those people had lost *all* their abilities? The presence of a fire-pool seemed to argue against that, but they might revere the fire without being able to use it or even to understand why they revered it.

As the convoy moved out toward the desert, Zaktar thought that in some ways it might be better if they had lost those talents. They could be taught again, and that way there'd be no danger of a fire-battle between them, something they all regarded as being the ultimate horror.

As they reached the desert's edge, they passed a Kapti division just returning from their first brief foray into that sandy wilderness. None of them had ever seen a desert before, and both the Kapti commander and Zaktar had agreed that they'd better familiarize themselves with it in case they too had to cross it.

For now, the Kaptis would remain at the camp, guarding the work force at the ruins and augmenting it with their own labors. But if the worst came to pass, they would move quickly across the desert to come to the aid of the Fire Warriors.

They drove into the dun-colored desert. Zaktar looked up at the sky and saw that even though it wasn't yet blue, it also wasn't the murky brown-black of a few days ago. He hoped that by setting out this quickly after the storms, they could avoid the primitive nomads they'd seen before. Surely those people left the desert during the storms and would take a while to get back, laden as they'd be with their belongings and their livestock.

The other reason for setting out quickly was that neither the black Warriors nor the residents of the compound would be expecting them this quickly. It gave them the added advantage of surprise.

The clear orders to the Fire Warriors were that they were to avoid any provocative behavior if they ran into anyone, and they could wield the fire only in self-defense and even then make every attempt to stun, rather than to kill. Wielding the fire was always tricky, but they all spent long hours perfecting their control over that awesome weapon.

The dark smudge that was the mountain range just beyond the desert was in sight when they crested a long hill of sand and stared down the other side to see a group of nomads approaching. Zaktar cursed his luck; they'd nearly made it. Then he closed his eyes and sent the message back to the truck behind him, from whence it would be relayed to all the others.

He signaled the driver to stop, then grabbed his glasses and got out of the truck. The ragtag band of 30 or so people had stopped, too. He estimated that they were a little less than a kilometer away.

The glasses revealed men scurrying for their rifles, which were strapped to the sides of the ugliest beasts Zaktar had ever seen. They looked like shaggy, misshapen horses. He knew they could never reach this distance with their old-fashioned weapons, so he climbed up onto the running board and told the driver to proceed slowly.

When they had closed about half the distance, they stopped again. The nomads hadn't moved, except to put their women and children behind them.

He'd preselected ten of his best men to join him in this eventuality, and they now scrambled from their trucks and hurried toward him, leaving behind all their weapons save the one they carried with them always. With Zaktar in the lead, they started on foot toward the group. Behind them, the rest of the Warriors had taken up positions before the trucks, rifles in hand but not aimed.

Zaktar knew it was important to project strength to these people in order to prevent them from attacking in the mistaken belief that unarmed Fire Warriors were without weapons. But to aim the rifles would be a provocation.

By the time they were only about 100 meters away, a dozen men had stepped forward, moving slowly and carrying their weapons, but thankfully holding them down at their sides. Zaktar kept walking at a steady pace and kept his hands in sight at all times, as did the others with him. That way, there could be no thought on the part of the nomads that they were about to reach for concealed weapons.

Zaktar had had some experience at communicating with aliens during that long ago battle that had made him into a hero. He knew that a smile helped, that even his stance was important, and that a great deal can be communicated without words. He hoped he could get across the simple message that the Fire Warriors meant them no harm and had only come in peace to seek out their kin.

Both groups stopped when they were about 20 meters apart. For a long moment, they regarded each other in silence. What Zaktar saw on the dark faces that stared at him was just what Taka had described to him from his encounter—fear and awe.

What did it mean? Did these people regard Cerecians as being gods or devils? It certainly seemed that they were being put into one of those categories.

Slowly, carefully, he extended his right hand, palm up. It was, he thought, a gesture that could only be interpreted as being peaceful. The nomads stared but made no gesture of their own. Then he began to speak slowly, hoping that perhaps some of these people might understand his language, but from their frowns and blank looks, he knew they didn't.

So he began to gesture, trying to tell them that they were merely crossing the desert and meant no harm to anyone. But as he gestured, he began to take note of individual faces within the group. Most of them were intent upon his gestures, their expressions more curious than hostile, but two were different, both in appearance and in manner.

These two, standing at opposite ends of the small group, were both larger and more muscular than the others, and even though their skin was dark, there was something different about it as well. He would almost have sworn that they had a paint or stain of some sort on their faces. Their rifles, like those of the others, were aimed downward, but unlike the others, they gripped them tightly.

Even as he continued to gesture, Zaktar spoke to his men, knowing he couldn't be understood.

"The two on either end—they don't belong. They could be Warriors in disguise."

There were murmurs of assent from his men. Zaktar repeated his gestures, then stood quietly awaiting a response. When it came, his worst fears were realized.

With lightning-quick speed that betrayed their military training, the two men he'd singled out raised their rifles to fire. One of Zaktar's men was quick enough to drop the one across from him, but the other one succeeded in getting off a shot before being engulfed in the green fire. There was a cry from one of his men, and Zaktar saw him crumple to the ground as a dark stain spread across his shoulder and upper chest.

The other Fire Warriors began to rush forward but at Zaktar's orders held their fire. The nomads simply stood there, mouths open in shock, rifles still dangling loosely from their hands. Behind them, frightened wails rose from the group of women and children.

Stifling his rage, Zaktar once again held out his hand. The desert men stared at it, then began to stumble backward to the rest of their group. They didn't bother to take their wounded or dead with them.

"You were right," one of the Fire Warriors said as he bent to peer closely at the one unconscious man. "It is some sort of stain."

But Zaktar's attention had turned to his injured

217

man as the Healer knelt beside him and held his hand just above the ugly wound. After a few seconds, he straightened up and nodded to Zaktar.

"He'll make it. The wound isn't deep, and the pellet exited through his back." He signaled to two men who waited with a stretcher.

"One of them's dead and the other one is just unconscious," another Fire Warrior reported after checking both the disguised Warriors. "The dead one is the one who shot Ravi."

Zaktar had guessed that. Emotions played a major part in one's ability to wield the fire, and it was difficult to be careful when your opponent has just fired at a comrade. He paused long enough to lay a reassuring hand on the shoulder of the Fire Warrior who had killed the man.

The group of nomads were still standing there, and Zaktar waved in the direction they'd been traveling, then turned back to the trucks, followed by his men. By the time they started off again, several of the nomads had come out to pick up the Warriors and carry them off.

It was, he reflected, not an auspicious beginning to their quest, but it now became even more important to make contact with their long-lost kin.

CHAPTER EIGHT

NAZLEEN AND LORETH STOOD TOGETHER IN THE GATE-
way to the compound, arms encircling each other.
Just beyond the gate, a group of Warriors waited,
the men staring curiously at the Pavla and their
horses pawing and snorting impatiently.

"This trip to Denra troubles me, Nazleen, although I can't say why. I fear . . ." Loreth stopped,
her gaze focused inward. "Events move quickly
now. It already may be too late."

"I must try," Nazleen stated firmly. "If there is
any chance that I can persuade Miklav to let you
contact the Fire Warriors, war could yet be
avoided."

Loreth nodded. They had been over this before.
Arguments on both sides had been stated and
restated. Although the Pavla foresaw much pain

and suffering just ahead, she clung stubbornly to her belief in the Augury—that the ultimate result would be good.

Nazleen stretched up to kiss the taller woman's cheek, then walked through the gate to join the Warriors. She smiled at Haslik, who stood holding the reins of her mare. She was glad that Miklav had sent him to accompany her to Denra, and she was eager to be on her way.

Haslik had arrived with the guard last night and had been invited to join Loreth and her for dinner. When they'd told him of Nazleen's plan to persuade Miklav to allow the Pavla to attempt contact with the Fire Warriors, he had remained noncommittal. Then, when she'd informed him of her pregnancy, he'd tried to persuade her to ride in the comfort of a carriage, rather than on horseback. But Nazleen had pointed out that she'd ridden to Cerece on horseback only a few days ago and that the Healers foresaw no problem with her doing so again.

Then he'd temporized, suggesting they wait for a few days before making the journey. The situation was too uncertain now, and Miklav wasn't expecting her yet.

Nazleen glanced at her brother as he rode beside her. Never before had she been so keenly aware of his divided loyalties. He must know of Miklav's scheme to start a war. Surely everyone at Denra would know when a large group of Warriors set out.

She glanced again at his handsome, aristocratic profile and wished fervently that they could be carefree children again, riding together in the royal forest. But Haslik was a Warrior and she was the

Liege, and those days were gone forever.

Just as they reached a bend in the road that would hide the compound from view, Nazleen turned to look back, once again seeing it in the mellow softness of early morning light. An inexplicable thrill shot through her. Unlike the last time, when she'd feared she might not see it again for a long time, she knew she would return here soon. She tried to examine that strange feeling that was gone as quickly as it had appeared. Had it been half-fear and half-anticipation?

All she knew was that it was some sort of premonition. Her training allowed her to distinguish between ordinary feelings and those that in some way foretold the future. Unfortunately, her talents were not that strong when it came to foretelling the future, and she was often left, as now, with nothing more than vague feelings.

Haslik watched his sister stare back at the compound and wished he'd been able to persuade her to stay there or go back to the palace, but his failure didn't surprise him; he knew her well. All he'd promised Miklav was that he'd do his best—and he had. The Warrior Chief wouldn't be surprised to see her show up, because he too knew her well, but he wouldn't be expecting her this quickly.

Haslik thought again about having the commander of this group send someone on ahead to warn Miklav, but there were only a dozen of them as it was. Even though it wasn't likely that the aliens had crossed the desert this quickly after the storms, he hated to decrease Nazleen's protection just to forewarn the Warrior Chief of her earlier arrival. Perhaps when they reached the Tren village, he could send one of them on ahead.

As Nazleen had suspected, Haslik knew Miklav's plans. The Warrior Chief had called him in when the request for an escort for Nazleen had arrived. Haslik had seen the group departing for the edge of the desert and had suspected their target, but the operation had been kept secret.

Miklav had opened their conversation by saying that Haslik's loyalties could be put to a severe test in the near future, and that if he wanted to leave Denra for some other fortress or for duty at the palace, he was welcome to do so. Haslik had appreciated the Chief's thoughtfulness, but he did not hesitate before telling him that his oath as a Warrior had to take precedence over his love for his sister. Had he not been absolutely certain that Miklav would never harm Nazleen, nor allow harm to come to her, he could not have made that statement.

Then Miklav had told him of his plan to start a limited war with the aliens in order to avoid a wider conflagration, and Haslik had found himself in agreement with the Chief, all the while knowing as Miklav did that Nazleen would never agree to this.

Miklav had then asked him to accompany the guard to Cerece and try to persuade Nazleen to remain there or return to the palace, and Haslik had agreed, although both men had conceded that his chances of success were very limited.

After that, the two men had shared a few drinks before the fire in Miklav's quarters, and Miklav had begun to talk about the future. It became clear to Haslik that once having seized power under the terms of the Compact, Miklav would never give it up again. But once again, he found himself not really able to disagree with Miklav's goals. Their society was changing; he'd tried to tell Nazleen that. What Miklav planned was, in Haslik's opinion, in the best interests of them all, although he knew that his sister would never see it that way.

The only thing that troubled him was that once Miklav had secured for himself the power he craved, he would never be content to rule Hamloor alone. Now that they knew there were people beyond the Fire Mountains, sooner or later Miklav would want to set forth to seek new conquests. The Warrior Chief would never be content for long to share the governing of Hamloor; he would want a new challenge, something that was his alone.

But perhaps, Haslik thought as he saw her turn away from one last look at the compound, his sister could present enough challenges to Miklav to last a lifetime. Certainly the Chief wanted her almost as much as he wanted power, and now they were to have a child.

The group wound their way down from the mountains into a narrow valley where the road curved along a small, swiftly running stream. It was a lovely spot, with thick fir trees covering the steep hillsides and the sun dappling the rushing water.

Then they were through the valley and ascending once more into the hills. The road here became quite narrow, threading its way around rocky outcroppings and in the process creating many blind curves. In recent years, there'd been discussions about widening this portion of the road, but the experts from the palace and from Denra had agreed that it would be a very costly and perhaps impossible task, since the area was nearly solid rock.

They rode now in double rows, with six Warriors ahead of Nazleen and Haslik and the other five behind. Nazleen turned in her saddle for one last look at the lovely valley.

Suddenly there were noises from up ahead, men shouting and horses whinnying. Immediately the Warriors behind her and Haslik, who'd been riding at her side, rushed forward, frightening her little mare so that Nazleen had to concentrate for a moment on keeping her seat and calming the animal.

She tried to see what was happening but could not see beyond a sharp curve where the Warriors had now disappeared. Then shots rang out, followed by more shouts and cries that were abruptly cut off.

At first paralyzed by shock that such a thing could happen in this lovely, peaceful place, Nazleen now began to fear for her life. She looked around wildly and spotted a barely discernible path that led up over the top of the rocky hill next to the road. Her little mare was far more agile than the Warrior steeds, and fear gave her even more fleetness as Nazleen urged her in that direction.

When she saw that the path led up to the very top of the hill, Nazleen leapt from the saddle and, after securing the mare to some bushes, climbed the rest of the way as far below the terrifying sounds of battle continued.

Cautiously and on trembling legs, she crept

across the hilltop to see what was happening. Before she could reach the far side, the noises below ceased, and the sudden silence became even more terrifying.

A cry started to force its way from her throat when she saw what lay below, but she pushed a fist against her mouth to stop it. Twelve Warriors lay unmoving on the road—including Haslik. Their horses were milling about, quivering and snorting as a huge group of green-clad men attempted to grab them and calm them. Even as she watched in frozen horror, one of the animals reared up before he could be grabbed and then trampled on an inert black-clad body.

Sunlight gleamed off the tops of golden heads as the men in green milled about, some of them tending the horses while others examined the bodies of the Warriors. From some fingertips came faint arcs of shimmering green fire.

They were talking, but between the sound of the wind and the roaring terror in Nazleen's head, she could hear nothing. Then yet another Fire Warrior stepped into view, and the others faded to a green blur as she stared at his tawny head. Zaktar! She knew it without seeing his face.

She saw that his uniform had gold stripes running across the shoulders and chest. He was their leader —the leader of the Fire Warriors who had killed her brother! A scream of protest began to well up in her, and she backed away from the edge. But just as she did, she saw Zaktar start to lift his head in her direction.

She scrambled back down to her mare, untied the

still-nervous animal and leapt upon her back, then urged her up to the hilltop and across to the far side, where she'd seen that the descent was easier.

"Five of them are dead," Staska reported to his leader. "That wouldn't have happened if we hadn't been surprised."

Zaktar lowered his gaze from the hilltop to meet the regretful look on his aide's face. "I know. You all did the best you could under the circumstances."

"It's these damned rocks," another man grumbled. "If it hadn't been for them, we'd have known they were coming."

Zaktar nodded. He'd been in just such a situation long ago in war. Certain types of rock formations interfered with their ability to sense the presence of others. They'd met this group at the worst possible place.

"What do you want to do with them and the horses?" Staska asked.

But Zaktar was once again staring at that hilltop. He thought he'd sensed someone up there, but he couldn't be sure. In the immediate aftermath of fire-battles, the extra senses were always dulled.

"Take two others and go around the bend to see if there's a way up to that hilltop," he ordered. "I thought I sensed someone up there."

Then he turned his attention to the black Warriors. "Bury the dead ones and mark their graves well, so they can be found later. We'll take the horses and the others with us. It'll slow us down, but I don't know what else to do with them. Tie them into their saddles."

"Better check them for other weapons, too," one man suggested. "These men are armed to the teeth."

Their trucks appeared at that point. They'd left them further down the narrow road while Zaktar and most of the Fire Warriors had walked on ahead to see if the road was passable. There was just barely enough clearance to get around the curve where they'd met the black Warriors.

A short time later, the search party returned.

"No one's up there now, but someone *was* there, all right. We saw hoofprints. Smaller than these, though. It could have been one of those little ponies we saw on our first trip."

The speaker was Taka, the youth who'd run into Trens while seeking the fire-pool.

Zaktar nodded. Probably it was one of those mountain men he'd described, but he'd seen another small horse on his previous trip—a beautiful white mare carrying the woman whose image had been tormenting him ever since.

He hesitated, staring once more up at that hilltop. What were the odds of her being here? Too great to consider.

"Let's get moving," he said reluctantly.

Nazleen rode down the steep hillside, weaving through the dense forest. No Warrior steed could have picked its way this sure-footedly, and the effort required to guide the animal and keep herself in the saddle kept her mind fully occupied.

Finally, she reached the road once again, but after a brief pause, she crossed it and plunged once more into the forest. The Fire Warriors had been on foot, but she felt sure they must have some of those strange vehicles around somewhere. At this point, her sole focus was on self-preservation.

When she felt the mare beginning to tire, she decided that she'd put enough distance between herself and the enemy to ensure her safety for the time being. So she brought the horse to a halt near a small waterfall where a stream tumbled down from the mountain.

Her legs began to shake as soon as she dismounted, but she led the mare to the clear pool at the base of the waterfall, then stood there dazedly while she drank. After that, she tethered the animal to some bushes and stumbled back to the pool.

The tremors in her legs wouldn't stop, so she sank to her knees and bent over to scoop up handfuls of the cold water, first dashing it on her face and then gulping some down.

The horror of what she'd seen had been waiting within her, and it now poured forth. Haslik was dead! The brother she loved more than any other living person had died in a blaze of sacred fire.

Zaktar! Now there was no question of his reality. It was he who had killed Haslik!

But she forced herself away from the immediate past to the present. Had he seen her on that hilltop? She couldn't be sure. But wouldn't his powers have warned him of her presence?

She sat back on the damp ground beside the pool, glad to have something else to focus on for a moment. She'd never wielded the fire, so she didn't know what it did to the user. But she did know that after the Auguries they all suffered a period of dulled senses—usually several hours, sometimes less.

That might well have happened to Zaktar and those others, too. It explained why they hadn't sensed her, but it didn't explain that sudden lifting of Zaktar's head.

How many of them were there? She closed her eyes and could recall nothing beyond many green uniforms and the dead Warriors—including Haslik. Still, there must have been more of them, since she was convinced that they couldn't have crossed the desert on foot. Somewhere, there must have been some of those vehicles the scouting party had seen and perhaps even more Fire Warriors.

Then she belatedly began to think about what they were doing on that road. They must be going to Cerece! She leapt up, then stopped, swaying slightly on her shaky legs. Her first instinct had been to rush back to Cerece, but some inner caution had brought her to a halt.

There were both Warriors and Trens guarding Cerece, and the Sisterhood had resumed watches from the newly rebuilt walls of the compound. At the first sign of the Fire Warriors' approach, the heavy gates would be closed and the Sisters would retreat into the cave of the fire-pool. Other gates could be closed in two different places to protect the cave, and the entrance to the tunnel was itself well-hidden within the compound.

She couldn't hope to reach Cerece before the Fire Warriors, because they had their vehicles and she would have to circle past them through the woods. The result would probably be that she would reach the compound after the gates had been closed.

Although her emotions pulled her in that direction, her common sense told her that she must go on to Denra. She couldn't reach it before nightfall, but if she returned to the road, she could at least reach a Tren village by that time and they could help her.

She walked unsteadily back to her mare and remounted. She still nearly turned back to Cerece, but then resolutely set out for Denra. She was Liege of Hamloor, and her first responsibility was to alert Miklav of the danger to them all. Even in the midst of her turmoil, the irony of the situation was not lost upon her. She had set out to prevent war, but she would now be carrying the news that would guarantee it.

The captive Warriors began to stir when Zaktar judged they were still several kilometers away from the compound. He knew how they'd be feeling—dizzy and weak-limbed and wracked with muscle pain. He'd seen that in prisoners taken during those old battles.

In a few moments the air was filled with groans and cries and words he couldn't understand. He was in the lead, riding one of the extra horses. Other Fire Warriors rode the remaining horses that had belonged to the dead warriors, scattering themselves among the now semiconscious group of black-clad men. Behind them, the trucks rolled along in low gear.

We make quite a picture, Zaktar thought with a bittersweet smile. We look like the collision of two periods of history. Those philosophers who saw time as a series of concentric circles just might have stumbled onto something.

He called a halt to the strange procession. The seven prisoners regarded their captors through half-focused gazes that began to resolve themselves into fear.

After ordering several men to get their rifles from the trucks, Zaktar told the others to untie the prisoners. They could still defend themselves with the fire if necessary, but since he didn't know what lay ahead, he preferred to keep that weapon in reserve.

The Fire Warriors untied the men in black and helped them down from their horses. One black Warrior, perhaps a bit more awake than his fellows, reached down for the knife that had been tucked in his boot, then fell on his face when his legs gave way. The knife, of course, had been removed.

Using gestures, he ordered the prisoners to walk about and to get water from a nearby stream. Both things could help them recover more quickly.

The men in black did as told, some of them helping their still only half-conscious comrades. By now, the looks they gave the Fire Warriors were more defiant than fearful; obviously, they were recovering. Zaktar knew they expected to be killed and must be terrified, and for that reason he respected their defiance. Courage was courage, no matter that it came from the enemy.

Within a few minutes, most of the men were moving about almost normally, a tribute to their excellent state of fitness. They were talking in their own language, and Zaktar saw the oldest among them, who was clearly their leader, counting his men with a grim expression.

Then suddenly he heard another of the black Warriors use the word "Cerecian". Zaktar stared at the man who'd spoken. He was as tall as most of the others but more slender, and his hair was the lightest of all of them. Among the Kapti, a dark-haired race, light hair occasionally showed up when there was a strong Cerecian presence in the family. His sister's hair was as light as this man's.

The man saw Zaktar staring at him and returned the stare, but his look was more one of curiosity than of hatred or fear. When Zaktar motioned him to step forward, he did so unhesitatingly.

An aristocratic face, Zaktar thought, and a regal bearing, too, even though he must still be in some pain. He judged the man to be in his early thirties.

"Do you speak the Cerecian language?" Zaktar asked, slowly and carefully.

"Yes."

Relief washed over Zaktar, followed quickly by an eagerness he could barely conceal. "Do any of the others?"

The man shook his head, and the motion brought a recurrence of his dizziness. As he tried to steady himself, Zaktar reached out to grip his shoulders. The two men stared at each other.

"Where did you learn it?" Zaktar asked.

"My mother was Cerecian," the man responded, his accent thick but still recognizable.

"Did your mother live at the compound up there?" Zaktar indicated the hill beyond them.

"No."

"But there *are* other Cerecians there?"

When the man said nothing, Zaktar went on in a

quiet voice. "We come in peace. I regret what
happened back there. We tried not to kill any of
you, but it happened too fast. We've buried the
others and marked their graves for you."

The younger man searched his face carefully and
asked, "Are you Zaktar?"

Then it was Zaktar's turn to stare at him. How
could this man possibly know his name? He then
asked the question.

The black warrior hesitated, then said, "My
sister saw you in a vision."

Eagerness rushed heatedly through Zaktar's
body. "Your sister? Does she live at the compound?" This man was obviously of noble blood, as
was the woman he'd seen.

But the man shook his head.

"But she was there recently?"

"Yes." Haslik was awake enough now for his
attention to focus on fear for his sister. Obviously
they hadn't captured her, unless she had died and
been buried with the others, but surely Zaktar
would have mentioned her.

"And she has hair the color of the setting sun?"

Haslik nodded again. So it *had* been Zaktar up
there on that hilltop that day. He stared at the man.
Zaktar was extraordinarily handsome—even another man could appreciate that. He guessed that if
he'd pictured what Fire Warriors would look like,
he'd seen them as smaller, more effeminate, because the only Cerecians he'd ever seen had been
women. This man was as big as their biggest
Warriors and looked as fit as any man Haslik had
ever seen.

Haslik could also see the eagerness in that green

gaze when he'd spoken of Nazleen. That thought chilled him. Perhaps these Fire Warriors did come in peace, but when he found out that she belonged to the Warrior Chief . . .

"Where is your sister now?" Zaktar persisted.

"She is in the city, in the palace," he lied. "Her name is Nazleen. She's the Liege of Hamloor. That's the name of this land," he added.

"The Liege? You mean she rules this country?"

"Yes." Haslik watched as various emotions played across that ruggedly handsome face. Finally, to Haslik's amazement, he broke into laughter.

"Ahh, the old Pavla would love this!"

The sun had slipped behind the hills and the shadows were lengthening on the road when Nazleen suddenly lifted her tired head to sniff the air. Woodsmoke! She must be near the Tren village. She urged the little mare onward, too dazed to consider her bedraggled and dirty appearance. After two more bends in the road, she saw the village just ahead.

Several older men lounged in the small square, smoking pipes and playing an old Tren game whose name her dazed brain couldn't quite recall. The mare slowed of her own will and headed toward them, no doubt thinking of food and a comfortable stable. The men saw her and paused in their game to frown.

Nazleen then realized just how bad she must look when it took several seconds for their frowns to turn to shocked recognition. Despite her green robe and the Royal White mare, they hadn't recognized her at first. Now they approached her hurriedly, gaping and bowing at the same time.

She quickly told them what had happened, seeing their horrified expressions when she spoke of Fire Warriors. Then she asked that someone be sent to Denra as fast as possible with the news. One of the men hurried away and returned with a sturdy youth. She explained it once again to him, and he ran toward the communal stable at the far end of the village.

A short time later, Nazleen was seated in the headman's house, being plied with enough food to feed an entire company of Warriors, all of it presented with deep apologies for its meagerness. She ate small amounts of everything, less from hunger than from a desire not to offend her flustered hosts.

Nazleen ached in body and in spirit. Her brother was dead, killed by the sacred fire, killed by the man who had invaded her dreams. Why hadn't that accursed Augury foretold his death? If it had, she might have prevented it.

And she longed to know what was happening at Cerece. She knew that the guards there couldn't hold off the Fire Warriors forever, and that sooner or later they would find the hidden entrance to the tunnel and get to the fire-pool where the Sisters hid. Could the guards hold them off long enough for Warriors from Denra to save them? And if not, what would happen to the Sisters?

She was so tired, drained of everything except anger and a bone-deep sadness. Her hosts noticed her condition and quickly offered her a bed. When she got up shakily, her hostess hesitantly took her arm, then led her back a small, dark hallway to a tiny but spotlessly clean bedchamber. She wanted to ask if she could wash up a bit, but when she saw the bed, she gave up that thought and fell onto it gratefully.

The Warrior Chief was a very happy man. His plans were proceeding perfectly. The scheme to provoke an incident in the desert had worked. He regretted the loss of a man, but deaths were an inevitable part of war.

He'd listened to the survivor's account of the Fire Warriors with avid interest, although admittedly with a touch of uneasiness, too. But Miklav believed he could win. The key, he thought, lay in their limited numbers and the limited range in which they could use their terrible fire.

He reasoned that if their numbers were great, there would have been more of them in the desert. His man had estimated that there could be no more than 60 of them, and there might be a like number protecting the camp.

He was also convinced that their fire was a very short-range weapon. Why else would those who had remained near the vehicles have carried weapons? And nothing more than rifles had been in evidence, although they were certainly superior to his own.

The survivor of the incident in the desert had arrived at Denra late in the afternoon, and now, scant hours later, the fortress was filled with the sounds of men preparing for battle. Two hundred Warriors would leave for Cerece at first light, since Miklav knew the Fire Warriors must be headed there, and another 100 would set out at the same time to join the force that already waited near the desert's edge. They would proceed across the desert to attack the camp of the aliens.

The only thing that troubled the Warrior Chief was that Nazleen was at Cerece, and in all likelihood the Fire Warriors would get there before his men could. Still, all that the desert survivor had told him indicated that Nazleen had been right. The aliens weren't really here to make war, and if that was the case, then surely they wouldn't harm their own kin. Besides, he didn't doubt that the Sisters could hide themselves somewhere in that compound, probably in the cave that held the fire-pool. They should be safe enough until he and his men could get there.

Miklav wondered about the man who was their leader. His instincts told him this was the man Zaktar, the Fire Warrior Nazleen had seen in her vision. He pictured the man as he'd been described, then summoned up an image of Nazleen—and his fists clenched.

He was asleep when the insistent pounding awakened him. For a moment, he was confused. Surely it wasn't time to leave yet. He felt as though he'd just gotten to sleep. He called out for the aide to enter, then sat up and stared at the flushed Tren youth who entered with him.

Zaktar kept the man named Haslik beside him as they rode on toward the compound. As soon as Haslik had fully recovered, he'd also become far more close-mouthed. Zaktar understood that; he knew he'd taken advantage of the man's disorientation.

But if he'd learned little else, at least he knew that there were Cerecians at the compound and that they still spoke their common language. And now he knew the name of the woman who'd taken over his dreams.

He smiled to himself. So she was the ruler of this land. That pleased him very much, since it meant that he would inevitably meet her again—or meet her for the first time in the conventional manner. The old Pavla had sent him out here to give him a new challenge, but Zaktar doubted that Nazleen was what he'd had in mind.

He glanced over at Haslik's handsome profile and wondered if brother and sister resembled each other at all. He'd already given Nazleen a face in his dreams, but he eagerly awaited the reality.

Then suddenly he was pulled from his thoughts by a very faint brushing against his mind. He turned quickly in his saddle and looked inquiringly at the others behind him. Most of them nodded; they'd felt it, too. Someone at the compound had discovered them. The question now was what they would do about it. Zaktar knew there must be guards, perhaps more of these black Warriors.

He signaled a halt. "I'm going to send this man Haslik on to the compound alone," he told the others as they clustered around him. "He will tell them that we do not seek war."

His gaze met Haslik's, and the younger man nodded. Zaktar could see dissatisfaction on the faces of some of the Fire Warriors, but he trusted this man. Zaktar considered that his greatest Cerecian gift was an intuitive understanding of others, and he'd learned long ago to put his unquestioned faith in those instincts.

He told one of his men to bring Haslik one of

their rifles, rather than his own old-fashioned musket. When the man brought it, Zaktar explained its workings to an incredulous Haslik, then handed it over to him. Haslik stared from the weapon to Zaktar and back again.

"It's a gift," Zaktar explained.

Haslik shifted the rifle into his one arm, then tentatively put out a hand to Zaktar. "Thank you."

The two men gripped each other's hands for a long moment, then Haslik spurred his horse and galloped off down the road. Zaktar watched him, certain he would try to prevent a battle and hoping he would succeed. He'd hate like hell to be shot with one of his own rifles!

They settled down to wait. The remaining prisoners stared at Zaktar with incredulity. Some of them clearly thought he was crazy to arm an enemy, and a few of them had a begrudging respect in their eyes. His own men appeared to be divided on the issue, too.

His aide suggested that they take advantage of this lull to climb the nearest hill and attempt to make radio contact with the Kapti army across the desert. Zaktar agreed, and three men went off to climb a nearby hill.

Time began to drag. Horses and men became impatient. Zaktar got up and walked a bit farther along the road, and when he rounded the bend, he could see the compound through the trees, high on its hilltop. He could also feel the unique pull of the sacred fire.

He continued to walk toward it, until he realized the foolishness of his action. He wasn't even carrying a rifle, and for all he knew, Warriors could be approaching him now through that dark, thick forest. He turned to start back, then whirled around again, gauging the distance between himself and the sharp curve in the road ahead as he heard hoof-beats.

The distance at which they could wield the fire wasn't as great as a bullet could travel, but in the case of the really proficient ones like himself, it was probably as far as a musketball could travel. Nevertheless, he moved quickly off the road, hiding himself behind some thick bushes as he watched the curve.

A moment later, he saw a flash of green, slightly lighter than his own uniform. Carefully, he eased forward, straining to get a better look. Then the figure in green came fully into view, and to his surprise he saw that it was a woman, riding with Haslik. He stepped out into the road, wondering why they would send a woman out to meet him, wishing it had been Nazleen—and finally beginning to wonder about their society.

Loreth rode beside Haslik, struggling to contain her excitement. Everything he'd told her suggested that the Fire Warriors were, at the very least, honorable men. And the man Zaktar was with them. She found herself intensely curious about this particular Fire Warrior, their leader.

It hadn't been easy for Haslik and her to persuade the Warriors to go to search for Nazleen and then to Denra to report what had happened, but Haslik had pointed out that Miklav would want no stone left unturned in their efforts to find her. Furthermore, given the fact that there were only 18

Warriors at Cerece and the alien Fire Warriors had had no problem defeating 12 men even when they were surprised, staying at Cerece was foolhardy.

The other guards were Trens, and since their loyalties lay more with the Sisterhood than with the Warriors, they had quickly agreed to return to their homes. All had finally left by the narrow road that led from the compound down to the nearest Tren village, the Warriors taking that way to avoid the Fire Warriors.

Loreth felt only a slight twinge of fear as she rode to meet the Fire Warriors. As a precaution, she'd sent the other Sisters down to the cave, with the gates locked and the tunnel entrance carefully concealed. But, even more than before, she had faith in the Augury. It was now clear to her what had been meant by an end to the Sisterhood and a new beginning.

Her only concern was for Nazleen's safety, but she agreed with Haslik that his sister wasn't the weak, defenseless female Miklav persisted in believing she was. Nazleen was healthy, resourceful and riding a horse that could easily carry her to safety.

She avoided completely thoughts of Miklav's reaction to all this. Miklav's death, she now believed, was the price that must be paid. Although it hurt her deeply, she trusted the Augury and knew, as Nazleen didn't, that it was inevitable.

Then, just as they rounded a wide curve in the road, a man stepped out of the bushes to meet them. Zaktar! There was no doubt that it was he and that he was the man she'd seen carrying Nazleen into the fire-pool.

"This is Zaktar," Haslik said unnecessarily.

What a handsome man, Loreth thought with a totally irrational rush of pride as Zaktar approached them with long, purposeful strides. She'd expected to find the distinctive features of their race very strange in a male.

He stopped before them, and Loreth put out her hand. "Welcome, Zaktar. I am Loreth, Pavla of the Cerecian Sisterhood."

Zaktar spared a moment to nod with gratitude at Haslik, then returned his attention to the tall, handsome woman astride the shaggy little pony. A female Pavla? And she'd said "Sisterhood." A strange thought crept into his mind, one that brought a pleased smile to his face as he took her hand.

"And I am Zaktar, leader of the Fire Warriors, Pavla. But we come here in peace."

Their eyes met, and Loreth nodded. He spoke the truth.

"Forgive me if I am asking what may appear to be a strange question, but I am unaccustomed to the idea of a female Pavla."

"We are all women, Zaktar. There are no male Cerecians . . . here, that is."

To her astonishment, he laughed aloud, revealing sparkling white teeth and dimples that made him look no less a man.

"Ahh, Pavla, I foresee some interesting times ahead. Our Pavla may yet regret that he approved this expedition."

When Loreth frowned, Zaktar hastened to explain. "You see, we are all males. We trace our ancestry back to a boy who was found wandering in the hills by the Kapti people with whom we live."

Loreth, by now, was wearing a smile of her own. "And we are all descended from a young girl who was also discovered wandering about homeless. It was just after a great explosion in the Fire Mountains several hundred years ago."

Zaktar nodded. "And I believe we have found the ruins of the village from which they both came." Then he chuckled again.

"Our geneticists will have their work cut out for them when they receive this information."

Loreth didn't know what geneticists were, but she assumed they must be some sort of scientist. Zaktar, in the meantime, had turned to Haslik to inquire about the Warriors at the compound. When Haslik explained that they had gone, Zaktar looked doubtful. Loreth decided that further explanations were in order.

"We persuaded them to go in search of Haslik's sister, Nazleen, the ruler of this land."

Zaktar's green eyes bored into her. "Why should they be searching for her? I thought she was at her palace."

Loreth shook her head. "Haslik did not tell you the truth because he couldn't be certain you were to be trusted. Nazleen was with him and the other Warriors you encountered earlier today."

When Zaktar's gaze returned to Haslik, the younger man felt one brief moment of fear, but the anger that had flared died quickly as Zaktar nodded.

"I understand," he said, even though he seethed inwardly that he should have been so close to her again. "But is she safe?"

Loreth nodded. "I believe she is. She will probably take refuge in a Tren village along that road." Then when she saw the doubt linger in his eyes, she added, "Nazleen may appear to be fragile, but that is not true. And she is very resourceful."

Zaktar's eyes flashed at Haslik again. "You will find her and bring her back here."

Loreth heard all the emotions in the Fire Warrior's voice, but before she could speak, Haslik had responded.

"I will go, but I think by then she will be at Denra, the fortress you saw from your balloon."

"Zaktar," Loreth said quietly in the tone of one who must deliver bad news, "Nazleen has chosen the Warrior Chief as her mate, and she is carrying his child."

She'd expected him to take the news badly, but she actually recoiled from the rage she saw in those green eyes. A sudden, incredibly sharp pain struck her between the temples, and she put up a hand and cried out. Immediately, the pain went away.

"I am sorry, Pavla. I lost control for a moment."

"I would like to meet the other Fire Warriors," Loreth said gently, "and extend an invitation to all of you to come to the compound. If you desire, you may use the fire-pool as well. And we have much to talk about."

"Yes, Pavla. Thank you very much," Zaktar said in a distracted tone as he turned to lead the way back to the others.

Loreth and Haslik exchanged glances. It was clear to them both that there could be no peace now.

CHAPTER NINE

MIKLAV FELT THE FIRST FAINT STIRRINGS OF UNEASINESS as he stood in his bedchamber, staring down at the mass of golden-red curls spilled across his pillow. By the time he'd reached the Tren village and found her asleep in the headman's house, something had changed her. There was no fire left in her, no more naive idealism, not even any of the iron-willed determination he'd seen in her all her life.

When he had awakened her, she'd told him the story of the attack and of Haslik's death. Then, almost as an afterthought and with no emotion at all, she'd added that she was carrying his child.

He'd wanted to keep her safe from all this, and he'd wanted to keep her beloved brother out of it, too—and he had failed.

Beyond the shuttered window, the two war parties were already assembled, waiting only for the first light of dawn to set forth. One group would march to Cerece, and the other would meet the contingent that awaited them at the desert's edge.

She stirred, then opened her remarkable eyes and stared at him silently. He sat down on the edge of the bed and brushed the curls from her face.

"I must leave now for Cerece. You'll be safe here. The physician will look in on you later, and old Aktra is just outside the door if you need anything."

She sat up and fixed her eyes on him intently. "You will die in this battle, Miklav. The Augury foretold it."

Miklav didn't hold much with Auguries, although he knew that this one had already proved to have some truth to it. He returned her stare, wondering if she cared. Was it his imagination, or had he heard concern there? Hoping he had, he reached out to touch her face.

"Auguries have been known to be wrong before, as you yourself have said, and in any event a part of me will live on." He rested a hand briefly on her belly.

Nazleen stared at him, then at her belly where his hand rested, and shook her head slowly. "No."

He didn't know if she meant that the Augury wasn't wrong, or that the child would not survive— and suddenly he knew that he didn't want to know, either. He bent to kiss her briefly, then got up and went out to join his men.

Nazleen watched him leave, then slid her hand to her belly. The coldness of death lay over everything. Haslik was already dead, Miklav would soon be dead, and she knew now that the child she was carrying would not survive either.

And all of this was the fault of one man—Zaktar.

Zaktar rose from the carpeted floor of the compound's main reception room with barely remembered fragments of a dream tormenting him. Nazleen. He knew only that it had something to do with her.

All around him, the other Fire Warriors began to awaken, too. Despite the troubling dream, he felt rested, thanks to the time they'd spent in the fire-pool. He was refreshed and ready for battle.

War was inevitable now. He'd sent Haslik and the other former captives back to their fortress and asked Haslik to carry the message to the Warrior Chief that he wasn't seeking war. The message would be delivered, but war would come anyway. Both Haslik and Pavla had said that Miklav was determined to have a war.

Zaktar sat up, thinking about his conversation last night with Loreth. She'd explained the history and structure of their society and the Compact, and she'd also told him how that Compact had forced Nazleen to choose a mate from among the Warriors. Zaktar clenched his fists in anger as he thought about it now. What kind of society would force a woman to take a man as her mate? It reminded him of the way his own forebears had once been treated by the Kapti.

He stood up and stretched, torn between the urge to return to the fire-pool and an equally powerful need to talk again to Loreth. Then the decision was made for him as the woman herself appeared in the corridor that led off the great room.

"You are welcome to use the pool again if you wish," she said after having greeted him. "Then we must talk."

Zaktar told the others to go ahead to the pool, then turned back to Loreth. "Perhaps we'd better talk now."

She nodded and led the way back to her personal quarters. A young girl appeared with fruits and berries and nuts. Zaktar smiled at her, but she stayed as faraway from him as possible and her hands trembled as she poured the fragrant tea.

"You know that a war party could be on its way here even now," Zaktar said as he sniffed appreciatively at the tea.

Loreth nodded. "Yes, I'm sure that Nazleen will have reached Denra by now or sent someone from the Tren village."

She saw the look on Zaktar's face and put out a hand to touch his. "You must remember that Nazleen is the Liege of Hamloor. Her loyalties are to Hamloor first, as they must be. In any event, according to the Compact, it is Miklav who will make the decisions now."

Despite her gentle tone and touch, Zaktar's hand clenched into a fist. Loreth went on softly.

"Miklav loves her in his own way, and she cares for him in hers. He may love the glory of war and the power it gives him more than he loves her, but he will never allow harm to come to her. Miklav and I grew up together, Zaktar, and I know that there is good in him. You may have to fight him, but do not hate him."

"She belongs to me!" Zaktar blurted out the

words without conscious intent, but then he met the Pavla's eyes unwaveringly. "I know this!"

"Perhaps she does," Loreth admitted as that vision of Nazleen in the pool with this man flickered through her mind. "But it will not be easy for either of you."

"And where do you and the Sisterhood stand in all this?"

Loreth stared into those deep green eyes. "We must remain neutral. All of us have kin among the Hamloorians and Trens, but our ties to you and your men are powerful, too, forged in the sacred fire."

Zaktar nodded. "Neutrality is the most I can ask for. We must leave here as soon as possible, so that the battle doesn't touch you."

Scarcely an hour later, Loreth stood at the gate to the compound and watched the Fire Warriors leave in their strange vehicles. Zaktar had told her that the army of their allies, the Kapti, would be meeting them after they journeyed across the desert. They'd contacted them with a little box that sent voices through the air. There was apparently no end to the miraculous machines their kinfolk had.

She turned and walked slowly back into the compound. Her heart ached—for this man Zaktar, whom she already loved as a brother, for Nazleen, whom she'd loved as a younger sister, and for Miklav, whom she loved with a love that was forbidden.

A long convoy of trucks and sturdy little vehicles called jeppas snaked its way through the desert. Along with Kapti troops, the convoy carried heavy artillery. In the middle of the desert, the convoy met a large group of black-clad Warriors. Fierce fighting followed, but the superior weaponry of the Kapti gave them the victory. Thereafter, a few trucks turned back to the camp, carrying prisoners and the Kapti dead and wounded.

The remainder of the troops then resumed their journey to meet the Fire Warriors.

Along the road to Denra, Haslik and the former captives met Miklav and the large Warrior force. When he saw Haslik, Miklav was grateful that he'd been spared after all. Some of the pain he'd seen in Nazleen's eyes would be gone when she got the news.

Haslik passed on the message from Zaktar, but he knew even as he spoke that the Warrior Chief could not be deterred from his course. Miklav then ordered Haslik back to Denra, but Haslik asked to stay and fight. He disagreed with Miklav's decision, but he too was a Warrior first.

In any event, they all heard the sound that Haslik identified as the vehicles of the Fire Warriors, and the battle lines were drawn.

The two forces met in the peaceful valley Nazleen had been admiring when the Fire Warriors had appeared. Each side took up positions at the valley's ends. Miklav was pleased at the small numbers of the Fire Warriors, but he was not about to celebrate prematurely.

Zaktar stared through his glasses at the Warrior Chief, knowing that this was the man who had the woman he wanted and trying to remember Loreth's admonition. It was obvious to him that Haslik had failed to dissuade this man Miklav, and despite the black Warriors' superior numbers, it was also obvious that they could not win this battle. The Fire Warriors could easily hold them off until the Kapti army arrived.

Haslik might be able to provide some information about them to Miklav, but he had not seen the weapons concealed in the trucks. Zaktar ordered them to be set up now—three powerful machine guns with a range far beyond that of anything the other side could have. Additionally, they had a small supply of grenades.

Then he saw, thanks to his powerful glasses, that the Warriors were sneaking through the brush in two lines on either side of the valley. He called for the men who were most accurate with the grenades, then ordered them to aim to frighten, not to kill.

A moment later, the valley exploded into fire and smoke, and the black-clad men stopped.

Miklav stared in stunned amazement at the dark column of smoke. What weapon did they use? Certainly not their green fire. Then he saw the two columns begin to inch forward again, and just at that moment, he also saw the signal being given by the men he'd sent around the hill behind the Fire Warriors. The men in the valley had been intended as a diversion only, while Miklav used his superior knowledge of the territory to get a large force of his men behind the enemy.

But the Fire Warriors had sensed the enemy presence this time, even before the first of them had signaled their leader from the hilltop. Two of the three guns swung in that direction, while others took up positions with grenades and rapid-fire automatic weapons.

The battle was not long. Black Warriors went down under rifle fire and were cut to ribbons by the machine guns. Grenades blew men into the air, and those who remained fell to the ground surrounded by a deadly halo of green fire.

Miklav signaled a retreat to Denra, and the remaining Warriors gathered up their wounded and rode out of the valley. Zaktar let them go as he awaited news about his own casualties. Two Fire Warriors had died and four more had been hit by musket fire, but none was seriously wounded and the Healer had quickly dealt with them.

Then they followed the black Warriors. On the outskirts of a Tren village, they caught up to them and killed and captured more men. But once again, Zaktar stopped, not wanting to engulf the villagers in the battle.

It was early the next morning when Nazleen received the news from one of Miklav's men who had been sent ahead to Denra. The aliens had reinforcements; an army of their allies had sneaked in under cover of darkness and attacked with the dawn. Furthermore, word had come that this army, or perhaps another, had attacked and either killed or captured most of the Warriors who had gone into the desert.

Nazleen heard stories about terrible weapons, about men being blown to bits by explosives hurled through the air like balls, about guns that fired so fast that they could kill a dozen men in the time it would take one Warrior to raise his rifle. And she heard stories about the green fire, hurled farther

252

than she would ever have believed possible.

Miklav had ordered a retreat to Denra, and they were even now on their way, pursued by the invaders. He'd also belatedly called for reinforcements from several other fortresses and was confident Denra could hold out until they arrived, two or three days at least.

"But how can we hold out," Nazleen asked, "if they have such terrible weapons?"

The man drew himself up proudly. "Milady, Denra could hold out for a year, even against them. We have our own spring inside the walls to provide water, and the storehouses are filled with food. Neither those guns of theirs nor the things they throw through the air can penetrate thick stone walls."

But Nazleen wondered. Perhaps they had even more terrible weapons they hadn't used yet.

The man who had returned from battle never thought to tell Nazleen that her brother was alive. He didn't know that Nazleen believed him to be dead, and Miklav, who did know, simply hadn't given it any thought as he struggled to formulate a plan that would turn defeat into victory.

A deep, cold anger settled over Nazleen as the old fortress rang with preparations for a seige. A large part of that anger was directed at herself. She was the one whose journey here had brought about the war—and Haslik's death. She was the one who had ignored Miklav's warnings when they might have defeated their enemy before reinforcements could arrive. And she was the one who had failed her people.

The other part of that anger was directed at

Zaktar. They were kin, part of an ancient and honorable heritage, sharers of the same blood, worshippers of the same sacred fire. If she had betrayed Hamloor with her foolish idealism, he had betrayed all Cerecians by using the fire to conquer instead of to defend.

As the retreating Warriors straggled back into Denra, Nazleen sat in the Warrior Chief's quarters practicing the exercises that would enable her to use the fire. Somehow, she would defeat this man who would destroy her realm.

When the Hamloorian Warriors had retreated beyond the tiny Tren village, Zaktar called a halt. By now the Kapti army had arrived, and he needed to confer with their commander. After assembling the village elders, he was fortunate enough to find one who spoke passable Cerecian, owing to a strong Cerecian influence in his family. Although he didn't know it, this was the same man who had journeyed to the compound to inform the Sisterhood of the Warrior army's march to the desert.

Zaktar carefully explained to the man that no harm would come to the villagers. He said that he would be leaving a few men there to guarantee the villagers' neutrality and also to guard the prisoners they had taken.

After that, he and the Kapti commander, a grizzled old veteran for whom Zaktar had great respect, began to discuss their plans for taking Denra. Since both men had spent the past several hours riding in jeppas, they decided to stretch their legs as they formulated their plans.

Just behind the little houses that faced the village

square were lush pastures where the Trens kept their ponies and livestock. Zaktar was describing the fortress to the Kapti commander when he suddenly stopped in the middle of a sentence and stared at the beautiful white mare grazing amidst a group of ugly ponies.

Nazleen had been temporarily thrust to the back of his mind under the pressures of more immediate problems, but now she filled it once again. Loreth and Haslik had said she would probably have sought shelter in a Tren village on the way to Denra. Could she be here even now?

Quickly, he explained to the puzzled Kapti commander about the woman he had yet to really see, but whose image filled his mind. Then he hurried back to find the man who spoke Cerecian.

The old Tren looked at the Fire Warrior's tense face and shivered a bit as he shook his head. "No, the Liege isn't here. She *was* here, but she has gone. We are proud to be caring for her horse."

"Where did she go?"

"To Denra," was the reply.

The Kapti commander, hearing this exchange and noting the look on Zaktar's face, knew that the plans they'd just been discussing would have to be changed. He liked Zaktar and knew his family well. He also knew, of course, about Zaktar's "mistake" years ago (although he privately thought that expecting healthy men to remain celibate was the equivalent of asking birds not to sing), and he suspected that the great Fire Warrior was about to run afoul of his Pavla once more. Of course, this woman *was* Cerecian, but she was also the ruler of a people with whom they were now at war.

Zaktar stared hard at the old man, tempted to demand that all houses in the village be searched immediately, but in the end two things prevented him from issuing that order. First of all, it would be an insult to the man to disbelieve him, and secondly, he was sure that Miklav would not have permitted her to remain here in harm's way.

The only question in his mind was whether Miklav had sufficient faith in the impregnability of Denra that he would have kept her there.

The next morning, Zaktar and the Kapti commander stood on a hillside not far from the fortress and peered through their glasses at those great stone walls.

"You know," said the Kapti, "it's almost a shame to destroy something like that. We once had such fortresses, but they were reduced to rubble when I was a little boy because no one wanted reminders of the past like that."

"We can't destroy it," Zaktar stated. "She may be inside."

"Yes," the man said, "there's that, too."

Both men knew that the mighty fortress could not long withstand their bombardment, but they could understand how the Warrior Chief might believe otherwise. As yet, they hadn't used the heavy artillery that had accompanied the Kapti army; there'd been no need for it.

As soon as he rode through Denra's gate, Miklav's eyes went to the windows of his personal quarters. She wasn't there, and he wondered if she had gussed that he wouldn't want to have her see him in retreat.

All around him, his men seemed to let go of their fear as they entered the fortress. Only Miklav himself knew that Denra couldn't hold out forever. His instincts told him that they hadn't yet seen all the arsenal in the enemy's possession.

He let his mind fill up for a moment with images of her, and in that moment Miklav came as close as he ever would to considering surrender. But as he had once told her, he was Warrior Chief first and a man second. He dismounted and went inside to make his plans.

Nazleen came out of her trance at the sound of insistent rapping on the door of Miklav's quarters. Tiny sparks of green fire flew from her fingertips, then vanished as she rose and went to answer the summons. At the same time, she suddenly became aware of the noise beyond the walls. A deep, powerful "whump" actually reverberated within the room itself.

Old Aktra stood there, his face grim. "Milady, the Warrior Chief has sent me to escort you to the dungeon. The fortress is under siege, but you will be safe there."

Another "whump" echoed through the room, punctuating his words. Nazleen nodded and followed him, pausing only to gather up her heavy cloak. A short time later, she was once again in that dank underground place, listening to the old Warrior's footsteps retreating into the distance.

She walked into the same cell she'd briefly occupied before and sat down on the hard bed. She was still feeling disoriented from her lengthy practice, so some time passed before she began to listen for sounds that might tell her how the battle was progressing.

But the sounds she heard were so faint that she couldn't identify them. She wondered what those strange sounds were that she'd heard from Miklav's quarters and shivered as she thought about their enemy's incredible weapons. Even now, she thought with surprising calm, the fortress could be tumbling down on her head.

If that were the case, then her only regret was that she hadn't had the opportunity to kill Zaktar.

Time passed, and still no sounds intruded into the chilled semidarkness. Several times she got up to light fresh torches and to stretch cramped muscles. Another time she felt a sudden twinge of pain in her belly and remembered the baby she carried. Somehow, though, she couldn't quite bring herself to believe in its existence.

Braced against the trunk and branch of a huge old tree, Zaktar kept his glasses trained on the fortress wall a half-kilometer away. They had been carefully shelling it for several hours, and huge cracks were already appearing in the rough stone surface. The stout wooden gate was also showing signs of splintering and could probably be destroyed with a few more hits. But Zaktar wanted an opening big enough to allow his men and the Kaptis to pour through in numbers large enough to end the siege quickly, so they were concentrating their fire on the walls to both sides of the gate.

Had he been willing to use their heaviest artillery, the walls would be down already, but the big guns were also less accurate on this difficult terrain.

Zaktar wanted to minimize damage to the buildings inside, one of which might well hold Nazleen.

The artillerymen were accurate. Only one shell had overshot its mark and landed somewhere inside. Not one Kapti or Fire Warrior had been so much as injured. The Hamloorians had fired their cannons regularly, but the old guns were hopelessly inaccurate and lacked any degree of mobility, their iron balls rolling harmlessly down the steep hillsides.

Atop the high walls, Zaktar could see great vats of something that was smoking, and he shook his head in bemusement. Did they believe for one minute that they would attempt to scale those walls? For one brief moment he felt sorry for the Warrior Chief. What would he himself do in such a situation? Would he be able to swallow his pride and surrender? He was glad that he wouldn't have to face that decision. Consciously or unconsciously, "death before dishonor" was the credo of every true warrior.

As yet another portion of the wall near the gate began to crumble, Zaktar's thoughts turned back to her. He set aside his glasses and closed his eyes to the destruction before him, emptying out his mind and then sending his thoughts across the walls. He knew it was unlikely that he could find her through all that stone, but he still tried until his head ached from the effort. He might have tried still longer had not a shout suddenly risen up from his men.

He came out of his trance just in time to see a huge section of the wall next to the gate collapse, taking the gate itself with it in a thundering cloud of dust and rubble.

Zaktar climbed down from the tree. Victory had come sooner than he'd expected.

From his vantage point within an interior tower of the fortress, Miklav stood with his senior aides and stared in open-mouthed disbelief as the wall and gate crumbled. He had never believed Denra could be breached this quickly and felt a fleeting but powerful envy of the Fire Warrior Zaktar, who had such weapons at his disposal.

Then he turned to his stunned aides, issued a series of orders and hurried from the tower. Before he joined his men in their final battle, he had one last matter to take care of.

Nazleen frowned as she got up once more from the hard bed. A short time ago some sound had penetrated to the dungeon, but she'd been unable to identify it. Now she heard more distinct noises, echoing through the subterranean hallways. Footsteps? No. As they came closer, she was sure it was the clip-clop of a horse's hooves. She ran out of the cell and was still trying to determine where the sound was coming from when Miklav suddenly appeared at the far end of the long corridor, leading a large gray mare.

Her gaze went from him to the mare and back again—and she knew. "Denra has fallen."

Miklav nodded. "You must leave now. There's a secret passageway that will take you under the fortress walls to a place far from the battle. Just beyond it is a shallow stream. Keep the horse in the stream to hide its prints. About an hour's ride from here, the stream passes beneath the road to Fetezza.

By that time, it will be safe for you to take the road."

When she said nothing, he reached out tentatively to stroke her face. "I am sorry, Milady. As Warrior Chief, I have failed you, but as a man, I have tried my best to be all you wanted. Perhaps it wasn't enough, but remember that I tried. May the ancient gods keep you safe and bring you a child to remember me by."

"No!" Nazleen startled even herself with her cry. "Come with me, Miklav! If Denra has fallen, you must get away to fight from Fetezza."

He shook his head slowly. "No, Milady, I will fight here. Gundra, the commander of Fetezza, is a good man with the capacity for greatness. He is my choice to be the next Warrior Chief, and the decision to fight on must be his."

He bent to kiss her, then groaned, pulled her roughly into his arms and kissed her again.

As soon as Zaktar had assured himself that victory was theirs, he plunged through a doorway into the main building of the fortress. There, in the cool silence with the final battle sounds dying away outside, he sent out his thoughts once more.

Very faintly, he sensed something. Following that elusive sensation, he ran along empty hallways, pausing at intersecting corridors to check again. He ran down several flights of stairs, with the feeling growing ever stronger. Even in his haste, he was careful to reach out gently, lest he hurt her again.

Then, at the bottom of a narrow stone staircase that led to what appeared to be a dungeon, he heard faint voices echoing from the walls. He crept forward slowly now, reining in his thoughts as he strained to hear the voices more clearly. One was male, the other female, and there was another noise that sounded like a horse's hooves striking stone. Then he reached another intersection and saw them.

She turned first, obviously having sensed his presence. Her green eyes widened as she saw him. He had only a moment to see that she was even more beautiful than his dream images, and then the man with her turned also.

"Tell him to put down his gun!" Zaktar shouted. "I won't harm either of you!"

Nazleen was so stunned at the sight of the Fire Warrior from her visions that Miklav had raised his rifle before she put a hand on his arm.

"Don't, Miklav! It's Zaktar! He says he won't harm us."

Miklav glanced at her briefly, and for a moment she thought he would do as she asked. But then he pushed her away from him, trying to get her behind both him and the horse, and raised the rifle.

A shot rang out, echoing loudly through the corridor, and then Miklav crumpled to the floor in a haze of green fire.

Nazleen stared from Miklav to the man who stood at the other end of the corridor, green sparks flying from his fingertips. Behind her, the terrified mare thundered off.

Her amazement at seeing him in the flesh at last vanished beneath that cold rage. He spoke her name and took a few steps toward her, but she ignored him and turned herself inward, summoning the fire. When she felt that tingling heat spreading through her to her fingertips, she raised her arm and pointed at him.

Zaktar saw those blazing green eyes, watched her raise her arm and knew what she was going to attempt. "No!"

But the fire leapt out and instinctively he parried it, striking out himself but still struggling to control its force. The space between them was filled with a shimmering haze of green, more vivid than anything he'd ever seen.

Then the fire struck him, sending wracking pain through his body and buckling his knees. As he fell to the floor, he saw her collapse into a lifeless heap of green.

His agonized "No!" rang out through the otherwise silent dungeon.

Loreth was at the gate to the compound when the truck arrived. She'd received the news earlier from two Fire Warriors who'd come in a smaller vehicle. Denra had fallen, Miklav was dead, and Nazleen was near death from a fire battle with Zaktar.

The passenger door opened first, and Zaktar slowly got out of the truck. That he was still in pain was obvious, but he followed the driver around to the back of the vehicle, then, when the doors had been opened, stood there as two more Fire Warriors who'd been in the back carefully brought out a stretcher.

Loreth gasped as she saw the still, pale face. She had been trying to prepare herself for this sight, but seeing the pallor of approaching death on one whose fair skin had always glowed with good health still came as a horrible shock.

She tore her gaze away from Nazleen's face to meet Zaktar's dark green eyes. She was ready to condemn him to eternal banishment from the fire, but the curse died in her throat. Never had she seen such anguish on a face. If Nazleen looked to be near death, Zaktar looked as though he would truly welcome it.

The stretcher was carried into the compound, and Zaktar stumbled along behind it, both unable to look at that pale, delicate face and unable to stay away.

How could he justify this? He was the greatest wielder of the fire among all their people. They all said that his control was nearly superhuman. But if she died, the fault was no one's but his.

And even if, the gods willing, she lived, she would hate him forever for having killed Miklav—and she'd be justified in doing so. He could have merely stunned the Warrior Chief; there'd been time to gauge his power carefully. He'd chosen to kill the Warrior Chief, because Miklav had the woman he wanted.

They carried her into a room where several older women, the Healers, awaited her. Their own Healer was overburdened with treating wounds just now, and he'd been afraid to work on a woman in any event. But he'd also expressed the opinion, shared by the Kaptis' doctors, that there was no hope.

Zaktar hesitated at the door, not wanting to leave her but knowing that his presence could interfere with the Healers' work. Then Loreth saw him and took his arm to lead him away.

She kept a hand on his arm until they had reached her suite, where she sent a young girl for tea and cakes. Both of them sat in silence for the few minutes it took the Novice to return with the refreshments. Loreth ordered him to eat.

"If you're going to be any use at all, you must regain your strength, Zaktar."

Obediently, he picked up a small cake, noticing disinterestedly that his hand trembled.

"Do you think she will live?" he asked, knowing that she couldn't answer.

"Yes, I think she will. I think it because I believe in the Augury, and I would have foreseen her death."

Zaktar wasn't much comforted by that, although he took care not to let the Pavla see that. A few silly old men among them still held Auguries, but even they seemed to think of them as being more rituals than predictions of the future.

Then, in a sudden burst of anger, he glared at her. "You said that none of the Sisters could wield the fire anymore."

Loreth recoiled slightly from the force of his anger, but her voice was calm and sad. "Yes, I know—and I believed that to be true. But Nazleen had always gone her own way. Because she isn't truly a Sister, she doesn't always feel bound by our rules and traditions. She must have been practicing on her own. The required exercises are well-known to us; we simply haven't used them since the signing of the Compact."

After that single violent outburst, Zaktar had

sunk back to despondency. "Should I leave here?" he asked. "Could my presence harm her in any way?"

Loreth regarded him silently for a moment. Despite the fact that this man had killed one person she loved and put another at death's door, she still liked him. If there had been an element of good in Miklav, there was, perhaps, an element of bad in Zaktar—reverse images—but Zaktar, she believed, had it in him to be a great man and furthermore was proving it now in his anguish.

"No," she said at length, "I think you must stay. She will need you, even if she won't admit it. Hamloor is in chaos. Someone must make decisions, and for the moment there is no one else."

"Haslik has gone to Fetezza. He said that it was well-known that the commander there was Miklav's choice to succeed him, and I have asked him to carry the message that we have no desire to continue this war. As a show of good faith, I have already sent the Kapti troops back across the desert. The few who remain are guarding the remnants of Miklav's army and working with them to rebuild the fortress."

"I would like to see those fortresses abandoned," Loreth stated.

"So would I, but such changes cannot happen quickly without causing great turmoil in your society."

Loreth smiled. "I think my faith in you is being justified, Zaktar."

"Do you forgive me for what I did to Nazleen?"

"It isn't for me to forgive you; you must forgive yourself. And the only way you will be able to do that is to stay here and help rebuild what has been destroyed, even if Nazleen wants you gone. Which she certainly will," Loreth added with a sigh.

For the first time since his fire-battle with Nazleen, Zaktar began to relax a bit. Loreth seemed so very sure that she would survive.

"I would like to see Haslik become Warrior Chief," Zaktar admitted.

"Then declare him to be so," Loreth replied. "He would be an excellent choice."

"But Miklav supposedly wanted the Fetezza commander."

"Miklav is gone, and you are the victor. Should I have to tell you, a Warrior yourself, what that means?"

"No, such a decision must come from the Warriors. To impose someone on them would be a mistake that your people would pay for when we are gone."

Loreth managed to hide her smile. Zaktar was truly all she had believed him to be. If only Nazleen could be made to see that.

"I didn't have to kill Miklav," Zaktar said suddenly, not looking at her and speaking in a voice so low she had to strain to hear him. "I could have merely stunned him."

"Then you must live with that knowledge," Loreth stated. And so must I, she thought.

"But it is my belief that Miklav would have fought to the death one way or the other. He would never have given up his power or Nazleen."

"She will always hate me for having killed him."

"When she is herself again, she will have no time to hate you. She is the Liege, and her power will be greater than ever, no matter who becomes Warrior Chief. The Warriors have been defeated, and they will therefore be discredited in the eyes of the people. She is the one who will have to pull our people together."

Zaktar thought about that, then realized that even though he knew he wanted her, he also didn't really know her. "What is she like?"

Loreth chuckled softly. "A strange question, coming from a man who says he loves her."

"I didn't say that I love her. I said that I want her. I think there's a difference."

Loreth smiled and nodded. "Nazleen is not easy to describe, even for someone who has known her from childhood as I have. She's highly intelligent, with that rare kind of mind that always seeks learning and then learns quickly. She can have a wonderful sense of humor, an ability to see ironies in things others often miss. And there is much kindness and compassion in her, as well as the idealism that Miklav so deplored.

"But she is also imperious, arrogant and often intolerant of those who disagree with her. She has been trained from birth to rule, and since she is blessed with great beauty, she has always been indulged by those around her. Even here, she received special treatment, despite the Pavla's orders to the contrary.

"She is also one of those rare people—or rare among us, at least—to whom the fire reaches out. Perhaps that is why she was able to learn so quickly how to wield it in battle."

"That is rare among us, also." Zaktar nodded, refraining from mentioning that he too was one of the chosen few—to his Pavla's unending displeasure.

At that moment there was a knock at the door, and when Loreth gave permission, the Chief Healer walked in, her handsome face taut with worry. The hope that Zaktar had so briefly allowed to flourish withered and died as he stared at her.

"We have done all that we can for the moment, Pavla, but I fear the worst. She has already lost the baby, and I think perhaps she has lost the will to live."

Loreth stifled a sob, and Zaktar got to his feet, turning away from them as he struggled to control himself. If he hadn't killed Miklav, she wouldn't be his, but she would still be alive. He had no doubt that she'd given up because Miklav was dead.

"No!" said Loreth succinctly as she grasped his arm and pulled him around to face her. "That isn't true! She didn't love Miklav. I think she cared for him in her own way, but she would not choose to die because of him."

Zaktar stared at her, not at all surprised or angered at her intrusion into his thoughts. "Then why would she want to die?"

"She has been through a great deal. She didn't want war, and she undoubtedly believes that war came because of her."

Zaktar frowned. "I don't understand. Why would she think that?" Then his frown deepened. "You mean that she thinks it started because of that incident on the road to Denra when she got away?"

When Loreth nodded, Zaktar explained that she was wrong, that Miklav had deliberately provoked an incident in the desert before that and that his troops were already on the move to attack the camp before that incident had ever occurred.

"Then she must be told that when she recovers."

But Zaktar thought there was less certainty now in the Pavla's voice.

Throughout the long night that followed, Zaktar remained in the Pavla's quarters, comforted by her presence and her continued belief that Nazleen would recover. He wanted desperately to go to her, but both the Pavla and the Chief Healer forbade it. The powerful emotions he would bring with him could tilt the precarious balance between life and death. Not even Loreth would go for the same reason.

In the early dawn hours the Chief Healer returned once more, her expression even graver. "The rhythms of life are very low," she said sadly. "I think it can make no difference if you go to her now."

Zaktar's head dropped into his hands. Loreth, however, drew herself up determinedly.

"Then I know what we must do. Listen to me, Zaktar. I didn't tell you this before because I don't understand it, but we must take the chance now.

"In the Augury, I saw you carry her into the sacred fire-pool. We all know that to enter the fire when one is not well is very dangerous because of the great energies there. Only Healers can channel the fire to heal. For that reason, I didn't connect that vision with her illness, but I now believe that I was being shown the way to save her."

"Pavla," the Healer said in a shocked tone, "she

will surely die."

"She will die in any event," Loreth snapped. "We've always known that there are probably rituals that were lost to us, and perhaps this is one of them."

Zaktar stared at her warily. "We too have always believed that only the healthy can go into the fire."

Their eyes met, and Zaktar felt again her unshakable faith. Slowly, he nodded. "Her death is on my hands in any event. Take me to her."

They went to the chamber where Nazleen lay surrounded by the other Healers. Both Loreth and Zaktar were shocked at her appearance. If she had looked deathly ill before, she now seemed totally devoid of life. Zaktar reached out to take her wrist. For a moment, he thought there was no pulse at all, but then he felt it, faint and irregular. Quickly, he slid his arms beneath her and picked her up, blankets and all.

"Zaktar, perhaps you should let us carry her to the pool. You are not entirely well yourself."

He shook his head as he started toward the door. He knew that Loreth was also warning him that he might not survive immersion in the fire either. It took the last of his strength to carry her, but now that she was in his arms, he would not let her go.

They hurried through the maze of corridors to the secret entrance to the tunnel. Loreth opened it, picked up a torch, then led the way. Zaktar kept his eyes focused on the Pavla, drawing hope from her faith as she opened her mind to him.

Loreth stopped at the mouth of the cave, where the torch's light was dimmed by the green glow of the pool. She reached out to touch his arm, then let her fingers rest briefly on the pale face within the blankets.

"May the sacred fire be your ally," she whispered.

Then she stood there as Zaktar carried Nazleen over to the edge of the pool and quickly stripped off his clothing, then knelt to unwrap her from the blankets. Two long, thin threads of fire reached out toward them as he picked her up and stepped into the pool.

Loreth watched her vision come true, then left them there and walked back through the tunnel, her faith stronger than ever.

CHAPTER TEN

ZAKTAR UNWRAPPED THE BLANKETS THAT COVERED
Nazleen and stared at the slender but unquestiona-
bly female body that was now exposed to him. He
was immediately shamed by the need that rose in
him and hurriedly bent to lift her into his arms.
Only when he had straightened up again did he see
the twin tendrils of fire that had reached out to
them both. He hoped it was a good omen and
stepped unhesitatingly into the fire-pool.

At first, the feeling was the same as always—a
deep, deep warmth and a sense of limitless, eternal
forces surrounding them—but then he realized
there was a difference. Although he was slowly
losing his self-awareness, he was not losing his
awareness of her.

He didn't know any words to say, so he concentrated instead on the woman he held, on his desire for her to live. Gradually, she became weightless in his arms but still very much there.

The vast energy surrounding them seemed different, still as powerful but changed in some subtle sort of way. For a while, he thought he felt something flowing out of him and into her, and he seemed to sense something entering him in return. There was an urgency to the feeling, a raw hunger.

After some unknown interval, he knew it was time to leave the fire without questioning how it was that he knew. He stepped from the pool, still feeling her more as an extension of himself than as a burden. He didn't look at her until he had laid her down again on the blanket. They were both bathed in a pale, shimmering green. He knelt beside her and picked up her limp wrist, knowing even before he felt her pulse that she was still alive. Then, as he stared at her, her hand moved slightly in his, and her fingers grasped his weakly.

He stayed there until her hand slipped away and she murmured softly and curled up on her side. Then he staggered to his feet and got the other blankets. He lay down beside her, covered them both and drew her carefully into his arms. He was asleep within moments.

Loreth crept quietly into Nazleen's chamber, signaling the young Sister who was keeping watch over her to leave them. Then she drew up a chair close to the bed and stared at her former pupil.

What have I done? she asked silently. I know that something has happened beyond the restoration of life, but I don't know what it is.

She'd just come from an unused wing of the residence that had been turned over to the Fire Warriors. There she'd found Zaktar, also deep in sleep, being watched over by a youthful Fire Warrior whose thoughts had been transparent to her. He too knew that something strange had happened in the fire-pool.

Loreth had gone to the cave after several hours had passed and had found the pair, wrapped in blankets and entwined in each other's arms. Ghostly tendrils of fire still encircled them. At first she'd feared they might both be dead, a lapse of faith she now regretted, but she'd quickly seen that they were both merely asleep.

Though the fire-pool warmed that which it touched, the rest of the cave was cold and damp, and Loreth had decided that they must be moved. After gently shaking them and receiving nothing more than murmurs of protest, she'd summoned some Fire Warriors and had them carried back through the tunnel. The gossamer fire-threads had vanished as soon as they were separated, and each of them had moaned in protest.

The Chief Healer had examined them and pronounced that they were merely in a deep sleep similar to the drugged sleep of those who remained in the fire-pool during an Augury. They would, she said, awaken in their own good time.

They had been put together in the chamber where Nazleen had earlier lain near death, but upon further consideration Loreth had decided to separate them. Allowing Nazleen to awaken in bed with the man she regarded as her greatest enemy could not be helpful to her recovery.

But she'd nearly changed her mind when they both protested their separation once more.

Nazleen struggled against the force that seemed to be drawing her up from some fathomless place. Vague, elusive memories slipped through her brain —sensations of warmth and some deep, powerful force far more powerful than anything she'd felt before.

She felt the memory of a touch—not the fire, but a human touch, also strong and gripping her tightly. This memory seemed to summon a different sort of heat within her.

There were other, disconnected memories—the sound of horse's hooves striking stone, a rifle shot, and the fire all around her. It was not gentle and welcoming, but horribly violent and painful. She cried out against that memory and put out her hand to ward off the bad fire, then felt it grasped by another, warm and soft.

"Nazleen, it's Loreth. You're safe. You're at Cerece."

Nazleen heard every word separately and put them together very slowly, but it was that dear, familiar voice, more than the words, that drew her up into the light again. With great effort she opened her eyes.

Loreth was bent close, smiling at her, but for one brief moment Nazleen felt fear coming from her.

"I'm all right," she said, pronouncing each word carefully in a thin voice that sounded strange even to her own ears.

"Yes," Loreth said, smiling now and pressing

Nazleen's hand to her cheek.

"How . . . ?" Nazleen asked, then temporarily lost her chain of thought as some of those memories intruded once more. "How did I get here? I was . . ." The memories flooded back, drowning her in pain. She ended with a cry.

Loreth squeezed her hand gently, and the pain subsided.

"Miklav is dead," Nazleen said. "Zaktar killed him, and I . . . Did I kill Zaktar?"

Nazleen faltered again, and Loreth saw confusion on her face.

"Zaktar," Nazleen repeated uncertainly.

"He is alive," Loreth said, guarding her thoughts so that she revealed nothing more.

She let Nazleen lay there in silence for a few moments, then Nazleen's hand fluttered down to touch the blanket covering her belly.

"The baby has died," she said softly but certainly.

"Yes," Loreth admitted.

"Miklav wanted the baby to live, so I would remember him."

"Miklav lives on in his other children, and you will not forget him," Loreth said gently.

But Nazleen's eyes had fluttered shut again, and her breathing had slowed. Loreth was about to get up and leave when Nazleen's low voice stopped her.

"Zaktar," she whispered again—and this time, her tone was caressing.

Nazleen sat propped up against the pillows, sipping the herb and vegetable broth that Loreth held to her lips. After she had drunk nearly all of it, she fixed Loreth with a look that was surprisingly close to the Liege at her most imperious.

"Tell me all."

Loreth hid a smile. The voice might be weaker, but there was no doubting that this was the Liege of Hamloor.

So she did as commanded, telling her about the fall of Denra, which Nazleen now remembered.

"The invaders have gone back across the desert to prove that they have no desire to continue the war. Haslik has gone to Fetezza and then to the palace to . . ."

"Haslik?" Nazleen stared at her, and for a moment Loreth thought that somehow she'd forgotten her brother.

"Haslik is dead. Zaktar killed him. He attacked when I was on the way from here to Denra before the battle."

Loreth then realized what must have happened. "No, he's very much alive. He came back here after that. Zaktar sent him."

"I saw him, Loreth. He was dead! They were all dead."

Loreth shook her head. "The Fire Warriors struck only to disable them. Some did die, but Haslik was among those who lived."

Nazleen searched her face carefully, and Loreth let her into her mind, knowing that she needed reassurance. She was rewarded by the first smile Nazleen had given her.

"Alive—and unharmed?"

Loreth nodded. "He should have reached the

palace by now. Captain Mevak stayed here to be assured that you were well, then went to carry the news to him. I am sure Haslik will be here as soon as possible."

Nazleen smiled again, but Loreth could see that the smile was more tentative. She was tiring again. The Pavla removed some of the pillows and let her slip down beneath the covers. Nazleen's eyes had closed, but once more she spoke almost inaudibly.

"How did I get here?"

Loreth considered the question, then spoke the truth. "Zaktar brought you."

Once again, Nazleen whispered his name.

"You seem to be yourself again." Loreth smiled at the tawny-haired giant who awaited her in her reception room.

Zaktar nodded, but Loreth could detect a small uncertainty in him. They had not discussed what had happened in the fire-pool, and Loreth suspected that Zaktar was himself confused about it.

"How is she? When can I see her?"

"She is awake more now but still very weak, and you cannot see her until she herself requests it." In her mind Loreth could hear Nazleen whispering his name.

"That will never happen," he said disgustedly.

"Oh, it will. After all, she is the Liege and you have just conquered her army. Sooner or later she will find it necessary to see you, whatever her personal feelings."

He sighed. "Well, at least she knows I didn't kill Haslik."

"Yes, you do have that in your favor," Loreth responded drily.

"Dammit, Loreth, I need to see her!"

"Why? What is so important?"

He hesitated, uncertainty creeping across his handsome face once more. "I don't know." Then he began to pace about the room, reminding Loreth of Nazleen in his restlessness.

"Maybe I'd better go back to the camp for a few days. The equipment needed to excavate the ruins will be arriving soon, and the gods only know how many more people with it. I've also decided to send the Kapti army home. The last of them left Denra yesterday. The fortress has been turned over temporarily to that Captain Mevak, Haslik's friend. He seems trustworthy."

"But the Fire Warriors will remain?"

He grinned suddenly. "I'm not sure they'd go even if I ordered them. Do you want some of them to remain here?"

Loreth considered that, not for the first time. The Fire Warriors and the Sisters were still uncomfortable with each other, generally keeping to their separate quarters, but she'd already observed one of the Novices walking in the gardens with the youngest of the Fire Warriors. The Pavla knew what the future held, and that knowledge hadn't required another Augury.

"They are not needed to guard us, but they are welcome to stay."

Zaktar smiled again. "One of the rules shared by both of us will soon be broken, Pavla."

"Not soon, I think—but, yes, it will happen."

And that, she knew, was the meaning of that

strangest part of the Augury—the end of the Sisterhood but without regret.

Nazleen lifted her face to the bright, warm sun. This was the first day she'd been well enough to venture out into the gardens, but she could feel her strength returning. She was already beginning to grow impatient, and that, she thought, was a good sign.

She could even feel the lure of the sacred fire, although she knew it would be quite a while before she could enter it again. But she'd also felt a strange fear of it, too. Loreth had said that perhaps it was a result of her having wielded it in battle.

She began to doze in her comfortable chair, lulled by the scent of herbs and summer flowers and the cheerful songs of the birds that flocked to feeders in the gardens. Haslik was due to arrive this day; word had come from the palace. At her request he would be bringing three of her most trusted Advisors with him. She was ever mindful of the need to keep them firmly under control, no matter how trusted they were. Advisors were by their very nature ambitious; otherwise, they would never have become Advisors.

She had almost drifted into sleep when from beyond one of the tall hedges she heard high, girlish laughter, followed by a lower but still youthful male voice speaking the Cerecian tongue with a strange accent.

She snapped awake, staring toward the unseen couple. Loreth had told her that some of the Fire Warriors were still here, although Zaktar had gone. Nazleen disapproved, but since Cerece was under the control of the Pavla, there was nothing she could do about it.

Knowing it was impolite, she still strained to hear the couple's words as they passed by on the other side of the thick hedge. They spoke in low tones, so Nazleen caught only a few words: ". . . changes," ". . . says it must be slow," then a full sentence as the young man spoke in disgust. "Pavlas are always slow to change."

In spite of herself, Nazleen smiled. His statement reminded her of those made by every Novice from time immemorial, and as far as she was concerned, this Pavla was changing entirely too fast. The very fact that those two were strolling about the garden was proof of that.

She continued to doze as the voices trailed off into the distance, and her thoughts drifted to the future of the Sisterhood. If that Novice was any indication, the young would have no problem accepting the presence of males, and accepting their presence would lead inevitably to accepting them in more intimate ways.

Those thoughts led eventually into that dark area she continued to avoid—Zaktar. She saw him suddenly as she had seen him in the dungeon—tall, powerful, his green eyes flashing, the fire sparking from his fingertips. Her eyes snapped open, but just before they did, she saw him another way, his eyes glittering with a different kind of light as he seemed to be bending over her.

When she had assured herself that he wasn't there, she drifted off again, but when another sound intruded, she opened her eyes to see the young couple, obviously surprised themselves as they came around a corner of the hedge. Nazleen recognized the girl—she was a distant relative—but her gaze fixed itself on the tall, slim youth at her side. He wore that hated green uniform, and his green eyes grew somewhat wary as he stared at her.

"I'm sorry, Sister," the girl apologized. "I didn't know you were here. We're all happy that you are feeling better now."

Then, when she realized that Nazleen's eyes were still fixed on the young man at her side, her face colored briefly. "Sister, this is Taka. He's one of the Fire Warriors that the Pavla invited to stay with us for a while."

She then turned to the youth. "This is Sister Nazleen, who is also the Liege of Hamloor."

The young man made a slight bow, not unlike the one given her by her own Warriors, although perhaps less practiced. He spoke somewhat hesitatingly. "We are also happy that you're well, Sister Nazleen." The title came after a brief hesitation, indicating that he was unsure of just how to address her.

"Thank you," Nazleen said, still scrutinizing him closely. He was clearly uneasy and therefore might be the perfect one to answer her questions. He'd be less likely to lie, and she more likely to notice if he did.

"I am curious about your people, Taka. Because of my illness, I've not had the opportunity to learn much about you. Tell me where you come from—your history."

Taka seemed to require no further prodding, and at her invitation, both of them took seats near her. He told her of his home beyond the Fire Mountains, then explained the history of his people. Nazleen noted that the youth had appeared in the land of the Kaptis at about the same time as Stakezti had appeared here. Taka nodded.

"We believe they both may have come from the village whose ruins we found just on the other side of the desert. They may have been the only survivors when the Fire Mountains erupted."

Then he went on, telling her of their enslavement by the Kapti and of their eventual uprising and victory. Only at one point did he become emotional.

"The Kaptis treated us as though we were prize animals, to be bred for our uniqueness."

Nazleen said nothing, but privately she thought that given that history, it was strange indeed that they seemed to get along so well with these Kaptis.

He had gone on to talk about the great war in which the Cerecians had thrown off their bonds. Then as he started to talk about the advances of their joint society, Nazleen interrupted to ask a question.

"What made you decide to come here?"

"There were several reasons. We fuel our engines with a crystal we call gewa, and it is becoming very scarce. So we hoped to find a new source, and we also hoped to find more of our people."

Then he gave her a boyish grin. "Some say it was also because the Pavla had decided he'd better find something for Zaktar to do before he got into trouble again."

At the mention of that name, Nazleen felt a tremor, but she managed to hide it from the couple.

"Why should he get into trouble?" she asked,

284

very much aware of the fact that she was treading on dangerous ground now.

"Zaktar is always restless, and he was seeking a new adventure once he'd finished designing his flying machine. He's our greatest hero," the boy stated proudly. "No one can fight like him."

Then he looked away quickly, his fair skin flushing brightly. Obviously he knew what had happened in the dungeons of Denra.

She declined to pursue his remarks and instead asked what a flying machine was. Did he mean that great balloon she'd seen?

No, Taka replied, a flying machine was different, shaped like a bird and not dependent on the wind currents at all. It was fueled by this gewa, too, and it was currently being built in their factories.

Nazleen was both fascinated and a bit horrified. Obviously, advanced weapons weren't all these people had. She was growing tired again, but she plied him with more questions about their machinery. He told her of things that not even Haslik could have dreamed of—homes and buildings and even streets lit by something he called electricity that also provided heat and ran all sorts of machinery, vehicles that moved by themselves such as the one she'd ridden in but hadn't seen, things called radios, which she realized were the boxes the scouts had reported that carried voices over very long distances, sometimes using tall things like needles pointed at the sky. He said they had a way of making pictures move and that soon there would be smaller machines that would do this in individual homes instead of large theaters.

She asked about agriculture and medicine and

heard wondrous tales there, too. There was no doubt in her mind that the young man was telling the truth, no matter how fantastic his tales.

Then she asked one final question as she began to grow tired. "You said that your Pavla is male. But what about women? Can they also be Pavla?"

He looked at her in surprise. "There are no women among us. There never have been, just as there have never been males here. Our scientists believe it is because our traits are gender-linked."

Nazleen didn't understand what that meant, but at the moment she didn't care. "And so you were seeking more of your people because your numbers, too, are diminishing?"

"Yes, Sister. Like you, we choose celibacy. In our case, it is because of the way the Kapti once bred us. Our numbers are declining because the gene pool has been diluted too much."

Nazleen nodded, knowing that she would hear more of this in due time. She thanked him for the information, then let them go, watching as they walked away. Their hands brushed accidentally, and both of them jerked away as though burned.

So the female half of their people had finally met the male half. No wonder Loreth had allowed them to remain here. To have tried to prevent it would be like trying to stop the arrival of spring.

And as she slipped into sleep, a strange half-memory stirred again—the fire-pool, something strong gripping her, something deep and powerful flowing through her.

Nazleen awoke as she felt a light touch, then opened her eyes to stare into the concerned dark eyes of her brother, who was carefully tucking a blanket around her shoulders. She must have dozed most of the afternoon; the garden was now in shadow.

"Haslik!" she cried, reaching out to him. "I thought you were dead!"

He hugged her, then finally backed off a bit to scrutinize her carefully. "You look so pale, Nazzie. How do you feel?"

"Much better now," she stated firmly. "I'm sure I'll be fine in a day or two."

Haslik knew from his talk with the Chief Healer that it wouldn't be that soon, but he also knew that if will alone could make her well, Nazleen would be herself very quickly indeed.

"Have my Advisors come with you?"

He nodded. "But I asked them to let me see you alone first."

"Good." She smiled, taking one of his hands in each of hers. "Oh, Haslik, I was so sure you were dead. I climbed up that hill, and I saw all of you lying there."

He saw her face cloud with anger and nodded solemnly. "When I came to, I was so worried about you, alone in the woods like that, but there was nothing I could do. If I'd told Zaktar of your presence, he would have gone after you, and at the time it seemed better for you to be lost in the woods than to be pursued by him."

"At the time?" she asked, thinking that it sounded as though he regretted that decision.

"Yes." He looked at her seriously. "Look, Nazzie, Loreth told me how you feel about him, but you're wrong. He's a good man, and he doesn't want war.

287

All they want from us is trade. We have plenty of that rock they call gewa—it's in caves all over the place—and they can give us their machines. They have incredible things, things I'd never even dreamed of."

She saw the eager look in his eyes and understood why he was so taken with Zaktar. "I know. I spoke earlier with a young Fire Warrior. But Haslik, have you forgotten that Zaktar killed Miklav and nearly killed you? And what about all the other Warriors who died because of him?"

"That was war, Nazzie. It wasn't murder. I'm sorry that Miklav and the others died. Some of them were my friends."

Nazleen couldn't understand that there was a difference. Death was death!

"Besides," Haslik went on, "Zaktar put himself at grave risk in order *not* to kill you and then brought you here so your life could be saved." He didn't tell her about the second time Zaktar had put himself at risk to save her. Loreth had told him about it but made him promise not to tell her. Haslik didn't quite understand what had happened and why it should be kept from her, but he trusted the Pavla's instincts in such matters.

"What do you mean? Put himself at grave risk?"

"When you struck with the fire, he had to assume you could kill him, and yet he held back enough to be sure he would only disable you. From what I've heard, Zaktar is the most powerful of all the Fire Warriors—and yet, here you are."

"No one knows what happens when fire meets fire," Nazleen scoffed. "For all we know, he might well have intended to kill me but couldn't."

"I don't believe that." Haslik, who had been among the ones who'd found the trio in the dungeon, could still remember the agony on Zaktar's face, how he'd cried her name over and over again as he fought to regain consciousness. Loreth had been right; she wasn't ready to hear that the Fire Warrior had saved her life.

"Loreth told me that Zaktar wants me to become Warrior Chief," he said instead, still surprised at this revelation.

Nazleen stared at him. "Why would he want that?"

"I think because he trusts me, and maybe because he knows by now that I'm more interested in science than in fighting."

"But Miklav chose Gundra. He told me that, just before Zaktar killed him." Bitterness made her voice taut.

"Miklav was trying to kill Zaktar," Haslik pointed out gently.

"If he's so good with the fire, as you say, he could have disabled Miklav, instead of killing him."

Haslik had nothing to say to that, since the same thought had also occurred to him. He suspected he knew why Zaktar had killed Miklav, but it wasn't a reason she would want to hear. Instead, he returned to the safer issue of a new Warrior Chief.

"Gundra knows, as we all did, that Miklav wanted him to be the next Warrior Chief. He's a lot like Miklav in many ways. He and I talked a lot when I was at Fetezza, and we both agree that maybe it's time to make some changes in the structure of the Warriors, especially in view of the changes to come."

He paused briefly. "There need to be many changes, Nazzie, and not just among the Warriors. I know you're too sick to be thinking much about this yet, but the new trade is going to change everything—and very quickly, too."

Nazleen saw the eager look on his face and knew that, like some of the Sisterhood, he too could not be held back. She asked what he knew of the Fire Warriors' and their allies' new machines, and when she learned that he actually knew about little but the weapons he'd seen, she told him what the young Fire Warrior had told her.

"A flying machine?" Haslik gasped, barely able to contain himself. "I've always dreamed of them. Some of the others even kidded me about wanting to build birds."

"Don't you see, Nazzie? This is the Golden Age you've talked about—and golden is a pretty good description for it, too, come to think of it." He reached out to touch her fiery golden hair.

"Cerecian gold."

Nazleen could not bring herself to prick his bubble of happiness. And when she met later with her Advisors, neither could she seem to bring them back down to reality, although with them she did try. Everyone, it seemed, was expecting fabulous things to happen, despite the fact that they'd just been defeated in war and had a huge army encamped in their territory.

She sorely missed Miklav. He would have lost no time in bringing them all back to reality. She thought about what he would have done and slowly came to the realization that she couldn't know. Miklav had been determined to die in battle, and so

he had. For him, life had been very simple—
victory or death—so he would never have faced the
difficult decisions she now faced.

For the first time, she felt a true sadness at his
death, not just anger at Zaktar for having killed
him. The Warrior Chief, in death as never in life,
had become a man to her—and a good man,
despite his many faults. That eternal conflict within
her when she thought about him was finally over.

Zaktar stood on a small rise, watching the work
at the ruins. A short distance away sat a sturdy little
jeppa, waiting to carry him back across the desert.
A week had passed, longer than he'd intended to
remain here.

He'd come back to learn that discoveries made
during his absence were leading the archaeologists
to suspect that the half-buried village they'd found
was actually only part of a much larger town,
perhaps even a city. The hardened lava and ash that
covered it had buried it unevenly. Some parts could
take years of careful work to uncover.

People and machinery swarmed over the site.
Not only the Kapti army had arrived; more and
more scientists, Kapti and Cerecian alike, had been
drawn to the discovery. Zaktar was very glad to be
able to leave the management of so many quarrel-
ing experts to Felka, their Chief Historian, who'd
been sent by the Pavla to supervise the dig.

On another hilltop across the way from where
Zaktar stood, a small cluster of Desert Trens
watched, too. They wouldn't come closer, because
the machinery frightened them, but it fascinated
them as well.

Just after his return, Kapti soldiers guarding the dig had discovered a small band of them, foraging nearby for herbs. With gestures and the few words of Hamloorian he'd picked up, Zaktar had told them that they could come and go as they always had so long as they didn't cause any trouble. Shortly thereafter, he'd received a visit from their Chieftain, who spoke passable Cerecian. After that, the Trens returned but left their weapons strapped to the saddles of those ugly creatures they rode.

With one final look at the slowly emerging homeland of his people, Zaktar strode down the hillside and climbed into the jeppa.

He'd been restless for days now, and yet he'd put off returning to the compound. His mind kept returning, in sleep as well as wakefulness, to their immersion in the fire-pool. Each time it did, he had the uneasy feeling that something more than a cure had happened there.

When he'd finally awakened, he'd immediately felt a sharp, aching sense of loss that still hadn't gone away. He could define it no further though, since it was unlike anything he'd ever experienced before.

He drove into the desert, his thoughts occupied with his plans. Trade had to be arranged as quickly as possible. Word had come over the radio relays that what had been believed to be a very large deposit of gewa at home had suddenly, inexplicably run out. Combined with a recent landslide and cave-in that had rendered another large mine useless for at least a year, this latest disaster meant serious problems. Gewa was the very basis of their modern society.

He'd told the Pavla and the Kapti Prime Minister that there should be no problem arranging trade, but his words were far more assured than his present thoughts. He'd kept the two men in the dark regarding the state of his relations with their future trading partners' Liege. If they knew how she felt about him, they'd order him home and send honey-tongued diplomats instead.

Surely she would be recovered sufficiently to give him at least a few moments now. If necessary, he'd be adamant with Loreth. But in truth, he'd be using the trade arrangements as an excuse to do what he wanted—needed—to do anyway.

Nazleen. He drew forth mental images of her as easily as always, except that they were no longer dream images. He saw that proud, imperious stance as she'd flung the fire at him, and he saw also that pale, fragile woman whose hand had so briefly clung to his. He wondered which one of them he would find at the compound.

"She's gone?" Zaktar stared at Loreth in dismay.

The Pavla nodded. "She returned to the palace yesterday. The Healers strongly advised against it, but she had already declared herself to be well—and that was the end of it. You will learn that at times the Liege of Hamloor listens to no one but herself."

"Is she well?" Zaktar asked, worried that she had left only in order to avoid him.

Loreth shrugged. "She has made a remarkable recovery, but she is still weak—in body, that is. Her spirit, on the other hand, has recovered quite completely."

Zaktar was annoyed. He'd spent the past few hours of his journey rehearsing every detail of his meeting with her.

"Well, then I shall go to the palace—that is, after you tell me what to expect."

Loreth smiled. "I have never been to the palace, but I think that I can probably advise you to some extent. It's unfortunate that Haslik has returned to Denra. He would have been your best source of information."

So Zaktar remained at the compound for a day and a night, talking to Loreth and asking questions. The fire-pool called to him, but he avoided it without quite understanding why. Then he drove to Denra to see Haslik.

He found he liked and respected Haslik even more than he had before. The two men shared a Warrior background and inquisitive minds and a talent for invention. Of course they also shared more than a passing interest in Nazleen.

Zaktar showed Haslik how to operate the jeppa, then rode with him as he drove happily along the roads near the fortress. They talked for hours, and Zaktar promised Haslik a jeppa as soon as one could be gotten. When they returned to Denra, the two men took it apart so that Haslik could understand how it worked. Most of the remaining Warriors watched them and asked questions, and Zaktar saw that many of them seemed more interested in gaining knowledge than in making war, especially the younger ones.

They told him that Miklav had stressed education, and although they spoke his name reverently, they didn't appear to hold any bitterness toward Zaktar.

Haslik had sent a Warrior to the palace to announce Zaktar's impending visit, and when Zaktar was ready to leave, he also suggested sending a Warrior with him so that his entrance into the city would be less frightening to the people. He also told Zaktar that Nazleen was quite fond of the man he'd chosen—a Captain Mevak—and that he might therefore be of help to Zaktar.

Zaktar agreed, although he had hoped to have Haslik himself come to the city. Since it was clear that Haslik was very busy at the fortress, he reluctantly set out with the Captain.

As they drove to the city, Zaktar began to appraise this tall, handsome Captain, who spoke fluent Cerecian and undoubtedly came from an aristocratic family. He was well-aware of the requirements of their damned Compact that the Liege must take her mate from among the Warriors. With Miklav now gone and the possibility that Haslik would become the new Chief, Zaktar couldn't help regarding Mevak as competition.

Clearly, the Compact—or at least that part of it—had to go. So too did Nazleen's disdain for what they called life-mating. Both Loreth and Haslik had told him about that. Zaktar was Cerecian, but he had been raised in a Kapti family and the Kapti had a very strong family structure. That seemed to Zaktar to be the natural order of things.

The two men drove down from the mountains into broad, fertile valleys that reminded him of his home. All along the way, field workers paused in their work to stare in awe at the sight of the jeppa, and those who were close enough also gaped unabashedly at the big, golden-haired man riding in it.

Zaktar had expected the city to be just that, and so he was shocked to see that although it sprawled over quite a large space, it was really no more than an extended village. No building was taller than two stories, although Mevak pointed with pride to a somewhat larger tower that had been constructed to honor the Compact. The streets were narrow and crowded with people and livestock and horse-drawn carts laden with all manner of goods.

Zaktar began to envision Cerecian and Kapti tourists coming to this place in large numbers and decided that they'd better discuss that, too. In fact, he now began to see that he had much to do here, and that pleased him. He'd feared that he would have no reason to remain here once he'd concluded a trade agreement—or rather that *he* would have a very good reason, but his Pavla would see it differently.

They were forced to creep along in the heavy traffic and consequently gathered quite a crowd of curious followers, but when Zaktar stared directly at any of them, not even his smile could prevent them from quickly averting their eyes. He wasn't sure if it was because he was the first male Cerecian they'd seen or because they had guessed who he was.

Then Mevak drew his attention to the palace. It was unmistakable, sitting as it did on the highest of the gentle hills amidst what looked like many acres of gardens and forest. It certainly looked far less forbidding than Denra, but he had a feeling it would be far more difficult to conquer.

Nazleen paced about amidst the splendor of the formal reception room. She knew that Zaktar was already in the city.

She was attired in her finest trappings of royalty, complete with the jewels and elaborate hairstyle she generally wore only on the most formal of occasions. Her maid had worked long and hard to erase any lingering traces of her recent illness, but powders and creams could not prevent the sudden weak spells that still came over her from time to time. She could only hope it wouldn't happen during her meeting with him.

She had considered surrounding herself with her Advisors, who could certainly look impressive as well, but in the end she'd decided to meet Zaktar alone. Most of the Advisors were still behaving like sycophants of a man they hadn't even met, and she had no intention of watching them make fools of themselves.

A great uneasiness hung over the palace these days, no doubt inspired by the Liege's own uneasiness. There was a strong sense that things were about to change, with or without the court's permission. Nazleen had decreed that her Advisors present her with a plan for coping with that change —one that would allow the people more say in their governing but still retain the court's power. Most of them had been reluctant, to say the least, and had gone away muttering about mob rule and the ignorance of the common people.

By now Nazleen was convinced that some

changes must be made, but she was also determined to retain the Compact. It had served their people well for all these years, and she was not about to let the promised riches of aliens change that.

As far as Zaktar was concerned, Nazleen had separated in her mind the enemy she'd fought from the trade ambassador who would soon be arriving. She regretted that she hadn't acquired more information about him from Haslik or from Loreth, since she had no real sense of the man with whom they must now negotiate. Was he little more than a golden-haired version of Miklav, a Warrior capable of occasional touches of kindness but still essentially a Warrior? Or did his Cerecian blood make for a different man altogether?

The majordomo glided through the open doorway as she asked herself those questions and announced that the object of her thoughts had arrived.

CHAPTER ELEVEN

THE MAJORDOMO RETREATED WITH HIS CUSTOMARY LOW bow, and Zaktar strode through the door. Nazleen drew in a sharp breath, then forced herself to let it out slowly. She hadn't expected the sheer physical force of his presence to be so powerful—and now she began to understand how Haslik and Loreth could have fallen under his spell.

In those terrible moments in the dungeons, she had seen him only as a shadowy enemy, and in her visions he'd been gone too quickly for her to truly see him.

He crossed the wide expanse of marble floor, his deep green eyes holding hers as he stopped just at the edge of her personal space, immediately creating the impression she was sure he intended—that of an equal.

For a moment she had made the inevitable comparison between him and Miklav. Both men were tall and powerful in appearance, and both wore uniforms adorned with the symbols of their rank. But Zaktar's was the simpler, although it made him no less imposing.

There the comparison died. Miklav had been born of humble origins, and even though he'd achieved the highest rank possible to him, something of those origins had always clung to him, giving her an advantage she'd used without ever having acknowledged it to herself.

She knew nothing of Zaktar's origins, but she knew she was dealing with an equal. Miklav's behavior had often made it seem as though he were demanding her respect; Zaktar assumed that respect would be accorded to him.

"I am happy to see that you have made a full recovery, Milady," he said, shattering the tense stillness of the room with that deep voice she'd heard in her dreams.

"And you too have recovered, I see," she replied, casting off the spell with some difficulty. As she spoke, she half-turned from him to indicate two chairs that had been carefully positioned to encourage conversation without also inviting intimacy, so she failed to see the smile her words brought.

Zaktar was now seeing yet another version of this woman who tormented his thoughts. First there had been the fire-wielding warrior, then the fragile female, and now the cool, aloof beauty whose every movement was calculated to create the impression of unassailability.

He himself had been born into a wealthy Kapti family of noble origins, and although the Kaptis had long since eschewed monarchy in favor of constitutional government, the old aristocracy still retained much of its former flavor. Self-confident by nature and somewhat arrogant as a result of his birthright both as a member of Kapti nobility and Cerecian blood, Zaktar had no doubt that he was a match for this woman, if only he could keep his desire for her in check.

Her remark about his recovery reminded him of Loreth's statement that Nazleen possessed a keen sense of humor. Under other circumstances, he thought, they both might have laughed. She certainly knew that their fire-battle had never been an equal one.

He took the seat she had indicated, deliberately not waiting for her to seat herself first. Haslik had filled him in on court protocol, but he decided that a statement needed to be made here.

She registered no surprise or displeasure at his improper behavior, instead indicating two crystal decanters set on a small table between them. "There is both wine and water. Please help yourself."

He poured a small amount of the pale wine, tasted it and then filled the goblet. She poured herself some water.

"It's very good," he said as he tasted it again.

"My mother had a passion for wines and spent a great deal of her free time supervising the royal winery. This was her proudest creation. I myself have little interest, although I enjoy it from time to time. Haslik shares her interest, but since he has other responsibilities, he can spend little time there."

The polite social conversation amused him. Cerecians tended not to waste time in meaningless talk; their discussions were usually scientific or philosophical. Needless to say, Zaktar's friends were scientists, but since he visited his family regularly, Zaktar wasn't uncomfortable in such situations.

"I have met your brother, as you know," he said. "In fact, I spent several days with him at Denra before coming here. I'd like to think we will become friends."

Her eyes flashed briefly with anger. "I find it difficult to understand how he could want to befriend a man who almost killed him."

"That is because you have no understanding of war, Milady."

"Exactly what he said, but I have no wish to understand it, either."

"We did not come here to make war," he stated, knowing that the brief moments of social politeness were rapidly drawing to a close.

"We had no reason to expect any encounters with other people, although we knew, of course, that it was a possibility. We came seeking gewa and seeking our origins. Were it not for deliberate provocations on the part of your Warriors, no battle would ever have taken place."

"Deliberate provocations?" she queried archly. "You attacked my guards and killed many of them."

"They fired the first shots," he replied calmly,

"but if such a responsibility had been mine, I would have done the same thing. However, that isn't what I meant. I was referring to the incident in the desert."

Nazleen frowned. "What incident in the desert?"

He searched her face in silence for a moment, then realized that neither Loreth nor Haslik had told her. So he related the episode in the desert. She listened carefully, her face expressionless. When he had finished, she looked away for a moment, then turned back to face him squarely.

"If you are lying, I shall know. Haslik either knows about this or can find out."

"If you wish to be sure that I'm telling the truth, there is a faster way to determine that," he challenged.

Their eyes met. She was the first to look away. "We consider thought-probing to be an invasion of privacy."

"So do we, but in this case I'm extending the invitation."

She got up and began to pace slowly about the room. He remained seated and watched her. When a shaft of sunlight touched her elaborate hairdo with fire, he had a nearly overwhelming urge to tear it apart and let the fiery curls tumble down over her shoulders.

"Miklav wanted war," she admitted after a moment, her voice low, "so it is certainly possible, even probable, that he deliberately instigated it. With war, he attained the power he wanted. That is part of the Compact under which we live."

"I'm familiar with the Compact," he stated. "Loreth and Haslik explained it to me."

Nazleen wondered what else they had told him. Had things reached the point where she couldn't even trust her brother and her dearest friend?

His revelation had truly unsettled her. Could he be blamed for the war if Miklav had instigated it? But she wanted to blame him for something. She couldn't give up her hatred so easily; besides, the alternative was far too troubling. She swung around to face him, her tone bitter.

"But it wasn't necessary for you to have killed Miklav. I'm told you are the greatest of the Fire Warriors. You could have merely stunned him instead."

To her very great surprise, he didn't immediately defend his action. Instead, his gaze slid away, giving her her first glimpse of uncertainty on his part.

"Yes, that's true," he said quietly.

For a moment, she didn't know what to say. Then, when she spoke, her tone was more questioning than accusatory. "Then why did you kill him?"

"I can't answer that because I don't know what went through my mind at that moment," he replied, wishing it were the truth. "It happened very fast, as you know."

"But you didn't kill me."

He had gotten up and now turned away from her as he pretended to examine a mural on the wall. "Perhaps I'd regained my senses by then, or perhaps I knew instinctively that you didn't represent such a threat to me. He had a weapon."

"So did I."

"But I didn't know that. Loreth had told me that the Sisterhood hadn't wielded the fire for many generations."

"They haven't. I practiced." To kill you, she thought, now finding herself uncomfortable with that hatred.

He whirled around angrily, his eyes flashing and his mouth set grimly. "And you damned near killed yourself in the process or forced me to kill you. It isn't a game to be played by amateurs, Nazleen. It's a discipline that requires many years of training and then constant practice. Do you have any idea just how close you came to death?"

She stared at him in shocked silence. She wasn't afraid of him, but she didn't understand his anger. He continued to glare at her for a moment, and then the anger slowly drained away as he ran a big hand through his tawny hair.

"Forgive me. That was uncalled-for. You couldn't have been expected to behave rationally in any event. I'd just killed your vezha."

"Vezha? I do not know that word."

"No, you wouldn't. It's the word in our language for . . . for one to whom you are joined for life."

"We do not believe in that," she retorted angrily. Miklav was my mate, chosen because . . ."

"I'm aware of the terms of that damned Compact," he cut in, his eyes flashing once more. "And while you may not believe in it, our people did. Otherwise, the word wouldn't exist."

"I have only your say-so that it does," she responded heatedly. "And the Compact has served us well. You are an outsider and have no right to criticize our ways."

He nodded, the anger gone again, shrunk back to a deep inner core. "That's true. Then you were mated to him only because of the Compact?" He had been told this but needed to hear it from her.

"Yes, but I did care for him. I'd known him almost all my life."

Zaktar heard the sadness in her voice. "I think no good can come of our talking about Miklav. He is gone. I killed him, but he would have killed me if he could."

It was true, so she said nothing, returning again to her chair. She was suddenly overcome with tiredness. The spells seemed to strike without warning, but she didn't want him to see her weakness.

Zaktar resumed his seat and picked up the wine goblet. When she reached for her own goblet, he saw her delicate hand tremble slightly. He cursed himself. She wasn't fully recovered yet, and he certainly wasn't aiding that recovery. Loreth had been right to have kept them apart. Fire seemed to flash between them even without conscious intent.

"I came here," he said formally, "to discuss trade between our peoples. You have gewa, and we have our science. Perhaps it would be best if I began preliminary talks with your Advisors."

"Yes," she said, struggling to keep her voice firm. "That would be best. A suite has been prepared for you here. I will send them to you."

He got up, and she summoned the last of her strength to arise from her chair. Zaktar was alarmed at her weakness but knew she wouldn't welcome his intervention. Still, he couldn't leave without at least touching her; his hunger was too great. So he took her hand in his, feeling her startled response, then bent to brush his lips against its softness.

Their eyes met again, and he was relieved to see

no hatred there, only a confusion that surely would have been hidden if she had been herself.

When Nazleen awoke several hours later, it was as though he were still there. For one brief moment she actually thought he might have broken into her bedchamber, and she sat up quickly to scan the empty room.

Their discussion kept replaying in her mind, jumbled now and fraught with unknown meaning. How much had been said and how much merely thought? And why had her dreams seem to be filled with such strangeness?

She began to think about a remark one of her teachers had once made. She'd said that since Stakezti, their common ancestor, had been merely a child, her knowledge of Cerecian customs and rituals had probably been incomplete.

The youth who was Zaktar's ancestor had been somewhat older and might have known more. She realized that besides knowing words and rituals she didn't know about, he might even know their written language, if such existed. She'd never thought to inquire about that, not even from Loreth, who seemed to have spent much time talking to Zaktar.

Those thoughts brought further thoughts about the ruins that his people were now excavating, and that led her to decide to do what she wanted to do in any event—see Zaktar again.

Although she felt much better than she had earlier, she knew she might have another attack of weakness. The dining hall was far from her quarters, and Zaktar wasn't the only one she didn't want to see her weakness. She summoned her maid.

"Please tell Zaktar that he is invited to join me here for dinner and then inform the kitchen."

Several hours later, when he was announced, she had begun to worry about what message she might be sending to him, and too late she regretted that she'd had her hair rearranged and chosen a less formal gown.

Subconsciously, she'd been clinging to the belief that since he was sworn to celibacy, she therefore had no reason to concern herself with physical attraction between them, but she was now thinking about that young couple at Cerece and should have remembered that earlier.

She was stunned when he walked in, still in uniform but now clean-shaven. Bearded, he'd been a handsome man, but now he was truly striking. She simply stared at that clean, firm jaw and the wide, sensuous mouth. Not even that small scar near his temple could mar his beauty. And then he gave her a dazzling smile.

"If I'd known you would be so shocked, I would have kept the beard, but I'd only grown it for convenience's sake. When Arthus told me that only Warriors wear beards here, I decided to change my image."

Arthus was one of the Advisors she'd sent to him. She didn't entirely trust the man, but he had the shrewdest business sense of them all and happened to own large tracts of land where gewa was common. So it would be in his self-interest to make a good bargain.

She countered his informality with a deliberately imperious manner. "Please forgive me for not holding a dinner in your honor. I will do so, but tonight I wished to discuss with you a matter that relates not to Hamloor but to the Sisterhood."

"Oh?" His golden brow arched questioningly.

"Yes. I wish to discuss the ruins."

They were then interrupted by servants who brought in the food. As she saw him looking at the dishes being set out, it occurred to her that she knew nothing of his food preferences.

"We are vegetarians," she stated, "but if you prefer meat, the kitchen can provide it. Both the Warriors and the Trens are flesheaters, so we always have it on hand."

"We eat meat, but it makes no difference to me. This is fine."

She was privately glad about that. The sight of meat always made her slightly queasy, and considering her present condition it might have been very difficult indeed.

They sat down at the small table, and the servants withdrew after filling their plates. Zaktar sampled everything, pronounced it excellent, then launched into a discussion of the foods of his native land. When a brief silence followed that, she gave in to her curiosity.

"What is your family background, Zaktar?"

He looked both surprised and pleased, and she realized that it was the first personal question she'd put to him and also the first time she'd used his name—before him, at least.

"My parents are Kapti, of course. Many years ago, the Kapti were ruled by an aristocracy—never just one ruler but a council of nobles. My family was one of those, tracing their ancestry back to one

309

of the great warlords. I had a brother who died in battle, and I have a sister two years younger. My brother was also Cerecian."

"Two in one family?" she asked in surprise. That was rather rare, although her mother had a younger sister who was Cerecian. She'd died in childhood.

Zaktar nodded. "My sister's son is also Cerecian."

"My own family also traces its ancestry back to the landed nobility of ancient times, and they were also warlords. The influence is strong with us, too. Haslik often teases me that he fears having a daughter just like me."

"How was it that your family was chosen to rule when the Compact was drawn up?" Zaktar inquired.

Nazleen smiled; her family's less than honorable history always amused her. "They weren't really chosen; they demanded it. Even though the Sisterhood was actually the victor in the wars, my family was the most powerful in Hamloor, thanks to some behavior we try to forget now. And as I said, the Cerecian influence was strong, too. Then, of course, it might also have had something to do with the fact that the Pavla at that time was a member of my family."

Her green eyes glinted with amusement, and Zaktar laughed aloud.

"There was an Augury, you see, to determine who should become Liege, but since the Pavla is the chief interpreter of Auguries, one would be justified in wondering if the results might have been suspect."

They both laughed, and in that moment Nazleen

knew that things were changing rapidly—too rapidly.

"Do you believe in Auguries?" he asked, still smiling.

"No, I never have. They're too vague. One can make them mean almost anything." Except for this last one, she thought with a twinge of uneasiness.

"A few of our men, mostly older ones, still hold them, but I've never had any interest in their mysticism. I put my faith in science." Then he paused and went on less certainly.

"On the other hand, Loreth told me of your recent Augury."

Nazleen avoided his gaze. Had Loreth told him about that part only she herself had seen, that vision of him carrying her into the sacred pool? A strange feeling crept through her. Was it something struggling to become a memory? What was it?

"Nazleen, are you ill?"

She jerked her head up to find him watching her intently. "I . . . I'm fine. You're right. This last Augury seems to have had some truth in it."

Zaktar resumed eating his dinner but kept glancing at her as she continued to avoid looking at him. He knew from Loreth that she apparently had no memory of their time in the fire-pool. Could she be remembering now? He thought about prodding that memory but decided against it. She wasn't ready to hear about it, and he wasn't sure he wanted to talk about it, either. An aura of mystery still hung over those hours.

When the food had been cleared away and the servants had brought tea for her and a thick, smoky-sweet wine for him, she brought up the subject of the ruins once more.

"I would like to have one of us—that is, one of the Sisters—at the site. What may be found there is important to us as well."

"And you don't yet trust us," he finished for her, but without rancor. "I thought about that as I was coming here. We would welcome their assistance, but will any of them be willing to come?"

"I think that some of the younger ones certainly would, and perhaps Sister Pilova can be persuaded. She is the most knowledgeable among us of our origins. She is past middle age but quite healthy, so I believe she could safely make the journey."

"The journey won't be any problem. We have the trucks and the jeppas, and we're going to be erecting buildings there to replace the tents. It's going to be a long-term project. The ruins are much larger than we'd originally believed."

She seemed interested, so he told her about the excavations and the plans. He wanted to suggest that he take her to see them, but he sensed that things hadn't progressed quite that far yet. Instead, as they finished their drinks, he stood up.

"I didn't really come prepared with gifts suitable for a Liege, but I would like to present you with a token gift until something more suitable can be sent. I took the liberty of leaving it just outside your garden gate. Arthus showed me the spot."

He was rewarded by a childlike glimmer of curiosity, so he reached out to take her hand and draw her to her feet. Even that contact inflamed him, and he was relieved when she withdrew her hand and preceded him into the garden.

They walked through the twilight to the gate

Arthus had shown him and he opened it, eager to see what she would think of his gift. He could only hope that her sense of humor was good enough.

"Ohh!" She breathed when she saw the ugly little vehicle that reminded her of a farmer's cart with a roof and doors. She began to walk all around it, bending to peer at the tires and then looking through the windows.

"There are far more elegant vehicles," he said with a smile, "but until your roads are improved, jeppas are the safest."

She pointed to the hood. "Is the horse in there?"

He laughed and reached inside to release the hood latch. "Yes, but I'm afraid it isn't nearly as beautiful as your white horse."

She paused in the act of bending to scrutinize the engine and stared up at him. "When did you see my mare?"

"I've seen it twice now," he said, then told her about the first time he'd seen her from that hilltop. "I'm sorry if I hurt you. You see, I had just realized that you were Cerecian, the first female of our race I'd ever seen."

He wanted to ask her why she hadn't reported his presence that day to the Warriors, but the time didn't seem right.

"As you were the first male I'd seen," she said softly, almost to herself as she bent to examine the engine more closely.

"You saw me?"

A long silence followed, and he thought that perhaps she wasn't going to answer him. Everything seemed very fragile between them at the moment, and he didn't want to push. Then she straightened up again and met his gaze.

"I saw you in a vision—or a dream, really—many months ago."

Both pairs of eyes darkened as they stared at each other in the gathering dusk. Neither of them consciously attempted telepathic contact, but it happened for just a moment. He felt her inner struggle over him, and she felt his hunger. She was the first to withdraw.

"How do you make this run?" she asked, moving away a bit and speaking a little too brightly. "With this?" She pointed to the steering wheel.

"That's how you steer it. This is what makes it run." He came up behind her, feeling her tense, and then pointed to the accelerator. "And the other one stops it."

"That sounds rather simple. I'd like to try it." She climbed into the driver's seat before he could protest, and he was glad that he hadn't explained how to start it.

"I think perhaps you'd better let me show you first, then you can try it."

With obvious reluctance, she moved to the other side, and he got in behind the wheel. When he turned on the headlights, she cried out in pleased surprise.

"This is like the lights Taka told me about, the lights for your homes."

"Yes, basically the same." The young Fire Warrior had told him about his conversation with her.

He started the jeppa. She sat close to him, her whole attention focused on his movements. He wished he could take her home to show her all the wonders of his world. Perhaps when the flying machine was perfected . . . He drove off slowly, thinking happily about their future.

"Can we take this road?" he asked. It was just barely wide enough for the jeppa but seemed to be well-maintained.

"Yes, it goes into the forest. I ride there." She was still sitting close to him, totally absorbed with his movements.

But before they had entered the woods, two Warriors appeared. When he stopped, she moved to her own side, fumbling with the window crank in an attempt to speak to them. He reached across to operate it for her, and his arm brushed briefly against the soft swell of her breasts. She drew in a sharp breath, but she made no attempt to move away from him.

After she had reassured the astounded guards, they proceeded into the forest, but he saw that she kept to her own side of the jeppa now, even though she continued to watch his every move.

Nazleen was thoroughly fascinated. She'd grown up listening to her brother's dreams of fabulous machinery, but even then she'd gently urged practicality on him. It wasn't enough to simply dream of some outlandish machine; that machine had to do something worthwhile. Haslik hadn't always given that much consideration.

Now she sat in the jeppa thinking of farmers bringing their goods to market more quickly and easily, of physicians being able to reach even the widely scattered rural folk, and even of the pure pleasure of being able to go anywhere at any time in comfort.

She'd already forgotten that moment when he'd

touched her. It was an act of pure will.

"Could this cross the desert during the storm season? And can it go in rain?"

Zaktar smiled. Haslik had told him that his sister had a very practical turn of mind. "The problem with the desert storms isn't the sand itself; it's the poor visibility. Even with the headlights, you can't see far enough ahead to know where you are, let alone where you're going. It's like driving in fog. But our roads have lines painted on them that reflect the headlights, so if you go slow, you're safe enough. If we could find some way to mark the desert, it could be done.

"Rain is no problem. It will even run through small streams. I know it doesn't snow here, but it will run in snow, too."

"It snowed once when I was little," she said dreamily. "It was beautiful."

Then that is another thing I will show you, he thought. It snowed too much in his land.

They were not moving any faster than her mare could run, although she assumed it could go farther than the horse could. "Can it go faster?"

He laughed. "Yes, but not here."

"Thank you for such a wonderful gift, Zaktar. Haslik will envy me."

"Oh, I plan to give him one, too, as soon as we can bring more from home."

"But if we sell you all our gewa, we won't be able to run our own vehicles."

"From what I've learned, you have enough for both of us, enough to last forever. And someday we should be able to make the crystals ourselves."

She made no response, and he brought the jeppa

to a stop at a spot where he could turn around.

"Nazleen, this will be honest trade. I'm not trying to take advantage of you and your people."

She met his gaze for a moment in the dim light, then averted her eyes. "It's very difficult for me to change my mind about you so quickly, Zaktar."

"I understand that. I also realize that I never told you how sorry I am that you lost your baby. I can't pretend that I regret Miklav's death, but I do regret your losing his child."

She turned away and stared out the window into the night. "I should be sadder about it than I am. Perhaps it was because I'd only just learned that I was pregnant and hadn't really started to think about it yet."

"Or perhaps it was because it wasn't a child conceived in love," he said gently and recklessly. He knew what her feelings were on that subject, and he regretted his words as soon as she turned back to him again, her expression scornful.

"A Liege has no time for such nonsense. Miklav understood that because he felt the same way."

He knew it was past time to stop this, but he went on anyway. "Love isn't nonsense. Making love is—or should be—the best thing that can happen between a man and a woman. And if a baby comes from that, it's even better."

For a moment, his words sent her back to that secret cache of love poems she and Haslik had found, but then something struck her and she frowned.

"How could you possibly know that? Taka said you believe in celibacy."

Zaktar sighed heavily. Now he definitely knew he

should have stopped this discussion or never started it in the first place. "I know because there was a woman in my life once, a woman I thought I loved."

So he told her all about it. She remained silent the whole time, and when he'd finished, he couldn't begin to guess what she thought of him now.

"Taka said that your Pavla sent you on this journey in part because he feared you'd get into trouble again. Is that the trouble he meant?"

Zaktar relaxed with a chuckle. "No doubt it was, although I'm the bane of his existence during the best of times. He's a rigid old man. He wouldn't have taken me back except for the fact that I was a war hero and a member of a powerful family, but he's never really forgiven me."

"Have you forgiven yourself?"

"Yes." Then he heaved another sigh. "Well, the truth is that I never really thought I had done anything wrong. I broke a rule, but it was a foolish rule to begin with. Men aren't meant to be celibate —and neither are women. If we were, how could there be a future? All that rule has done is to put us on the verge of extinction. I can understand the feelings of the early Cerecians, given what they'd gone through, but we've been at peace with them for years now. It's a perfect example of rules being set in stone and then never really questioned." He almost added, "like your Compact," but managed to hold his tongue.

"But that will change now in any event," she said in a tone that suggested she might prefer extinction.

"Of course. I spoke with the Pavla by radio when I went back to the ruins, and he's actually considering lifting the ban, not that it much matters at this point. Even he couldn't stop nature from taking its course."

Zaktar thought about his last visit to the compound. He'd seen men and women mingling freely now, although they were clearly not all comfortable with each other yet. But the very air of the place was heavy with promise. He wished they were there right now. When he began to feel that now-familiar stirring in his loins, he hurriedly restarted the jeppa.

"I will drive now," she said. "I understand how it works."

Zaktar recognized an order when he heard one, but he didn't mind. She could order him around for the rest of his life—and probably would, too. He might even listen most of the time.

He got out, and she slid into the driver's seat. The jeppa was made for tall men so she had to sit on the very edge of the seat to reach the accelerator and brake. As soon as he had gotten back in, she started it jerkily, then quickly eased off the accelerator.

He was lulled by her initial caution and failed to anticipate what would happen when they came to a curve. She steered too sharply and the jeppa wobbled badly, sending him against her. Even so, she managed to get it under control quickly. He moved back to his side regretfully, fighting the inevitable result of that brief contact with her soft body, and he noted with pleasure that her hands on the steering wheel shook slightly. Of course, that could have been the result of their near-accident.

Nazleen concentrated on her driving, but everywhere their bodies had touched, a gentle heat lingered. Then a strange, vague memory came to her, a memory that couldn't be. She must be somehow confusing Zaktar with Miklav. She pushed it from her mind as they came to another curve.

Then they were back to the palace, and she stopped the jeppa outside her garden gate. But as soon as she got out, a weakness came over her. She leaned momentarily against the jeppa, then straightened quickly when he came around to her side.

"I enjoyed this, but it is late and I'm tired," she said, her voice once again formal. Summoning up the last of her strength, she started toward the gate.

Then she uttered a startled sound as he came up behind her and scooped her into his arms. "Put me down!" she ordered, although even she could hear that her tone wasn't as emphatic as her words.

"No one can see us," he said close to her ear as he kicked open the gate and started across the garden. "And I give you permission to be tired."

The sound of her own laughter embarrassed her, but she couldn't seem to find the energy to become angry with him.

"I think you had better get back to the compound and let the Healers check you. I can drive you there tomorrow."

"No, there is too much to do here." She didn't add that she couldn't afford to leave court again, for fear of what her Advisors might do in her absence.

"The Healers warned me that I would have these spells for a while."

"They also told you not to leave."

"I had to come back here."

"You came back here so you could impress me with all the trappings of your position. You've impressed me. Now you can go back there and get well."

"Zaktar," she sighed, "there is much you do not understand."

He had carried her through the open doors into her reception room. He paused there for a moment, then continued on to her bedchamber. When he set her down on the bed, she looked up at him and that strange memory stirred again—their bodies entwined, surrounded by a circle of green fire.

He was watching her closely. She looked away. Was it a vision of the future, perhaps somehow connected to that vision of Loreth's? But it felt like a memory.

"Zaktar . . ." she began, then faltered.

"What is it?"

"Please summon my maid for me. Just tell the guard at the door."

He hesitated for just a moment, then left the bedchamber. She didn't expect him to return and pulled herself tiredly from the bed to the dressing table, so the maid could undo her hair.

But then she looked into the mirror and saw him there. He hesitated again, then reached around to undo the clasp that held her shawl in place. He pushed it from her shoulders, then slid his hands slowly along her bare arms as he bent to kiss the top of her head. Their eyes met in the mirror.

"One day soon," he said in a low, hoarse voice, "I will show you what love is."

The maid walked in at that moment, and her startled cry followed him as he turned and left without another word.

Over the next few weeks, Zaktar saw little of Nazleen—by design on her part, he soon realized. He cursed himself repeatedly for having moved too quickly. He should have been more patient or at least a bit more discreet in his speech. Even if she hadn't loved Miklav and hadn't had time to care about the baby, she'd still suffered a double loss, not to mention a fire-battle. He'd never been more aware of the fact that patience wasn't one of his virtues.

He continued his negotiations with her Advisors, but things proceeded at a pace so slow that it seemed to him they were at a standstill. He was increasingly frustrated over this, then frustrated still further by her absence.

He made two trips back to the ruins to check on progress and to make use of the radio relay system that currently had its terminus there. He spoke with the Pavla and also with the Kapti Prime Minister and knew that they were both growing impatient with his failure to produce a trade agreement. They began to hint that perhaps the role of negotiator didn't suit him well. It didn't, but he wasn't about to tell them that.

On both trips, he also stopped at the compound where progress certainly *was* evident. Loreth begged him to talk with the Fire Warriors, who had adapted somewhat more quickly to the presence of women in their lives than the Sisters had adapted to them.

It wasn't an easy task, given his own situation, but he counseled patience, then threatened to send home immediately any who became too persistent. Then he decided it was likely he'd have to send himself home if Nazleen didn't soon accept him into her life.

He told Loreth that the Pavla would soon be sending an official delegation to the compound. He was too old and frail to come himself, but he was sending the man believed to be most likely to replace him. Given the Pavla-to-be's nature, Zaktar wasn't at all sure he wanted to be around when that meeting took place. Loreth might decide to throw them all out.

In order to justify remaining at the compound, the Fire Warriors had begun to renovate the old wing of the residence and also to undertake some new construction. Zaktar obtained Loreth's permission to build a radio relay tower on the highest point of the compound. When it was completed, it would permit direct communication between his home and the compound and—unfortunately, for Loreth's sake—between the two Pavlas as well. It would have to be constructed of wood until steel could be brought from the Kapti factories.

Only to Loreth did Zaktar speak of his frustrations both with the negotiations and with Nazleen's behavior. The Pavla was gently sympathetic but too distracted to offer much in the way of practical advice.

Then it gradually began to dawn on Zaktar that there might be a hidden reason for the Advisors' seemingly interminable bickerings over the terms of the trade. This possibility occurred to him during one lengthy session on a warm afternoon when he remained imprisoned in the palace with them while looking out the window to see a distant figure galloping off into the forest.

Their arguments sounded to him as if they were being staged specifically for his benefit, and as he watched Nazleen disappear from view, he decided it was time to take some action. He'd seen her only twice during the past two weeks, both times when she'd been surrounded by her Advisors or other court officials. She'd been gracious, smiling—and distant.

At night he'd lain in his bed and imagined himself sneaking into her chamber through that garden gate. One night he'd even walked near there, but just as he was about to give in to temptation, a pair of guards had appeared.

He requested a private audience with her and was politely rebuffed. So after another fruitless bargaining session, he sought out Captain Mevak, with whom he'd become much more closely acquainted during the past weeks. Mevak always accompanied him on his trips back to the ruins and out into the countryside. During these trips, the Captain also helped Zaktar polish his Hamloorian, which he was learning from a palace instructor.

What had begun as an attempt to keep an eye on a possible competitor had been transformed into a friendship. That was helped considerably by Mevak's disclosure that he had a lover within the palace and they wanted to life-mate, but the woman feared losing the job she loved if it became known.

He found Mevak just finishing a meeting with two Warriors who'd ridden in from Denra. The

Captain dismissed the two, then smiled at Zaktar.

"It appears that Haslik has worked out most of the details under which he and Gundra will share the responsibilities of Warrior Chief. Haslik himself will be here in a few days, and he sends his regards. He might have done better to send his sympathy," the Captain finished with a wry grin.

Zaktar flung himself into a chair with a muttered curse, bringing laughter from Mevak, since the curse was in Hamloorian.

"Mevak, is it possible that the Advisors could be deliberately stalling for some purpose of their own?"

The Captain looked at him appraisingly. "What makes you suggest that?"

So Zaktar explained his feeling that some of the disagreements seemed staged, and Mevak's handsome features darkened.

"It wouldn't surprise me. Most of them can be trusted only to look after their own interests, and in this case those could be considerable. Let me look into it. I have some reliable sources of information in the city."

"Can Nazleen really be so blind that she doesn't know what kind of people she has working for her?" Zaktar asked in frustration.

"In a word—yes. She became Liege when she was only twenty-two, and most of her Advisors are much older and were already in place when she took over. Her mother was a highly intelligent woman, but she had a blind spot where that group was concerned. If they were loyal to her, that was all that mattered.

"Nazleen, to her credit, is far more concerned

about the welfare of the ordinary people than her mother ever was, but between her wishes and the actual putting into place of programs and reforms, a lot can get changed. For example, she decreed that education should be free and available to everyone, but her first Education Advisor saw to it that the teachers for the common people were barely literate themselves. That's changed now, because the man died and the new one set things right.

"And that's just one example from many, believe me. Haslik could give you many more."

"But hasn't Haslik told her about this?"

The Captain nodded. "He tells her, she berates her Advisors and orders them to correct whatever it is, and they pretend to do so."

"Then what must be changed is the entire system," Zaktar stated.

Mevak smiled. "Ahh, a revolutionary after my own heart."

Then he leaned back with a sigh. "You're right. The system must be changed, but it's very difficult for Nazleen to stand alone against her Advisors."

She wouldn't have to stand alone if she'd let me into her life, Zaktar thought.

The next evening, Mevak appeared in Zaktar's suite, his expression grim. "I've got some very interesting news," he said after accepting a glass of wine.

"It seems that the Advisors and their friends have been very busy buying up all the land they can find that has gewa deposits. They've been taking advantage of farmers and other rural folk who know nothing about your interest in it. There are even rumors that a few who refused to sell have been burned out of their homes."

"Nazleen has to know about this—now!" Zaktar stated, crashing his fist into the arm of his chair.

"I agree," Mevak responded. "Since you seem to have trouble seeing her these days, why don't I ask to see her instead?"

Zaktar's face relaxed into a smile. "Has it been that obvious?"

"Palace gossip has it that the Liege finds your company very, ah, discomfiting." Mevak grinned. "Perhaps your patience ran out at an inopportune moment?"

"You could say that." Zaktar chuckled. "Can we see her tonight?"

"I'll try."

CHAPTER TWELVE

"DID CAPTAIN MEVAK SAY WHY HE WISHES TO SEE me?"

"No, Milady, but he did request to see you this evening, if at all possible."

"Very well. You may tell him that I will see him now."

When her aide had departed, Nazleen narrowed her eyes thoughtfully. Could this be some sort of ruse on Zaktar's part to see her? She knew that Mevak and Zaktar had become friendly, and she couldn't think of any reason why the Captain should fell such an urgent need to speak with her.

Well, at least if this was a ploy on Zaktar's part, he would be forced to see her in the presence of the Captain.

She knew she couldn't avoid Zaktar forever, and that wasn't her intention. She simply wanted time, and after that episode in her bedchamber, she'd become convinced that the impatient Fire Warrior would not allow her that time. Furthermore, she didn't trust herself, although she very much disliked admitting that.

He wants too much of me, she thought. And an inner voice replied, perhaps you want too much of him, also.

Being under the same roof with him for these past weeks had been an ever-increasing torment. On those occasions when she'd been forced to be in his presence, the tension between them had been so powerful that she knew it had not gone unnoticed by others.

Her Advisors told her that he was deliberately prolonging the trade negotiations, constantly changing his demands and generally being very difficult. The two of them were playing a game. She was constantly seeking new ways to avoid him, and he was prolonging his stay until she couldn't avoid him.

Perhaps his patience had finally come to an end, and he'd asked Mevak to intercede on his behalf. Although with Haslik due to arrive soon, it was strange that he hadn't waited to utilize him for that purpose.

But he's already winning, she thought wryly. I have succeeded in keeping him away in the flesh, but I can't keep him out of my dreams. Scarcely a night passed that she wasn't tormented by that strange vision that persisted in seeming like a memory—the two of them in each other's arms beside the fire-pool, surrounded by strangely entwined tendrils of sacred fire. She'd never seen the fire behave like that. Certainly it sometimes reached out to certain people—she was one of those—and often after an immersion a soft glow would surround one for a brief time, but she'd never seen or heard of anything like this.

She desperately needed to discuss this with Loreth. She'd considered writing to her about it, but she felt an urge to talk about it, rather than struggling to put her feelings onto paper. But she couldn't go to Cerece until the trade agreement had been concluded, and for that she needed Zaktar's cooperation.

When the guard announced both men, Nazleen was actually relieved.

"I have asked Zaktar to accompany me, Milady, because it was he who first raised this matter."

Nazleen's gaze went very briefly to Zaktar, then back to Mevak again. She felt a quiver of uneasiness. She'd expected to see guilt written all over the Captain's face, but instead she saw anger there.

"What is this matter that seems to be so urgent?"

So Mevak told her what he had learned. Even in the midst of her growing shock over Mevak's story, she was aware of Zaktar's steady gaze on her.

"Are you quite sure of the reliability of your sources, Captain?" she asked, even though she knew that through his family, Mevak would have excellent contacts throughout the realm.

"Yes, Milady."

Finally she was forced to address Zaktar. "And you are saying that my Advisors, not you, have been delaying the negotiations?"

"I am prepared to sign any reasonable agreement. We urgently need to begin this trade, since time will have to be spent bringing our gewa miners here to train your people to cut it. The methods required are very precise or the gewa is worthless.

"They keep changing their requirements. Then, when I agree to the new ones, they change them again, often during these arguments among themselves that seem staged to me."

Somewhere in her brain, his words were registering; they were too important to ignore. But a part of her was lost—lost in those eyes, lost in a world where only sensuality existed. She dragged her attention back to Mevak.

"Please wait while I think about this."

She left them there and went out onto the terrace that led to her garden. Why hadn't she been more shocked at the duplicity of her Advisors? Had she really believed them to be capable of this?

Sadly, she knew she did—and always had. She'd forced those doubts down every time they'd surfaced, because there had seemed to be no alternative. She needed them.

A Liege's circle of knowledge is so small, trapped as she is within her role. The Council of Advisors tended to come from the same few noble families generation after generation. In theory, she could choose whomever she liked, but in reality she could only choose from among those she knew.

Haslik had been right; things must change. But she still wanted that change to be orderly. To fire the lot of them would mean chaos, just at a time when great upheaval would come to Hamloor in any event as a result of this trade agreement.

331

She mused sadly for a moment about power, the power she had that Miklav had wanted so badly he'd died for it in the end. It was an illusion. If she had true power, she could issue a decree and change it all and it would be done.

Then she began to consider what she *could* do. After a few moments, a smile came tentatively to her troubled face and grew still more. Miklav would have approved of this. Her mother would have appreciated it. She went back inside.

The two men rose from their seats when she walked in. She waved them back again, but only Zaktar sat; Captain Mevak was clearly uncomfortable being seated while she paced about the room.

"I think I have found a solution. I know that both of you can be trusted, and I need to know if you think this will work." She glanced at both men to see them nod. The irony of the situation nearly made her smile. Here she was, bestowing her trust on a Warrior and a man whom she'd believed only weeks ago to be her greatest enemy.

"We will sign a trade agreement. From what you've told me, Captain, my Advisors and their friends have by now bought up most of the large deposits, so they should be ready to conclude this matter. I will make it known to them tomorrow that I wish it to be completed quickly so that I can journey to Cerece.

"Then, as soon as the agreement has been signed, I will tell them that I have decided that all gewa deposits will become the sole property of the Liege. I can do that; it's in the Compact, even though it's never been done before. I will also appoint a Special

Commission to oversee the collection of this money and its distribution to the people."

She turned to Mevak. "In fact, Mevak, it strikes me that your father would be an excellent person to head that Commission. His reputation for fairness is unequaled in the realm—not even the Advisors could challenge such an appointment—and he can present me with a list of others he knows to be honest and fair."

She paused and smiled, very pleased with this new idea. It was an excellent way to bring new people into the court, so she could gradually get rid of the current Advisors. Mevak's father, although a member of the old nobility, had remained aloof from court. She now suspected he'd never wanted to taint himself through association with her Advisors.

"Well, what do you think?" she asked, barely able to contain her excitement.

Mevak's broad smile answered before he did. "I think it's a brilliant move, Milady, and I am sure my father will serve you in this manner. The Advisors will be unable to protest too strongly because of fear that they might reveal their duplicity."

She nodded, smiling herself. "Not only will they not gain anything, but they will have lost the money they paid to the owners of the gewa. That pleases me even more."

Then she turned to the silent Zaktar questioningly and felt a momentary chill when she saw his frown. He dragged his gaze from her and addressed Mevak instead.

"Just how treacherous are these Advisors and their friends, Mevak? Will doing this put her in danger?"

Mevak answered before she herself could. "No, they'd never go that far. They wouldn't dare. The most they'll do is to scheme to find a way to get their money back. But just to be on the safe side, Haslik can speak to the Commander of the Palace Guard. He's a good man, totally incorruptible. That's why Miklav sent him here."

Zaktar nodded and then smiled broadly at her. "In that case, I think it's a perfect solution, and I ask only to be present to see the looks on their faces when they find out what you've done. It may repay me for these weeks of frustration."

She laughed and nodded, but she also felt the silent message that the Advisors weren't the only ones frustrating him. Even Mevak shot an amused look at the big Fire Warrior.

"Then it is settled. I'm sure Haslik will agree with my plan, but I will wait for his arrival before signing the agreement."

Captain Mevak bowed. "Good night, then, Milady."

"Good night, Captain." She turned to say good night to Zaktar, but the words remained caught in her throat. Mevak left, and as soon as the door closed behind him, Zaktar got up from his chair and started toward her.

She stood her ground, but in an attempt to defuse the situation, she spoke hurriedly.

"Tomorrow I will tell the Advisors that I wish to conclude the negotiations quickly. Then Haslik should arrive the following day, and we can sign it then."

"And after that I will take you to the compound and to see the ruins if you like. I will need to return there to report the signing of the agreement."

She wanted to go to Cerece and to the ruins as well, but she feared those long hours with him. She also feared leaving court just now. As Mevak had pointed out, they would certainly begin scheming to get their money back at the very least. She shook her head.

"No, I really can't afford to leave the palace just now. There is no one I can trust who has the authority to control the Advisors and keep an eye on them."

"There is Haslik. Surely he can be persuaded to remain here while you are gone."

"Haslik has no authority here. He is the Warrior Chief."

"Doesn't the Compact make any provisions for the absence or incapacity of a Liege?"

She looked at him sharply, wondering if he'd read the document. She knew he'd been learning the Hamloorian tongue.

"Yes," she admitted, "it does provide for the Warrior Chief to assume temporary control in such events, but that part has never been used." She didn't bother to add that no Liege had ever trusted a Warrior Chief enough to hand over the power even briefly.

"In this case, since the Warrior Chief is also your brother, surely no one could question it."

She nodded, feeling trapped but not entirely

unhappy about it. After all, she wanted desperately to see Loreth, and she wanted very much to see the ruins, too. She could make certain that they were not alone on the journey. Warriors would insist upon accompanying them in any event.

He reached out suddenly and lifted her chin to force her to meet his eyes. "Nazleen, please don't avoid me any longer. I'm sorry if I frightened you. It won't happen again. I'll wait for an invitation."

"An invitation you know will come," she replied as heat spread through her from his light touch.

He nodded, then drew his fingers slowly along her cheek before saying a husky "good night".

In the end, Denra was added to their itinerary and made the first stop. From there, they would proceed across the desert to the ruins, then finally to Cerece. When she protested that she wished to go to Cerece first, Zaktar had all sorts of reasons why the itinerary he'd chosen was better. She thought he might have some hidden purpose, but since she had one herself, she finally agreed.

The decision to stop at Denra followed a long discussion between Nazleen and Haslik. He suggested it because it was a way to reassure the Warriors that their Liege still held them in the highest regard, despite their defeat in battle. Nazleen had at first balked at the idea, even though she understood Haslik's reasoning. Denra, she said, shivering at the memory of those moments in the dungeon, was too filled with ghosts for her.

"Then perhaps going there will lay them to rest," Haslik had urged gently.

In the end, she realized he was right. Miklav was

entombed there in a great vault deep within the fortress that was reserved for Warrior Chiefs, and she knew that she had to go there to lay to rest his ghost. She had never loved him, but he'd occupied a very special place in her life. He represented a past of which she knew she had to let go.

Haslik had been delighted with her solution to the problem with the trade agreement and had agreed with Mevak that she would be in no personal danger as a result.

The division of responsibilities that had been worked out between Haslik and Gundra gave Haslik the role of educating Warriors and supervising the new sciences with which they were about to be deluged. To Gundra went the old Warrior responsibilities for defense and preparedness. Both men would hold the title of Warrior Chief.

Haslik was quite willing to assume temporary control of the Court while she was gone, stating that he would use the time to explain to her Advisors the new Warrior structure. And because he'd always been very popular at court, he would have no problem dealing with them.

As for the Advisors, many of them had been visibly shaken when she'd announced her decision —in the presence of both Haslik and Zaktar as well—but they made no serious objections. However they recovered quickly enough to begin proposing names for the Special Commission, a decision Nazleen said she was leaving in the estimable hands of Lorevar, Captain Mevak's father. Their expressions at that announcement gave her such pleasure she was barely able to maintain her regal demeanor.

The trip to Denra was accomplished in a convoy of two jeppas and a truck, with some very happy Warriors trying out their newly acquired driving skills along the way. It took less than a full day; on horseback, it was usually a three-day journey.

They arrived at the old fortress late in the afternoon, driving through the partially rebuilt gate to encounter long lines of Warriors awaiting their Liege. Their expressions told Nazleen that Haslik had been right; these were proud men who needed some reassurance. Even some Warriors who were clearly still recovering from battle wounds had been brought out for the occasion.

Nazleen had worried that Zaktar's presence would not be welcome, but once again she was faced with that peculiar Warrior mentality that somehow bore no grudges against a man who had bested them in battle. Of course, the shipment of new rifles that Zaktar brought with him may have helped, too. Pleased as they were to see her, they were even more eager to take possession of these new weapons.

As Nazleen was helped from the jeppa by Denra's temporary Commander, she spotted a group of young recruits, among them Miklav's son, Kyetki. She told the Commander that she wished to visit Miklav's tomb and asked that the boy accompany her. When he was summoned, his pleasure at the honor was obvious.

So the two of them walked through the ancient stone corridors and down winding stairs. Thinking that perhaps it might be difficult for the boy to remain here at Denra now, Nazleen asked if he intended to continue his Warrior training.

"Yes, Milady. My father would have wanted it, and I too want it. Chief Haslik offered me a post at the palace, but I would prefer to remain here." Then he gave her a quick, shy look. "I mean no offense, Milady."

"No offense has been taken, Kyetki. I am pleased that you will stay here, and I know your father would be proud."

They stopped as they reached the great stone archway that led into the vault. The names of Warrior Chiefs were inscribed in stone on crypts lining the walls. In the center of the room a flame leapt from a stone urn filled with oil. Through the wavering flame, she saw Miklav's crypt with his name and dates of service already inscribed.

She circled the flame, aware of the fact that Kyetki had remained in the doorway to give her privacy. The tears welled up unexpectedly as visions of the man filled her mind. It was difficult to believe that such a strong presence in her life was here in this lifeless place. Slowly, she reached out a finger to trace his name.

"Miklav," she whispered, "I never gave you all that you wanted, but I gave you what I could. You deserved more."

Then she turned to his son, grateful that he at least had survived, as their son had not.

"Your father was a great man, Kyetki. He was also the greatest of the Warrior Chiefs, but I think he would understand that I consider it more important that he was a great and good man."

"Th . . . thank you, Milady," the boy said, his lips trembling as he tried to maintain control.

She wanted to take him into her arms, but out of

deference to his brave attempt to be a true Warrior, she simply took his hand.

The Warrior Chief's quarters, which would soon be occupied by Haslik, had been put at her disposal, and it was there she went, her mind still preoccupied with thoughts of Miklav. Old Aktra awaited her there, to see if there was anything she required.

She saw immediately that Miklav's personal effects had been removed from the suite, but that made it even easier to spot the pair of gold earrings lying on a table. Frowning, she went over to pick them up. The old Warrior cleared his throat.

"We found them among the Chief's things, Milady, and were certain they must belong to you."

"Yes, they do," she said in a choked tone. "Thank you for returning them." She'd worn those earrings the first night she'd slept with Miklav.

She chose to spend the night alone, dining in the suite and then wandering about, remembering. Sadly, she knew that she would never be able to put Miklav into a single category in her memory. Friend, foe—even, perhaps, lover. He would forever remain suspended somewhere in between. If only they hadn't been Liege and Warrior Chief . . . If his nature had been different or hers had . . . But they'd both played the roles they'd been destined to play, and now it was finished.

Somewhere in that long night, Miklav's ghost was indeed laid to rest, and Nazleen began to face the future.

In the morning, she breakfasted alone, then went out to the courtyard. Zaktar stood there with Mevak and another Warrior who would accompany them on the remainder of their journey, and the Denra Commander also waited to see them off. Green eyes met, and without conscious intent, their minds touched for a moment. She felt understanding, and he sensed that she had let go of the past.

A short time later, when they drove out of the fortress, Nazleen turned at the base of the hill to look back at the mighty stone walls. Denra would always mean Miklav to her, and she knew she would not want to return to it again.

She rode alone in a jeppa with Zaktar, followed by Mevak and the other Warrior. He drove in silence for some time, then finally turned to her.

"I too visited Miklav's tomb this morning. I hope you're not offended."

She was not, but she was surprised.

"I spent the evening with the men who knew him best, and I came away thinking that if circumstances had been different, he and I might have become friends. Whatever his faults, he was a man who looked to the future, and I think he would have liked the future that will come to Hamloor.

"I also spoke to Kyetki this morning and told him that I deeply regretted having killed his father and that he had fought bravely. He's a fine boy who shows great promise. I've been thinking about arranging some sort of educational exchange between our peoples, and he'd be an excellent candidate for that."

Nazleen merely nodded, but she was taking that first small step into the future. She'd gone from hating this man to a cautious neutrality combined with a growing need, and now she thought for the first time about all the kindnesses he'd shown, the fairness he'd demonstrated, the gentleness that seemed so uniquely his.

In short, she stopped drawing comparisons to Miklav and began to see the man for the first time, but a small measure of caution remained because that was her nature.

They entered the desert, which Nazleen had never seen, and she was fascinated by the unending panorama of sand and bleached sky. But that fascination soon gave way to discomfort at the intense heat. If it hadn't been for the breeze created by the jeppa's passage, she thought she might have suffocated. Not even a brief stop at a campsite of the Desert Trens revived her, and Zaktar was watching her with concern. As they were about to leave, he drew her aside.

"Do you think you could give up being Liege for a while to be comfortable?"

She gave him an uncomprehending look, and he handed her a package he had taken from the jeppa's storage compartment. She opened it and saw a simple white shirt and a pair of loose trousers that were in fact the same as the clothes he himself was wearing.

"I borrowed them from one of the women at the campsite. She might be a bit taller, but I think you're close to the same size. They're not the robes of the Liege of Hamloor or the gown of a Cerecian Sister, but they'll be much more comfortable."

"But I couldn't put them on here," she said, feeling the lightness of the fabric. "The Trens would be horrified to see me in such attire."

"Then we'll get out of here and find some place

for you to change," he said, leading her back to the jeppa.

Just beyond the campsite, they found a spot where a tall dune afforded her some privacy, and while the men waited, Nazleen put on the strange garments. In design, they weren't much different from the loose pajamas she sometimes wore at court, although there was no adornment of any kind. The moment she put them on, she felt cooler.

She also felt very conspicuous as she returned to the waiting men. Both Zaktar and Mevak grinned at her, and the other Warrior tried hard to avoid staring.

The remainder of the trip was far more comfortable as the breeze cooled her skin beneath the loosely woven clothing. And then it was over. They were through the desert and driving through a semi-barren land that separated the desert from the jagged Fire Mountains that loomed in the distance. The air became almost instantly cooler as the sun sank slowly out of sight behind them. It had nearly disappeared by the time they crested a small hill and she saw the ruins for the first time.

Zaktar stopped, and they both got out to stare at the landscape littered with emerging buildings and walls and strange machinery and many people dressed much like she was.

"Progress has to be very slow," Zaktar explained. "In some places, they actually have to sift through the sand and dirt with small sieves so they don't miss anything of importance."

"How big is it? Do you know yet?"

"As far as we can tell now, it went from that

hillside all the way across the valley and perhaps beyond. The estimates have been revised every time I've come here."

"I can feel the fire," she said. "Not strongly, but it's there."

He nodded. "We think it's buried very deep, and we may not have even reached the top of the building they must have constructed over it."

She turned to him with a smile. "Somehow it no longer seems appropriate to call the Sisterhood's home Cerece. *This* is Cerece."

They got back into the jeppa and drove down into the ruins. All work ceased the moment they arrived, and several dozen pairs of eyes became riveted on Nazleen. Belatedly, she realized that none of the Kaptis had yet seen a female Cerecian, and neither, apparently, had the handsome older Cerecian who now approached them, smiling delightedly at the sight of her. Zaktar introduced him as Felka, their Chief Historian, who was in charge of the work.

"Welcome to the true Cerece, Milady. We are honored. I eagerly await the arrival of Sister Pilova, who I understand will be joining us soon. I look forward to many long and enlightening arguments."

Nazleen laughed. She was afraid that poor Felka couldn't possibly know the half of it. Pilova was inclined to rigidity where their history was concerned. She was glad that Felka had a sense of humor; he would need it.

The work ended as twilight approached, and Nazleen went with Zaktar to the campsite, where those who had been charged with food preparation had already gotten the evening meal ready. They were evidently aware of her diet, since a special meal had been prepared for her.

Nazleen was utterly fascinated by these people, who treated her with respect but certainly not the deference to which she was accustomed. To her surprise, she discovered that they all spoke Cerecian. Zaktar explained that both languages were taught in all their school.

The Kapti were a handsome people, dark like the Trens but taller. There was a casualness to all their speech and activities she found to be unique and very interesting. Nazleen, who was without a maid for the first time in her life except for her years with the Sisterhood, was astonished to learn that there were no servants of any kind here, either. They all took turns with the various chores, including the Fire Warriors who were at the site.

She spent some time talking to Felka about his interpretation of their people's history and found that it didn't really differ in any major aspects from what she had been taught. At one point when she was telling him about the history of the Sisterhood and she mentioned Loreth's name, a strange feeling came over her.

"I think you would like Loreth," she said before she could quite stop herself. "I hope you will find time to visit the compound. Or perhaps she can be persuaded to come here."

Felka may have picked up something from her tone because he smiled. "I will arrange it as soon as possible. As the senior man here, I should at any rate check on the behavior of those Fire Warriors."

Nazleen also talked with the young Kapti woman

who generously had lent her the clothing and now offered more for the return trip. She sat there in her dusty shirt and trousers with streaks of dirt in her brown hair and told Nazleen that her family were part of the old Kapti nobility, related distantly to Zaktar's family. She was here because like many of the others, the Cerecian influence was strong in her family. One of the Fire Warriors now at the compound was her brother.

She also gave Nazleen an interesting glimpse into Kapti society. Women, she said, had been treated equally before the law for many years, but only now were they achieving distinction in other ways. She spoke of the man she intended to be her mate, who would be arriving soon to supervise the construction of permanent buildings here, and she frowned uncomprehendingly as Nazleen explained their own disdain of life-mating or vezhara, as the Cerecians called it.

"But how unhappy everyone must be!" she exclaimed. "How can men and women not want to stay together?"

Nazleen would have willingly talked the night away, so great was her interest in these people, but the others, who had spent their day at hard labor, began to drift off to their tents as the full moon rose in the sky. Zaktar, who had disappeared some time ago, now returned and extended a hand to help her up.

"Would you like to see Cerece again before you retire?"

She nodded, having already thought of that when she saw how bright the moonlight was.

They took the jeppa and drove the short distance

to the ruins, where they left it and began to stroll amidst the crumbling walls and buildings that were all sharply etched in the silvery light.

"Do you think that we will find much here that can tell us who we are?" she asked as she stared at the ghostly tableau and felt again the lure of the green fire.

"I hope so. Much depends, I think, on whether or not they had a written language. Let us hope that our old tales are correct."

He'd explained to her some time ago that while Metak, the youth who had founded the male line of their race, may have been able to write, the ability had been lost during their enslavement.

"Felka also believes that this place is so ancient that they might well have evolved even as they lived here from some ancient form of writing to a more modern one. That means we could even discover two written versions."

They reached the end of the excavated area and turned to go back to the jeppa. Then their eyes met, silvered by the moonlight, and they stared at each other as the faint touch of the buried fire surrounded them.

Tomorrow, she thought, I will find out if I have been seeing the past or the future. Somehow, as she looked into his eyes, it became less important.

The next morning, as they were touring the ruins for one last time, a shout suddenly went up from the small group at the very middle of the excavated area. From all over the site, people came running, including Felka, who forgot all about his dignity as he scrambled excitedly down from a hillside.

They all crowded around the young Kapti woman Nazleen had talked to the night before. She stared at them, awestruck, as she held up a surprisingly thin stone tablet with a strangely smooth surface. Felka bent to examine it, then smiled at everyone.

"We have found a written language. It's very ancient and may not be the form they were using when the end came, but it will surely help us. Let's hope that many more such tablets have survived."

Nazleen bent over it herself, peering at the strange carvings. "But it's pictures, not writing."

"Yes," Felka agreed, "but the Kaptis also wrote with pictures many centuries ago. I'm not really familiar with their ancient writings."

"I am—a little, that is," the young woman who had found the tablet said. "And I think I see some similarities."

When Nazleen looked confused, the young woman explained that some of their scientists and historians believed that the Kaptis may have descended from the Cerecians as what she called a mutation.

"There are old tales among the Kaptis, written many, many years ago on tablets similar to this, that speak of the golden gods who were their ancestors, and they were often associated with a symbol for fire."

Nazleen got down on her hands and knees to examine the tablet more closely. Zaktar knelt beside her, amused at the sudden abandonment of her royal dignity.

She saw that some of the characters were readily identifiable—Warriors, farmers, mothers with babies—but many others were less easily translated as lines and waves and other shapes. The symbol they all accepted as being the symbol for Cerecian did not appear, but Felka, when she pointed this out to him, said it was possible that it had a sacred significance and was used only for certain writings.

She went through the lines, trying to fill in the gaps between the easily identified pictures and the unknown symbols. Then one picture caught her attention. There were scratches over it, as there were in various places on the tablet, but as she stared at it, a chill crept along her spine despite the warmth of the day.

It appeared to her to be a picture of a man and a woman holding hands as they walked toward a fire-pool. Or could they simply be standing before an ordinary fire? It was impossible to tell.

Others were crowding close and pointing out various features as they wondered aloud about the meanings. Nazleen wanted to ask Felka about that particular picture, but something held her back. Then Zaktar leaned forward, pointing to the same picture.

"Felka, what do you make of that? Is that a fire-pool?"

Nazleen held her breath as the Historian produced a round, thick glass and examined it through that.

"Yes, I think it may be. It probably represents some sort of ceremony. Vezhara would be my first guess."

The chill that had crept through Nazleen now froze her in place. She felt Zaktar's eyes on her and sensed a sudden tension within him.

"We should know more when we find their library or temple or wherever they kept their public records. I suspect this may be simply one family's record of its life," Felka stated as he straightened up again.

Then he chuckled. "In view of the discovery of the female half of our race, I think finding such records of ceremonies should be a matter of the highest priority."

Zaktar got up, too. "Yes, I agree."

But Nazleen heard the vagueness in his voice, and when she glanced up at him, his eyes were still on that picture.

CHAPTER THIRTEEN

ZAKTAR CAST YET ANOTHER GLANCE AT THE STILL, SMALL figure who sat beside him in the jeppa. His few attempts at conversation had met with no response. She'd said barely a word since they left the ruins several hours ago.

He wanted very badly to probe her thoughts, privacy be damned, but he couldn't do it without her knowledge. They were acutely sensitive to each other.

That pictograph haunted him, and he thought that was the reason for her silence, too. He'd taken Felka aside before they left and told him about their joint immersion in the fire-pool. Felka had been shocked that they'd survived it, and he'd agreed that it was a matter of highest priority to find those ceremonial records.

"Could we have unknowingly taken part in a ceremony?" Zaktar had asked.

"What you're asking for is an answer, not just one man's speculation," Felka had replied gently. "If you believe, as many of us do, that the sacred fire has a will of its own, that it is in some way unknowable to us, alive, then the answer to your question would have to be yes."

Zaktar thought about that now, as Nazleen continued in her silence. He'd never been much for all the philosophizing about the fire that characterized so many Cerecian discussions. He accepted it and used it, period. Such speculation had always seemed pointless to him. One day science might provide a means to analyze it, but until then he could contain his curiosity about it.

Now, however, he wished that he hadn't spent his classroom time daydreaming about fighting great battles or designing a machine that could fly through the air. He could only hope that Felka was wrong in his guess that it might be months before they found and excavated the central storehouse of records.

He felt her gaze on him and turned quickly, but she turned away just as quickly. Forgetting about politeness for the moment, he tried to probe her thoughts, but she had blocked them quite effectively and for good measure threw him a disapproving look that probably melted her courtiers on the spot. In response, he tried a disarming smile.

"Don't do that, Zaktar."

"It got your attention."

"I'm not in the mood for childish games."

"You're obviously not in the mood for conversation, either."

"No, I'm not." Then she sighed. "Don't you feel overwhelmed by all this?"

He wasn't quite sure what "all this" encompassed, so he made a noncommittal sound.

"Do you think the fire has a life of its own?"

He stared at her, knowing she couldn't have heard his conversation with Felka. Was she reading his mind without his knowledge? Surely she couldn't do that.

"What makes you ask that?"

She affected a casual shrug that didn't quite work. "Nothing. I was just curious."

"I've never had much interest in philosophy," he replied. "Do you think it's alive?"

"I don't know. We used to talk about it endlessly in school. It's certainly a possibility."

"Well, if we find their records, we may have the answer—or at least their beliefs on the subject."

But she had turned away again, and he could feel her withdrawing into herself. Ahead of them, the dark mountains of the Trens were gaining definition.

Zaktar looked forward eagerly to their arrival at the compound. He knew that the stop at Denra had helped her put Miklav into the past, but he wasn't sure just how ready she was to face the future— their future.

It was late afternoon when they reached the compound, and Nazleen left him quickly to seek out Loreth. A truck filled with Fire Warriors had followed them across the desert, and they hurried off to seek their companions—and the Sisters. Zaktar paused for a moment to watch several

353

couples walking in the gardens, then went to check on the construction of the radio tower.

"Is it a memory, Loreth?" Nazleen demanded. "Did that vision of yours come true? Did he take me there when I was unconscious?"

Loreth stared at her former pupil who now stood accusingly before her. "Why didn't you ask him?"

"Because I'd rather ask you and know the truth before I talk to him."

Loreth nodded slowly. "Yes, it came true. Zaktar carried you into the fire-pool in a desperate attempt to save your life and at great risk to his own, since he too was still recovering from your fire-battle.

"It was my suggestion. The Healers had given up, Nazleen. You were very near death. I believed or hoped that my vision had been pointing a way to save your life."

"But we've always believed that only the healthy can go into the fire, that when one is sick or injured the Healers must channel it to cure us."

"Zaktar's people believe that, too, but we were desperate. And we've always known that some of our beliefs could be wrong. All we know came from a child."

"And this memory I have of the two of us sleeping together beside the pool, with those strange entwined fingers of fire surrounding us— that actually happened?"

"Yes. I found you there, and I saw the fire as you've described it. I'd never seen that before, and neither has anyone else."

"Does Zaktar know about that?" she asked.

Loreth shook her head. "Strangely enough, he

and I have never discussed it. He's never told me what happened when you were in the fire, and I've not wanted to pry. I think he may not know himself, actually."

"That's impossible. *He* wasn't unconscious."

"No, but you've stood an Augury and you know that those who are in the fire don't know what's happening then."

Nazleen simply stared at her in silence, then left to bathe and change from her dusty desert clothes. Loreth watched her go and wondered what she would do if it turned out that she and Zaktar had indeed performed the ceremony she called vezhara —or had it performed *for* them by the fire.

She left her office and walked through the building and the tunnel to the fire-pool. They'd devised a system of notices to guarantee that men and women used the pool separately, and all had agreed to that without question, as though they knew instinctively that to enter it together meant something. Both signs had been down, indicating that no one was there now, but when she emerged from the tunnel, she found one of the Novices and the youngest of the Fire Warriors standing there, staring into the shimmering flames, their hands clasped.

"No!" she said, not loudly but quite clearly.

They both turned to her guiltily, but they continued to hold hands.

"We just wanted to walk down here, Pavla," the girl said defiantly. "We weren't going to do anything."

"Why can't men and women go into the fire together?" Taka asked in the same tone.

The Pavla sighed. "I don't know, but I have a

feeling we'll find out soon enough."

Then she shooed them away and stood for a long time staring into the flames.

Nazleen sat in the ornate bath and lathered away the desert sand with the herbal soap the Sisters made themselves.

Was it possible that Zaktar had known exactly what he was doing when he carried her into the pool? If the men had that knowledge, then Felka too must have lied, since he'd claimed to be uncertain about that picture or the ceremony of vezhara.

But they admitted that they knew such a ceremony existed.

At any rate, even if he hadn't known what he was doing, he must know what had happened, unless Loreth's comparison to the Augury was correct.

She wanted to trust Zaktar, and that in itself was a new experience for her. Lieges trusted no one; her mother had drummed that into her from early childhood and demonstrated it in her own behavior many times.

Nazleen did not bestow trust on anyone and with good reason. Her Advisors had betrayed her. Miklav had hidden things from her. Haslik had even kept from her his knowledge of Miklav's plan to provoke war. And Loreth, the one person she had always believed wouldn't lie to her, had kept the truth from her until now.

She thought about how she could get at the truth about Zaktar's role in this, then she slowly began to smile. Of course. Had she forgotten that he too was Cerecian?

She left the bath and dressed in the simple gown

and short vest of the Sisterhood. The only adornment to the flowing green lines was the gold chain
with the medallion of Cerece that she hung around
her neck. Her hair was left long and loose, since she
had no maid to dress it for her. It shimmered like
the last rays of the sun sinking below the great sea at
the edge of Hamloor.

Then she went to seek out Zaktar.

She found him in the midst of a group of men
and women enjoying the shadowed coolness of the
gardens. For a few moments she stood quietly in the
deeper shadow of the building, looking at a scene
that neither she nor anyone else could ever have
expected to witness.

The very air of the place seemed subtly changed.
Men and women walked in pairs, golden heads bent
close together in private conversation. A few of the
younger ones were openly holding hands as they
moved slowly along the paths between the flower
beds and hedges. Light, musical, female laughter
mingled with the deeper male tones, drifting on the
breeze that carried the scent of flowers and herbs.

What I am seeing, she thought, is truly the end of
the Sisterhood. How could it come so quickly after
all these years? If I close my eyes and will myself to
wake to this place one year hence, what would I see?
What will become of us?

Then she felt a tug at her thoughts and saw Zaktar
coming toward her.

As soon as he stopped before her, she said, "I
wish to speak to you privately."

He nodded and took her arm. "Let me show you
the radio tower that we're constructing. When it's
finished, which should be within a few days, Loreth

will be able to speak directly with our Pavla, not that she's going to find that much of a pleasure," he said with a chuckle.

"We can talk there."

They left the garden and walked to the far corner of the compound where the ground sloped to its highest point. There Nazleen got her first look at the strange creation of crisscrossed logs.

"It certainly doesn't add to the beauty of the compound," she remarked as she stared up at the thing.

He laughed. "It isn't meant to be beautiful. When it's finished, those pieces of metal will be placed on top and that wire will run to the radio itself. One day these towers will stand all over Hamloor, linking the palace with the fortresses and connecting all the communes and mines."

"Then we'd better find some way to make them more attractive."

"That can be done by thinking them into being attractive," he countered. "Most people will find them so useful they'll ignore their appearance. The same will be true of the wires that carry electricity."

"Electricity?" She tried out the unfamiliar word. "Oh, you mean the thing that makes lights and runs machinery. They have to have wires, too?"

He nodded. "They're strung up high on poles to keep them out of the way. Sometimes they can be buried underground, but that's more expensive."

She continued to peer up at the tower. "I'm not sure that I like this new world you're bringing to us, Zaktar."

"You'll learn to like it. The advantages far outweigh the disadvantages. What did you want to talk with me about?"

His abrupt shift caught her off-guard. She'd been thinking about the beautiful countryside of Hamloor and the mountains of the Trens being despoiled by poles and towers and wires and the gods knew what else. She drew in a deep breath and moved away from him a bit.

"I want to know why you carried me into the fire-pool."

He nodded. "I thought that was it. You've remembered at least enough to make you seek the truth from Loreth."

"Yes, but she doesn't know what happened. You can tell me more."

He shook his head slowly. "No, I can't. I don't know what happened, Nazleen. You were near death, we were desperate, and Loreth told me about her vision."

"But what happened in the fire?"

"I don't know. I don't even know how long we were in there. I didn't wake up for nearly a day."

She frowned. "But you must have said something, recited some ritual."

"I said nothing. I didn't know what to say. I just wanted you to live. That's all I can remember thinking."

"Don't you remember coming out of the pool?"

He hesitated, running a hand through his thick hair as he looked at her warily. "I remember a little of it, but not much."

"Well?"

"Well, it was cold in the cave, and I remember that I was very tired. I hadn't completely recovered from our fire-battle. I put you down on the blanket in which I'd carried you, then fell asleep beside you. Loreth found us later."

"Do you remember the fire around us then?"

He frowned. "No, I don't think so, unless you mean the glow that's always there after you've been in the fire."

"No, this was different. Loreth told me about it. Why didn't you ever talk to her about it?"

"I didn't know what to tell her, because I didn't know what had happened."

"But didn't you think she might know?"

"Nazleen, I'm not one of your Advisors or some criminal that you can question like this."

She was momentarily taken aback by his vehemence, but so too was he, because his anger drained away quickly.

"The truth is that I didn't talk to her because I felt that something had happened and I didn't know what it was, and I thought that maybe if I waited a while, it would come back to me. But it hasn't." He paused and threw her an accusing look of his own.

"And why did you go to her instead of coming to me?"

"Because I wasn't sure I could trust you," she replied honestly.

"Has that changed, or do you want to be sure I've told you the truth?"

She shook her head. That's exactly what she'd intended, but it wasn't necessary. She believed him, and she told him so.

"Well, what do we do now?" he asked.

When she said nothing and started to turn away, he reached out to take her arm. "Have you been into the fire-pool since then?"

"No."

"Why not?"

"I was still sick."

"But you aren't sick now—and you still haven't gone down there?"

"Have you?" she challenged, already certain of the answer.

He shook his head. "I don't know why. I did go down there the last time I was here, but I didn't . . . couldn't go in. It didn't feel right."

"Maybe it's because of our fire-battle," she suggested.

"No, it's not that. Don't forget that I've wielded the fire before."

She remained silent. He waited, but his patience was wearing thin.

"We could go down there together now," he suggested with a very careful casualness.

But she shook her head and walked off into the darkness without another word. He stood there staring after her, then finally followed.

Nazleen had no idea what had awakened her, and for a moment she just lay there quietly, listening to the silence in the compound. She'd gone to her room early and stayed there, falling asleep while she listened to the distant murmur of voices in the garden and in the hallway. Now all was silent; the hour must be late.

She moved around in the bed, seeking that perfect position to send her back into a blessedly dreamless sleep, but something kept pulling her back, even as she felt herself slipping into that welcome oblivion. Finally she gave up and sat up in the bed.

It was then that she finally identified it—the fire—but it felt different. She had gotten out of bed and was putting on a robe to ward off the night chill before she stopped herself.

What on earth was she doing? Was it because she'd been away from it for so long? No, this was definitely not that familiar longing she felt whenever she came here. Even as she thought about it, her body seemed to be moving on its own, seeking her slippers in the darkness, putting them on her feet. She lifted her hands to her face and saw in the dim light from the oil lamps in the garden that she was trembling slightly.

The fire beckoned again, a deep, powerful thrumming that vibrated through her body. She left her room and hurried toward the tunnel entrance. There she paused only to light a torch before moving on toward the source of that vibration.

Then it stopped just as suddenly as it must have begun. The moment she came through the mouth of the tunnel into the cave, she was herself again. She set down the torch, then walked slowly to the edge of the pool, staring into the roiling flames, but she felt no desire to go in. In fact, she felt quite the opposite. The flames did not seem welcoming. No ghostly finger reached out to her as it always had in the past.

"Wh . . . what do you want from me?" she asked, the words out of her mouth without thought.

But the flames merely continued their unique dance, oblivious to her question.

The chill of the cave began to seep through her

robe and her slippers, but she was strangely reluctant to leave. She felt certain that something was
about to happen.

There was no sound in the cave; the flames were
always silent. Then she felt something—not the
flames but something else—and just as it had in her
room, her body seemed to know what to do. She
turned toward the mouth of the tunnel just as he
appeared there.

Zaktar set down the torch and stared at the small
figure outlined in front of the flames. That insistent
call that had pulled him from his sleep had stopped,
and he was confused. Was she really there? Was he
really here? He walked toward her across the cold
stone floor.

Their eyes met, reflecting the fire more powerful-
ly than ever before as it began to dance more wildly.
Then they both turned toward it as two thin threads
reached out, twining about them and twining about
each other. They shed their clothes without even
knowing they were doing so, then walked hand in
hand into the flames.

The green fire leapt around them, pressing
against them with a substance neither of them had
ever felt before. They turned to each other questioningly, then answered the unspoken question by
the blending of their bodies. The pressure of the
flames fell away, taking with it their own substance
and their separateness.

They both heard the soft murmurings, voices just
at the limits of hearing. For a moment, it seemed
that they were hearing simultaneously the voices of
everyone in the world.

Then there was silence once more and a returning

awareness of themselves and of each other. They moved apart, touching only with their hands, and walked from the pool. The glow surrounded them, and the intertwined threads of green came, too.

They had discarded their clothes in a heap on the floor, and they lay down on them now, still surrounded by that glow and the twining threads. Their bodies flowed together again, hungering and wanting. Time stretched out, but neither of them felt the cold of the cave as they touched each other, tasted each other and grew still hungrier.

Then the walls of the cave echoed with their mingled cries as they found that incomparable oneness and clung to it until they both fell asleep. The flames reached out then with many tendrils, curling around them, warming their exhausted bodies.

Inside the flames, there were soft murmurs of approval—and then silence.

A WANTED MAN.
AN INNOCENT WOMAN.
A WANTON LOVE!

Renegade Heart
Madeline Baker

When beautiful Rachel Halloran took Logan Tyree into her home, he was unconscious. A renegade Indian with a bullet wound in his side and a price on his head, he needed her help. But to Rachel he was nothing but trouble, a man whose dark sensuality made her long for forbidden pleasures; to her father he was the answer to a prayer, a gunslinger whose legendary skill could rid the ranch of a powerful enemy.

But Logan Tyree would answer to no man — and to no woman. If John Halloran wanted his services, he would have to pay dearly for them. And if Rachel wanted his loving, she would have to give up her innocence, her reputation, her very heart and soul.

____2744-5 $4.50